The
California
Voodoo
Game

BY LARRY NIVEN
PUBLISHED BY BALLANTINE BOOKS:

THE KNOWN SPACE SERIES:

A Gift from Earth
The Long Arm of Gil Hamilton
Neutron Star
Protector
Ringworld
The Ringworld Engineers
Tales of Known Space:
   The Universe of Larry Niven
World of Ptavvs

OTHER TITLES:

All the Myriad Ways
Convergent Series
The Flight of the Horse
A Hole in Space
The Integral Trees
Limits
The Smoke Ring
A World out of Time

WITH STEVEN BARNES:

The California Voodoo Game

WITH DAVID GERROLD:

The Flying Sorcerers

WITH JERRY POURNELLE:

Footfall
Lucifer's Hammer

The California Voodoo Game

Larry Niven
and
Steven Barnes

A Del Rey Book/Ballantine Books/New York

A DEL REY BOOK
Published by Ballantine Books
Copyright © 1992 by Larry Niven and Steven Barnes

All rights reserved under International and Pan-American
Copyright Conventions. Published in the United States by Ballantine
Books, a division of Random House, Inc., New York, and
simultaneously in Canada by Random House of Canada Limited, Toronto.

Library of Congress Cataloging-in-Publication Data
Niven, Larry
The California voodoo game / Larry Niven and Steven Barnes.--1st ed.
    p.   cm.
"A Del Rey book."
ISBN: 0-345-36598-4
I. Barnes, Steven. II. Title.
PS3564.I9C3 1992   91-72881
813'.54--dc20   CIP

Manufactured in the United States of America
First Edition: February 1992
10   9   8   7   6   5   4   3   2   1

Selected Dramatis Personae

Dream Park and Cowles Industries:

ALEX GRIFFIN—Chief of Security
MILLICENT SUMMERS—financial operations officer
THADDEUS HARMONY—Chief of Operations, Dream Park
TONY MCWHIRTER—Data operations, IFGS liaison
SHARON CRAYNE—Cowles Industries security executive
MITCH HASEGAWA—Dream Park Security
DOCTOR NORMAN VAIL—Dream Park psychologist

International Fantasy Gaming Society (IFGS):

ELMO WHITMAN—Game Master
DORIS WHITMAN—Game Master
RICHARD LOPEZ—Game Master of international reputation
MITSUKO "CHI-CHI" LOPEZ—Game Master of equal renown
ARLAN MEYERS—IFGS arbiter

Gamers:

The University of California "Manhunters":

ACACIA "PANTHESILEA" GARCIA—Loremaster, Warrior
CORBY "CAPTAIN CIPHER" CAULDWELL—Magic User
MATI "TOP NUN" COHEN—Cleric
STEFFIE "ACES" WILDE—Engineer/Scout

TERRANCE "PREZ" COOLIDGE — Warrior
CORRINDA HARDING — Thief

Texas Instruments–Mitsubishi "Cyberjocks":

ALPHONSE NAKAGAWA — Loremaster, Warrior
CRYSTAL COFAX — Engineer/Scout
MARY-MARTHA "MARY-EM" CORBETT — Warrior
PEGGY "THE HOOK" HOOKHAM — Engineer
FRIAR DUCK — Cleric/Magic User
OSWALD "OZZIE THE PIKE" MURPHY — Warrior

Apple Computer "Troglodykes":

TWAN TSING — Loremaster, Magic User
TAMMI ROMATI — Loremaster, Magic User
"MOUSER" ROMATI — Thief
APPELION — Warrior, Magic User
GORDON REESE — Scout
GEORGE "INDIANA" HOWARDS — Warrior

Army:

MAJOR TERRY CLAVELL — Loremaster, Magic User
CORPORAL S. J. WATERS — Scout/Thief
LIEUTENANT MADONNA PHILLIPS — Warrior
LAWRENCE BLACK ELK — Cleric, Magic User
GENERAL HARRY "EVIL" POULE — Warrior/Scout
CHAIM COHEN — Cleric

General Dynamics:

NIGEL BISHOP — Loremaster, Magic User
HOLLY FROST — Warrior, Thief
TREVOR STONE — Magic User
TAMASAN — Cleric
ILSA RADICHEV — Warrior
MIKHAIL RADICHEV — Warrior

Glossary:

THE BARSOOM PROJECT — the ongoing attempt to transform Mars
    into a habitat suitable for human life. Named after the Martian
    locale in novels by Edgar Rice Burroughs.

CHARACTER—a role played by a Gamer, in broad categories such as Magic User, Scout, Engineer, Cleric, and Warrior. Characters are often continued from one Game to the next. During Games, Gamers accumulate points, talismans, and treasures, which strengthen their characters. Gamers can also "split" accumulated points to create a character with abilities in two different areas: for instance, a Scout/Warrior.

COWLES INDUSTRIES—Dream Park's parent corporation. Driving force behind the Barsoom Project.

GAME MASTER—one of those responsible for designing and guiding Dream Park "Gaming" scenarios.

LOREMASTER—one of those who plays within a scenario, recruiting and guiding a team of Gamers.

MIMIC—Meacham Incorporated Mojave Industrial Community.

NPC (NON-PLAYER CHARACTER)—an actor who performs within a Dream Park scenario. Often, but not always, in opposition to Gamers.

PALO MAYOMBE—Congolese variant of voodoo. Generally thought to be violent and death-oriented.

SANTERÍA—a Latin American variant of voodoo.

SCANNET—MIMIC's security system.

VOODOO—a belief system, or system of magic, incorporating African and European cosmologies.

The California Voodoo Game

Prologue

For seventy minutes now, the murmur of five thousand throats had built steadily into a cacophony. The lobby well of the Dream Park Hyatt was filled from mezzanine to rafters with cheering, stomping, hooting fans. Banners streamed and flickered in the wind like the tails of small dragons. Faces from a dozen countries were animated, eager, expectant.

At the lobby floor was a multileveled crystal dome with a narrow, tapering top. Beneath that dome lay a miniature city that sparkled as if riven from diamonds or carved from ice. Within its walls, lights crawled like glowing snakes, panels slid like ships through oiled seas, and braziers pulsed with scented smoke. Any lurking minotaurs would have felt right at home.

This was the Crystal Maze. It was covered by one-way transparent plastic, allowing observers on the mezzanine and upper levels of the Hyatt to witness the duel to come. Vid cameras would broadcast everything to thousands of room monitors and hundreds of thousands of homes and gaming venues worldwide.

A whistle split the air, stilling voices. A door opened at the western edge of the lobby. Four combatants advanced to the mark.

Tammi Romati's ash-blond hair was tied back by the band of her slimline Virtual goggles. She was beautiful, a vision in white leather. Tammi had the physique of a semipro bodybuilder. Her energy and intensity intimidated most men even before they learned her sexual preference.

Beside her, enfolded in a red cloak and an emerald sheet of flames, was Twan Tsing, Magician. Twan's black hair was chopped short and hidden under the emerald skullcap that incorporated her Virtual apparatus. The green-tinted liquid crystal lenses of the Virtual gear leached the color from Twan's Cantonese eyes but couldn't disguise their intensity. She was half a head shorter than Tammi, and more smoothly muscled. She gestured mystically, fingers intertwining in arcane, angular configurations. Her aura flared until it matched and then surpassed the radiance of all the Hyatt's lights, then silently subsided.

To her left stood Tammi's son, Mouser. He was clad in gray leather, a silver saber weighting his belt at the left hip. He was a Thief, if not a reaver or slayer. Two months shy of his fourteenth birthday, he combined an adolescent's narrow-eyed insolence with an adult's cold-blooded self-assurance. His thumb tested the edge of his blade.

Beside Mouser was the Warrior Appelion. He was everything Mouser was not: tall, sinewy, black-bearded, and ferocious in countenance. He balanced a single-headed battle-ax easily in his massive left hand.

Both wore their own versions of the Virtual gear, video equipment that would enable them to see specialized overlays on the holographic and mechanical illusions to come.

All four raised their hands to the assembled multitude, graciously receiving a deafening ovation.

And then, the eastern portal swung open.

Again, the first through was a woman, Acacia Garcia. She was dressed in the leather body armor and chaps of a nomadic warrior. Not as muscular as Tammi Romati, Acacia was a lithe, athletic blend of Pueblo Indian and Spanish with a dash of Moor. She was sloe-eyed and wide-mouthed, quick to laughter or anger. Her long black hair gave her an air of sensuality that quieted the room and evoked a clearly audible "Jeeeesus Christ" from somewhere above her. She scanned the room almost absently. She relaxed, shoulders slumping . . . then in a flash her sword appeared in her hand, with only the hint of a blur to suggest a draw. She stood perfectly balanced, as alert as a hungry leopard.

Behind Acacia came a short figure in a nun's habit, with a tranquil, sun-bronzed face. The roar "Top Nun!" rose from the crowd. The Cleric inclined her head solemnly, her fingers tracing a Star of David on her chest. A small, pale, chunky man followed her: Captain Cipher, Magician. And beside Cipher was a man with the height, color, and weaponry of a Zulu warrior. His name was Terrance Coolidge.

All wore slimline goggles or costuming incorporating the Virtual lenses.

The Crystal Maze shuddered before them, groaning and weeping as if it were a living thing.

"In two days we're going head-to-head with the Troglodykes in the California Voodoo Game. They're used to winning. We've got to shake them now. Establish dominance, or at least gain respect—or they'll motor over us. I've got a strategy," Acacia had told her team. *"It may seem crazy, but you have to trust me . . ."*

Now, looking into the vid monitor and the coldly confident gaze of Tammi Romati, who had never lost a game of Crystal Maze, Acacia wondered if her confidence had been misplaced.

The door to the Crystal Maze opened to a cloud of flamingo-pink smoke.

A little man walked out of the smoke. He stood only waist-high, his thick gray skin mottled with warts the size and shape of half-dollars. His hand brushed smoke from his stubby nose, then waved Acacia and her companions forward. "This way," he whispered, raising a gnarled finger to his lips.

Acacia followed the troll, trusting in her instincts and sword arm to save her. Her opponents hadn't had time to subvert the locals . . . had they?

The wall slid shut behind them.

"Eyes open for a double cross," she whispered to "Prez" Coolidge, the tall, stocky African-American at her left. His eyes were focused intensely. He would miss nothing, and she had seen him catch flies in midair, on a summer day . . .

The walls of the Maze throbbed around them like the chambers of a titan's heart. Faces flared momentarily behind crystal panels, mouths leering or laughing. If she turned to look at the faces they dwindled, then vanished altogether, their laughter echoing mockingly through the corridors.

Acacia glanced at her wrist monitor. She brushed a button on it and gained an aerial view of the Crystal Maze. The Troglodykes were clearly visible as a cluster of red dots. She could keep track of them—it was the only sane thing to do. But the monitor's special vision had cost dearly.

Both teams were expected to struggle to the center of the Maze. Then, equally drained of power, they would slug it out for the pleasure of the audience. There might be another, better way . . .

She punched buttons, disabling the wrist monitor.

"What are you doing?" the slender Zulu whispered.

"Trust me," Acacia told him. "I have a plan."

"Jesus. Don't they all?"

A bone-chilling buzz vibrated the walls of the Maze, and Acacia tightened her sword grip. It sounded like . . . what? A swarm of flies? Bees?

Light flared ahead, light that moved with such impossible torpor that it bounced back and forth between mirrors in a visible sheet. Still, it moved much too fast for her to dodge or avoid. When it struck her face, the world was instantly seared white. Then black specks rose in a mass, black against a screen of white, and swarmed toward them.

Bees. Swords were useless. "Top Nun!"

The small, dark-cowled woman pushed past her to face the approaching swarm. She raised her arms high and began to chant. "*Oy gevalt!* For honey, bees are good. One of your better ideas, God. Stingers on the other hand, *pfui!*"

A brisk, irresistible wind flared up behind them, striking the bees just as they reached Top Nun's hood. The entire swarm tumbled away, down the corridor and gone.

Acacia hissed air. Top Nun had probably won them five hundred points right there, but . . . "Too close. Any stings?"

Top Nun scornfully held up unblemished arms. "Stings *schmings.* Am I a *shmegegge* now, or what?"

Chapter One

New Dreams

Late afternoon shadows crept across MIMIC.

Meacham Incorporated Mojave Industrial Community was one of the largest structures in the world, for all of its ruined grandeur, a testament to 1990s optimism and the vision of the late Nicholas Meacham. Built forty miles northeast of Barstow, about twenty miles west of the California-Nevada border, MIMIC looked east with a facade that resembled a nineteen-story rust-colored sandwich board with a vertical convex crease. A thirty-foot-high horizontal row of letters spelling M.I.M.I.C. divided the crease from the tenth to the twelfth floor. The flattened top extended acres of concrete roof onto Clark's Ridge, a natural mesa. At the bottom, MIMIC measured nearly half a mile across.

According to documents found among Meacham's effects after his demise, MIMIC was intended to be the "linchpin of a planned community, an ever-expanding prefab metropolis poised to house and employ the excess population which, in years to come, will boil out of the Los Angeles basin like a crazed yeast culture."

As one might guess, Meacham's genius lay in construction, design, and financing, rather than the realm of prose. If not for a little seismic misunderstanding in 1995, MIMIC might have been all he anticipated.

After the Quake, MIMIC lay cracked and rotting for almost fifty years. Myths about the abandoned hulk multiplied. There was a live nuclear reactor in its guts; mutants prowled the ruins, shambling semihuman Morlocks with a taste for trysting teenagers . . .

Then, abruptly, the nightmares were dispelled. Life began to return.

And with new life came new dreams.

The rooftop stretched to a convincingly distant horizon, a concrete flat etched with pools and gardens, shadowed with California stucco. Newly installed sensors scanned sun-bronzed tennis enthusiasts as they swished their rackets about. Monitors translated sounds of thudding feet and gasping lungs, waste-heat silhouettes, and cheerfully exhausted visages into multisensory data for the security banks. Like glowing ghosts, guests roamed through three minimalls, lounged in tiny parks and arboretums, or chased golf balls through the flames of purgatory and the gilded clouds of paradise in Dante's, the best miniature golf course in the state.

A swimming pool glittered in the sun, like a pond touched by King Midas. Here its border was a white sand beach; there a rippling frictionless slide with a vertical loop; elsewhere were black basalt cliffs for diving. A hidden wave generator sent seven white crests rippling across the surface every minute. Here was an expanse of cattails sculpted of bronze; there, swimming in a programmed curve, was a weed-and-palm-covered island. Explorers would find it to be a huge lethargic flatfish with feelers the size of hawsers writhing about its mouth. In the center of the pool rose an island shaded by an artificial banyan tree, beneath which a grass-roofed tavern tinkled with laughter and the clink of glasses. One could swim to that tavern, or stroll a glass pathway hidden beneath the artificial waves.

Four hundred Dream Park employees were partying hard: swimming, minigolfing, playing dominance games, drinking.

Sixteen stories beneath them in level three, Tony McWhirter licked his lips. *A drink? Later.* He focused on the work at hand, his fingers and thumbs dancing in the holographic display of a keyboard.

He was an intense man in his middle thirties. Light red hair ran thin above a lean face with chocolate eyes. His fingers were long and almost delicate, his forearms still wiry from years of college wrestling and gymnastics. Muscles bunched and corded as he typed. A window jumped into place, superimposed on the projection of the roof. It focused on a view of the bar beneath the island.

Tony knew the man and woman busily mixing drinks: Elmo and

Doris Whitman. Both were white-haired, pink with sun, and as oval and solid as potatoes. They meshed like well-worn gears.

Tony made adjustments. His viewpoint floated in closer, as if his camera were mounted on a skimmer. He was staring into El's face. Capped teeth and sun-peeled lips filled the visual field at point-blank range.

Sound: the computer picked out El's voice from the surrounding gibberish, matched it to his lip movements, filtered, and compensated.

". . . part-time for eight years. Never really thought about being full-time until . . ."

Doris glided onscreen. She was chunky but esthetically firm and rounded. Her legs looked damn good beneath the barmaid's skirt.

"Tttequillla—"

The computer made a fast adjustment, backed itself up, and now she was a vocal pattern, locked into the bank. "—Sunrise for table six."

Doris Whitman's face was pink with sun, pleasantly plump, and invariably glowing with some private amusement. She plopped her tray down on the counter and kissed El behind the ear as he juggled bottles and glasses. She said, "We met at drama school, metro N.Y., did a lot of summer theater, a little off-Broadway. I guess we never quite made it big, but we always ate, which is more than most can say. Anyway, we gave it up maybe six years ago when an old buddy offered good jobs at a restaurant at Kennedy International. Lugbot jockeys, off-duty stews, mostly. They went automated, we grabbed our savings and got out. El, I said, what would we rather do than anything in the world?"

Tony pulled farther back as another voice came in, high-pitched and lightly accented. "I know your answer."

Chi-Chi Lopez was the prettier half of the world's most famous team of Game Masters. Her cheekbones were high and angular, but softened by ringlets of shoulder-length, jet-black hair. Her eyes were just as dark and sparkled with mischief. "Richard and I used three of your DreamTime routines before you even went pro, Doris."

"Tribute from a master," Elmo said, putting two drinks on Doris's tray.

"Later. Our room." Doris arched her eyebrows. "Tribute from a mistress?"

"Rrrrr!" He swatted her affectionately. She dimpled, sashaying away.

Barmaid's walk, Tony mused. Efficient, no-nonsense sex appeal. She was old enough to be his mother, but she'd been a private fantasy for months. Was the Whitman marriage lockstepped?

Chi-Chi watched them and then turned her attention to her husband, Richard. Tony remembered the wan little man. More specifically, he remembered playing the South Seas Treasure Game, designed and executed by the Lopezes. Their reputation had been well earned: lethal, unpredictable, but basically fair.

Richard spoke, and the computer automatically adjusted for decreased volume and pitch change: Richard had lost a lung four years back.

A small dark man with introspective black eyes and a pencil-thin mustache, he always hesitated over his words, as if writing them on a mental slate before speaking. "This is the Game I always wanted to conduct," he said. "I am happy to have you with me, El. Doris. This one will be remembered."

Hell, yes. It would be argued about, debated, and replayed for years.

And even after costs, and dividing up almost seven million dollars in guarantees among the players, the Park would still profit mightily. Worldwide pay-per-view, Virtual simulations, theatrical re-creations, and licensing rights would reap over thirty million dollars.

Damned little of which would find its way into Tony McWhirter's hands.

Richard and Chi-Chi huddled silently against the bar. How long had it been since Tony had seen them? Eight years? Chi-Chi was tall and slender even when seated, the elegant curve of her back accentuated by a fluff-fringed yellow dress that clung like body paint. If anything, she looked younger and more alive. Richard, smaller and darker, seemed shrunken. Could his health be a liability in the coming Game?

No. Richard Lopez never gave less than one hundred percent. Never. It was what made him great.

They were all great, in their individual ways—the Lopezes with their holograms and overall Game design, the Whitmans with their choreography of Virtual mimes and Non-Player Characters.

Four Game Masters. And Tony made five. A junior member he might be, but, by God, a member.

Tony's fingers tapped again. A window zoomed on the shoreline, framing schools of bathers. All those Dream Park employees tended to cluster, leaving lots of empty space. The roof was too big for them, dauntingly large.

The water was green, covered with lily pads and shoals of moss. Pure artifice, it looked as if half a thousand years of neglect had allowed a real swamp to take over Meacham's toy bayou. But that was Game reality. In truth there hadn't been water in the rooftop lake since the Quake of '95, when the tilt of the roof changed and the lake emptied into the desert.

There had been several levels to the roof, even before the Quake. Now it sagged to the west, and the whole western edge had collapsed. Twelve thousand gallons a minute flowed from the swimming pool through a safety grid and over the edge, plummeting two hundred feet to a fountain below. What was the rate of evaporation? It boggled his mind—only the power of the Cowles fusion distillery in Long Beach could have furnished sufficient cheap water to make the lake viable.

Tony zoomed in on the roof party: some of the celebrants were almost at the edge, near the vine-camouflaged barricades. Narrow focus: he watched them enjoy the view. Meacham's architects had never planned that waterfall, either!

"Barsoom Project" was the designation for the projected terraforming of Mars. The dead planet would gain a breathable atmosphere, arable land, and enough water for an expanding human population. The Barsoom Project would take decades, and would involve the natural, industrial, and scientific resources of almost every nation on Earth, but MIMIC would house the beginnings. The vast spaces within Meacham's arcology, and the spaceport now being built nearby, would *be* the Mars terraforming project for decades to come ... unless thirty Gamers and four hundred Non-Player Characters, under the supervision of Tony McWhirter and four senior Game Masters, tore the building apart during the California Voodoo Game.

Something *buzz*ed at the edge of his attention.

Tony ignored it—not a computer sound, not an alert, nor yet the sound of data disappearing in randomized bubbles—as unimportant. A notion had come to him. Fingers and thumbs tapped as inspiration took hold. Pictures jumped around him on the white half-dome of MIMIC Security: windows into all the corners of the huge building, windows projected onto windows.

Conversation behind him, a woman speaking. " ... Voodoo Game is ready?"

A man's. Deep and musical. "Yeah. McWhirter wanted to tear the building apart. Travis said no."

"So El Boss finally did something right. Aside from being born into the right family."

Tony recognized voices: Alex Griffin, and that woman from Cowles Security in Tacoma. He couldn't resist a comment. "Buildings are hardware. Software is as cheap as dreams."

"Tony?"

"We did our work in DreamTime. You'll think we spent a billion dollars. I'm finished here in a minute, Griff."

Out of the corner of his eye he watched Griffin, Dream Park's security chief, a tall man who carried his seventy-five inches and two hundred pounds with animal assurance. His hair was shaded a burnt strawberry, dark enough to make Tony look almost blond. When Griffin answered "Fine," his voice exuded enough casual confidence to make Tony wince.

The woman at Alex's side was a stunning brunette. Sharon something . . . Court? Griffin's left hand lightly touched her arm, while the other gestured with the relaxed authority of a plenipotentiary. "Sharon, there's working room for sixty people here. MIMIC—"

"You like that name?"

"Seems appropriate."

"I like 'Meacham's Folly,' " she said. "That's what the locals call it."

"All right, *Folly*. ScanNet breaks it into overlapping quadrants, with variable scan depth. The entire building gets a standard four-stage coverage, but some countries have contracted for more. Half a billion dollars' worth of security. Quite a system."

"Are you jealous?" she asked innocently.

"Cowles asked me to join up. I get all the stretch I need at the Park." Irritation had touched Griffin's voice, very lightly.

Tony's fingers kept moving in the hologram, sensors picking up finger movement and wrist position, inputting far faster than any mechanical keyboard. The sensors "learned" eccentric movements and habitual errors, the individual shorthand of the operator, and together with voice cues created an ideal programming environment. Minimum size of portable units was no longer limited by the physical dimensions of a keyboard. He was trying to keep his mind on programming. The last thing he wanted to think about was Alex Griffin. But it wasn't working.

Persecutor . . . betrayer . . . woman-thief . . . savior.

Eight years before, a disguised Griffin had entered one of Dream Park's infamous live-action role-playing games to solve a case of industrial espionage. In the commission of that crime, a guard named Albert Rice had died. *Very* accidental it had been, but as even Tony's own lawyer had observed, dead is dead.

Griffin had taken six years of Tony's life.

He had also taken Tony's lady, Acacia Garcia. Eventually, she had taken him—or somebody had dumped *somebody*. Tony had never been sure which.

Alex pointed in the video windows, picking out familiar faces in the rooftop press. "Quite a party."

"Everybody's getting the time off?" Sharon asked.

"Sure. The Folly's almost finished. The Barsoom Project is cooking. Fiftieth anniversary of groundbreaking for Dream Park is right around the corner. Everybody's feeling pretty good. Dream Park's closed to the public for a week. Some folks are taking off. Four hundred of us are staying right here as Non-Player Characters—NPCs." He stretched, yawning hugely. "Nice to be just another head in the crowd. For once."

"Say not so. The Griffin actually taking a day off?"

"Scout's honor." He squeezed her waist, glanced back at Tony, and released her.

Good old Griff. So considerate. So quick to hire Tony out of Chino, get him a job, set him up with psychological readjustment sessions. Mother hen . . .

And why did something at the very core of Tony McWhirter take offense? How could he respect this man, and be grateful to him, and never warm to him at all?

Because you're an ungracious bastard, McWhirter. He shut Griffin's voice out and began building dreams again.

After all, what good is a dream without internal consistency, hard edges, mappings, and a rigorous timeline? A good dream had all of those things, plus special effects to make the dreamer relax and submit to the illusion.

Tony had become very good at computer dreaming during those six long years. Dreams and computers, after all, were all he had had in Chino State Penitentiary.

Alex Griffin, like so many security execs before him, had decided that anyone good enough to beat his systems was a man to recruit. He had turned Tony loose in Dream Park, then gone further still. He had pled Tony's case with the International Fantasy Gaming

Society, the organization that monitored and brokered points for Gaming worldwide. They had screamed foul, but Dream Park hired its own personnel, and Griffin chose McWhirter. Tony went on-line as Dream Park's liaison to the Game Master, coordinating security and computing time.

And now, not two years later, Tony McWhirter, novice Gamer turned gentleman thief turned

(murderer)

turned . . .

The current wasn't buzzing through his fingers anymore. Hard-edged ideas dissolved into a mushy jumble in his head.

Dammit, when would he forgive himself? He had made good. Now he was coordinating the efforts of four Game Masters as they unleashed their finest work. The killing was behind him, his debt for the untimely, unintended strangling of Albert Rice paid in full.

(Okay with you, Albert?)

At the moment he was at work on the setting: a dreamscape superimposed on the real, redesigned MIMIC, a building intended to feed, house, and entertain 25,000 people. Fifty years earlier, water had poured down the wrecked building, into broken balcony doors and windows, until the tilted rooftop swimming lake was nearly empty. Now the waterfall flowed again. In the context of the California Voodoo Game, the roof and its artificial lake housed a fishing and farming community half a thousand years old. Who knew what supernatural terrors lurked beneath its filthy waters?

The Shadow do. McWhirter chuckled nastily.

Scattered within the California Voodoo Game were a total of fifty talismans, far more than the number necessary to win. Some were in the rooftop lake, requiring scuba gear. Currently, such gear was available on the Mall level, but could he make it easier? "Of course," he muttered, and his fingers began to move.

"Of course what?"

"Of *course* it's obvious." He couldn't delay acknowledgments any longer. "Hi, Griff. Hi, Sharon . . . Caine?"

She was small and dark-haired and pretty; she looked quite military in her crisp, blue Cowles Security uniform. "Crayne. Sharon Crayne. Good evening, Game Master." Her smile was incandescent. He wondered how it tasted.

He bet Good Ol' Griff knew.

"I'll finish this later. How goes?"

"You're changing the Game," Crayne said disapprovingly.

"Is a bear Polish? But only just a little bit, Sharon, and I'll record all changes for Security, and it's trivial anyway. We've put snorkels and scuba gear in the Mall level, right?" His fingers were a floating blur in the keyboard. "The Gaming teams have to use it on the flooded levels, but getting it there will be an exercise in masochism."

"That's a fair description of the whole Game," Alex Griffin said. "Five teams of masochists submitting themselves to the tender mercies of Tony McWhirter."

"Well . . . me and four other gentle souls." Tony felt warm and chummy. Alex could do that to him, if they were face to face. It was easy to forget the intense intelligence behind those dark green eyes and the tremendous strength and technique that had once held Tony McWhirter as helpless as a baby. Tony grinned like a minstrel. *Yas, boss.* "Isn't it obvious? If there was diving gear for sale before the Quake, somebody must have been *buying* it. So I'll put some in the upper apartments, too."

Griffin chuckled. "You're getting sly in your old age. Why aren't you partying?"

"I thought if I went through the territory again, I'd come up with something more."

"You've got four hundred NPCs out there, all partying their hearts out in the forty hours left before your Game begins." Alex Griffin was being just a little bit careful with his tongue. Might have been drinking, yes? Never seen Alex drunk. Might be interesting to douse his punch with a little Kleerlite 190 proof. "Why not go out and get a little adulation? Your public awaits."

"Uh-huh." Tony's cheeks were getting tired, and he relaxed the grin. "What are *you* doing here?"

"Routine check. We need our screens back, Tony. Wrap this up, would you?"

"Oh, Lord. How long?"

"Give me an hour. If everything checks, you can have it all back. The damn Game is *done*, isn't it?"

Tony bit back a retort: *No Game is ever complete while the authors live, Alex.* He stood up, and Alex slid into his chair.

Dream Park's security chief was at work almost instantly. He had a running view of the train depot on levels one and two. Then the Mall on level three. The Mall extended up to level six, with another two stories of light-well. Escalators ran from there down to the train gates. The gates had been there already, but with only one set of track laid, a split-level station carved into the ground and the cliff face.

"How much of this did you actually build?" Sharon asked.

Griffin didn't seem inclined to answer, so Tony said, "We cleaned out the broken glass and planted merchandise in the stores, and bombed out the stinks and the vermin. Otherwise we left it alone. There're some clues in the Mall—"

"What about the rest of the building?"

"Ah. Well, most of it was in place. MIMIC had eleven thousand in residence, and was going slowly broke, on May twenty-third, nineteen ninety-five."

"The California Quake," said Sharon.

"Yep. You can see for yourself, the place wasn't totaled. California's always been antsy about quakeproofing. MIMIC stood up pretty well. Part of the west face is sagging. See how it's distorted, like someone slammed the oven door on the soufflé? Maybe two thousand people were trapped. Rescue was a long time coming, because the whole damn state needed rescue. Over eight hundred died. The building wasn't a total loss, but who'd want to live here after that? Cowles stole it at auction. Hell, everything in California was going for nickels."

The scanner's eye shifted just north of the vertical ridge on the west face, to focus on the waterfall. The western edge of the rooftop lake cascaded over the broken masonry in a silvery flood. The viewpoint moved down the torrent in jumps.

"When we finish, we'll turn this back into industry housing. Home base for the Barsoom Project. But first, we get to play with it. We'll run the California Voodoo Game from roof to basement, the biggest role-playing game ever.

"We flooded levels ten and eleven, Sharon. There'll be more flooding by the end of the game. We clean it up afterward. The waterfall, that'll stay part of the building forever. Along the crease"—*taptap*—"here we go. This was what Meacham called 'the modular wall.'"

The view was from the desert floor, straight up the crease. A central track ran the crease, with tributaries splaying out and up like Christmas-tree branches. There were egg-shaped bulges on some tracks, each the size of a camper. Half-crushed eggs lay at the base of the building. One egg hung three hundred feet up from cables that looked no larger than threads.

Griffin spoke. "Tony, you're not going to *use* those?"

"Oh, hey, Griff, they're not dangerous. Not anymore. I watched the work."

"But you've got a whole apartment dangling there." He leaned closer. "Crap. That's not *mine*, is it?"

"Ha ha. Your apartment is down a few levels, and anchored tight, Griff. You don't trust me at all . . ." Could Griffin veto his use of the modular wall? "It's a mock-up, just a bedroom and office and some storage."

"Does it move? Crawl up and down the wall like the others?"

"It does that."

"It looks dangerous."

"Exciting, Griff. It looks exciting. This is a Level Ten Hazardous Environment game. They don't get tougher. Lawyers worked overtime on the waivers, believe me. If Gamers or their families even whisper 'lawsuit,' their firstborns disappear in baby-blue puffs of smoke."

"Exciting, huh?"

"Yeah." A distraction? "Griff, hope you don't mind, but I tied some of the Gaming monitors into ScanNet. Seemed a shame to waste all that wonderful full-spectrum imaging technology—"

Sharon's pretty face creased with irritation. "And how did *you* manage *that* trick?"

Griffin clucked with feigned weariness. "Don't ask, Sherry. There is madness to his methods."

Tony's grin was pure evil. "Yesss. Seems a shame not to get some use out of it. After all—ScanNet will be obsolete in ten years. Five if the Japanese don't sit on their hands. Maybe three—"

"Leave the poor woman her illusions."

"Sorry, Griff. Heh heh. Anyway, even if you don't need it yet, I do, to run the Game. Is *that* stuff in place?"

"We're still mounting scanners. Sharon, let's do a run. Tony, you can stay or you can party." When Tony seemed inclined to stick around, Griffin added, "I'd party if I were you."

"On my way, chief." Tony saluted and spiraled out of the chair.

He was at the door in three breaths and paused there, casting a final glance behind him. Alex and Sharon were standing close together, generating enough heat to make the air shimmer.

Do you remember Acacia Garcia, Griff? She'll be here, for the Voodoo Game. Did you look at the roster, Griff? Do you know? Do you care?

Tony cared, enough for it to create a sour, aching void in the pit of his stomach. Enough to wonder where she was at that moment, and what she was doing.

The back of Acacia's neck burned with the touch of Wizard's eyes. She longed to check her coordinates on her "location finder," but dared not. She had to save that juice! Tammi would be closing in on her with lethal intent. Tammi would be expecting Acacia to prepare an ambush, or to select the best possible location to stand and fight. Neither approach would work. Tammi was too good at selecting her own sites. There would be no way to sucker the Troglodykes.

But there was one stratagem that had never been tried.

She walked rapidly and spotted a telltale reflection only an instant before her nose bumped an invisible barrier. Thump.

She edged around, both hands spread, searching for the ends of the glass. There had been nothing, just another endless crystal vista, and suddenly—

Acacia stood on the edge of a waterfall. Victoria Falls? Niagara, in some prehistoric age? The air churned with foam, a million acre-feet of water per second cascading into the dizzying depths.

There was no way across? Her team might well fight and die here . . .

"Captain Cipher!"

An odd, fat, pale little man came waddle-jogging to join her. Corby Cauldwell was as nimble as a somnambulant geriatric. He had the personal hygiene habits of a water buffalo. A bumper crop of potatoes could be grown on his scalp. But his alter ego, Captain Cipher, was not only a certifiable genius, but also one of the highest-ranking Magicians in the International Fantasy Gaming Society.

She needed him now. "There's a way across," she said urgently. "Find it for me."

Light erupted from Cipher. Its radiance revealed a loop of rope sitting on a tree branch beside the abyss.

Acacia reached for it, then hesitated. What was the trick? Was it as easy as that? She sensed nothing menacing . . .

"Reveal danger," the Captain whispered.

At first, nothing. Then . . .

"Look," Acacia whispered. On the far side of the falls danced a tongue of red fire.

"This is your baby," Cipher said happily.

Acacia retrieved the coil of rope and balanced it in her hand. There was something wrong with it—a metal bulb buried in the trip? But a quick scan by Cipher showed nothing. That meant that it was Dream Park business, not hers.

She made a long cast over the water—

The rope stood straight out—

And hung there, like an Indian rope trick performed on the horizontal. And then the rope elasticized, began to stretch out and out . . . until it connected on the other side.

Acacia's tummy did a sour little dance, recognizing the next part. She reached out a sandal-shod foot and tested the cord.

It would bear her weight.

"Vision," she said brusquely. "I want magnified vision."

There on the other side of the abyss was the rope bridge. The rope didn't quite reach. Someone would have to cross and attach a lariat to the magical bridge, and then haul it back across.

Or could her team cross on the rope? Hand over hand? Tightrope walking? "Captain Cipher? Do you think that you could—"

"Captain Cipher loves your sense of humor," he said.

"Just checking." She shucked her pack. "All right. Let's see what we've got."

Acacia drew her sword, balancing it easily in one hand. Her Physical rating was high enough—she could actually perform a fifteen-foot tightrope walk without Dream Park assistance. But in winds, and over a gorge, and in a Game—that made it a little scary.

She stepped out on the line . . .

Tammi stretched out a long, muscular arm and shushed her companions. There was a bridge ahead of her, a catwalk rising on crisscrossing wooden supports that rose up from a deep gorge. The bridge led nowhere, terminating against a sheer crystal cliff. A perfect location for an ambush, Garcia-style.

She looked at her wrist sensor and noted Acacia Garcia's movement patterns. Acacia was approaching the center of the Maze, but taking the long way around. Tammi's esteemed opponent was famous for direct assaults. The apparent indirection had to be a trick. To assume anything else would be suicide.

She called to the thin young man behind her. "Mouser, what do you think?"

He touched his goggles absently. "I can see a door," he said, his voice adolescently nasal. "I think I can riddle the lock, or break it."

Mouser tested the bridge and then walked out into the center. It swung gently from side to side. Below it glistened a field of fire blossoms. They were much like morning glories and grew on long, glassy stems. Their petals unwound slightly, hissing.

"Kiss my pistil," Mouser hissed back.

"Mouser!" Tammi warned.

"Sorry, Mom," he said sheepishly, only mildly chagrined. His Gaming buddies at Medford Academy would howl when they heard that line. He was sorry that he'd gotten the gender wrong, not that he'd said it. "Kiss my stamen" had like zero impact.

The bridge was narrow enough that he had to be cautious with every footfall. Above him, through the ceiling, he saw the sun, or something that could have been the sun, rising. As it rose, the petals of the flowers opened. Tiny flaming mouths shimmered within them.

As he watched, the mouths spit threads of fire. Flames began to crawl up the bridge's support struts.

Mouser smirked, humming with cavalier disregard for his own safety. He had at least fifty seconds. He knew this world; he understood its rules.

He removed a lockpick from his leather belt pouch and faced the blank wall.

His Thief's vision revealed a tiny flutter in the crystal. A keyhole. He slipped his key into the slot and began to manipulate it.

Two eyes, a nose, and finally a mouth appeared in the crystal before him. They watched him speculatively. "Hello there, young man. Are you ready for a test of skill?"

"Bring it on."

The pick slipped in, and his field of vision expanded. He could see the workings of the lock. Within his gloves, his fingers tingled. It was a pleasurable sensation, not yet a warning buzz; it felt rather like snowshoed ants scampering in rhythmic patterns over his knuckles. The flames were closer now. His vision was edged in flame even when he focused his attention down to a narrow line. Now he felt as though he actually were hot—in fact, he was burning up. The air around him was crackling, and the flames were closer . . .

He maintained focus on the job at hand, and suddenly the flames disappeared. There was a crack in the crystal wall, one just tall enough for Mouser.

The metal framework of the catwalk remained, and he beckoned to the others. *Come on over!*

His teammates swarmed across.

Tammi checked her scanner and chuckled grimly. That task had netted seven hundred points, easy. Her adversaries were just the other side of this tunnel. She would take the lead, and with just the smallest bit of luck—

The adventure would be won in time for lunch. She shucked her cloak and wiggled through the crack.

Chapter Two

ScanNet

Alex adjusted his reimaging field, zooming in on one section of the fractured, inverted L shape that was MIMIC.

This was no holographic animation or DreamTime synthesis. Most of the rotating image was piped in from thousands of scanners, coordinated by ScanNet's Cray 181 computer.

Sharon was perched on the edge of her seat, watching every move intently.

Alex chuckled contentedly as the image rotated like a pie in a microwave oven. "Want to see?"

"How deep can you scan?"

The building wheeled until they were behind it, gazing west across the rooftop recreation facilities. He zoomed out far enough for the roof to look like a roof, a three-story cap of glass and concrete built onto the shelf of rock called Clark's Ridge. Alex's fingers were a soft blur. "I'm not totally sure," he murmured. "Shall we see?"

The visual field flashed from hyperrealistic to an X-ray display. Rock and steel became transparencies, MIMIC's awesome bulk a glass model barely three feet tall.

MIMIC blinked red on the third floor of the southeast quadrant and then expanded to fill their field of vision. They passed through the walls, then phased into a world of computer reconstruction. ScanNet was only forty percent operational at the moment: unsecured zones were represented by pulsing orange light. When fully implemented, the system would turn the concrete, steel, and plastic of MIMIC into a kind of ant farm, with every ant individually tagged.

Thousands of tiny human figures labored and strove within that maze of walls and corridors. With the merest touch, Alex dove in, guided them smoothly through the maze, and brought them to level three.

Eerily, they were looking into the circular security room. Its white-domed ceiling arced away, desks and workstations collected at the central axis. In the center of the room sat Alex and Sharon.

"Hall of mirrors, isn't it?"

Sharon reached out and pushed her forefinger into her own miniature back. "Can we rotate that?"

"Easy." His voice dropped and steadied. "Rotate one-eighty." As if mounted on a carousel, the entire image flipped. Sharon was facing herself.

She stuck out her tongue, then waved her right hand. The mirror image waved its right hand, too.

"Want that reversed?"

"Nah." She examined her flawless complexion, leaned close, and wiped a strand of blond hair away from her forehead. "Scan me, baby," she said huskily. "Scan me good."

A stream of physiological data materialized in the air beside her image.

Height: 69 inches
Weight: 140 pounds
Body fat: 14%
Pulse: 54

Alex brushed her throat with his lips, and the pulse corrected to 67.

Temperature: 98.8

"I've always been a tick warm," she said.

"I'd noticed."

"Do you mind?"

"Please, Miz Fox, don't throw me in that briar patch . . ." He shut down the scan. "We'll be able to do a full medical on anyone in MIMIC, and they'd never know it. Impressed?"

"Be more impressed if you promised to stay off duty for the next four days. You've got the leave." She nibbled on his ear, wrapping her arms around his neck. "Things got interesting last night. At least I thought so."

"Want to see a playback?"

"Alex!"

"Joke! ScanNet doesn't peep into executive bedrooms."

She pushed herself away from him a little. "It wasn't a joke to me, Alex. Maybe it was a mistake to get involved on the job." Her mouth curved in a calculated pout. "I'm not sure you're a free man."

"So I'm married to the job—"

"These are the Fabulous Fifties." Her eyes were challenging. "Cheat a little."

"Just wait till the Voodoo Game is over, and we get Barsoom on line." He snaked his arms around her and pulled her in close. She smelled of strawberries and lime and healthy female animal. He kissed her throat. "I promise I'll make it up to you."

"Uh-huh. When Barsoom is on line, you'll be back in la-la land, and *I'll* be up to my ears." She intertwined fingers with him and leaned over, soft and warm and supple as they kissed. Then she pushed herself away, suddenly one hundred percent professional. "I've seen your dossier, Alex. I know people who knew you in Intelligence. You're wasting yourself at Dream Park. The terraforming of Mars will bring out the very best and worst of humanity. Worst is your domain, yes?"

His eyes had become distant.

She stopped. "I said something wrong."

He managed a dry, unconvincing laugh.

Sharon took the hint. "Let's leave that, okay?"

"Might be best."

"Truce. All right—I know the internal ScanNet system is coordinated with the externals: synchsec satellite network, ground-level sensors, that stuff. You have to teach me the rest."

Suddenly, levels seven through twelve flashed with orange neon urgency.

"Another damn blackout," he muttered. "Bugs in that software."

"It should be finished by now."

Alex was relaxing a little—he understood the irritation in her voice. "I've heard it was a miracle ScanNet got written at all. The problem isn't gathering the information, the problem is organizing it. ScanNet's an artificial brain. Well, if the scanners are eyes and ears, and the central processor is the frontal lobes, then according to Norman Vail, ScanNet's substations are the reticular activating mechanism."

"Duh . . ."

Alex laughed. "They filter the information. Each substation decides what is important and what isn't, before it sends it upline. Only about a thousandth of that reaches the main banks, and that's still probably a gigabyte a minute."

"How much of ScanNet was developed in-house?"

"Nobody said. 'Need to know' and so forth." His eyes narrowed speculatively at her. "Come to think of it, I should be asking *you*, lady."

A sphinx.

"Yeah. That's what I thought." He remembered the complete briefing. ScanNet was a massive neural-modeling project, an outgrowth of speech-recognition and artificial-vision research in the last century. It was able to sample, digitize, and record any sound, light, or vibration in MIMIC. Thousands of miles of copper wire cocooned the corridors, acting as antenna, impedance sensor, and Faraday cage, alternating between modes several thousand times a second. All transmissions would be either authorized and filed, or monitored. ScanNet could block unauthorized transmissions in a few milliseconds.

Sharon interrupted his reverie. "Alex," she asked, "isn't it dangerous letting Gamers in with the system incomplete?"

"There's computer equipment and tools in shops . . . maybe some industrial diamonds. But those areas are sealed off, and ScanNet's external shield is solid—nothing comes in or out unless we know. We can scan Gamers before they leave. Should be pretty safe."

Sharon brooded. "There are a hundred and sixteen countries participating in the Barsoom Project. Most are bringing their best resources into the fold: technology, the nimble minds, raw materials, money. If we don't keep them safe, the Barsoom Project fails."

Virtually indistinguishable black and gray dots, a stream of lilliputian workers labored in MIMIC's central well.

MIMIC rose sixteen stories tall against the cliff, and another three stories above the edge. Light-transport landing systems were up on Clark's Ridge at level sixteen. Heavy cargo chopper pads were at MIMIC's base. Four miles away, landing strips for Earth-to-orbit cargo and passenger transports were under construction. Roads and railroad tracks splayed out from the "ground" floor.

Pull out the convertible floor panels, close down the Mall levels, and MIMIC's industrial capacity tripled—with a considerable loss of population density. The internal structure was being reworked. Foamed steel struts and monofilament from Falling Angels' lunar-orbit research-and-manufacture facility allowed a level of flexibility beyond anything the original planners could have dreamed. Immense inner spaces were open for shops. Twelve stories of eastern wall could roll to the side, to allow repair or modification of gargantuan machinery.

Point of view shifted again and again: now they were completely outside the building, floating at about the eleventh floor, facing the raised bronze letters spelling out M.I.M.I.C.

Now they were above it, a view provided by geosynch satellite, or survey plane, or perhaps computer animation. DreamTime technology was simply too good to show a difference.

"The power of a dream," Alex said contentedly. He leaned back in his seat. "You know, there must be a thousand stories about Earth uniting to face a threat from space. Who ever thought we could do the same thing peacefully?"

"Travis Cowles and all the little Cowlettes?"

"Cowlettes? Are those like raingear for little duckies?"

Sharon scooted in close to the console. "May I?"

Alex watched her fingers sink down into the holographic matrix, felt sympathetic constrictions in his throat as she slid into the controlled mumble an experienced computer operator used in the information maze. "Sharon Crayne," she said. ScanNet accessed her file, analyzed her personal collection of fricatives and glottal stops, and was ready to go.

As she began moving effortlessly around inside the security guts of MIMIC, Alex felt an uneasy mixture of pride and alarm.

The project was so *big*.

And Dream Park had been essential to its creation. Although the actual physical park lay seventy miles southwest, its influence infused MIMIC's every level.

Sharon was deep into her routine, exploring the labyrinth that was MIMIC. Within a few weeks, he would hand over responsibility of the structure to Sharon, and whomever the board of directors appointed security chief for the Barsoom Project.

And when he no longer carried the weight of both MIMIC *and* Dream Park, perhaps he could be more human with her. Between now and then they would discover everything they needed to know about each other, and just maybe . . .

If the "real world" would just leave him the hell alone . . .

But for now they were firmly enmeshed in different worlds. Sharon didn't even seem to notice as he slipped out the door and into the outer corridors.

Tammi exhaled as fully as she could and squeezed through the gap in the crystal caverns. She felt the walls pulse. Was that music? No . . . wait . . . the walls began to shift, molding themselves to her body.

The walls clamped on her until there was just barely room to breathe. She found enough space to turn her head and look back at her teammates. Interestingly, the walls seemed to flex to make each of them uniformly uncomfortable. From what she could see, Appelion was almost exactly as cramped as little Mouser.

There was no room to pull a dagger, let alone a sword. It would have been smarter to let Twan go first. In the Crystal Maze, magic was often stronger than steel.

Tammi stopped in her tracks, chilled by a crackling, creaking sound. She squelched a quick flare of panic. Where had that come from? It sounded like ice breaking . . .

Tammi had played Crystal Maze seven times, but had never been through this corridor. It might be new. Common sense told her that things were about to get deadly.

The crystal in front of her cracked open. Something disturbing wormed its way out.

At first it seemed like a sea anemone—a tiny sprout with tentacles, protuberances that wavered like fronds in a sea bed.

There were four little fronds, and then . . . it budded an opposing thumb. A tiny hand as large as a newborn child's. It reached for her . . .

And where it touched, its tiny fingers grew crystal claws. It raked, leaving scarlet creases along her skin. Evil, impish laughter echoed through the Maze.

Tammi strained and reached back along the corridor, breathing gone suddenly ragged. "Appelion!" she panted, and he reached out his hand to her. "Get Twan!"

Appelion reached back and linked hands with Twan, and Twan began to mutter a spell.

As she began, the wall erupted with tiny infants. They laughed insanely. They had pale dead eyes, and red, crinkled skin. And crystal knives for fingers.

Acacia was halfway across the bridge. Wind and mist boiled out of the abyss, and she tottered—

(Someplace in Dream Park, a computer rolled its electronic dice, and she was saved . . .)

She extended her arms to the side, windmilling for balance. She crouched into a ball, steadied herself, and waited.

From the far side of the gorge came a high-pitched chittering sound.

A crystal monkey . . . baboon . . . orangutan? It was perhaps three feet tall, with long hairless arms and a fixed grin. It chittered again and then screeched in challenge. It stepped out onto the rope and hopped up and down experimentally a few times, and came on.

It swarmed down the rope so quickly that she barely had time to prepare herself. Acacia whipped her sword into position as the ape jumped off the rope, catching itself with a single paw. It dangled there and then swung up, sweeping at her ankles.

Acacia jumped back, sucking air. She couldn't cut at its hand without cutting the rope. And yet, if she didn't do something, she was going to be shaken off.

She had a choice. She backed up and hunkered down.

(Curious, but the rope felt, well, broader than a mere rope. Eighteen inches wide, perhaps. She grinned at what could only be interpreted as an interesting kinesthetic illusion.)

She wrapped her legs around the rope and edged forward. The crystal monkey eyed her from its upside-down world. She swept the sword at it experimentally.

It skittered back, chattering. It crept closer . . . and closer . . .

Acacia readied her sword. It was almost close enough—

A sudden realization stayed her hand. At no time had the creature actually attacked her. When one came right down to it, all that it had done was come close and investigate. Might it not be friendly?

She smiled, as broadly as she could. She said, "Pretty thing. Friend?"

The monkey's expression didn't change. But it reached out a long arm, a limb as clear and hard as diamond. It touched her arm and left no mark. The monkey smiled, and the cash register ran in Acacia's head. Another eight hundred points?

Hand over hand, it returned to its side of the gorge. Acacia followed. Then, as if sharing a secret, sacred knowledge, it showed her how to extend the bridge . . .

Twan's magic was irresistible. Tammi and her team glowed blinding white, and before that aura, the crystal hands retreated. Her team was scarred and bloody, but they were almost out of the caverns.

Tammi crept out first and saw Acacia's team ahead of her on the bridge.

Tammi screamed, "Attack!" and they swarmed down.

Terrance the Zulu Warrior met Tammi's attack coolly. His assegai jutted at her. She swept the short spear aside and lunged. Terrance blocked twice with a tak-*tak!* rhythm, then disengaged and stabbed for her chest. He was good, better than Tammi in a confined space. She had discovered that during a previous encounter. But for all of his speed and coordination, he was weak on tactical maneuvers.

She used the blind pressure of her charge to force him back a little, where she had more room for swordplay.

Mouser saw an opening and slipped past Terrance, and headed for the bridge. Then Appelion was able to join Tammi—

With Acacia on the far end of the gorge, and with no time for Top Nun to launch a spell, Tammi would have the Zulu down and dead in another moment. Terrance fell back to the mouth of the rope bridge. They were piling up. Only Captain Cipher had made it across. Top Nun was still at the halfway point, with Mouser in hot pursuit. If Tammi could fight past Terrance, Appelion could pepper Acacia with arrows—

"No!" Tammi heard herself shriek. Incredibly, Acacia had bent to the line and was sawing away! With her own teammates at risk? What manner of insanity was this? "Back!" Tammi yelled.

It was already too late. The bridge was falling. Top Nun, Mouser, and Terrance plunged screaming into the gorge, lost in the rushing current.

The rope dropped away from under Tammi's feet. She fought back for safety, too late. Falling, she managed to grasp a rope. The wind whoofed out of her as she smashed into the spongy cliff face.

Tammi hung there, twisting in the mist, and stared shuddering into the heart of the falls. What the hell had happened? Acacia had lost two: Top Nun and Terrance. The Troglodykes had lost one: Mouser.

A poor, and almost incomprehensible, sacrifice.

There were no individual points in Crystal Maze. Only team points. Still, a two-for-one loss?

Tammi climbed to the top of the gorge, helped the last few feet by Appelion and Twan. She stared back down, and then across.

Acacia and Captain Cipher were gone. And worse . . .

In some odd fashion that Tammi couldn't quite grasp, Acacia had gained a delicate advantage. Tammi knew it, but couldn't identify it.

Some unnervingly complex and subtle trap was being laid out right under her nose. She was certain she had all the necessary clues, but she still couldn't figure it out. Whatever was going on went beyond Acacia's capacity for guile.

In fact, it had a touch of the Bishop about it.

And if that was so . . .

Then the rumors were true.

Chapter Three
Old Dreams

As he opened the door, the sights and smells of backstage MIMIC hit Alex Griffin in the face. Smelting, lifting, loading, painting. Stenches, vibrations, roar, and whine. There were always a thousand minor jobs left undone until the last minute. Some were part of the California Voodoo Game, some were unrelated aspects of the Barsoom Project.

But Barsoom and Dream Park were part of the same thing, weren't they?

Share a Dream ... Share the Future. That slogan, emblazoned on a billion stickers in a hundred different languages, had become a catchphrase, a battle hymn, a mantra for an entire generation of Earthlings.

A neat irony. Mars, the god of war, had brought peace. And Dream Park was a place of illusion, whereas the Barsoom Project would pound and carve the planet Mars into a habitable world: not an illusion at all.

Griffin remembered a conversation with Norman Vail, chief psychologist for Dream Park. Halfway through an excellent bottle of Tanaka "White Plum" '02, Vail had held forth on the mythic power of dreams.

"In dreams we walk through phantasmagoria, our judgment sleeping," he had said intensely. Vail was sixty-seven years old, but a superb exercise and nutritional regimen had bought him the health and appearance of a forty-five-year-old outdoorsman. His skin looked more weathered than wrinkled. Tonight his bright little blue eyes were a bit unfocused. "Our drowsy judgment cannot distinguish reality from fantasy, the possible from the absurd. An inanimate object rears from the mist, snarling. We greet it lovingly, and in the greeting transform it into a friend, an ally, to help us on our journey."

"Well, that's dreams for you." Alex took another sip. The wine virtually sang on his palate. Its bouquet was clear and warm, sweet to the teasing edge of cloying, but not an inch beyond.

"Alex, you see, but you do not observe. A poor trait for a detective."

Alex placed his hand at his waist and bowed without standing. He kicked his heels onto a footstool and surrendered. "Please instruct me, Holmes."

"Quite. Do you perceive the parallel between dream and human existence?" Vail leaned forward eagerly. "From the perspective of our covetous misery, our neighbor's chattel often seems the solution to our own poverty. Isn't the history of human interaction the conversion of neighbors into enemies? Or into nonhumans, that we might deprive them of said chattels, or life itself?"

"Ah . . . I'm not following you. Maybe you're a little drunker than I am. I'd better catch up." He poured himself another glass of Tanaka.

"The atom bomb was supposed to kill us all. I say it transformed us into a cave full of troglodytes, up to our knees in gasoline, armed with cigarette lighters. No option save learning the other man's grunts and clicks, eh?"

"How I Learned to Stop Worrying and Love the Bomb."

Vail looked peeved. "Don't you see?" He snatched the bottle from Alex's hand. Actually, it took two tries: he missed the first swipe. "The weapon of war creates the necessity for communication. The god of war becomes the symbol of peace. Five billion people, speaking a hundred languages, dream the same dreams at night. They seek to create their wealth, rather than loot it. Finding new friends in old enemies."

"My my. Aren't we in a philosophical mood this evening."

"Treasure it, heathen. You shan't see such again."

Alex had been warmed by Norman Vail's unusual burst of optimism. But when one came right down to it, wasn't Vail right?

Dreams were the ultimate intimate language. Mankind had always struggled to bring its dreams into reality. It mattered little whether they were fantasies of bloody conquest, yearnings for love, or hopes for a brave new world. Whatever the images and intent, man needed to dream, and to share those dreams.

And hadn't books, films, radio, and multivision paved the way for understanding?

Through them, a new vision of mankind had been forged.

Griffin remembered a holographic diorama at Carnation's Feed the World exhibit in Dream Park. The first image had been a midwestern Dutch-American mother breast-feeding her baby. No sooner had the eye absorbed it than she began to darken, her eyes narrowing, her sun-blond hair drawn back into tight braids as she became African . . . and then Asian . . . and then Polynesian.

To the strains of music drawn from a hundred cultures and miraculously woven into a single skein, the concept of motherhood burst all cultural boundaries to strike a single nurturing chord. Through the cinematic eye the cornfields of Kansas became the rice paddies of Vietnam, then the banana plantations of Jamaica, and then a million acres of sugar cane in Hawaii. Earth became one vast farmland tilled by a billion callused hands, feeding ten billion hungry mouths.

It was an image whose time had come.

Alex Griffin's thumbprint summoned a glass-walled elevator tube. He began to rise through the floors. He waved to workmen as he slid past them, dwarfed by the multileveled enormity of MIMIC.

Dream Park, like Disneyland before it, brought together all the myths of mankind and displayed them on a single stage. Cultural prejudice withered before such an onslaught of fantasy.

As individuals, human beings are weak and vulnerable. Families to tribes to nations were an inevitable progression. Mankind was ready to take the next step.

Why should Alex Griffin quit his job at Dream Park to control the North American headquarters of the Barsoom Project? Dream Park offered all the responsibility any one man could want.

The walls and floors buzzed and thrummed with activity. Elevator banks were being disguised behind secret doors and hidden panels. Workmen could ferry equipment up and down MIMIC, from one end to the other, without interrupting the Game to come.

At the bottom of MIMIC's central well, lights flashed and glittered like a flaming silver mine. Was that reality or illusion?

At the sixth floor Alex stepped out, then threw himself back against the wall as a synthesized voice chanted, "Please take care, wide load coming through."

An oval mosaic as immense and mysterious as a Mayan calendar hummed past, balanced impossibly on its edge upon a little robot cart. The cart flashed red lights and droned its ritual warning as it slid past, blithely made a ninety-degree turn, and trundled merrily on its way.

It had almost disappeared before he recognized the oval as a mask rendered in strips of hide and lengths of bone. It was ten feet high, striped and curlicued with dusky earth tones. Its lower teeth pierced the upper lip jaggedly.

It was hideous, then suddenly comical. The eyes were platters of ancient flattened cola cans, the nose a plastic crucifix stenciled with the name of a popular chain of motels. How many other bits of cultural effluviums could he spot?

The floors and walls jiggled as the Cowles Mach VIII speakers ran their testing sequences: peals of maniacal laughter, bursts of rain, jolts of thunder, the chilling rumble of a hundred thousand pairs of jackboots. Sudden sharp explosions and shrieks of agonized pain.

Far down the central well, cranes that looked like toys prepared shuttle bays for the coming Game. Just above Security, on level four, automated tractors plowed ground and workers planted tombstones in a voodoo graveyard.

Griffin trotted up four flights of stairs to the tenth level, which was now flooded waist-high with warm water. A pontoon catwalk bobbled around the edge. Balance was tricky, even more so since he was already drunk with the sights and sounds, the hot acid stench of burning metal.

Voodoo! Naked slaves praying for protection to dead gods, gods rotting in graves left half a world away. An impotent religion embraced by the lost and degraded. *Why voodoo?*

Because Richard Lopez, Game Master extraordinaire, *loved* the notion! As McWhirter explained it, voodoo was a cultural maze. It was African shamanism and pantheism touched with Muslim influences and transplanted to the New World. There it absorbed Christianity and eventually held millions of worshipers in thrall beneath the very noses of the oppressors. Eventually it found its way back to nineteenth-century Africa, carried by repatriated descendants of slaves. There it absorbed gods from India and Asia, and bounced back to America in the hearts of African immigrants. It ate everything, surrendered nothing.

As a coherent mythology, voodoo was a jellyfish—interesting but difficult of purchase—until Lopez had grafted in a spine from an obscure twentieth-century text . . . Tony had smiled mysteriously and would say no more.

From thirty feet away there came a blinding flash of light. A twenty-foot-long amorphous shape reared up from the water. It had no features; it had no detail. It was just a blot of dancing incandescence. It wavered like an obese sea serpent, for a moment resembling something half-man, half-crocodile . . .

Then with a wall-trembling belly flop it disappeared back into the pool. Wave generator, or underwater bomb, or just hologram and sound effects?

It burst up again, and this time Alex could make out vague details of form and feature. It was a bronze, taloned thing, or maybe a copper flame crawling in slow motion.

Crazy place. Alex Griffin walked lightly through a realm of devils and demons, slipping around the inner rim of the tenth floor. He thumbed a hidden panel and chuckled delightedly as it rotated to admit him into its shadowed secrets. Pink footlights guided him down a twisting staircase.

He passed a corridor recently sealed off: the engineers had yet to evaluate the quadrant's structural stability.

A chunky woman of indeterminate age prattled rapid-fire to an attentive circle of Cowles officials. She had very short black hair tucked under a construction cap. Her raiment was eccentrically diverse: ancient yellow ski pants, a blue velvet tunic belted at the waist with a bicycle chain, thong sandals cut from sheets of corrugated plastic.

A squatter.

For fifty years squatters had haunted MIMIC. They ate whatever they could find in its cupboards, sold whatever they could scavenge. It was squatters who had promoted the myth of radiation-spawned mutants.

When Cowles had actually begun to develop the project, there had been sticky legal problems. What belonged to whom? Did squatters have homestead rights? A few claimed to be descended from tenants marooned in the building. When Cowles lawyers took them seriously, suddenly *everyone* was descended from tenants.

The situation could have become comically complex, but a battalion of social workers and attorneys had moved in, offered schooling, jobs, vid rights for the squatters' stories. In two sticky cases Cowles lawyers had demanded sixty years' back rent, and that fixed *that*. Dozens of the elder squatters had been hired to act as guides, experts on the Folly's structural stability.

The squatter peered at Griffin shrewdly as he passed. She was telling the senior engineer, "The floor in here is about twice as stable as you'd expect, seeing as the Snake's alive on level eight."

The senior engineer, a short round black man named Ashly Mgui-Smythe, wiped his forehead with a plaid handkerchief, then folded it prissily and tucked it into a back pocket. "You . . . said that the Snake was alive on eleven, and the floor turns out to be stable."

She cocked her head. "Welll . . . maybe it was gone by the time you got there. But it bit pretty sharp on eight, section two, now, didn't it? And it's here. I *feel* it."

Grudgingly, Mgui-Smythe nodded. "Eggers—give me another check on this level. Folktale or not, if they've got record of quake damage here, maybe we missed something."

"On it, Ash."

Mgui-Smythe turned around and brushed his fingertips against the wall. "Be safe—wall sector six off. I don't like the cracked floor." He traced a jagged line of ruptured concrete with his toe. The crack had been filled with a bonding compound, but it extended across the entire corridor, vanishing under the far wall. It made Griffin nervous, as well. "Check level eight, too. Hazardous Environment Game or not, losing Gamers is bad for business." His expression warmed. "Hello, Alex."

"Ashly. More squatter stories?"

Mgui-Smythe shrugged. "Can't take any chances." He glanced at his watch. "Thirty-eight hours to go."

"Gonna make it?" Alex's eyes sparked challenge.

"Two gets you five."

"Good enough for me." Griffin moved on. Moments later he reached a door labeled with an hourglass symbol in Day-Glo red, as eye-catching as a black widow's underbelly. *Radiation.* Griffin thumbed the lock and entered his apartment.

MIMIC was only eighteen minutes from Cowles Modular Community by tube, but a four-day Game was coming up. Alex preferred his sleeping quarters close and snug to the action. It had been easy enough to have his personal living pod skimmed in from CMC and hooked up to MIMIC's modular wall. Some small adjustments to the electrical fittings, a water line, fiber optics, and *bang*: instant home. In four days it would be flown back over the hill.

His kitchen, bathroom, and living room were standard issue. Bedroom and personal office were modular hookup, could be bolted down and shipped anywhere in the country in twenty-four hours. Meacham hadn't been *wrong*, he'd only been too early.

There were rooms to spare at MIMIC. This was a converted office, not one of those shaky monstrosities that slid up and down the modular wall on tracks, though Tony had had it touched up to look like the older shells.

In the two weeks Alex's module had been at MIMIC, Sharon was the first person he had entertained.

Quite a night. He still felt smug and steamy at the thought of it. All they had needed was bedroom and kitchen. And bedroom.

He stretched out on the mattress and felt it mold to fit him, felt it purr and knead.

Very little sleep last night. Like most first encounters, it had been a whirlwind evening, a veritable symphony of mutual exploration with a sinuous and greedy lady. He could always catch up on sleep— one rarely had so fine a reason to miss it.

He had four days off, and Dream Park was about to hold the greatest Game of all time. He and Sharon would share in it—not as Gamers, but Actors, NPCs, two of those who shaped reality for the players.

He ground his palms into his eye and stared into the mirror across from his bed. A big, gangling stranger stared back at him, body taut from countless hours of training, a certain rakish hollowness surrounding the pale green eyes. They were algae green, emerald with hints of blue and black swirled together. The lips curled naturally into a smile just now, flat but not quite cynical.

Sharon's scent was still in the air. Quite distinctly, he remembered her legs, their silken warmth as he peeled her nylons away. She had whispered wordlessly, feverishly, as the two of them sank back onto his bed. It had molded to their bodies, adjusted to their thermal patterns, and given back precise waves of heat and vibration, the exact levels of firmness and fluidity necessary to maximize pleasure.

He was lost in the bed's undulations. Swept away in Sharon's pungency, the smell and taste of her, the way she whispered his name, or clung shuddering to him as she tumbled over the edge and into the long, long descent.

Dammit, he just plain adored her, even the imperfections. Assiduous study had found only two: a discolored molar at the top right of her mouth, and the featherlike remnant of an appendix scar. In every other way, the lady was just too damned perfect.

He remembered the flash of coolness in the moments directly afterward, when she turned away from him to light a cigarette.

A spark of light, followed by the brisk tang of contraband. She inhaled harshly.

"You ready to do three months in County?"

"You turning me in?" she asked. She made a rustling sound. "Want one? Tennessee Tornado." Her voice was cool. She had given him so much, so completely, almost submissively, but then something inside her drew a curtain, retreated into observer mode. *That's all, folks.*

"Later, maybe."

"I'll leave the pack."

The sound of an exhalation cut off all possible communication. Nothing special, or even unusual, in Griffin's life. Just an abrupt cessation to closeness, then a pat on the butt as she rose to shower.

Griffin felt a surge of panic, swiftly suppressed as he realized he wanted more.

He lay in darkness, absently scratching at an existential itch.

Postcoital irritation? His hand searched out and found the plastic pack of contraband tobacco. He shook one out halfway and slid it into his mouth. Found her lighter and sparked the cigarette into smoke. Drew shallowly at first. He savored the burn, the quick hot dizziness spreading out from his lungs.

And thought of her.

Sharon Crayne sat at ScanNet's console, doing what she had to do, what she had committed herself to do. For a moment, she thought of Alex Griffin, and her resolve weakened.

He was just a man, she told herself. Just another man who had used her body. And that made Griffin an animal, like all the others. Something to be used and then thrown aside. Maybe they could have been friends, but that potential had ended the moment he went for the bait, the moment he let her coax him into bed. The moment he had entered her, no matter how gently.

No friendship was possible, and yet her head sagged, and something inside her cried out in loneliness, in need ignored for years. There was something different about Alex, something good and gentle and strong. She was ashamed to have used his loneliness.

Just perhaps, if all went well, they could start over again. Perhaps, if he could forgive her for what she had to do, she could forgive him for what he had done. He needed someone, as she did. He didn't really *love* her, he was in love with the *idea* of love. Enthralled, and perhaps amazed, that he still believed in love.

And what did Sharon Crayne believe in?

She didn't know, and wouldn't have time to find out, not until her task was done. So for now, focus on that task. Let nothing interfere.

"I'm coming, sweetheart," she whispered. "Mommy's doing everything she can."

Chapter Four

The Crystal Maze

Tuesday, July 19, 2059—9:00 P.M.

Acacia Garcia calmed her breathing. She wiped sweat out of one eye at a time for fear of obscuring her vision. She was ever alert for symptoms that the Crystal Maze was preparing to shift.

The Maze's forest of glass and plastic mirrors crawled and crackled with slow lightning. A vaguely mint-scented mist roiled around her knees. Sometimes tentacled things writhed in its depths.

All of the lights dimmed, and she held her breath. A ploy? Laughter. Fanged reptilian mouths materialized in shifting demonic faces, dancing in the wan light. Then the glowing image of Tammi floated through the darkness.

Acacia swiveled, back flattening against the wall. Tammi's face was an illusion: its eyes didn't track her. Perhaps lurking behind her back? Close enough to breathe in her ear? . . .

Acacia checked her wrist monitor and punched in TAMMI. She got a heartbeat and respiration rate, a blood-pressure reading. If she chose to monitor it long enough, she might be able to tell when or if Tammi was getting ready to spring a trap. But it couldn't give her Tammi's location.

And of course Tammi had a monitor, too.

Six hours before, at the beginning of what was supposed to be a three-hour exhibition Game, Acacia and her team had entered the Crystal Maze.

Wrist monitors were supposed to give each team a complete

readout of the other, plus a rough location within the Maze, making general strategy easier and melees more complex.

But . . .

Team leaders had monitor bands operating on a five-hour rechargeable battery. Acacia shut hers down, then employed the bridge-cutting strategy designed to confuse and infuriate the volatile Tammi. In order to have any chance against the unbeaten Troglodykes, Acacia had to force Tammi to play Crystal Maze to an alien rhythm.

By that dreadful fifth hour it seemed that Acacia's strategy was madness. Both teams were exhausted, but the Troglodykes had lost one player, and Acacia had lost two.

Then Tammi's locator died. Acacia had watched Tammi's panic register in the biomonitor: a sudden surge of respiratory and heart rate. Grimly satisfied, Acacia switched her locator back on.

Acacia sat tight in the Maze, waiting for Tammi to do something irrational.

Waiting . . . and waiting.

If Tammi was impulsive, Twan, her other half, was as nerveless an opponent as Acacia had ever faced. As a team they were too damned dangerous.

She had to shake their confidence *now*.

From the balcony around the edge of the lobby, the Maze looked like a jeweled city. The spectators wore costumes from a hundred lands and eras. Some weren't human. They wore prosthetic plastic or makeup, and, in a few cases, moderately effective holographic shrouds to give them the appearance of lizards, or glass-skinned damsels from the planet Wyndex, or denizens of worlds yet undreamed of. There were minstrels, and warriors from Africa and Japan and the Aztec empire. There were costumes from the English Regency and the Italian Renaissance and the antebellum South.

Wagers were offered and taken as the contestants crept about in their arcane patterns, deployed their various stratagems, and engaged in bloody battles.

In their thousands, Gamers surged at the rails and crowded about monitors in every Dream Park hotel. These were the legions of the IFGS, having the party of their lives. Confetti streamed from the top level. Party rhythms wafted from the rooms, from Waltz to Big Band to Salsa and Elf Hive Hop. A different era and beat blared forth every twenty feet or so.

Hotel security men eyed each other nervously as the press increased. Even for Dream Park, this crowd was decidedly weird.

Without turning, Acacia knew that Captain Cipher was beside her. No sound had betrayed him, and certainly Acacia had no sixth sense. She was merely unfortunate enough to be standing downwind of him.

Sweat plastered his red hair down and painted dark pungent stains in the armpits of his red tights.

"Captain Cipher," she whispered.

"At your beck and/or call, milady," he whispered, with a sweep of an imaginary hat. He was slow straightening. He had been on his feet continuously since five that morning and was starting to fade.

The glass walls around them glowed red. In a few moments the glass might clear again, and their antagonists would know exactly where they were.

"Listen," Acacia said urgently. "We're going to die here in a minute—"

"But you think Captain Cipher can save the day?"

"Yes," she said wearily. "Captain Cipher can save the day. Look at this."

She tapped out the first five notes of the *Starship Troopers* theme on a crystal keyboard inset in a wall. A hidden plate slid up.

Within was an old-fashioned computer console keyboard. Its screen revealed the remaining three members of Tammi's team as they crept through the mist.

So, they were together, not separated into a pincer movement. That was valuable information, but she needed more. She needed their location.

"Look," she said. "We've accumulated twelve thousand three hundred points. With seven hundred more, we get a tunnel through the mirrors. But we have to gamble seven to win seven, and this is a Fourth-Level puzzle."

She tapped out a request, and categories appeared:

1) Historical Trivia
2) Famous Battles
3) Killer Konundrums
4) Minor Masters

Corby blinked his rather protruding eyes rapidly. "'Famous Battles.' Erk. History was always Captain Cipher's weakest subject."

"I might be able to handle that—"

"Not at Level Four. Nine-nosed Napoléon, milady—they'll pull out some fourth-century Mesopotamian ca-ca, trust me. Minor Masters is probably eighteenth-century Italian card sharks and street mimes. Captain Cipher likes Killer Konundrums." His round little eyes grew shifty and distant as he considered. "If it's a classic, I'd probably know it. Even if it's brand new, it might be a reframe of a classical puzzle. Or I can logic it out. I mean, it has to be solvable, you know?"

She rubbed his shoulder affectionately. "I'm gonna trust you."

"With a face like mine, who can blame you?"

It was a face, Acacia decided, that only a mother or a desperate Loremaster could love.

She made her choice with the touch of a finger. The screen cleared. A cool synthesized voice spoke while matching words crawled across the screen.

"A hunter leaves home one morning. He walks a mile south and finds nothing. He walks a mile west, sees a bird, runs it down, and spears it for his supper. He walks a mile north and is home again. Tell me: What probable color is the bird, and why?"

Acacia stared, perplexity creasing her lovely face. "I've heard that one," she said. "It's too easy. The bear is white."

"*Bird*, not *bear*. So the answer can't be 'It's white, it's a polar bear, he's at the North Pole.' So."

The Maze around them began to throb, smoke pouring from beneath the nearest sliding panel.

Captain Cipher's eyes defocused. "Spears it. Runs it down and spears it. That takes . . ."

"Can you solve it?" They could take their loss and scamper, or try to answer the question. Every second cost them another five points.

"I've already got half of it, milady. The bird . . ."

Acacia decided to let him work. She raised her sword high, set her back against the Captain's, and waited, ready for danger, but never forgetting for a moment to keep tummy tucked in and chest lifted high for the camera. The eternal "Cheese."

Her body, once lean as a runner's, was now carefully ripened, so lush it almost burst out of her costume. Fashions change, she told herself, but mammalian response remains the same.

In every Game, players had a variety of factors going for them. Stamina, fighting skill, intelligence, luck, memory of obscure trivia . . . all these figured in the actual playing of the Game. An additional quality was needed to create a champion:

Showmanship.

A true champion needed to spend an inordinate amount of time playing the Games, traveling from one area of the country and the world to another. In order to do that, she had to be popular with the players, the NPCs, and ultimately the millions of people who would never play a Game but would pay to watch it. Professional Gamers competed to divert as much of that loot to their own pockets as possible.

To that end, as well as the others, Acacia had deployed her considerable charms. She considered her alter ego, Panthesilea, to be the best mixture of brains and beauty, brawn and bravado in the Gaming world.

The Warrior-woman's past was sketchy. Panthesilea was known to be the great-granddaughter of Hercules and an Amazon queen, a second-generation product of parthenogenesis.

Acacia had played Panthesilea for almost ten years, had nurtured her carefully. She had never died in a Game. She had ascended through time and effort to become one of the most powerful and highly ranked Player Characters in the International Fantasy Gaming Society.

During Games Acacia disappeared, immersing herself completely into the Warrior-woman from afar.

The mirror behind Captain Cipher flamed red. A mouth had appeared in it now, glowing brightly, a vast, grinning diamond shape, chockablock with needle teeth. Flames danced within. Insane laughter rang in her ears.

The demon of the Maze. This was the final trump. If Captain Cipher failed, all of their accumulated points might vanish. If he succeeded but she was killed by the materializing demon, the Troglodykes would hunt Cipher down and fillet him.

"Have you got an answer?" she hissed.

"Never published. Brand-new puzzle. Lovely!"

And the demon leapt.

Acacia screamed Panthesilea's battle cry (an assiduously practiced blend of Johnny Weissmuller and Ella Fitzgerald) and—

The demon froze in midleap. Captain Cipher had begun to answer the question. Mutilations were temporarily suspended.

She peered anxiously over Cipher's shoulders.

He had typed, "Black and White. Penguin."

A politely inquisitive demon appeared on the screen. "Why?" he/she/it asked sonorously.

Cipher looked around. "The camp is one plus one over two *pi* times *N* miles north of the South Pole."

Acacia stared. "What?"

"The hunter runs it down, yes? The bird's flightless. Penguins. The tuxedoed darlings are found only near the South Pole." He was typing furiously:

1 + 1/2Pi(N) miles north of the South Pole (N a positive integer)

"Just so the demon knows Captain Cipher means business," he said arrogantly. "Now, Hunter set his tent just north of the pole, right? He walks a mile south, toward the pole, then circles the pole. That takes him a mile west, see? If he's closer yet, he can circle the pole two or three or four times. Then he backtracks, one mile north, and he's back at base camp. Only place he can do that is at the South Pole."

She felt dazed. Captain Cipher waited coolly, matching gazes with the ruby-flame apparition dancing in the glass before him.

"Dinner," it said, "is served." Its mouth opened wider, wider. A tunnel to the beyond. *"Bon appétit,"* the demon said in a very bad French accent.

Acacia whispered, "Stay here" in Panthesilea's husky voice, and stepped through the portal.

The entire Crystal Maze revolved around her with a barely audible vibration. The path beneath her feet remained stable.

The important thing was that she could see the enemy, but they couldn't see her. The three surviving Troglodykes had found their own console and were attempting to defeat their own demon. If they made it, both teams would have an equal footing, and Acacia was doomed.

As always, Tammi was stunning. Her icy-blond hair framed fashion-model cheekbones and blue eyes that burned with a challenge few men could ignore, and none surmount. Makeup made her pale skin even paler. Her shimmering white costume was radiant in the rotating lights. Her partner Twan Tsing was busy at the console. What would their chosen category be? Acacia had no idea and couldn't afford to guess.

Just concentrate on the action to come. Brain and brawn. Beauty and bravado. The Troglodykes were said to be the Crystal Maze's

Dynamic Duo. Better than any individual, better than any other team.

Like hell.

Tammi kept her staff at the ready, as alert as a cobra. Behind the walls of glass, lights slid past like the eyes of disembodied jinn. Her nerves burned. What was it? Could she subliminally sense approaching footsteps? Or a change in noise level from outside? Or was the tension simply beginning to get to her?

Behind her, Twan labored through a three-dimensional maze. A rolling red ball guided by a set of delicate finger controls crept its way through a forest of swinging axes and flopping trapdoors, toward an opening at the top of the screen.

The Troglodykes had invested two thousand points here, but if they made it, the entire Maze would turn transparent. Superior forces would trample what remained of Acacia's team.

"Almost . . ." Twan said.

Tammi glanced at Appelion, the Warrior Warlock at her side, with satisfaction. He was a burly, hairy brute in matching black leather, and a stalwart companion. He growled, "I want first crack at Panthesilea—"

—who promptly stepped out of the wall and scythed him down. He squeaked incongruously and started to swing, then (hearing the death-buzz in his ear) toppled.

Tammi screamed and leapt.

Terrifying. Acacia had never confronted Tammi, the Warrior half of the Troglodykes. Tammi's staff, padded composition plastic imbued with a mystic glow, blurred to the attack. Panthesilea's sword swooped to counter.

Her sword was pure Dream Park. The components of a hologram projector were woven around a rigid, padded core, with a gyroscope in the handle to simulate weight and heft. She could parry and block with it in safety, while the holograms simulated a web of glittering, razor steel. This was where genuine proficiency, the grueling hours of saber or iaido or Filipino escrima, paid off.

They spun and dodged, Tammi taken aback and disadvantaged momentarily by the need to defend Twan, now fighting to keep her ball floating on its track.

Sword and staff leapt and swished and clacked. Now the sounds of cheering from the gallery were piped in. From behind Acacia's eyes, Panthesilea exulted.

If only she'd brought Captain Cipher! The little man could certainly have handled Twan. But she was winning! Scenting the kill, the cheering throng above them was going nuts.

Block and spin, a lethal tornado of motion. Low feint, trap the staff down, kick to the head blocked with the other end of the staff—

Acacia saw her opportunity. She accepted a shattered rib to touch Tammi's right arm. Ribs and arm glowed red. Cursing, Tammi dropped her weapon.

Twan screamed, "Excellent!" The red ball dropped neatly into its hole.

The demon of the Maze appeared. "Your pleasure?"

Panthesilea froze, and Acacia's personality emerged, figuring the odds. Twan could kill her right then—her Magic User rating was high enough. Then she would stalk down Cipher.

But before the spell worked, Acacia would kill Tammi. For the first time in Crystal Maze history, one of the dread Troglodykes would die.

What would she do? Twan squinted up at Acacia owlishly. "Stand by," she said to the demon.

"As you wish," it hissed.

The crowd was silent.

"I offer a draw," Twan said.

"Not quite," Acacia reminded her. "If we quit now, it's even kills, but you're a few points up."

"Draw. Take it or leave it." Tammi's eyes wouldn't leave hers, wouldn't look to the left . . . she was about to leap for that damned staff. She'd continue the fight left-handed.

"Accepted," Acacia said, and lowered Panthesilea's sword.

Chapter Five

The Phantom of Dream Park

The mezzanine thundered its applause, echoed by five thousand hands in surrounding hotels.

Dream Park's twenty-six hundred acres was surrounded by dozens of fantasy-theme hotels. Some were owned by Cowles Industries, many were not. All were touched with the Dream Park magic; all were a tram away from the most fabulous amusement park in the world. At the moment, most of them were operating at minimal capacity.

Dream Park was closed.

In thirty-six hours, four hundred of the Park's employees would be involved in the greatest Game in its history. For one week, the management would take a rare opportunity to shut down, to perform as much maintenance and overhaul work as they could.

The Arabian Nights Hotel was a prickly forest of minarets under a canopy of laughing jinn. It was raucously noisy now, swelled to capacity with Gaming enthusiasts.

If Dream Park, crown jewel of the Cowles empire, was momentarily subdued, it still burned in the night like far Damascus. At this precise moment, to one special observer, it seemed to be blazing upside down.

A man hung by his heels from the roof of the Arabian Nights. His calf-boots were snugged in a loop of synthetic filament the approximate thickness and weight of a spiderweb. It had a breaking strength of twenty-seven hundred kilograms.

His was an unusual figure: wasp-sleek, perfectly muscled, moving beautifully beneath a leotard-thin shadow-black jumpsuit.

Surprisingly, the wind blowing off the Mojave carried a mist of rain. It slicked his face, dropping the temperature to below fifty. He hadn't reacted to the heat, or to the exertion, and now had no reaction to the wet.

The sky above crackled with lightning and a distant roll of thunder. The wind stiffened, and the rain became a pounding curtain.

He hung, a spider weaving its web in a torrent. Unmindful, he watched the inverted phantasmagoria of Dream Park and sighed. It had been . . . what? Seven years?

He spoke a quiet word. His visor fogged. On its clouded interior was projected an image stolen from the Hyatt's security cameras. Excellent. The crowd was still congratulating Acacia on her rather plebeian draw.

The *Troglodykes.* Tammi Romati and her brat, and her lover. Did they think *the family that slays together stays together*? He snickered.

He breathed another word into his helmet. A thermal sensor triggered. The pod at his belt scanned the room for sound and heat, bounced a beam around and off the walls, and then reconstructed the interior for his visor screen.

Not home, Alphonse? Heat blurs, but nothing more recent than a half hour. Still some warmth in the bed, a feathery tangle of bodies, fading even as he watched.

Stepping out on the pregnant wife? Alphonse! I'm shocked! Does Saray know about this? A hint dropped, say, three hours before the beginning of California Voodoo, could result in a disturbing phone call from a hysterical, pregnant woman. A juicy confrontation might ensue, leading to split attention at a vital moment . . .

Sun-tzu said: The highest form of generalship is to disrupt the adversary's will to compete. The next highest is to disturb vital personal relationships and alliances.

He grinned and broke the five-digit emergency code that sealed the window. Another twelve seconds defeated the alarm system. The window slid open.

Silence.

He hitched his weight onto the sill, shook his foot out of the loop, and dove into the room. He rolled with perfect coordination and came to balance squatting on the balls of his feet, silent. Black against black. Drops of rainwater puddled on the carpet beneath him.

His reimaging system picked up sounds and heat impressions from the hall beyond, transmuting the walls to glass.

He giggled with pleasure and dried his hands on a used bathroom towel. A quick sweep found luggage. It was sealed with a mechanical lock, which the intruder broke in less time than most men would have spent fumbling for keys.

It contained nothing worth stealing. But there was another suitcase—

It was tougher. The lock looked the same, was the same, but the case didn't open. He probed patiently . . . there was another lock, hidden . . . There.

Inside, a few data cards. All right, then: Alphonse Nakagawa used a personal data system, and kept it with him at all times. But he would have encrypted backups.

The intruder didn't know what system his adversary would use, but he would break it.

And he had time. Alphonse, like a good little Loremaster, would be watching Acacia's lackluster performance over at the Hyatt. Most IFGS members could watch in their rooms, but the LMs had to be present for the kill, had to parade themselves in front of their public. This the intruder had counted on.

Swiftly, without any fuss, he drained the data, then replaced the cards in their pouch.

Proximity. People approaching from the hall.

The intruder's wraparound visor sparked with data. Auditory channels amplified, filtered, scanned, and attempted to identify. No match.

He snapped the luggage closed again and slid it back into its place.

Voices closer now. Could Alphonse have loaned his key or code number to some stranger?

The voices stopped in front of the door. The intruder sprang to the window, his foot in the loop. A whispered word started a remote circuit and triggered a tiny powerful motor that reeled him up and out of the room. A second word slid the window closed a moment before the door opened.

The intruder smiled coldly, suspended forty stories above the ground. The rain had stopped. He breathed deeply, watching the subdued lights of a closed amusement park as they dwindled even further.

He chortled melodramatically. "The Pink Panther is gone missing again," he whispered, and it took all of his considerable self-control to keep from laughing with unabashed, urchin glee.

What a lovely evening.

Acacia Garcia was surrounded by admirers as she rode up in the Hyatt's elevators.

"Captain Cipher predicts we'll kick serious butt, milady."

"Tammi may have a different opinion, Cipher," she said. She was exhausted, and boggled that this strange little man would rather talk than crawl away somewhere and slip into a coma.

She couldn't bring herself to snap at him: his eyes were worshipful, as guileless as a puppy's. She placed her hand on his, and he almost swooned. "Listen. We make a good team?" She mustered enough strength to make intense eye contact. "I need rest."

He tried to peek around her shoulder, peering into the room beyond. "*He*'s in there, isn't he?"

Fatigue vanished momentarily. She stood hipshot, head canted to the side, smiling mischievously. "And just who are we talking about?"

"Oh, milady—it's not a secret really, everybody knows you and Bishop are an item. When's he coming out?"

"Man of mystery." She changed the subject. "Corby, we'll be on public display tomorrow. I want you *clean*. That means soap and water and maybe a wire brush." She slid the door shut without waiting for a reply.

She sighed relief and collapsed with her back against the panel.

The room was entirely dark.

If she stood motionless and opened her senses, Acacia imagined that she could hear the slightly husky sound of his exhalations. She imagined that she could smell his sweat. And *that* thought triggered a wave of heat that drove away all fatigue.

For the thousandth time, she warred with her own instincts. *Just turn around. Walk back out the door. It's not too late.*

But then he'll never touch you again.

Lightly, she moved into the room, into the darkness.

In the dark a computer screen flickered pale green, like the face of a ghost. Its fluctuating luminescence flowed with numbers and letters and symbols.

Nigel Bishop was at work. She watched as his fingers manipulated the stylus and tapped at the keyboard, as he whispered into the throat monitor.

He was swathed in shadow, his wiry body sheathed in a leotard that was darker still. Occasionally the light reflected on his torso. He was whipcord slim, chest and back more knotted and corded, more sinewy and powerful, than any she had ever known—except one.

And Bishop was wirier, denser than Alex Griffin. Quicker. Maybe not stronger. The thought of Bishop atop her, or she astride him, the pressure of his hands, the taste of his mouth, his faintly sweet and musky scent filling her senses . . .

She felt dizzy, and hollow, and confused. Did Acacia love Nigel? Or was Panthesilea in lust with the Bishop?

Sometimes she hated that hot-blooded bitch.

His hands were a blur, switching from longhand to typing as the mood struck him. The computer synthesized writing and shorthand typing and whispered cues seamlessly together. Without turning, he said, "You were superb, darling. Your variation on the Horshact maneuver was nonpareil. Excellent trial for your team. You pulled them together, and sacrificed them at just the right moments."

He paused for effect, or perhaps lost in a parallel train of thought. She could never be sure which. "Did you know that you are just a teensy bit ruthless?"

"I wonder who I learned *that* from?" She came close enough to peer over his shoulder.

On the screen was data on each of the five teams entered in the California Voodoo Game. Bishop already knew his team, of course, and Acacia's team. But the other three were supposed to be mysteries, their identities and personae concealed until the last possible moment.

One face after another flicked onto the screen. Bishop tapped out notes.

"Did I keep them long enough?"

"Just," he said, bending back to work. A network of lines and curves appeared, fluctuated, and expanded from the screen into three-dimensional abstracts.

"What is that?"

"Preliminary chart," he said. "I now know the full IFGS records of every team." He grinned up at her, his smile brilliant in his night-dark face. His watch beeped. "Ah. Appointment time."

"Appointment?" she asked. Sudden sharp disappointment made her feel hot, flushed, and embarrassed.

And damn the bastard, he knew it. He grinned up at her again and shut down his computer. "Business before pleasure, sweetheart. The lady can't wait."

The lady can't wait. And I can? "Lady?"

"Tsk. Jealousy? From you?" He spun to his feet, swirling her into his arms with the same motion. "You, more than anyone, should know my aversion to ladies."

"Bastard," she whispered. He laughed, and with two fingertips brushed her eyes closed.

"Shhh," he said. He backed her into the bed and folded her down onto it. The sheets rustled against her neck as she sank down into them.

"Just quiet," he said. She shivered, knowing what was to come.

She felt the slight, liquid pressure of his lips and tongue as they drifted over her, touching her at the nape of her neck, behind her ears, brushing her eyelashes. His teeth nipped at her earlobes. Reflexively, her body began to arch, but his thumbs ran along the edge of her hips, pressing, calming them back down, as his mouth nipped and played along the long, warm column of bare throat.

His fingers twined in hers, pressed her hands into the bed as he caressed her for what seemed an hour, but could only have been a few minutes.

When her breath was explosive, her entire body shuddering and molten, she felt his weight leave the bed, and heard him say:

"I'll be back." His voice was neutral. "Be ready for me."

The door sighed shut behind him. Acacia waited ten seconds, feeling the tension build inside her until she thought she would explode. Then she screamed in the soundproof room, shrieked until her throat ached, and hurled her shoe against the back of the closed door.

The rain-swept town of Yucca Valley, just south of Dream Park, was a warren of exploitation, a boomtown of auxiliary entertainments and service facilities designed to catch the trickle-over from the world's largest tourist trap.

An astonishing variety of pleasures, ethereal or mundane, legal or illegal, could be found there. There was a thriving red-light district, as well as a Buddhist temple, a Methodist church, a Catholic mission, and a Kingdom Hall of Jehovah's Witnesses.

Alcohol was available all over. Cocaine, marijuana, and tobacco could be had in every alley and parking lot along the central strip. Nigel Bishop breathed it in, reveling in the sights and sounds and smells of human degradation.

They were pawns, every one of them. Even more amazingly, they *liked* being pawns. All the easier to use.

A hot-eyed pair of hustlers watched him as he pulled his car into the lot across from the Mate 'N' Switch Adult Emporium. He paid the toll and nosed his car up to an idle charging post. It clicked as the couplings mated and the trickle of current began.

The charging light blinked, splashing the bottom half of his face with green. Despite the darkness, he wore sunglasses of a tint similar to his visor.

He checked his watch. One fifty-five. In five minutes it would happen. He stepped out of the car, sniffing the air. It smelled humid but clean.

His watch beeped. His eyes scanned the Mate 'N' Switch. Just another fantasy sex trap, like any of a hundred in a fifty-mile radius of Dream Park, or a thousand others in southern California that catered to the very special needs of jaded flesh.

There was one difference, a difference known to only a select clientele. In addition to the usual mechanical accoutrements and procurement services, the Mate 'N' Switch offered a commodity increasingly rare in a high-security world: anonymity. They guaranteed it. Pay with cash, and they were notably lax about records, recalled no faces, and routed all phone messages through a cutoff satellite service subscribed to by a select high-security clientele worldwide.

The blocky stucco building was sleazily unassuming, but its customers had included some of the most powerful men and women in the world—by their own very private admissions. The Mate 'N' Switch would never comment. Managers paid their fines for non-cooperation, or served their time for contempt. When the place was eventually closed down, the shell corporation owning it would dissolve. Weeks or months later the owners would form a new shell and open a new hot-sheet special. Once again the word would spread along the grapevine that privacy was available.

Bishop flicked his cigarette away. It spun, striking sparks against the rain-slick pavement. He cinched his trench coat and crossed the street with studied casualness. His door lay in a shadowed alcove, away from street lamps.

He fed bills into a slot, carefully keeping his back to passing cars.

The door opened into an elevator. He punched in a room number. The lift capsule shuttled him up a wall and around the edge of the building, finally coming to rest in a corner slot.

No Mate 'N' Switch guest ever needed to encounter another. Undoubtedly there were entrances even Bishop knew nothing about.

The door opened on an otherworldly garden, reeking with hot citrus. Glimpsed between flowering trees, fertile fields and green-speckled hills stretched off into the horizon. Flocks grazed. Birds cawed in looped melody.

The Garden of Eden? How déclassé.

He whispered, "Scan," and the room's genuine dimensions appeared, banishing the phantasms.

It was a mere cubbyhole, an area marked off by the shadow of a single towering fig tree. Beneath it was spread a blanket.

And on the blanket sat Sharon Crayne. Her face was as expressionless as a waxwork.

"Bishop."

His gaze slid past her, examining the room, ignoring the illusion. Bathroom. Wet bar. A closet of possibilities. It opened for him, and he brushed the hanging garments with the back of his hand.

"Sharon. Delightful to see you again." He slid his hand into a long glove that felt like fur-lined silk. It breathed into his hand, tickling and caressing.

He lost the sensation of his arm. His hand felt long and graceful and fragile . . . feminine.

"This is really rather decadent," he said, smiling. "Shall I slip into something comfortable? And then you can be Adam, and slip into me. I'm certain that all of the anatomical bits are quite clever."

He pulled it free from the closet, holding it in front of him. It was some kind of stretch material. Breasts, now flaccid, would doubtless grow firm if he donned it. Was there a menu of shapes?

Her smile was mirthless, meaningless, tacked on like a doll's glass eyes. "Let's stick to business, shall we?"

"You're just no fun anymore." He slid the woman suit back into the closet and let the door shut and disappear.

Back in the garden.

Sharon spread a series of slender packets out on the blanket. "This is what you want," she said flatly.

He sat cross-legged. "That," he said, slitting one open with his thumbnail, "remains to be seen."

He doffed his sunglasses and slipped a projector-viewer from his trench-coat pocket. He inserted one of the flat crystals. A six-inch model of MIMIC appeared and revolved on the table before them.

"These are the most recent updates?"

"I got you the entire map of ScanNet emplacements. It's only forty percent operational now. In a month, you'd never be able to beat it."

"Yes," he agreed merrily. "But then in a month I'll be in Acapulco earning seventeen percent, darling."

"I don't teach strategy to Nigel Bishop. You can see where the improvements have been made—foundations shored up, new support struts. Where the floors have been lifted or lowered. And where you'll be entering the structure on Thursday morning. I think that I've lived up to our bargain, don't you?" The emotionless mask had started to crack.

"Umm-hmm," he answered. He fished something from an inside pocket and tossed it to her. "Indeed you have. Yes, I think that this will just about do."

Her hands shook as she opened the packet. There were pictures of a small girl with a sweet, sad smile. The girl might have been six years old. Accompanying it was an official genetic-code scan, and the confidential file marked *Embryadopt* identifying the donor mother. "What is her name?" She was unable to control the tears now, and they streaked both cheeks.

"It's all there." Bishop rotated MIMIC this way and that, humming to himself. "Tricia, I think. Should be twelve by now. Supposed to be a bright kid. Living in Kalamazoo, Michigan."

"I've got to get her," she said, as if to herself.

"Indeed." He nodded, not really paying attention. "How fortuitous was our meeting, dear girl."

She seemed lost in bitter memory. "I was twelve." Her voice went venomous. "I hope his balls rot off."

"Such a mouth. Hmmm. Eighth level . . ."

She seemed to be trying to justify something, talking even though Bishop wasn't really listening. "I didn't have an option," she said. "Fetal adoption was the only choice."

"And a child always yearns for Mommy." He grinned and hummed as he worked, almost ignoring her. "Tricia's foster parents are going to have paperwork problems. Terrible for them. Lucky for you. I always keep my bargains—see that you keep yours."

"How did you get this?" she asked, confused, slipping back out of her trance. "I tried every connection I had. I tried money—"

"It's love, not money, makes the world go—" Bishop was sliding the crystals back into their envelopes and starting to turn when his world went red and blue, and the illusions vanished completely.

Sharon flinched as the whites of Bishop's eyes turned dark blue. "What the hell . . ."

His hand snapped up in command. "Shut the fuck up," he snarled. "This room is being scanned."

To Nigel Bishop, the walls had become blue glass. He saw and evaluated holographic projection equipment, fiber optics, electrical and plumbing, communications . . .

Communications.

He turned, quiet and deadly. "One can't even rely upon mother love anymore. You don't want her, do you?"

More than the question had taken her by surprise. "How did you . . ." She was confused, startled, but questions and possible answers were formulating at breakneck speed. She went into a crouch and moved back, away from him.

His eyes no longer resembled human eyes. And all of the slightly arid amusement had disappeared from Nigel Bishop's demeanor. He had become, in a moment, something not entirely human, and not at all sane.

"Scleral lenses?" she asked. "You've got DreamTime technology in *contact lenses*? That's not available to the public! How—"

He raged about the room, ignoring her implied question. "Morals? Attack of fucking ethics? Enchanted with the single life?"

Toilet, sunken bath, floor mat. Walls. Yes. A triangle of light pulsed next to the bathroom door.

A monitor. Recording, not transmitting.

Sharon's face slackened, sick with sudden understanding. "You're not a Gamer at all, are you?"

Suddenly he relaxed. Totally. Shoulders. Arms. Face. Sharon, watching, attuned to him, felt her own body slacken. Felt confusion course through her. Where a moment before he had seemed as deadly as a rabid snake, now he projected total harmlessness. Her nerves burned, but she couldn't stop herself from relaxing, dammit . . .

Nigel chuckled delightedly, as if sharing a wonderful jest. "For a moment there—" He slid sideways, and his left arm flickered out faster than a blink. The ball of his thumb dug into the nerve plexus at the base of her ear. Pain erupted, sudden and unbelievably severe. What defense? Kick? Elbow? Knee?

But all of her lovely defense techniques had been learned in a state of clarity. A mind screaming with pain cannot think. A body denied balance and breath cannot respond.

His right thumb dug for a nerve cluster at the elbow. Attacked by two entirely separate sources of pain, Sharon's body spasmed and froze. She couldn't even speak.

Bishop brought his face into her line of sight. It seemed carved from black ice, all bone and muscle and terrible, animalistic fury. "An application of *aiki-jutsu*, you faithless bitch." She couldn't understand the venom, the sheer murderous hatred in his words.

"It isn't as if I trusted you, whore. But if you didn't care about your word, or your life, you might have given a *shit* about your *child*." He screamed the word, and she cringed, expecting a blow that didn't come.

"I should have known," he said, and increased the torque, intensifying the level of pain until her face turned pasty. Then he released it a little, letting her breathe.

She gulped air. Maybe if she explained. "I—just wanted some insurance . . ." His face had become impassive, except for those animal eyes. The eyes promised death. All hope drained from her, and with it, much of the fear. "Who are you?" she asked dully. "What do you really want?"

"Surcease of sorrow." He ground his thumb against the nerve again. Then he mashed the cartoid artery. She twitched hard, shivering, locked between pain and oxygen starvation, and then went limp. Sharon Crayne slid bonelessly to the floor.

"Tsk," he said.

He could see no flaw in the featureless cubicle's walls . . . ceiling . . . rim of the pool? Nothing, and seconds were becoming minutes. On a hunch he dialed Eden again, then changed the setting. A castle and moat. A wilderness of ice, a seal hole exposing black water . . . what was that, an insect? A lifeless beach beneath a vast sun made of red-hot fog, and the same lone insect hanging in the air.

It was a flaw in the liquid crystal display that sheathed the walls. His thumbnail scraped aside white plaster and revealed Sharon Crayne's tiny scanner.

His body was shaking, and he realized with a start that he was afraid. Everything could come apart, right now, unless he thought clearly.

Why had she bugged the room? And why the hell hadn't he put the sunglasses on before letting her know he had seen it? No mere

Gamer had Bishop's level of technology. It took very special connections. The kind that could pierce an Embryadopt screen . . .

And now Sharon knew. And that eliminated his options.

Nigel Bishop slipped a knife blade from the tip of his belt, slid it
under the liquid-crystal wallpaper, and peeled the paper back.

He was still trembling as he lifted out a video-audio recording
device no bigger than his thumbnail. Probably stored an hour of
image in bubble memory. With this in her hands, she'd thought to
hold him captive, to threaten exposure to the IFGS.

Stupid *bitch*. Bishop fought with his breathing, using his hard-
won muscle control to quell his shakes. It took twenty seconds, but
finally his stomach unclenched.

Perhaps Crayne had thought to prevent future blackmail. Stupid.
"I keep my bargains, Sharon."

A quick search of the room revealed no more nasty surprises.
Did she have an accomplice? Unlikely. Was there a device in another
room? Unlikely. The sensory cubicles had input but no output—
part of the privacy guaranteed by Mate 'N' Switch's exorbitant
prices.

In all probability, this was the only nasty she had.

What to do?

Bishop closed his eyes, ran a dozen possibilities past his closed
lids in as many seconds. When he found his answer, his eyes opened
again, blinked once, and then regarded Sharon without emotion.

He peeled her out of her clothes with impersonal efficiency. He
hoisted her onto the bed as if she were a rag doll. He rubbed her
hair into the pillow. Rubbed her shoulders into the blanket.

He sniffed where her skin had touched sheets, vaguely recognizing the scent as Apéritif by Chanel.

Slip bug in pocket.

Ready.

He ran his fingers over Sharon's arm, found the pain hold that
he wanted, and then checked his watch. Three o'clock. He heard
nothing outside. The Mate 'N' Switch was silent, clients either
sleeping or humping feverishly away in fantasyland.

Adrenaline boiled in his veins. He clamped his mind back down
on the fear. There was still much to do, and not much time in which
to do it.

He slung her over his shoulder and carried her to the sunken tub.
When the illusion was on, this would be the lagoon, hot springs,

alien sea, Trevi Fountain, whatever. Bar soap was hidden in a recessed shelf at the edge. He dipped a new bar into the water and then squeezed it out of the wrapper. He balled the paper up and pocketed it.

Now. Very carefully, he set her heel down on the wet bar, let her weight mash it and skid her sideways. He let her fall, changing grips at the last moment to add the drive of his palm to her forehead so that it smashed hard against the tiled edge. She slid down, the white enamel now dappled with blood.

The water slid up into her nose. Her eyes fluttered open weakly. Dazed and almost helpless, Sharon Crayne fought for her life like a sick kitten. A thread of blood drifted out of her nose. She pushed feebly at his hand.

A few bubbles flowed out of her mouth.

And then she was still.

Bishop stood, wiping his palms against his pants with genuine distaste. "It wasn't in the game plan," he said flatly. "It isn't elegant. Bad call, Miss Crayne."

Moving swiftly, he checked the entire room again, minutely, remembering everything that he had touched, wiping every object and surface clean. He popped the wrapper into a disposal unit, then the child's picture, and watched them flash to flame. Good.

He stepped into the elevator capsule. Ran his actions back through his mind. When he had done this three times and found no flaw, he touched the pod at his belt. The illusion sprang to life once again.

Palm trees swayed in a gentle, fragrant wind. Somewhere distant, a lute played sadly.

And Sharon Crayne floated sideways in a blue lagoon.

The elevator door closed.

Acacia went from deep, druglike sleep to wakefulness in a slow beat. "Nigel?"

He didn't say anything, just pressed himself against her. His skin felt cold.

He was shaking. He pulled himself close to her, then closer still. In the room's dim light, she turned to look at him, touching his face and hair, surprised at his vulnerability.

"Nigel?" She felt sudden alarm, but he shushed her. With strong thin fingers he rolled her onto her back. He parted the veil of her nightgown, ran cold fingers along her warm flesh.

"Shhh." His lips brushed hers. Only his upper body, his cheeks, felt cold. His legs and thighs, his crotch, were fever-hot. "Shhh . . ."

She gasped, inhaling harshly as his weight came down on her. "Nigel?"

"Not a word, darling," he said. He began to move rhythmically, and despite all of her will, questions and speculations began to dissolve in sensation.

"Everything," he said hoarsely, "is just fine."

Chapter Six

Old Friends

Wednesday, July 20, 2059—10:00 P.M.

Acacia glided through the ballroom, nodding and accepting nods, flirting and accepting flirtations, saving an edge of her awareness for her team.

Corrinda Harding, her excellent Thief, was dancing with Terrance "Prez" Coolidge. They looked like Mutt and Jeff: Prez was almost a foot taller, although they weighed about the same. Corrinda wasn't fat, but she was one beefy Wagnerian Valkyrie, a picturesque contrast to Terry's Zulu Warrior.

But Corrinda was nursing a knee injury suffered two weeks earlier in sword practice. Damn it, even with the pneumatic cuff, that knee might cause problems. At least she and Prez were slow-dancing, working a little more of the stiffness out. One could assume that was their intent . . .

The music became a hurricane shriek. Corrinda stepped back. Terry snatched at Mati "Top Nun" Cohen's hand and seemed to go into rhythmic convulsions. Top Nun's habit flipped to the music. The little Israeli had no skill but sufficient grace to make her fun to watch.

Where was Steffie? That was Steffie's chair, and twelve feet of huge pike propped upright between chair and table. Steffie must be dancing with Ozzie the Pike. They were old friends. Maybe she could learn something.

Oswald Murphy was with Tex-Mits on this roll, and he was a hell of a dancer, too.

Captain Cipher orbited somewhere near Acacia's elbow, as he had all night. On the breast of his jacket rode a green tag emblazoned *Universities of California.* His own attendees had kept him from being a nuisance. Yes, Captain Cipher had fans, and tales to tell, as well.

Look at those pudgy hands swooping through the air. Let the fans listen for enough years, and one day he would talk well. He'd play with his image, get a suit that fit and a tie with less flash and more imagination . . . She'd seen it happen in others.

The Universities of California were one of the strongest teams. Captain Cipher was from UC Irvine. Steffie "Aces" Wilde and "Prez" Coolidge were from UCLA, Corrinda from San Diego, Mati from Berkeley. Acacia was something of a ringer. She had homelinked courses in Polynesian Cuisine and Archaeology through UC Berkeley. She had never actually seen the campus, had never entered a classroom even in Virtual mode. She hated cooking. The thought of digging up old bones made her yawn. She probably had enough life-experience credits from the last few years of Gaming to get undergraduate degrees in either. It was just barely within the rules, and no one complained loudly enough to make a difference.

She was one of the highest-rated players in the United States. There had been sly offers of "part-time" employment at Texas Instruments, and a proposal for a very temporary enlistment in the Army. UC's cash scholarship offer was a token at best, but their team actually had a chance.

She had chosen and crafted well. She had one Cleric, one Thief, a Warrior, a Magic User, and an Engineer/Scout. Panthesilea would compete as a second Warrior.

A newsman drifted up to her. He was short, with pink cheeks and long white hair. A vidbot trailed behind him on a tripod dolly, balancing upon its slender stalk. Both fixed her with dreadfully serious gazes. "Panthesilea?"

She winced. "Acacia, please. Jimmy Crest?"

The reporter from *Star and Shield* magazine dimpled and half bowed. "Acacia, isn't it a bit unusual for rival team captains to be . . ." He paused, rolling his adjectives around, searching for the one that would give the proper impression of reluctant intrusion.

"Romantically involved?" she offered politely. She tried not to look at her own image, suddenly vast above the crowd, a bronzed goddess surveying her subjects.

"Well, yes. There are no rules against it, but there really isn't a precedent, either."

"There isn't really a precedent for Nigel, either, is there? Or me. We don't break rules, but we bend the hell out of them." There. She could almost hear the little delighted intakes of scandalized breath, all across the wide, wide world of sports.

"Are you sure you can do your best against a man you are involved with?"

"*Especially* against a man I'm involved with," Acacia said. "I know his soft spots, and I never back off. He'd better watch his sweetbreads."

They laughed. Women nearby applauded. But that was Panthesilea talking: Acacia Garcia had retreated into silence, miserably wishing that it was all true.

Seventy miles northeast, in MIMIC, Tony McWhirter watched his vid sourly, feet up on a bolster, drinking a fifth beer. He was drunk, and didn't care. He wished only that he dared switch to Scotch.

"But I have promises to keep," he said to himself, to the walls, to no one in particular. He wadded up the beer pod and hurled it at the wall.

He had known she was coming. He had kept the knowledge buried somewhere inside him, hidden deeply enough for him to cope with the pain.

She didn't have to look so damned good. She didn't have to sound so fine. He remembered that voice whispering warmly in his ear, encouraging him, urging him, cooing and caressing.

She didn't have to . . .

"Damn," he said sourly, and pressed himself back into the chair and closed his eyes hard.

"It's delightful being a scandal," Acacia said breathlessly. "Everyone should try it at least once."

Every eye was on them. Acacia Garcia and Nigel Bishop roamed the expo pavilion, sampling hors d'oeuvres, nibbling at a cherry cake sculpted in the shape of a dragon. They walked like a pair of strolling tigers, perfectly matched for stripe and muscle. Her dress was cut from *here* to *there*, exposing every curve to best effect. Nigel wore a custom-made ensemble, an elegant meshing of a traditional African dashiki and a tuxedo. The jarring contrast probably wouldn't have worked for any other couple.

"It's good for the Game, don't you think, Mr. Crest?" Nigel asked over the edge of his champagne glass.

"Well, maybe, but . . ." The little reporter lowered his voice conspiratorially. "There was some controversy about you being top-seeded after all of this time. What do you think about that?"

"I had to pass my preliminaries. I'm completely conversant with all of the recent IFGS rule changes, and we conducted six pure strategy sessions. My physical fitness has been rated 'superior' by two separate panels of experts. I'm not sure whether people think I'm being exploited for my reputation, or whether General Dynamics has purchased an unfair advantage . . ."

The convention center was crowded with Gamers from all over the world. There were exhibits on every side, Gaming systems, costumes, makeup, weaponry, logic crystals for every make of Gaming computer on the market, sign-ups for Games with a display of options. Gaming tours that would take players into exotic lands and match them against environments in Africa, Asia, and even one to be played in a cluster of shuttle tanks anchored near the Falling Angels lunar industrial complex.

Gamers strolled in costumes, in armor, in holographic projections—and nude. She tried not to giggle, but some of them strutted about absolutely starkers, with grotesque genital prostheses in every conceivable configuration.

These, of course, didn't show to the naked eye. These Gamers were broadcasting on one of the Virtual Kink channels. Acacia wore slimline glasses/movement sensors—cost a damned *fortune*, way more expensive than a standard helmet system—and her decoder brought in every public channel, including the adult lines. Some Gamers were broadcasting multiple images simultaneously, some explicitly X-rated.

A man with a pink, prickly organ that would have cored a rhinoceros smiled slyly. Acacia realized that she must have been staring and quickly turned away. She let him see her program her glasses to filter out the porno.

She waved when she recognized friends. Friar Duck . . . was with Texas Instruments–Mitsubishi this trip, wasn't he? Normally a burly gentleman with a wide mouth and large feet, he was projecting as *Dirty* Duck, a squat, cigar-chomping alcoholic mallard from the Golden Age of the *National Lampoon*'s comics section.

She thought for a moment before returning another woman's smile. Felicia . . . something. Played as Dark Star. She wouldn't be in California Voodoo—Felicia had been caught cheating once or twice. Acacia . . . hadn't.

There were millions of dollars' worth of equipment on display in the three tiers of the expo hall. Security personnel roamed everywhere, alert for trouble.

She searched for a familiar face, and didn't see it.

Alex, where are you? Do you still work for Dream Park?

Do you think of me? Of Acacia? The fanfares here were for her alter ego, Panthesilea.

Arlan Meyers took the podium, way down at the other end of the hall. He was bald and lemony, with a thin, prissy mouth and a manner that suggested a life of library excitement. He had been one of the great Magic Users, and a driving power behind the IFGS.

"Testing—is the image all right?" Arlan bowed his head to speak the words low, and then came up grinning again, greatly enjoying himself. The hologram system made of him a dumpy-looking thirty-foot giant. "I would like to welcome everyone to the opening of the tenth biannual IFGS sweeps."

Applause rippled through the crowd.

On the holoboard above the hall were betting lines on the teams, with every team member, his personal stats, and lifetime scores listed in full. Team organization strategies weren't there, but it was enough for the Vegas boys to establish odds in all of the major categories.

UC was the second-highest-rated team. First came Apple Computer, the team headed by the Troglodykes. Army was ranked third, and only because of their familiarity with War Games in the Gaming domes. General Dynamics would have been last, instead of Texas Instruments–Mitsubishi, but for the presence of Nigel Bishop. Bookmakers in Vegas and Atlantic City gave them a shot based on Nigel's presence alone. It was hard to fault their logic.

The IFGS had existed for sixty years, primarily as a brokerage house. They established rules and point-exchange protocols between the thousand separate and proudly independent Gaming groups around the world.

Does blitzkrieging a balrog in Brazil equate to slicing samurai into sashimi in Singapore? Ask the IFGS.

Game Masters, Loremasters, and the categories of Wizard, Warrior, Cleric, Thief, Scout, and Engineer were cross-referenced for hours of supervised play. Points could be earned by accumulating experience or taking standardized tests of mental and physical skill.

The results were integrated into a central processing system, and the rankings allowed players from different parts of the world, playing entirely different rules, to come together and enjoy each other's poison.

Oh, the infighting was dreadful! But the end result was worth it.

". . . and a very special thanks to Travis Cowles," Arlan said, "grandson of Arthur Cowles, and presently Chairman of the Board of Cowles Industries. Travis?"

Wimp, Acacia thought. At least he didn't glance down at notes. But his eyes flicked left, slow right, quick left: his notes were displayed on his glasses.

"We here at Dream Park feel that we owe you a debt. You helped keep the dream alive. You have supported us from the beginning. You helped us test the technology that sold the Barsoom Project to all the world . . ."

She spotted a watchful but unobtrusive security man. It was hard to read his broad oriental features, but he looked, she thought, concerned, uneasy. She pulled herself away from Nigel and went to speak to the guard.

His name badge said MITCH HASEGAWA. "Mr. Hasegawa?"

His worried expression cleared immediately. "Yes, can I help you?"

"I was wondering. I guess you know Alex Griffin?"

"Yes, ma'am." His expression grew watchful. Protective?

Acacia looked inside herself, noted the spark of joy, and was happy that she could still feel it, that she wasn't too far along whatever path Nigel was leading her. "He still the boss?"

"Sure." His smile looked freshly pressed, folded, stuck neatly into place. Acacia felt uncomfortable again.

"So if I just rang him up, you think I could talk to him? I used to have his personal line. He changed it."

"Sure." His eyes had already focused beyond her, as if there was something infinitely interesting just over her shoulder.

Acacia's skin crawled. Something wrong here. He wasn't playing the game. Dream Park Security interacted well with Gamers. Alex Griffin had Gamed himself, once, a lifetime ago. He may have continued. She'd shared his bed, and his life, a little; she'd known the security people . . .

Not this one. Hasegawa was new, or moved in from outside. But he didn't respond to her as a Gamer, a customer, a woman, a person. Coolly polite. Flinched at the Griffin's name. *Why?*

In a Game she would have tiptoed out with extreme caution and waited to learn more. Here . . . She excused herself politely and wandered back into the crowd, looking for Nigel.

He was swamped in the middle of a crowd of autograph hounds. She watched him, his black face shining, laughing, in total control.

"Representing the Army team, we have Major Terry Clavell," Meyers said. "Major?"

They loomed gigantic above the stage. Clavell was small, dark-haired, and wiry but not bulky. Give him a few pounds and he would have looked a little like Napoleon. He might easily have been mistaken for a desk warrior were it not for the messianic intensity of his eyes.

"Good evening," he said. "I would just like to assure you, especially those of you on the Armed Forces Network worldwide, that I will uphold the honor of my regiment. We invented war games. These . . . civilians . . . don't know what they're up against."

" 'Cacia!"

Now *that* was a familiar voice! Acacia turned just in time to miss being blindsided by a ball of muscle and wrinkled skin, about four feet one of solid energy.

"Mary-em!"

"The very." Mary-Martha Corbett scanned Acacia approvingly. "I see you've put on a few curves, girl. Playing to the crowd?"

"Aiming at the big time! I didn't know you were here. You're not on the big board."

Mary-em lowered her voice, forcing Acacia to bend almost double. "Traveling incognito. Nakagawa-san is nervous about security. Wants to keep everyone off balance. It's been, what—five years?"

"Since the Diskworld Game. Ah . . . Hamburg."

"Umm-hummm."

Acacia savored the sight of Mary-em and the memories of three Games they had played together. She was an enemy this time out. It didn't matter. When all was said and done, one got points by destroying one's enemy, but made money by cooperating to make the best holovid possible.

She searched her memory. "How's your brother . . ."

And knew immediately. The little woman's face fell. Deprived of the outflow of maniac energy, she showed her age. She must be in her sixties now. In mountain-climber shape, to be sure, but still a woman on the verge of serious retooling. Would Mary-em have the money for that?

"Patrick died two years ago, spring," she said. "I'm sort of dedicating this Game to him."

"That's wonderful," Acacia said. There was a swirl of crowd, and she was suddenly surrounded by eager hands with tabs and slates. She began signing signatures as quickly as she could, aware that she was being separated from her friend.

"Mary-em. See you in the Game!"

Mary-em raised a stocky arm and fist, and the sadness was gone. Not submerged or hidden, but genuinely gone, and Acacia was filled with warmth for the little woman, as if she were a symbol of a simpler time, before Acacia had become Panthesilea.

Before Nigel Bishop.

It was another hour before Acacia could sneak out of the hall, into a service elevator, and back to the room she shared with Nigel.

She sealed the door behind her and panted, relieved.

Nigel's computer was still on. The security files would be closed, but she didn't need those. He had shown her how to activate the High Pass program, invading the simplest levels of Dream Park Security without chance of trace-back.

Some of the channels were broadcast rather than direct-line. The computer picked out the right frequencies, unscrambled them, and let her sort. She queried: ALEX GRIFFIN?

The computer scanned. Within twelve seconds the program found the name "Alex" in a conversation. Then "Griff." It queried her to verify the dimunitive, and cross-referenced.

Lines of text began to appear on the screen. She sorted through them as the computer found Griffin's personal code and a nonsecure file giving his location.

Yucca Valley, California, four miles out from Dream Park . . . in a ratty section of town, she thought. Nigel's program was still at work. A moment later it had found a voice.

". . . sure how she died yet. Apparent accident. Drowned in a fucking bathtub."

"Dammit, what was she doing there last night?"

"Assignation."

"Wasn't she on duty?"

"No."

Acacia listened to the freeze in the speaker's voice and then realized that she was listening to Alex. The voice was flat, almost metallically emotionless. "What do you think?"

She knew that tone, knew the pain it concealed. The dead woman had meant something special to Alex Griffin.

As much as she, Acacia, had meant?

More?

"I want the complete forensics report by noon. Preliminary workup in two hours. Sheriff Osterreich will handle any interviews."

"Griff?"

"Yes."

"I'm sorry."

Pause. "So am I." He sounded tired.

Then Griffin signed off.

Acacia sat staring at the screen, troubled.

Someone close to Alex Griffin was dead. An employee of Dream Park, so it seemed. Drowned. Freak accident.

No real concern to her, except . . .

Where had Nigel been last night? He'd come back powerfully in rut, and in the morning had data she'd never seen, coded against theft. Not so strange, that, but was it new? Stolen? And what had caused the frenzy of sexual excitation?

She rubbed her eyes and killed the computer screen, trembling.

Her brain chattered reassuringly to her even as her gut twisted with suspicion. Acacia was proud of herself: she made it two-thirds of the way to the bathroom before champagne and hors d'oeuvres and cherry-frosted cake came spilling back up over her lips, marking her trail to the toilet.

Chapter Seven

Mate 'N' Switch

Alex Griffin dialed through a series of nine preprogrammed illusions. An igloo next to an ice hole, a castle and moat, a tropical isle and moonlit inlet, an alien world with a vast red sun and a foamy, crimson sea . . . Each had its own sour smell, its own irritating soundtrack.

He dialed 0. Once again he faced bare walls, a bed mat with rounded corners, a rug/floor with a wide, wild range of textures, a big oval sunken spa with shower heads above it. There were enough hooks, magnets, and suction devices to support a whole wonderful world of sexcessories. An alcove was stocked with sensory skinsuits, direct-nerve-induction stuff.

There was a hole chipped into one wall, high up, the size of his smallest toe. Below it on the rug was a trace of powdered plaster. Vacuuming would have picked it up: it had to be fresh.

Here in this dreary little box, Sharon Crayne had died.

The service door stood open. Local cops streamed in and out, searching, checking, finding little, trying to pretend not to notice his anguish. Failing.

Within the featureless cube of the Mate 'N' Switch building was an open, central well. It was lined with catwalks and resembled the backstage or substage at a Broadway show, or maybe a low-level Gaming area. Gaming Dome X?

The pleasure palace was shut down while Moshe Osterreich,

Yucca Valley's understaffed, overworked sheriff, attempted to extract information from the staff of Mate 'N' Switch.

Sharon's body was gone, removed by the county coroner. Again Alex scanned the room, shrinking from its stark and vulgar utility, and found no excuse to edit the pictures in his mind.

Sharon had checked in of her own will, in health, unaccompanied. He—surely not *she*, or *they*, though the evidence showed nothing of . . . He had entered sometime later, and together they had romped in the big bed.

Afterward, the lover had left. Sharon, perhaps tipsy and too relaxed after being well laid—though there was no evidence of alcohol or other funny chemicals—had taken a bath. Her foot slipped, and her head cracked into the rim. It was flush with the floor, but nothing else was hard enough to raise a bruise. She must have flipped like a gymnast. Momentum had carried her rolling into the bath . . .

More likely: *Thump. Ouch!* She rubs her head, curses, and slides into the sunken tub. Arms wrap around her head. She's making a keening squeak of rage and pain, like when she stubbed her little toe against the doorjamb in Griffin's mobile apartment. Doesn't know how badly she's been hurt. Blood leaks into brain tissue, shorting signals. Her head slips under the water . . .

Hours later, shortly after checkout time, a maintenance crew finds her as dead and cold as the water around her.

Who, then? Whom did she meet?

Alex tried to retain a modicum of professionalism, but it wasn't working. "I'm getting out of here, Moshe," he said to Osterreich.

The sheriff was a thin, wiry man with Groucho Marx eyebrows and a hawklike nose. "It's been a long day for you, Alex," he said. "Usual six A.M. roust?"

"Up at five. I'm beat, but I can't sleep. Not yet. See you later."

Alex shouldered his way through the door and fled to his skimmer. His blunt fingers dug into the dashboard.

He was under control. You have to stay under control, or life will eat you.

He said, "Home," thinking that the skimmer would take him to Cowles Modular Community, not really remembering that the beacon had been reassigned to MIMIC. The vehicle rose to its legal altitude of two hundred meters and hummed out across Yucca Valley, the community surrounding Dream Valley.

The Town that Cowles Built.

The car more or less drove itself, leaving him no distractions. He needed to put his mind somewhere; there were too many questions.

As security chief of Dream Park, he had immense leverage in Yucca Valley, but the truth was, he had no real right to interfere with Osterreich's investigation.

But Sharon had died in that sleazy sex shop after a sleazy assignation. Her life would be sieved by the minds guiding the Barsoom Project. Griffin's relationship with her would be dissected and analyzed. If, at the end, her only business at the Mate 'N' Switch had been the scratching of a physical itch, they would hand back the fragments of his memory, say "Sorry," and let him carry them meekly away.

Griffin guided his skimmer in toward MIMIC's rooftop landing pad. It was almost midnight, and the roof parties had died. A few robots scooted about picking up trash. He stepped out of the car. As soon as he slammed the door, it took off again, spiraling up and over the lip of the roof, down to the parking structure at MIMIC's base.

The elevator sank down toward the security hutch. Griffin was still brooding.

God. So fast. Everything had fallen.

She meant so much to me, and so quickly . . .

And he hated himself for the next thought:

Got under my skin quick, didn't she?

At the Security Center he found Hasegawa and a couple of other people. The room was mostly empty. Condolences had already been offered, but were offered again.

A cold wedge of pepperoni pizza stared at him from a cardboard coffin. What little nudge of hunger he might have felt vanished instantly.

Mitch was offering coffee. Alex sniffed it. Tasted it, glad that his ulcer hadn't bothered him recently.

Hadn't, in fact, since meeting Sharon.

Splash. Coffee stain on the cuff. *Shit.*

Numbly, he mopped it up.

Sharon. What were you doing in that place? Your tastes weren't that exotic. Why couldn't you have met him in your room? Or his?

Because they work here. At MIMIC. She didn't want me to know.

Griffin's eyes wanted to water. He clenched his eyelids against the sting.

A buzzing sound penetrated his concentration, and he punched up the line. "Griffin."

"Osterreich here."

"Yeah, Moshe. Go ahead."

"We have the preliminary coroner scan. Full workup in about five hours."

"Pump it through."

Sharon Crayne appeared onscreen. First the usual stats of inches and pounds. Then scars, muscle tone, apparent age. Makeup and recent beauty treatments. The prescription of her contact lenses. The plastic pin in her left wrist.

More intimacies: the nutritional content of her last meal. An ounce and a half of dark rum imbibed an hour before death. No other funny chemicals whatever.

And . . .

There was no semen in her vagina. Or her throat, or anus . . . or anywhere on her body . . . or anywhere in the room.

Okay, Mr. X hadn't screwed her yet. Maybe she was getting ready for him.

But the bed pad was wrinkled. Had it been used?

He studied the report. Traces of her perfume and body oils, a few cells, a strand of hair . . .

But no one else's. Nothing at all that didn't match her. Not male, or female, and as for the llama and the spayed gerbil . . . nothing.

Did she check in to masturbate, or what?

What were you doing there, Sharon? What was in the wall?

All right. Let's think this through. You had an assignation with a married man. You were in love . . .

Alex's ego wouldn't allow him to think that. There had been no one in her heart. There had been room for him. He knew it. He'd felt it. It *had* to be true.

Then— *Sharon:* You *wanted to call the affair off.* You *agreed to meet him one last time.* You—

The hole in the wall was right for a wide-angle scan. Sharon could have gotten her hands on a pinhead camera.

All right. *You wanted . . . he wanted?* Sharon checked into the motel. *She* would have had time to mount the camera. *He* wouldn't.

She wanted evidence. Information . . .

And that other, nasty thought coiled and hissed in his hindbrain. *She got under your skin mighty fast, didn't she, Griff?*

You let her into the security lines, past your defenses faster than you had to, because she was going to be taking over in two weeks. So she had access. To what?

May I? she had asked.

"Playback," he said. "Last access Sharon Crayne date July nineteenth security files."

There was a momentary pause—more, he suspected, for the psychological benefit of the user than from any need of the system. Then the screen flashed NO ACCESS CODE THAT DATE SHARON CRAYNE.

He thought of Sharon poring over the files. A smile struggled to surface, succeeded but lost its warmth along the way. It hung there on his mouth, cold and lifeless.

How long have you been dead now, Sharon? Thirteen, fourteen hours? And a file that doesn't exist is the last thing that you looked at.

The smile was deathlocked onto his face. He felt ghastly.

Somebody walked by his workstation and dropped a plastic data sheet off next to him. With an unoccupied splinter of attention he heard a rustle, saw a shadowy figure, heard somebody talking behind him.

He refused to come up from his search, even when he felt the hand on his shoulder.

"Griff!" Tony said, louder this time.

Alex jerked and stared up at the sympathetic face above him. For the first time, it was Griffin who looked away, who couldn't meet and hold his gaze.

"You want to know what Sharon was looking at last?"

"Just . . . want to look at it."

"I can do better than that. I have a complete playback loop. Every word, every command. Sometimes you get a weird effect in programming and can't figure out how you did it, so you'd like to go back and—" Tony sat next to Alex, and his fingers became a blur. "—watch over your own shoulder . . ."

Alex, still numbed, watched without enthusiasm. He wanted to tell Tony to go away.

"Funny," Tony said. "I can't pull up her visual . . ."

"Why would that be?"

"She may have put a block on it? Let's see the keystrokes." Tony continued to work while Alex watched. "I've still got some tricks."

"Breaking and entering type tricks?"

"I'm shocked, *shocked* that you would—" The structures of MIMIC began to appear. The view rotated, then zoomed in. "—accuse me of such a . . . preposterous . . . *There.*"

Suddenly Alex was watching Sharon again, and his heart broke.

She was totally absorbed in her work, busy, typing and writing occasionally, triggering some of the inputs with eye and head movements alone. She was alive, and he knew that he loved her. The urge to reach out and touch her, to speak the words he had never spoken, lashed him like a bitter wind.

"Griff, it looks like she called up the ScanNet system for the entire Gaming area."

Tony pulled back to a broader image of MIMIC, encompassing all nineteen floors. Some of the corridors flashed red: Sharon had been into them.

"Here, here, and here," Alex said, "we have the radiation signs."

"Why would she want those locations?"

"Don't those signs seal out Gamers?"

"They do. Strongest mantrap in IFGS: cost of opening that door by any means, one absolute death. No saving throws, no defense."

"Cute notion," Alex said. "Yours?"

"Doris and El." Tony sat back, and watched the play. "You know, Alex . . ."

"What?"

"We don't have a playback from the correct angle, but the way she's doing this reminds me of something."

"What?"

"Well, it's the way she's acting. The pattern. Trying to block the record, that too. She's recording ScanNet sensor locations."

"Maybe she wanted to look at the whole thing later, at her leisure."

Tony choose his next words carefully. "Maybe, but why not just have it pumped into her room?"

Alex sat stonily.

"Sorry, Griff. I didn't mean to imply anything . . ."

The air around Alex seemed to crackle. "Go ahead. What were you about to say?"

"Well . . . say I saw this. Say I didn't know Sharon, which I don't. Say I didn't know she was your friend."

"Will you cut the bullshit?"

Suddenly, unmistakably, the potential for physical violence normally submerged deep within Alex Griffin was quite close to the surface. Tony considered backing off. Instead he said, "I'd say she was recording this to give to someone else."

And there was a bugging device in the wall at the motel.

"We don't have any sound," Alex said, controlled again. "It looked to me as if she was saying something. Can you get that for me again?"

Tony tapped out commands. They were looking at Sharon's mouth. Griffin moved his lips along with her. *"I'm coming, sweetheart. Mommy's doing everything she can."*

Tony McWhirter froze. "What the hell?"

Alex stood. "Thank you, Tony."

"Sure," Tony said, still confused. "Any time."

Alex left the room.

Tony McWhirter let six seconds pass before he exhaled again. His armpits felt damp and clammy.

In Chino there were men who spent their whole lives at the edge of violence. Tony had never seen Alex Griffin like that. It disoriented him to learn that the man was human after all.

And, drown it, if he was thinking what Tony had already thought, it was no wonder.

Chapter Eight

Earlybirds of Prey

"Loremasters have five major weaknesses: If they are reckless, destroy them. If too cautious, capture them. If prone to anger, ridicule them. If proud, humiliate them. If they are, or have been, sexually or emotionally involved with their teammates, harass them.

"Study your opponent's weaknesses, and never miss an opportunity to exploit them."

—Nigel Bishop, *The Art of Gaming,* 2052

Thursday, July 21, 2059—4:25 A.M.

Gaming Central was alive on level three now. In two hours everything would begin.

Richard Lopez entered the domed room to a standing ovation from the technicians and took his place to Tony McWhirter's left, at a console opposite Mitsuko. She had arrived an hour early to run her checklist.

With every touch, every movement of foot or hand, every whisper of voice, shapes and sounds came alive in MIMIC.

The circular room was separated roughly into thirds, with Tony McWhirter's control console in the center. Backup technicians and assistants were behind him at consoles and holo stages. To his right, on the far side of a glass wall, was a multivision stage. Upon it, a troupe of mimes twisted and turned through their movements, practicing. El directed, and Doris led by example.

She was superb. Every movement, every torsion of the head and arch of her spine, transformed her into a different animal, a different entity. She ranged from subhuman to human to transhuman with the flicker of an eyelash. Her troupe was no less adroit. Skills thousands of years old matched perfectly with twenty-first-century Virtual imaging techniques.

The Virtual images in Tony's field of vision flickered from shape to shape, trying this and that. The hologram projections, computer-based Virtual illusions, makeup, and backdrops, combined to create the effect they called DreamTime.

Tony felt like a voyeur, a mere observer in the process, but there wasn't much he could do. For now, his task was that of an overseer.

"Richard?" he said.

The little man turned to look at him. "Yes?"

"Have you run your testing sequences?"

"Working on that now, Tony."

Richard Lopez moved like a man prematurely aged. A touch of arthritis, perhaps? But when he sat down at the board and began to bend the machine to his will, when he fell into the thought and movement patterns he understood and loved so well, it was as if Richard Lopez swelled in size, becoming another person entirely. Then he was like a concert pianist in his prime.

Images flowed through the computer, Virtual images perfectly matched with the holograms and the backgrounds.

It was realer than real. Tony watched the DreamTime unreality that flowed and shifted, then looked back at the room around him. It made him dizzy. In comparison, reality seemed rigid and colorless.

Acacia had almost finished packing.

All equipment was designed to nest precisely together, fitting into her backpack or belt pod with a maximum of balance and a minimum of strain. She inspected every inch of her costume, then peeled the seam open with her thumb and slipped into it. She pirouetted in front of her mirror. Perfect. She lunged and recovered, shadow-fencing.

She felt the two pounds she had gained in last week's nervous eating. But thirty-two ounces be damned: balance felt good, costume looked good, and she was electricity in tights.

Except . . .

Nigel.

He was still asleep on the bed that they shared. He lay on his back, respiration down to three breaths a minute, arms out to his sides in *savasana*, the corpse pose that led him directly from meditation into sleep.

His control was something close to total.

Even—or especially—when they made love. Every trick she knew, everything she tried, every sensual exertion that broke the control of ordinary men, brought them gasping to the brink of climax and beyond, merely amused him. Occasionally, a light dew of perspiration glistened on his forehead.

For Nigel Bishop, control was like a religion.

Especially last night. She felt like a woman of glass. He had peered into her, seen all her secrets, and perceived the unspoken.

She had turned and writhed, atop him yet completely under his control, his fingers light upon her wrists . . . light, unless she tried to twist away. If she attempted escape, they became like manacles.

"Acacia. Pet," he breathed into her mouth. "You're nervous."

"Shouldn't I be? My God, Nigel, what we're doing . . ."

He smiled, his teeth very white and clean in the darkness. "Why yes, yes, you should be." He paused. "Is there . . . anything else?"

He arched his head up and caressed the side of her neck, nibbling. His teeth touched the pulse point on her throat, closed about it subtly. Acacia wanted to scream, but didn't. But didn't speak her mind, either. And somewhere deep inside her, where all of his gentle, brutal assurances could never reach, she was afraid.

One final time, Acacia evaluated herself in the mirror. Backpack. Sword. Panthesilea, hello again.

Time to meet her team.

Five seconds after she left the room, Nigel Bishop's breathing began to speed. He opened his eyes.

Yes, he thought. She knows something is wrong. She isn't sure what. She will justify and rationalize, because she thinks she is in love, and that should carry her well into the Game. And then?

Nigel smiled. He didn't have the faintest idea.

Alphonse "The Barbarian" Nakagawa, Loremaster for the Texas Instruments–Mitsubishi team, was a tall, thin half-Japanese from Austin with a golden halo of Jesus hair and the thin, angular body of a stork. His grandfather had been a shrimp fisherman in the Gulf of Mexico, his father an oil rigger. For him, the California Voodoo Game began with his wife's image on a hotel phone screen, too early in the morning.

"Saray? Heck fire, woman—what time is it?"

Was she glaring? "It's six forty-five here. The Game starts in two and a half hours."

"Christ. I feel like I was ate by a coyote and shit off a cliff."

"I see you're working your shitkicker routine overtime. Sorry, but we've got to talk."

"Ah . . . right. Okay, I'm sitting up."

"Al, someone really wants your balls."

"I'm a Loremaster. Goes with the territory."

"Phone call, black screen, anonymous, twenty minutes ago. I took that long to think it through before I called you. I couldn't really tell the gender, even. Male, I think. 'Guess who's sleeping in your *husband*'s bed?' "

"Damn! Let me in on the secret, would you?"

"Crystal Cofax, I assume, I should *hope*! I hung on long enough that he could have said. I don't think he knew. So I got tearful and hysterical and called you a bug-fucking pederast Tex-Nip prick and swore I'd call you that instant and demand explanations."

"*Just* right. But . . . um."

"It *is* Crystal, isn't it?"

"Sure. Yes, dear, honestly. She's back in her room, but you could call her."

"Okay. What means *um*?"

"Well, could be Bishop. Rumor has it, he's crooked as a bucket of snakes. Either he's bluffing, or he knows I've got a little friend up here. Thinks I'm cheating."

"Why didn't he give me a name?"

"Maybe he's playing another game. He's sharp as a rat turd, but maybe he doesn't know . . ." Alphonse felt his thought processes coming unstuck. "Doesn't know. Just peeked at an unmade bed. But that'd mean he was here in my *room*." The last came out as an indignant squeak.

Saray laughed. "You're in the security wing of the Arabian Nights, dear. Aren't you letting your imagination run away with you?"

But Alphonse wasn't watching her anymore. He was studying the door, imagining Bishop overriding the lock, or bribing a maid, or stealing a key from the front desk, or emergency-coding the central processor, or . . .

"Al?"

"Huh? Oh . . . I was just wondering how he did it."

"You can't be serious."

"Serious as cancer," Alphonse said thickly. "This is war."

He had to check his valise. Was it gone? Did Bishop have all of his data cards?

"Alphonse? Alphonse? There you go again. Listen, call me back when you have a flash of sanity, however brief."

"I'm gonna hurt that boy."

She grimaced and was gone.

He checked the closet and found all of his gear. Bishop for sure. If something had been misplaced, it would mean he faced a lesser adversary. But if Nigel Bishop had targeted him . . . researched him . . . and why not? Alphonse Nakagawa was the only real threat to the Bishop.

So Bishop knew Saray was pregnant, but he must think their marriage was lockstepped. That was reasonable. There were only two couples in the world—and once there had been three—that Saray and Al would swap with. During a Game he kept, as the expression went, his pecker in his pocket. He believed it improved his performance.

Thought you could bitch me up? Well, Bishop, when I'm finished with you, there won't be anything left but fur and claws.

But I'll keep my smile tight for a while. I'll let you think it worked. The only question is—were you in my room?

Alphonse stalked the room, peering under the bed, searching behind the cabinets for bugs, checking and rechecking the locks on his valise a dozen times before finally, reluctantly, concluding that he was probably overreacting.

But if Bishop's stolen my strategy notes, I'm fucked, faded, and laughed at.

It's too late to change everything now. What to do? One chance: if Bishop doesn't know I know . . .

The knock on the door jolted him. It was room service, with breakfast. Al the Barbarian ate as he dressed. He tried to convince himself there was no real problem, that it was all, as Saray suggested, a paranoid fantasy.

Ha. As Grandpappy Nakagawa used to say, *that* dog wouldn't hunt.

The room was small and stark and reminded Panthesilea more of a locker room than anything else.

Captain Cipher was the first to notice her in the doorway. He peered up at her through his oversized helmet with its blue visual shield. "Milady," he said. There was no whining in his voice now, no uncertainty. There was a different quality to him. He even smelled clean.

Acacia looked at the rest of her team.

Steffie "Aces" Wilde, Engineer/Scout. Mati "Top Nun" Cohen, Cleric. Terrance "Prez" Coolidge, Warrior. Corrinda Harding, Thief.

Each nodded, a silent salute as she came into their ken. They were appropriately busy stretching or checking their equipment.

Acacia checked her watch. "0515 hours. Crack of dawn. Game starts in two hours. Any last-minutes to discuss?"

Corrinda pumped a pneumatic cuff around her bad knee, checked the pressure, eased off a little, flexed it . . . and tried to hide her grimace. "It's fine," she said. "Just a little stiff."

"We'll keep the jogging to a minimum."

Top Nun adjusted her hood. "How are we going to protect Cipher, and to what degree will we be expected to?"

A reasonable question. The rest of the team were all athletes. They pumped air, did grueling hours of yoga and martial arts, ran, swam, worked the rings. Cipher was a couch potato right to the eyes.

"Crystal Maze was a special situation," Acacia said. "I knew we'd need him more than we needed the other categories. Here, we know from the preliminary notes—" She lifted a thin sheaf of notes entitled "California Voodoo," then dropped it again. "—that no Gaming category is dominant."

She checked through her own equipment as she considered. "Prez? Work with me for a minute."

"Prez" Coolidge, the tall, stocky African-American, slid an assegai out of his back sheath. The spear balanced like a willow wand in his gigantic hand. He flicked on the monitor, and a holographic blade projected over the slender sensor. Gyro switched on. Acacia dropped the Virtual shield in front of her face, and the spear became even sharper and more fearsome.

"What it boils down to, people, is that we're the best-balanced team that I could assemble. Cipher is our voodoka, so to speak—" Acacia weaved to the side and, despite Terrance's best parry, touched him along the ribs.

He was fast—faster than she remembered, actually, but Panthesilea was the wind. Her parries and strikes were economical and unpredictable. Her every attack followed a new angle, created a new rhythm.

After a thirty-second display of swordsmanship that left the others speechless, she called it off.

"*Soberbia. Gracias.* Now—" She noted her heartbeat as it began its swift descent to a stable 50. "Cipher will save our hash as often as we save his. We protect him, and take his physical skills into account exactly as if we lived the adventure. From the moment we enter California Voodoo until it ends, I want everyone in character. That means during the breaks. That's at night during the rest. We think, eat, sleep as a team. And if you get lucky and tepee-creep to the bushes, by God you'd better screw in character, too."

They nodded, and chuckled a little.

A knock at the door, and a rounded older man with a peeling sunburn entered. "Elmo Whitman," he said. "I'm here for final check on Virtual diagnostics. Helmets and headsets, please."

Every player had a different headset, but in the most important particulars they were alike. Liquid-crystal visors could clear to become transparent; these gave each player his enhanced senses. Scouts could see paths, Wizards could see auras, Thieves were sensitive to treasure or hidden doors. These things appeared to them as overlays on the basic designs of prop, makeup, and hologram.

Steffie went first. Her helmet was ultralight, not much more than silvered goggles and earpieces. The complete illusion could be accurately conveyed despite the streamlined equipment.

El Whitman ran it through a complete diagnostic. "Please hum what you hear."

"La la la la la la la."

"All right. Fine. Next—"

Major Terry Clavell inhaled sharply as he entered the locker room. He tried to suppress a rather childish grin and, he believed, succeeded grandly.

His team looked ready. Clavell was wishing he knew them better.

Corporal Waters was in because of his IFGS experience; he'd never played in the armed forces war games. It might make all the difference.

Lieutenant Madonna Philips was a thirtyish, hatchet-faced brunette with a linebacker's drive and a cheerleader's body. She was here because Waters had insisted that they needed a woman. "Men and women keep secrets from each other in most cultures," he'd said. "If we're all men or all women, we'll miss some of the briefings."

Philips had silvered in fencing at the '48 Olympics before joining the Army. She was wearing a chain-mail bikini, as useless a piece of fighting gear as could be imagined, and not a man was looking at her narrow, angular face.

Mind on business. "Evil," he said sharply. "Is the team in order?"

General Harry "Evil" Poule snapped to attention and saluted. Clavell enjoyed the moment. Pulling rank on a general! At another place and time, beyond the shadow of a doubt, the general would certainly make him pay, but for now . . .

"Everything is in order, sir. Except that Black Elk needs a new ROM for his spell computer. Some of his blessings come out as seduction spells."

"Can't have that. Get on it."

The general was junior to Clavell in Gaming experience. He'd pulled rank to get in—and he still wouldn't be there save for his willingness to retrain, to upgrade his sword- and stick-fighting; and literally because he might frighten the other Gamers.

He was a frightening man. At fifty-four years of age he had seen combat in six tough NATO war games and countless simulation drills. He bore an awesome collection of scars, and he loomed over Clavell like a battered mountain.

Playing as Warrior and Scout, "Evil" Poule was a big, powerful blue-eyed blond of mainly Scots ancestry. Once he must have been built like a basketball player. Now his thin hair wrapped a fist-sized bald spot on the back of his head. His belly was grotesque but as hard as a drum. Poule would order junior lieutenants to punch him in the belly. It didn't sag; it rode squarely between his short ribs, making him look like he'd swallowed a smallish liberal Democrat.

Giving orders to a general was going to be awkward for Clavell. It would help if he could swallow his grin . . . "General, you've been in Gaming A . . . four times?"

"Yessir. Blue Team all four times, won three."

"Have an opinion on what's coming?"

"Corporal Waters has studied a lot of Games within the last month. Waters?"

The youngest member of the team spoke up. "The usual mistake seems to be hotdogging. I expect that to be a problem on Bishop's team. Gamers tend to go for publicity, whereas our only mission is to win."

Clavell could trust that opinion: Waters was a Gaming addict. He had entered basic training stringy and soft. The Army had put muscle on him. He was still no Schwarzenegger, A., but he looked like he could trot through a war game without breathing hard.

Better yet— "Waters, you're here because you know Gaming Dome B. We've always used Gaming A for war games because it's bigger. This time they tell me—"

"They tell you right, sir." Waters remembered the *sir*, but he did like to interrupt. "Just because there are thirty of us doesn't mean they can't fit us all into B, or even something smaller. We could have a locked room mystery, or a *Star Trek* clone with transporter rooms, no real distances involved. Or they could use B *and* A and link them with a temporary tunnel. Bring in the Gravity Whip too." The corporal grinned. "You just never know with Dream Park."

"You're familiar with the A Dome, too." Not a question: Waters's record showed that he'd played the South Seas Treasure Game eight years earlier, shortly before he joined the Army. "In fact, you played as an Engineer. You should have told me that."

"Nosir. My Engineer got killed out, dead-dead. There's nothing left, no skill points, no talents. I had to build my Scout/Thief from scratch."

Pity. And Waters didn't seem to want to talk about it. Clavell asked him, "What do you think they'll hand us?"

"Sir, if you were a cartoonist, what could you do with a concept like California Voodoo?"

They debated the question. They had all been in Gaming A, four repeatedly. Waters hadn't been in there since the South Seas Treasure Game, but he'd been four times in B. Dream Park might give them permutations of A and B, secret connecting tunnels and trapdoors, sliding elevators and walkways, the possible integration of rides such as the Gravity Whip . . . they could hope for that. If Gamers found themselves unexpectedly required to perform in free-fall, Army would win that test.

The infernal ingenuity of Dream Park filled their time while they stretched, and dropped afterthought items into their packs, and re-checked each other's equipment and their own.

Expect *anything*.

Clavell believed he was ready for that.

Acacia took the elevator down. The tube car disengaged, slid sideways into another slot, and presently opened into the train station.

The tension had started to build. Acacia's stomach ate at her. She couldn't think or plan or project into the future now. Only the next moment was real.

The train was small. Five small shuttle cars—labeled Tex-Mits, U of C, Gen-Dyn, Army, Apple—and a bubble-domed club car hovered two feet above a maglev rail sheathed in nonconducting foam plastic.

There were hundreds of spectators standing behind the security lines. Most wore costumes, though the quality varied from hologram-augmented alien creatures to twenty feet of Doctor Who scarf. They cheered and chanted the names of their favorites and held placards aloft. Some—UClink, TEX-MITS—were mere scrawls, or elaborate calligraphy in several colors. Some from GEN-DYN were 3-D displays. Psychedelic Day-Glo 1960s letters twisted in the air to spell ARMY! A toothy apple chewed up Apple Computer rivals and snapped at spectators.

Acacia's mood took a palpable upswing. Difficult not to, with such a send-off!

With very conscious grace she swayed to the rear of the platform. Without breaking stride she tossed her hair over her shoulder, a much practiced gesture that brought all of the carefully nurtured highlights to the fore. In the same motion she stooped and entered the U of C compartment with the easy flow of an eel.

Her team followed. They stowed their gear under the seats. Captain Cipher reclined his chair, ready to snatch a last nap, while the rest gazed out the windows at the crowd.

Steffie said, "Quite a show, eh?"

"Quite a show." Acacia felt her skin tingle. Regardless of the surroundings, regardless of what anything seemed to be, the Game had begun.

Laughter and a tinkle of glasses echoed down the corridor. The connecting passageways were open. Somewhat curious, she motioned to the others, and together they streamed down the passageway to the club car.

They had to go past the other compartments. Two cars were still empty, but backpacks, helmets, and weapons were scattered on the seats of the Army and Texas Instruments–Mitsubishi cars. In the club car they found others waiting.

The Army players had clustered along one side of the bar, as if for defense. Five men and one woman, with Lieutenant Philips in the center. She'd changed out of that silly chain-mail outfit. A tall woman with long bones and long, hard muscles, she was dressed for rugged terrain, with lots of pockets and a saber on her back— hey, that chain-mail bikini was just a ploy, wasn't it? A fairly sophisticated one.

Beneath their expected stiffness the Army boys looked uneasy— except one. One had dancing eyes and a smile just for Panthesilea.

She said, "Congratulations, Corporal."

He glanced at his shoulders. "No stripes showing."

"I hear things. Damn, you grew muscles! You look a lot better than last time we met. Then again, you were two days' dead."

"Then again, I was a wimp. That's why I joined up. Today I think I can outrun you, Panthesilea."

She laughed. "You are more than welcome to try, Waters. Meanwhile, what do you suppose is happening to your odds in Vegas?" She rounded the bar without waiting for an answer.

She knew the Tex-Mits crew by names and rankings, knew their Gaming histories in detail, even if she didn't know them all as individuals. Ozzie the Pike, bearded and capped in steel with a Virtual visor, grinned at her in open admiration, a feedback loop that pleased them both. Friar Duck smiled at her and babbled happily, the buzzing gibberish of a still-famous movie star. But Alphonse Nakagawa sprawled back against the wet bar, sipping orange juice, loose and gawky, hostile gray eyes following her.

"Small world. Panthesilea herself."

His apparent awkwardness didn't deceive her. Acacia had seen Al the Barbarian in recorded combat. He seemed to coast on invisible ice skates. He had incongruously blue eyes, and a deep, golden tan to go with that jarring accent.

She said, "Naw, we sent this duplicate instead. Much cheaper, but still too good for *you*."

"I ain't drunk enough to listen to this shit." His hostility made Acacia uneasy. Friar Duck, embarrassed, turned back to the bar.

So: this concerned nothing that Al the B could share with his team. Could he know that Nigel had been in his room? With anything more than a suspicion, he could complain to the IFGS.

So why the attitude? At this stage in the Game, wouldn't he normally be seeking an alliance? Or pretending to? Unless he had some unbeatable advantage . . .

Unless he could set her to watching and wondering about Al the B, instead of reacting to current events—as in Nigel's translation of *The Art of War*. The book was thousands of years old, by a Chinese named Sun-tzu, and was still relevant:

"Simulated disorder postulates perfect discipline; simulated fear postulates courage; simulated weakness postulates strength . . ."

If Alphonse simulated anger, he might only be trying to make her think he was out of control.

She smiled blissfully at him.

The Troglodykes were already squeezing through into the club car. Acacia did a quick survey. There was room for maybe fifty people, if they were all friendly, if only a handful wanted to sit. Normally that would mean room for, oh, twenty-five Gamers.

The crowding could be deliberate. No room to fight, but they could bicker.

A bar box slid down the counter and politely inquired as to her choice of beverage. She asked for fizzy grape juice, and it spritzed her a merry concoction, swiveling to place it before her.

She sauntered up to Tammi Romati, who was peering out the window. "And so it begins."

She got a wolfish smile in return. "Place your bets, Panthesilea. Where are we being taken?"

Acacia shrugged. "Nowhere in Dream Park. The Army team's going nuts. Fifty man-years of experience in Gaming A, straight into the recycler."

"I mean in Game reality."

"California Voodoo Game. Voodoo was—is practiced in California. Usually called santería? Our notes say it has wealthy patrons. Out of the barrio and into the boardroom."

"Is that an answer?"

"No hablo Inglés," Acacia said. And she almost leapt up as Nigel entered the car.

There was a momentary hush. Then conversations returned to their former level. The rest of the Gen-Dyn team followed him in. Holly Frost, Thief, remembered her and lifted a spear in salute. Acacia hadn't met Trevor Stone or Tamasan, the Japanese-looking Shinto priest; but she'd read their dossiers. The Radichevs were impressively muscled Warriors, a married couple who Gamed and fought as a team, and generally died that way, too. Why had Nigel picked them? Or had Gen-Dyn assigned them, like Trevor Stone?

The door sealed shut behind them, and Nigel worked his way up to the front, making eye contacts as he came.

Al the Barbarian . . . His eyes lit, burned on Nigel, and then he turned his back. Suppressed rage? Jealousy? *Al might know what we did,* she reminded herself. *Watch your back.*

With a barely audible hum, the train began to move.

Nigel gave Acacia a single wolfish grin before he turned to the bar—just in time to miss what was happening beyond the windows.

Chapter Nine

"Do We See This?"

Well-wishers, Gamers, media gadflies . . . all waved good-bye. But in the last twenty seconds or so before the train slid into darkness, they'd mutated subtly.

Acacia could see it in their stance (beaten down, prematurely old), their clothing (primitive, crudely made), the plaintive expressions on their gaunt faces. Crude placards in paint or charcoal on wooden boards read "Godspeed to our united forces," "Power to the Five Peoples!" "Crystal, come back to us."

Then they were lost in darkness. The mundane world slipped away from her. If she were to survive here, Acacia had to become Panthesilea, she of a dozen epochs, a hundred missions, and a thousand deadly skills.

The train floated silently through a black tunnel. A voice said, "Somebody get the lights?"

Tammi bellowed, *"Lights!"* The car juddered slightly. *"Lights? Dammit."*

The sensors didn't respond to a verbal command. Circles of golden light glimmered in the hands of various players: here a magic aura, there a flashlight, there a corpse candle. Grins were yellow-white arcs. *It begins!*

"All right. Let's see if I can find the circuit," Corporal S. J. Waters volunteered. He reached high, along the rim of the roof, for something his special vision must have pointed out: a metal panel

Acacia hadn't noticed at all. He thumbed it open. He jiggled a few wires, and—

One of the big windows lit up and became a vidscreen.

A somber woman dressed in gray tones faced them across a worn, wooden desk. Her shoulders were slumped with care, her face heavily lined. She looked like George Washington in drag. "Greetings, once again," she said. Her eyes and chin flicked sideways for an instant, as if she feared eavesdroppers.

An uneasy ripple of murmurs ran through the club car. The image said, "I must add a few words to what has gone before—"

Army Lieutenant Madonna Philips snapped, "Before *what*?"

"Quiet!" Bishop commanded. Philips glared.

". . . true that you must cooperate with the other four cohorts. But you six have a greater obligation, and a greater destiny."

Acacia's mind whirred. "California Voodoo," the game's artfully vague information packet, had arrived on her fax a week earlier, although the title had been known for months. Twenty single-spaced pages contained just enough information to tantalize, and to send frantic Loremasters on a frenzied last-minute data hunt.

But this was the real briefing. She triggered a recorder at her belt pod, knowing that a dozen other hands were doing the same thing.

So far, she was pretty certain that the vid had been "accidentally" triggered. This was to have played to only one . . . cohort. She glanced down the corridor. Screens were alight in the shuttle cars, too.

"Two hundred years ago, the Age of Miracles ended. Earthquakes, pollution, global warming, and famine struck a world already drastically overpopulated. Nuclear, chemical, and genetic warfare followed. Nations fell, supplanted by isolated states and townships. Through years of delicate negotiating, diplomatic communication between the five great North American enclaves has been reestablished—but much unpleasant history has had to be censored to control public opinion. What I was pledged not to say to you, but find I must say, is: Do not trust the others."

A hush stole over the car. Beneath Acacia's feet the train hummed toward its destination. Vaguely, through the partial shadows, she saw the silhouettes of other Adventurers as they nodded uneasily. Teeth gleamed.

"Meacham's Folly is the world's last hope, true enough. There, across the desert, lies the last working power plant capable of running a city. We had neither the resources to reach it, nor the means, until a robot repair system on the old tramway was activated. That required cooperation among the five enclaves. It is therefore reasonable and right that each enclave send emissaries to MIMIC.

"It is also prudent. With the fall of technology, the old magic returned with a vengeance. Arcane techniques useless for centuries have become viable once again. Whether due to human mutation or a shift in the Earth's magnetic field, no one knows. But you have as many magicians and clerics among you as soldiers and scouts.

"By common agreement no team carries guns. Guns would make it too easy for one team to slay another in its sleep.

"For, mark my words: as soon as you have reached MIMIC, scouted its mysteries, and determined what will be needed to conquer it, at that moment the other teams will have no further use for you. They will try to slay you. You must be alert, and dispose of them when the opportunity arises."

Now the grumbling in the car was audible. Acacia's ribs itched, expecting a dagger's point at any moment. Instead she felt a vulnerable back pressed against her in the darkness. Her hand wandered toward her own dagger . . . and paused.

Who knew what skills would be needed? The woman on the vid had said, *"After you have scouted out MIMIC . . ."*

After.

Defeat might well be the penalty for killing off another member too soon. She would have to wait and see.

The woman was winding up her spiel. "My brave ones, you fight for all of us. You are the best of us. You are our only hope. Do not fail us."

The image flickered and died. Moments later the train emerged into daylight. Gamers blinked out at a yellow-white desert whipping past them in eerie silence.

They watched each other cautiously, all amusement suspended. Which team was expected to play the double-cross game? Thumbs edged nervously toward daggers. Magical staffs and shields glowed at low level.

Nigel Bishop raised his hands. "My friends—" he began, with such high-octane sincerity that no one protested his presumption. They waited, and grinned and nodded when he continued. "—and trusted allies. We love our cities, but their war, and their past, is their own. We are sent to start a new world! Surely we can leave the treachery of the past behind us? Surely we need not accept their legacy of hatred?"

The Bishop was in his pulpit, and his congregation was in thrall.
There were solemn or half-solemn nods. Hands dropped away
from blades. The teams turned to each other, faces wreathed with
saccharine smiles, and brawny arms draped about broad shoulders.
Looks like Christmas Eve on Death Row.

The train raced a few feet above the brown-and-yellow desert, at
just under the speed of sound. Here windblown sand had covered
the track. The train shivered slightly, but magnetic levitation didn't
fail. They passed a forest of worn metal stumps, and suddenly Acacia
knew where they were. Those had once been hundreds of propellers
turning on posts: experimental designs for windmills. That made
this the Mojave, north of Joshua Tree National Monument; and
hundreds of years in the future, given what time and wind had done
to those propeller mounts. Or had it been the hot breath of a ther-
monuclear fire-mushroom?

Time had made other changes. Plants close to the shuttle track
flashed by too quickly for detail. But those farther away seemed . . .
alien. Like twisted, mutated skeletons. Joshua trees had been weird
enough, but stranger plants had invaded.

So this was the world shaped by . . . ecological disaster? A shift
in the earth's magnetic field? Biochemical weapons to cause genetic
mutation? Whatever; but the woman had spoken of magic, too.

Of course, that could be mere superstition. Acacia played her
recording back into her earpiece. One never could tell what one
might find concealed in a briefing.

The Adventurers crowded close, shifting like seabottom currents
as some sought access to the bar. Old friendships were here, and
new ones forming. No Gamer would trust another forever, but
Gamers took relaxation when they could.

Trevor Stone of Gen-Dyn was a brawny middle-aged English-
man, a Gamer before Dream Park erected the Domes. He was
second-in-command on Bishop's team. He was speaking of the old
days, and most of the University team was lapping it up.

"We used any kind of land we could get access to. Marsh, mountains, whatever. Once we used a Scottish castle. We'd march four
groups through the Game site in a day . . ."

Funny how no team had returned to their private cars. Were they
wondering, as Acacia had, whether it was possible to detach one of
the cars, seal it off, and simply leave it stranded in the desert?

"So we weren't supposed to use the whole bloody castle, because it was up for sale—the rental agency had made the arrangement with us, and they were also showing parts of it to prospective customers. Movie people, a bed-and-breakfast outfit, so forth. We went through the wrong door at full battle alert, and found ourselves face to face with a Girl Scout troop. The Loremaster stared at them for a moment—there we were dressed up like mad folk, you know, swinging these great padded swords and axes. I think the lassies were close to fainting—and our Loremaster says to the Game Master, 'Do we see this?' "

Steffie and Prez looked puzzled. Top Nun said, "Pray tell, what then, *bubele?*"

A shrug and a smile. "It wasn't in the Game. The Game Master shook his head, the Loremaster waved his hand and said, 'Away phantoms,' and back we marched to the other room. We could hear the girls going doololly, and couldn't really blame 'em."

Cheerful he was, and most amused by his own story. It was a dominance game, of course, even if largely unrecognized. Acacia understood the code.

You challenge *me?* Trevor was saying with polite incredulity. *I've been at this infinitely longer than you have, children. I'm the Wizard from Afar.*

His eyes flickered to Bishop and back. His smile lost some of its life. Acacia amended Stone's internal monologue: *and I should have been the bloody Loremaster, not that upstart Bishop.*

A thin, sharp elbow in her ribs. Zulu Warrior "Prez" Coolidge was pointing with his nose, through the window and ahead of the train. She looked.

Hills loomed, and something angular, artificial, hard to see because it was the same sand color as the slopes. She'd seen it before, or something like it, but where? The half-buried track was a ridge in the sand, curving left toward that building . . . that very distant, *tremendous* building.

And the ride was becoming bumpy. Acacia remembered riding an imitation mining car at Dream Park, dodging avalanches, rocking back and forth as dynamite explosions thundered about her, and holding on tight to . . .

Tony McWhirter?

Yes—and she smiled to herself, a sad, lost smile that vanished like a drop of sweet moisture on an oven window . . .

This felt the same. And the sound was the same—

She and Twan barked simultaneously, "Buckle in!"

Easier said than done. Massing in the club car had been a mistake: twenty chairs divided by thirty Gamers equals chaos. Acacia got into a seat somehow. Other Gamers pushed through the door and into the shuttle cars. They were still swarming when the train underwent a lurching deceleration.

That was what her eyes had been trying to tell her mind. She couldn't see the end of the track! It ended under a hill of dirt or sand.

The train shuddered and ripped apart. The club car grated over rock on its metal belly. Just outside the windows, one of the shuttle cars was rolling, bouncing, jolting, getting the shape pounded out of it. Friar Duck was ripped from his seat and went rolling along the bar, yelling, thudding into more bodies. Acacia closed her eyes as screams rang out in the constricted space.

The car's nose was smashed violently sideways. The car rolled, sliding uphill, and came to rest on its side in a final lethal lurch. The scream of grit or sand or dirt grinding in gears ran down to a destructive halt.

"What happened?" Major Clavell yelled.

The air was filled with moans, whimpers of disbelief, and a few muttered prayers of gratitude or oaths of vengeance.

"This damn door is wedged closed." That sounded like the normally unflappable Twan, and Acacia managed a smile.

Somebody got a flashlight working. She saw a mass of bodies, a bizarre forest of arms and legs sticking up and waving about. Corrinda promised Mouser castration unless he removed a strategic portion of his anatomy from her eye.

A creak. The door was opening. As it did, a torrent of sand and dirt flowed into the compartment, half burying Trevor Stone before it stopped.

Acacia wiggled toward the door. It was overhead now. Sand trickled down into her face. She lowered her visor. Surrounded by the harsh rasp of her own breathing, she crawled up and out, gasping, using knees and elbows. Once free, she grabbed Trevor's big, bony hand, braced herself, and pulled until he had leverage to make his own way.

He was puffing. "Thank you, Miss . . . Panthesilea?" He had big square teeth, too perfect to be all his.

The tram was half buried in a spill of rocks and sand. She skinned elbows and shoulders crawling up.

Cracked, even earth and ruined ridges of sunbaked mountains

surrounded them. She turned as a spray of cool mist wet her cheeks, and found herself looking straight up along a sheer cliff—a cliff partly made by men.

It was the largest building she had ever seen. It wasn't tall—though a twenty-story fall will kill—but its weather-blasted, sand-scraped, dull red walls stretched perhaps a mile along the base, bending to fit the contours of the mountain. Twisted, ruined cables dangled free from its east face, swinging in a wind that blew from somewhere in the south. Halfway down the building, a row of immense, raised stone letters spelled the word MIMIC.

Water cascaded from the rooftop, tumbling in the early light like a fall of emeralds. It impacted with balconies or outcroppings until only a fine spray reached the ground, deflected into them by that mild southern wind.

MIMIC seemed completely abandoned. The windows were all sealed up, and there was no obvious means of entry.

The slope of sand and rock had been part of the natural cliff. The Quake of '95—or a later one?—must have caused an avalanche. Hundreds of tons of rock covered the maglev track.

Over later centuries sand had softened the contours of the rubble slope. It still stood four stories high. The six cars following the track had slammed into it, ripped loose from their magnetic confinement, and continued moving uphill until their momentum was lost. The club car had reached the third story. The five shuttle cars hadn't gotten that far. Gamers were crawling out and up toward Acacia.

Acacia got her heart back down out of her throat and turned to her companions.

There were only thirty Adventurers. Hardly enough to search a single floor. That mountain of masonry could be full of . . .

Anything. Or Things.

With a spate of coughing and sputtering, a thin, muscular arm waved up out of the passenger compartment, seeking assistance or purchase. Acacia grasped it. She heaved with all of the considerable muscle in her back and long steely legs, and hauled Twan up.

The wind whistled low.

"Formidable."

Acacia nodded. "At least they have water. Probably power, too."

"An Engineer, and a Scout." Twan snapped her fingers twice. "Evacuation, then evaluation—" She stopped, and seemed to be wrestling with a notion. "Panthesilea?"

Acacia nodded acknowledgment.

"Truce. Straight up. Twenty-four hours." Twan's oval, very Asian face was firmed by resolve.

"Can you control Tammi?" the Warrior-woman asked. "She wants my ass. Pardon. My hide."

A tiny smile. "Affirmative."

Acacia glanced at her watch—7:46 A.M.—and thrust out her hand. "All right. Truce." They soberly extended hands, touched thumbs, and waggled their fingers to and fro. Neither laughed.

The wind spawned dust devils at MIMIC's base. They danced away into the distance, or dissolved in the wet spray to the south.

There were no lights in any of the windows, and when she scanned the grounds around them, there was nothing but desolation, and a long, low ridge of dusty mountains.

Acacia called, "Aces!"

"Yo!" Steffie Wilde was still down in the car. She lifted her bulky pack through a window. Acacia helped her with it, and then hoisted Steffie out.

"All right. We need a way in."

"Pathfinder, do your stuff." "Aces" Wilde punched a combination code into a bracelet, and her face visor glowed.

The Scout would be seeing details denied to Acacia the Warrior. Acacia flipped her visor up and watched the entire building.

It was pitted and streaked, as if a thousand years of neglect had all but destroyed one of the great giants of architecture. This was Meacham's building, wrecked by the '95 Quake—the place they called "Meacham's Folly."

But within the California Voodoo Game, the facts would vary. What had she heard of MIMIC? In her . . . girlhood in the enclave? Yes. Had Panthesilea known of it? *What* would she know?

Aces lowered her glasses. "Fourth level. See? There's a ledge, and it's marked for entry."

Acacia strained, but couldn't make it out. "Marked for entry?"

"Oh, yeah—someone's in there all right. Count on it. We might be watched right now."

Acacia's hand unconsciously strayed to the blade at her belt. "All right. Keep a watch. Let's get everyone out."

The teams had to split up and somehow get into their various half-buried shuttle cars to get their gear. Major Clavell supervised the extraction of two of his team members, but he was repeatedly distracted.

"Corporal," he said under his breath. "Where *are* we? This *is* real, isn't it?"

"It's real," SJ said. "Smell the wind, Toto. I don't think we're in Dream Park anymore."

Together they hauled Black Elk up, Clavell muttering, "Serious snafu. We'd better revise tactics, and fast. First break, report to me."

But SJ was staring up at the Folly, his expression somewhere between anger and admiration.

Despite their growing alarm, within three minutes all Army personnel and equipment were out of the train, armed and ready to go.

"Trevor!" Bishop yelled. "Find us a way in." His voice was abrupt, imperious. Trevor Stone's eyes narrowed, but he pulled Aces aside and began to confer.

They formed in single file, staggered with no real concern for teams, and worked their way up a fall of twisted rocks and construction rubble. The mound was so weathered that it took Mouser and SJ, both experienced Scouts, twenty minutes to pick their way to the fourth floor.

Footholds and handholds had been cut by unknown artisans. It was true: others had been here. Somewhere in MIMIC, frightened eyes might be watching. Angry lips were whispering deadly secrets somewhere out of sight. MIMIC seemed impossibly old and evil.

Hands hovered above weapons.

Stifle the melodrama, Acacia snapped at herself. *One step at a time.*

It was hard not to pay attention to her instincts, hard not to wonder, not to speculate.

One step at a time.

She extended a helping hand to Black Elk. A moment later, he saved *her* from a twisted ankle. One step. Then another. And another.

And then they were at the top; they had climbed a tumbled fall of rocks that took them to the brink of the fourth floor, only five feet from the window.

Behind her there was a commotion. Boards were pulled out of a heap of rubble and passed forward. Alphonse said, "Looks like these are used in an emergency. Must be a more reliable system inside. Let's see."

Alphonse, moving with the assurance of a circus acrobat, helped them steady the boards against the ledge. He tested it with a halberd, felt the board jiggle, and then looked down: a nasty spill. Not fatal, but it would probably incapacitate.

"I can make it, but I'm not sure—" Alphonse said.

"Then move aside, darlin'," Mary-em said, and tested the board with a booted foot. "Piece of cake."

She spread her arms out for balance and tested one board, then the other. When she was satisfied, she strolled jauntily across.

She hunkered down onto hands and knees to peer through the window. Then she nodded as if confirming something. "Dark in there," she called back. She wiped at the sill with a gloved hand. "No dust. Somebody's been here. Recently. This is it."

She drew a torch from her belt and shone it around inside. Then she crawled in.

Acacia's nerves burned for a few moments, and then Mary-em reappeared. Now she had another plank of some light plastic. It was broad, with raised rounded edges, like a big chunk of surfboard. She laid it atop the other boards, anchored it on her end, and beckoned them across.

And what would Panthesilea be feeling? The wind was still moaning. The entry was open to hidden and hideous dangers. Their transport was six smashed maglev cars.

Acacia played with Panthesilea's thoughts. *How are we going to get home? What if the legends are wrong? We could all die here.*

She was giving herself the creeps, and it was her turn to cross the bridge. She sheathed her sword and stepped carefully across. Just before she stepped into the window she took one last glance at the outside world.

In for a penny, in for a pound . . .

Panthesilea hopped inside, leaving the world of the known behind her.

Chapter Ten

Nakagawa's Law

"Generally, an artful Loremaster will ensure that his lines of support, supply, and information are well maintained.

"He needs Barbarians and Magic Users for speed. Armored Knights for heavy combat. Locally (game-world or real-world) recruited troops and allies for cannon fodder. Actual provisions are usually supplied by the Gaming facility; therefore one need only stock nonstandard material relevant to strategic play within the Game-world; but these must be thoroughly stocked. Caches must be hidden and mapped, and strong backs recruited to carry them."

—Nigel Bishop, *The Art of Gaming*, 2052

Thursday, July 21, 2059—8:20 A.M.

You expected glitches. Of course you did. You waited for them . . .

Those doors were supposed to lock, isolating the Gamers in their respective cars. The message would reach each team separately. The club car, empty, was to be shredded in the crash. Five cars would slide to rest within reach of five entries. Five teams would enter MIMIC separately, wary of enemies, fearing each other more . . .

Tony McWhirter was swearing under his breath, but it wasn't slowing him down. He put in quick requests for a repair team to examine the train and report to him. Not that they'd be using the cars again, but he had to know what had gone wrong. It would tell him where else to look for problems.

They'd worked around it. They hadn't shredded the club car; the Gamers were alive and walking. The secret message was no secret now. There would be less paranoia, and alliances among the five enclaves, probably. Not a ruined Game, just an altered one.

Still, it was a bad omen. Glitches were a lot like cockroaches. If you didn't catch them in time, they'd scuttle off into someplace dark and warm and begin to breed.

Alphonse Nakagawa was third through the door, his adrenaline pumping hard.

Nakagawa's Law #1: *Something in the next shadow is waiting to eat your face.* He never let himself forget that. It was this conviction that kept him alive—often.

Fool-Killer, where are you?

For the moment, nothing. But it was lurking. Al knew it, and the beast knew it. If Al wanted to keep his face, he would have to remember that the beast knew he knew it.

First: search the room. There were broken boxes and scraps of plastic everywhere. Peels of paper littered the floor. Madonna Philips pulled twenty pounds of anonymous metal motor part from under some torn cardboard boxes, hefted it, and discarded it. Storage room? Over the decades, scavengers would have stripped it clean. Probably.

Nakagawa's Law #2: *Probably doesn't count.* There might be weapons here, or clues, or traps . . .

"They've rifled this stuff a hundred times," Corporal Waters muttered.

"Search it anyway," Alphonse said. Acacia flickered him an approving glance, but possibly for the wrong reason.

Corporal Waters was right, of course. There was no treasure here that he need fear to leave in the hands of a rival team. Let *them* spring the traps. Al wanted an overview. Was there any clue to the nature or contents of this vast structure? What did the locals consider worthless? What valuables should have been there, but were not?

The others were piling in through the window. The room was getting belly-to-back pretty quick.

"Nothing here, children," Mary-em said, flinging a torn carton aside. "Let's go kick some heinie."

The others were gathering by the door. Al the B picked up the carton. Mary-em had seemed too casual. The box was empty, the logo illegible . . . the trace of a sketch remained: girl in a raincoat?

Drop the box before someone sees. Stand by the door. Check the hinges. They seemed in good repair, not too likely to squeal embarrassingly.

Let someone else open it. (When it rains it pours. Salt! The raiders had valued salt. Not a grain remained. There wouldn't be any tinned meat either.)

Another exchange of nods between the Troglodykes, and Tammi turned to Mouser, her Scout. "Enhanced hearing," she whispered. "Anything out there?"

The boy placed his fingers to his temples and tilted his mop of copper hair sideways. "No . . . distant. I hear feet. Distant. Shuffling. I don't like it."

California Voodoo. Images of sun-bleached beach bunnies cavorted nakedly around a titanic bottle of sunscreen lotion . . .

Tammi slipped through the door, followed by the hulking Warrior Appelion. He gave Alphonse the Evil Eye as he passed. It was impressively evil, too. It was his left, and it was swollen and bloodshot. A blue flame glowed in its depths.

Alphonse waited to see if the Fool-Killer was waiting outside. It seemed to be elsewhere. He chanced a swift, sliding passage through the door, halberd at the ready.

All about him, halls as wide as city streets stretched off to concrete horizons. The ceiling was ten feet above his head. A balustrade lipped a central well larger than most airports.

"Horseshit and gunfire," Alphonse muttered. The central well's ceiling was at least four floors above them. *One man's ceiling is another man's floor.* Who lived up there? Were they home? How could his people find their way in so vast a structure?

"We could spend a week mapping this place," Major Clavell said.

The hallway seemed empty in either direction. Alphonse tiptoed to the rail and looked down. An ocean of mist raged down there. It curled, lapping at the lower levels like some semisentient primordial soup.

Alphonse was a Warrior-Magician, with a spell or two of his own. His halberd, enhanced by past adventures, gave him a little extrasensory data.

With the tip of the blade he traced a symbol in the ground, a complex curlicue of power. Immediately he heard a chorus of low groans, a herd of shuffling feet. *Something Wicked This Way Comes.*

Tammi was already looking down in that direction. "All right," she whispered to Acacia. "Let's get the others."

Why did he get the feeling that these ladies were in bed together, pardon the pun? In addition, Acacia/Panthesilea might well be allied with Bishop the Living Legend. *That* notion put a spider in his shorts, for sure. Alliances were fencing him in. Al the Barbarian had best watch his backside.

A few at a time, the Adventurers filed out of the room and crouched down in the corridor. They coalesced into a loose diamond formation. Almost without design, the five individual teams formed themselves again.

Mary-em was right behind Al, with Crystal Cofax, his favorite Scout. His Engineer and Thief were with him, and he was damned glad.

Because something was waiting to eat his face.

The halls were musty, and reeked with decay. The corridors stretched off in all directions, fading in the mist. Vague light shone through the fog. It swallowed more than light: it was a sound baffle. Something that might have been voices, machinery, footsteps (or the Fool-Killer), echoed around out there, hovering just below the threshold of hearing.

Crystal had sensed a distant glow. She stared through her visor, flipped it up, and looked again. Then she motioned with one hand and crept down the hall.

So they filed through the darkness, keeping torches shielded and pointed at the floor. They passed the shattered, ruined shells of stores now: a shoe store—with a sale still on, a TWELVE HOUR SALE!!! lasting for a thousand years. Al had a sudden, mad urge to rummage around and see if there was anything in a size 11.

A frozen-yogurt parlor. Next to that, a transdress shop offered over three thousand color designs per processor. Just plug it into the transparent dresses and dial a new fashion every day! He had heard stories of women whose batteries had died while they were walking down the street . . .

The entire column had suddenly stopped, and Al went to the alert. A moment later he saw why.

They had passed the commercial sector and were entering a park of some kind. Perhaps long ago it had been an alluring, restful pit stop for the overburdened, overstressed shopper. Now it was a graveyard. Epitaphs had been carved in elaborate, almost illegible curlicues on plastic rectangles that slanted at irregular angles from piles of dirt. Ancient topiary was wildly overgrown, to bizarre effect: rabbits seemed toadlike, a lion had grown tentacles and extra, misshapen heads.

A few graves were lying open. He inspected two of them. Their headboards bore different dates: Joseah Miller, died 2234. Millie Washington, died 2189.

He whispered to Mary-em, "Unburied?"

"It was a warm night. They kicked the dirt off." She touched her holstered, telescoping staff. She didn't bother to say, "Voodoo implies zombies," and neither did anyone else.

They continued deeper into the cemetery, spreading out as they did. There was little sound, but the ground thrummed with an irregular vibration like distant machinery going bad. Drumbeats? Lights flickered, hundreds of meters away. A far lantern . . . or glowing gases of decomposition?

From that direction came a distant scream.

There followed a quick, efficient pause during which everyone checked his or her equipment. Weapons up; visors down; *duck* as Ozzie the Pike assembled his twelve-foot weapon; noncombatants safely protected in a center pocket. *Go.*

It felt very strange to be moving en masse like this. Damn it, a section of floor could open up . . . anything could happen.

The Adventurers were stretched out in a thin line. Alphonse felt his heart in his throat. And if some of the others had made truce, or deals—when would the backstabbing begin?

Right after we figure out the Game.

Meanwhile, keep an eye on Da Gurls. Give me half an inch and sayonara, suckers. Pearl Harbor time.

Drumbeats? Machinery? And smoke, or something like smoke, boiled out of the corridor ahead. Alphonse raised his hand just before it engulfed them. "Crystal," he whispered, and his Scout tucked her nifty little derriere beside him.

Crystal's body emitted a soft phosphorescence. Immediately, Alphonse could see crouched, misshapen figures creeping toward them through the smoke.

The Beasts awaken. Could they see in this smoke? Probably. Still, Al wouldn't give away his position by warning the others. If they didn't have enough sense to call for a Scout . . . "Stay behind me," he whispered. "Mary-em?"

"I register outlines. They flicker. I'll be okay."

Mary-em's staff, like his halberd, had seen enough campaigns to have magic of its own; her Vision rating was phenomenal.

Could the enemy see him? Couldn't they? He had to keep in contact with Crystal.

"Watch your hand, boss."

"Just business, darlin'."

"Get your business a little higher, then. Or let me." Her hand closed on his belt. "Leave your hands free to fight."

There were four attackers ahead, maybe more elsewhere. They carried maces of some kind. Bludgeoning weapons, and nasty ones at that. Shards of metal and glass projected at odd angles from the knobby ends.

One zombie shambled right at him.

All he had was a vague outline. When he twisted to avoid the mace, he broke contact with his Scout: as Crystal's hand left his belt, the attacker winked out of existence.

Duck! Where'd the beast go? He felt wind as the mace swished past his shoulder.

The combat computer in his brain figured angle and momentum, and he backhanded with the halberd. Nothing, and he was overextended.

If I were him . . .

Al the Barbarian rolled and brought his weapon up, and felt the blade slam into legs. Heard the unearthly howl of . . . pain? Did zombies feel pain? Wrath, maybe. *The terrible beast, spawn of the undead, no longer recognized pain . . .*

Or soap. Shitfire, they stank! Then again, rotting does that to a person.

Decomposing? Ordinary antiperspirants still leave 'em gagging downwind? Try new Vlad the T's, deodorant for the undead—

His thoughts returned to the matter at hand as a body thudded atop him. Teeth bit into his arm, through the thin fabric, and it *hurt*. Screaming, Alphonse kicked the zombie away from him and hacked at it until it stopped quivering.

All around him in the fog pealed screams of pain and fear, labored breaths, the groans of the undead. He rose shakily to one knee. "Crystal!"

"Here."

Behind him. He backed up cockroach-quick, staying low to the ground, until her hand touched his ankle.

As they touched, glowing zombie outlines reappeared. They were almost upon him. He parried the swing of a mace, shattering it. Careful not to lose contact with Crystal, he backhanded the halberd into a face and saw the head peel back and open. Something thick and black bubbled out—

Elmo Whitman caught that one. The blunt edge of Alphonse Nakagawa's composition-plastic halberd had hit one of his zombie actors. He was always nervous about that, even with extra padding in face masks and at neck and groin and knees.

Some of the stuntmen had dotted red lines at arm or neck, visible only through Virtual visors. Strokes there produced an especially messy special effect, for the pleasure of the home viewers. *Let's see . . . should be breakfast time about now. Watch that over your Rice Crispies. Snap, crackle, and who ate Pop?*

Live interactions were his responsibility, and as the actor stumbled back, El watched the program register a "kill," producing the requisite disgusting effects. He keyed in the stuntman's code and got an A/V link.

"You all right? Blow looked solid."

"Little English on it, but didn't penetrate. My nose stings a little." The stuntman chuckled softly.

El rang off and went to wide-angle again, watching the combat. Nobody had ever been seriously injured in one of *his* combats, but he had heard rumors . . .

Behind Alphonse, Acacia screamed, "Top Nun! Lift this fog!"

Even as her scream faded, Al heard Top Nun say piously, "Though there was darkness in the land of Egypt, Israel's *mishpoche* had—light!"

Light exploded behind him, and the fog disintegrated.

"Excellent, Sister," Acacia said.

"Darkness has its points," Top Nun remarked.

The undead enemy became partially visible. They seemed to wink in and out of existence. Their skin was pasty, like Caucasians smeared with mud, or Africans daubed with ash. A mixed breed they were, perhaps human and baboon, hair a beaver's nest of mud and sticks, facial skin drawn so tight across the bone that they resembled some heretofore-undiscovered tribe of mutant Java men.

Friar Duck threw fire. The spell was simple and dependable, if expensive. Two zombies came straight through it—*unfair!*—and slashed him with dirty claws. Friar Duck went down in a swirl of brown robes.

Corrinda threw salt. The monster grinned and licked the crystals from its lips with a long, greasy pink tongue. Corrinda scuttled back to safety, limping on her bad knee.

Then Al had no more time for judgment or appreciation, because they were around him. A glancing blow hit his left shoulder, and the arm glowed red; if he tried to lift that arm, red would fade to black.

He saw Madonna Philips die. It shouldn't have claimed his attention, but it was a mistake so classic. The Army team had her enclosed, protected. She stood tall with her saber straight above her head, unable to do anything, letting her frustration show. Then Clavell faced left to block a zombie's club, Evil Poule clove an enemy with a left-to-right swing of his scimitar, and Lieutenant Philips stepped forward and split a zombie head-to-crotch. Overwhelmed with her success, she took a classical fencing pose and thrust into another zombie's body. Her telescoping blade collapsed as she ran him through.

Al saw her snarl of triumph change to dismay and knew what had happened.

A little whisper in her ear. The Game Masters, damn their souls, had just informed her that her sword was stuck fast in the body of an undead.

Instead of springing back to the protection of her comrades, she tugged, hoping to get it free—

And a zombie threw her to the ground and bit her throat out. For an instant she seemed about to bite back; then she must have believed the voice and collapsed, dead.

Al got his attention back in time to block a blurred motion, a club that would have split his head.

He had lost Crystal again, but the spell shielding the zombies was coming apart now, and he had enough glimpses of them to zero in. He twisted sideways, heard a mace *shoosh* over a shoulder, drove his halberd into a stomach. Yerch—it actually stuck there. Some kind of mucilage sack?

The zombies were an arc around Ozzie the Pike, who fought alone, back against a wall. For an instant Al considered trying to reach him. In his first Game, Oz had played as "The Great and Powerful," a Magic User. He'd frozen up and been killed out. An accountant, he'd admitted later, with no imagination. The pike had been the saving of him. He was agile and strong and he could wave that pike like a magic wand . . . and he was too far away and doing fine without Al.

A zombie approached from behind, and Al wrenched his halberd free and drove it into the juncture of neck and shoulder. A red-black gash opened up, splitting the undead from chest to crotch.

Mary-em got behind him now, and they formed a protective sandwich around Crystal. Mary-em's staff spun in figure eights, and she bounced it from head to crotch to ribs, leaving glowing red and black wherever it touched. "Hiyahhh!" she screamed, and drove its end into a face with a horrific crunch.

If she had put the boot to a beetle's carapace, the effect could have been no more dramatic.

The face actually crumbled. The zombie flapped its arms and stumbled back against the wall. Its (un?)dying scream was a gurgle, oily black fluid splashed in a starburst, and it slid to the ground, arms and legs flopping. Locusts crawled out of the shattered head, fluttered their wings, and flew away.

Mary-em was hypnotized for a moment—

Then she ducked as a mace whizzed over her head. She howled with battle fever as she cut the zombie's legs from under it.

One leg came *off*. The zombie crumpled at her feet. Filed teeth filling a hideous, limp twitch of a grin.

As quickly as it began, it was over, except that in the mists around them, from every direction at once, came a horrific moaning.

Then the mist disappeared.

Alphonse turned over one of the bodies with his axe.

"Is it dead?" Crystal asked breathlessly.

"Too late for that," he muttered. The body had two black borders undulating about it. Dead-dead. Somebody upstairs was a joker.

It had dropped its weapon. Al hefted it: a stick with a tin can wired to the top, and a chunk of concrete wedged inside the can for weight. Nasty.

One zombie was still "alive."

He was pale-skinned, and again the flesh was drawn so tightly across the bone that he seemed to have just barely enough substance to animate him.

Nigel Bishop pushed his way through a phalanx of groggy Gamers and shook blood from the end of his sword. He knelt over the creature. "Who is your master?" he asked.

Nothing but a hissing sound. The creature writhed.

Nigel struck a pose, and he swelled with a sudden, fierce inhalation. "By my forefathers!" he called to the ceiling. "Spell of revelation!"

Alphonse leapt back a step.

Light pulsed, and something peeled away from the zombie's body. It hovered in the air above him like glowing smoke, but smoke with eyes and ears.

Its eyes were dead flame. As they watched, it expanded, then dissipated, seeping through the walls.

"Goddamn," Alphonse whispered. "What was that?"

Nigel shook his head. "That's what we were really fighting. Demon of some kind, wearing a mutated corpse."

Alphonse kept quiet, watching as Acacia joined Bishop. Captain Cipher crept up beside her. "Ridden by the Loa, milady. Possessed," Cipher stage-whispered. Then, briskly, "Voodoo or santería deity. Loa or Orisha. Possession's a way they use to get around."

The zombie hissed and tried to get up. Nigel was lightning, pressed his sword into it. The creature's back arched as if it were a serpent. Its mouth overflowed with black fluid. Then it lay still.

The Clerics scuttled about, healing what wounds they could. There were enough wounded to allow them all to test their powers in this unknown domain. Chaim Cohen, Top Nun, Friar Duck, Black Elk, and Tamasan chanted in five languages. Gamers winced at the hideous chorus.

Black Elk, blocky in leather chaps, beads, and medicine feathers, reported to Clavell. "We've lost Lieutenant Philips." His impressive facial scar was peeling a little at the lower edge.

Waters said, "I saw her go down. She tried to macho it."

"It looks like every team's down one or two," Black Elk said.

"Now we're screwed," Waters said. "Without a woman on our team, there are things we just won't learn. Major, think hard about forming an alliance somewhere."

Clavell's face set. He didn't like losing Philips so fast.

Alphonse was already scanning his own team. He had lost an Engineer and a Cleric: Peggy the Hook and Friar Duck.

Al did some quick addition. In the first engagement there had been six fatalities: one each for Apple and Army, two each for Tex-Mits and General Dynamics. Acacia, damn her soul, hadn't lost anyone.

Al felt queasy. "Well, we got stretched a mite. Hardball, is it?"

Smoke tendrils still wafted through the graveyard, muffling the anguished sobs of the injured and mourning.

Nakagawa's Law #3: *There are no expendables. A Loremaster takes the best he can get, in every slot, and loses them only when he must.* Law

#3 fit the California Voodoo Game better than most. Each dead Gamer was a serious loss.

Alphonse shook himself out of his trance. "Scout!"

He got Crystal, and Acacia's Scout, Corrinda. "Scan, please."

They joined hands and pointed toward a side corridor. Warriors Holly Frost and Appelion joined them.

En masse they moved down the corridor, Alphonse in the front. He tested the flooring with the tip of a toe. "Crystal, can you do a structural check?"

Crystal Cofax checked her power ratings and gritted her teeth. "I can give you an eighty-percent yes. Best I can do, chief."

"Let's get it done."

"All right." He studied the older man. "No offense, Trevor."

Trevor's smile was tight and plastic. "None taken."

The weeping was closer now, and Alphonse flattened himself against a wall.

A woman's voice: "Please. Please help us . . ."

She was no more than twenty, and dressed in rags. She was dark-skinned, with a face like a Michelangelo cherub in negative, but her nose was narrow and her lips were thin. What was she? A darkly tanned white person?

At her feet lay a young boy.

"*Oy gevalt,*" Top Nun whispered.

He'd been eviscerated.

But was still alive.

The girl looked up at them earnestly, sniffling, wiping tears away from her cheeks. "Oh," she said. She batted huge, incongruously blue eyes at them, and then continued rapid-fire. "My name is Coral, and this is my brother Tod, and those zombies got him all icky and everything and he's like probably going to die if we don't do something but I can't figure out what to do 'cause like there's guts *everywhere* and did you like maybe bring a Band-Aid or something?"

A beat of five passed in shocked silence. Then somebody passed a Band-Aid to the front. A big one. Alphonse watched, aghast, as she put the adhesive strip onto a rubbery wet red length of intestine. She looked up at them brightly, an edge of hysteria in her voice. "There," she said. "That should be all better now—"

Then fell over sideways in a faint.

Chapter Eleven

Mallbeasts

Thursday, July 21, 2059—9:50 A.M.

The native girl had fainted twice more, but managed to last long enough to lead them through a labyrinthine network of corridors, catwalks, and stairwells, going up, down, and sideways.

Al thought that they *might* be on the second floor. Crystal would be mapping, and he could catch up later. Meantime, keep the eyes open.

Tod was alive but hardly lucid. He babbled to himself while his frantic sister babbled to them. "Thaddeus sent us looking for coffee. He's sort of our leader. Some of the boutiques still have a little of it, if you know where to look."

"Why coffee?" General Poule asked.

"Ceremonies. We don't—" Coral paused. "Well, they don't always let us in the other ceremonies."

"Which ones?"

Coral combed her fingers through her tangled hair and cast sad blue eyes at her brother. "Poor Tod. He found two shakers of that low-sodium salt-substitute stuff, you know, for diets? I told him it wouldn't work against zombies . . ."

And she was off again.

After a few more attempts to communicate, Nigel had given up. Whatever benefits voodoo conferred, intellectual agility was not among them. She led, and twenty-four remaining Gamers followed, but with no great confidence.

Every team had lost someone, except the UC Manhunters. Al

had graciously offered his services to Tammi and Twan as official Beheader, *just a precaution, wouldn't want old friends to get up and go sniffing for kidneys* . . . Tammi had responded with a string of invective that should have peeled off her lipstick. Then she'd performed the task herself. God, he loved Gaming.

The rabbit warren of tunnels opened out into what had been a main Mall area.

Alphonse was shocked.

Despite marquees and displays gone cryptic with burnt-out light panels, it was as well lit as an outdoor pavilion. There were few machine-tooled items for sale in the stores, but the shelves were stocked with arts and crafts and handmade items of every description. Fresh meat? Vegetables? Handmade clothes? Scuba gear? These people had impressive resources.

And power! Neon and incandescent bulbs burned with no thought to economy.

Coral's clan strolled the Mall like Angelinos out to enjoy a summer day. Her people were every color of the human spectrum, from coal black to pale white. They dressed in a wide range of fabrics and colors. Alphonse looked more closely at Coral's clothes: they weren't rags, really, just eclectic and stained. Seen in this improved lighting, they might have made an attractive ensemble, a bizarre fashion statement scavenged from a dozen different scrap heaps and consolidated by a blind seamstress with eight thumbs.

Tod had been sheet-wrapped and strapped onto a makeshift stretcher. His ranting had ceased, and Alphonse couldn't guess whether he was dying, or something worse.

And Coral kept up her line of mad chatter. It was driving him to distraction.

All two dozen Adventurers had collected in the center of a Mall walkway before anyone noticed. Then a tall barrel of a man in a Hawaiian flower T-shirt and a neatly trimmed beard saw them, and yelled in pleasure. "Visitors!"

He dropped his hoe (dropped a potential weapon!) and ran over to them, shaking hands like an incumbent running for reelection. "Why, as I live and breathe. You're outsiders, aren't you?"

"We have one of your people here," Nigel said. "He's badly hurt—"

"Why, as I live and breathe. You're right!"

A crowd of people had gathered around them. Concerned, polite, and speculative, but still a crowd. Al felt twitchy.

"My name is Thaddeus Dark," the big man said. "Coral! Dear child! I was worried about you." She tried to twist away from the immense arm that Dark draped around her, but he just chuckled at her efforts. He hustled Coral off to the side and whispered to her genially while she squirmed.

Finally she said, "No!"

Coral and what was left of her brother were guided off together while Dark returned to the Adventurers. "Now then. Unfortunate, of course, but we warn the children not to go snooping about on the upper levels. Dangerous, you know."

Acacia's lips curled faintly. "Evidently."

He draped that arm around Acacia now, imprisoning her right arm, her sword arm. Alphonse saw her left hand flex; a small knife dropped into it. Dark didn't notice. "Let's do lunch! Tell us all about your voyage. We so seldom see new faces . . ."

They were welcomed by an amazing swarm, at least several hundred people. Every palm Al pressed, every grazing shoulder, was flesh and blood. Damn! Wasn't *anybody* a hologram anymore?

Scouts scanned for traps and Clerics for spells. They found nothing.

Al managed to get up next to Dark, matching his long stride. "You people are pretty comfortable here."

"Yes." Dark smiled. "The gods have been kind."

Which gods?

They passed dozens of children, and hundreds of adults. Maybe two or three hundred just within easy range of sight. More traversed bridges in the Mall, talking and shopping, and others worked at craft boutiques.

Without being too obvious, Al stepped to the edge of a railing and peered down into MIMIC's central well.

They may well have been on the second level, but there were at least three more levels beneath them. Something pulsed greenly down there. Alphonse grabbed Twan Tsing.

She languidly set her fingernails against his knuckles. "Remove," she said sweetly.

He lifted his hand. "Twan. Down three levels. Something glowing. What do you think?"

"Take your distance," she said, but looked.

She adjusted her visor, whispered some words, and then turned back. She bowed. "Most grateful, honorable barbarian." And she hurried off to tell Tammi what she'd seen.

He'd lost his own Engineer. He would have to perform a ceremony later, raise Peggy the Hook from the dead and try to get information that way . . .

Damn, damn, damn.

They were taken to a restaurant named Brio, on the edge of the pavilion. It was the kind of restaurant that tried to evoke Parisian street scenes, with limited success. Little tables were crested by multicolored metal umbrellas, surrounded by metal frame chairs with wicker plastic seats.

They were seated, and Dark lauded them.

"Once, we filled this building," he said, "but we have been driven down by the walking dead above!" His people gathered around in a ring, sealing the restaurant off from the rest of the Mall. Alphonse took a count. Roughly fifty, among twenty-four remaining Gamers. He felt nauseated with alarm.

". . . are powerful. They are the minions of the voodoun of the upper levels."

Captain Cipher woke up. "You practice voodoo yourselves?"

"Oh, no." Dark smiled. "We are good Christian folk."

And a minute ago you said, "The gods have been kind."

Dark's smile deepened. He said casually, "We hear you have powerful magic. That you were able to see them despite their cloak of night. Is this true?"

Nigel answered without a pause. "We were lucky."

"Ahh . . . I think that you are modest as well as powerful. A true mark of greatness!"

He raised his arms, and Alphonse noticed that they were thick with old, heavy muscle. Dark ate well. Those teeth . . .

"My people! We have powerful visitors! Together we may be able to wrest our rightful heritage away from the blood-eaters of the upper levels!"

Waiters appeared. Natives emerged from the shops, dressed in wild variety, chattering and peering curiously. They smiled. Alphonse waved cheerily. *Just folks, you betcha!*

"Little lady, can you keep your right hand on your sword and pass that catfish with your left?"

"Let's see," Acacia said brightly.

Muzak bleated a tired melody as toothy, cheerful, perfectly tanned waiters with weight-lifter physiques brought trays of catfish, fresh hot bread, and endless streams of orange juice. The plates were decent china, badly chipped, from several sets.

"Where does the bread come from?" Alphonse asked Dark. "And the orange juice?"

"We trade with those on the upper levels," the big man answered. "They have things that we lack. We have things that they need. The balance is all that has kept us alive!"

Alphonse had lost his Cleric. Gen-Dyn's Tamasan was seated at his table, but out of earshot; and he was Bishop's man. Mati "Top Nun" Cohen was closer.

Al bent sideways and said, "Truce. If there's an attack, you can tuck in next to me."

"That comfort failed Friar Duck," Top Nun said conversationally.

"Cut him from asshole to appetite, but it wasn't *my* fault."

"True, he was a klutz. Let's hear the offer, *bube*."

"Bless this food, little lady. Add my power to yours. If you can detect anything—poison, whatever—let me know."

She thought for a moment, and then said, "Tell you what—you truce with me for the rest of the day?"

"Sure."

"*Mazal tov*—so you've got a partner." Top Nun spread her hands. "Our Father who art in heaven, bless this nosh, from knish to schnapps. Reveal any and all *meshuge* traps. Amen."

She shut her eyes hard and then opened them again. "Clean as a whistle."

He looked over at the other tables. All surviving Gamers had performed similar ceremonies, if Cleric or Wizard were available. Bishop's rounded little Shinto monk didn't look happy, but he was eating everything in sight.

Not the slightest hint of trouble.

Al's neck itched.

Top Nun, her little brown face a pleasant oval in her hood, nibbled daintily at her catfish. Her enormous brown eyes widened even further, pronouncing it good. "Eat, eat. You're a skeleton," she complained.

Thaddeus Dark stood and raised his glass. "Let us toast our new friends—"

Alphonse wasn't listening; he was scanning the food. Clean. It was common to provide meals during a Game, and the food tested clean . . . but it was Game Time, and anything could happen, and Thaddeus Dark was too bloody massive . . .

Hunger won out over caution, and he bit into a catfish fillet. Delicious.

And one at a time, all of the Gamers were dropping their defenses, concentrating on the meal at hand. A few Magic Users still surreptitiously scanned, but there just wasn't anything wrong with the food.

In fact, the catfish was crispy and hot, the croissants fluffy. The orange juice must have been fresh-squeezed.

Captain Cipher approached Top Nun and whispered something in her ear. They huddled.

The back of Al's neck, never completely calm, began itching furiously. He didn't much like Cipher. The man was—how do you say? Fragrant? Alphonse wished for a breeze, a breeze to put him upwind of the good Captain.

Cipher and Top Nun linked hands and began to chant.

Cipher blinked hard, said, "Whoa," and then linked up again. He spoke in hushed tones, but Alphonse could still hear them. "Whoa. I'm getting the—"

"Brother Cipher, you're such a *mensch.*" Top Nun said. She cast around the table and finally settled on Alphonse. "Brother Alphonse, if you want in on this, give me thy hand."

Al flipped down his visor. Everybody around the tables looked the same as before. Then he linked hands—

Aw, shit.

An aura flickered red/black/red/black around half of the Adventurers. His own hands bore the same mark.

"We're being poisoned."

Alphonse's fingers gripped the table. "This really chaps my ass. How could it *happen?*"

Cipher's protruding eyes rolled in something near panic. "It isn't just magic and it isn't just chemicals. Magical poison . . . not a strange concept, not at all. Witches and shamans always used poisons and magic both—"

"Stop wringing your dick and get *on* with it."

"Game designers *never* use magical poison. It makes for too short a Game. We can't fight this," Cipher gulped. "It's too strong. It's not fair . . ."

So maybe it was something else, Alphonse thought, dropping out of character for an instant. Maybe it was a spell to make Gamers crazy, paranoid, to make them attack new friends. He stood and raised his weapon.

The halberd's Virtual-display blade wobbled in his hand, almost out of control. His arm was bordered in red. If he tried to move, the red ran to black. *Poisoned. Really.*

His hosts began to shapeshift, their flesh melting away, humanity dissolving even as he watched. *It's going to be a short Game.*

A few of the Adventurers hadn't noticed, and were still caught up in eating, didn't have enough juice to *see* the transformation going on right in front of them. Then it was damn near too late.

The Mallbeasts were fanged, rough-skinned things. Not zombies; something halfway between human and demon.

Music burred in his ears. Pulsating. Hypnotically seductive. As if it were impossibly loud music playing terribly far away.

His vision began to cloud.

God! No! It couldn't be over so soon! Not like this! To die without reaching any goals, without having any—

The Bishop stood, sweating, one hand on his stomach. His back was to the other Magic Users, who cried out as the Mallbeasts approached. Alphonse couldn't hear the spell, but their bodies suddenly exploded with light.

For a moment—but only a moment—the beasts were driven back. Then they began to advance again.

Nigel Bishop's dark, normally confident face was crinkled with worry, with a familiar *what the fuck?* expression normally reserved for lesser mortals. It was almost worth dying to see it.

And then the air crackled.

There was a wet smell. An explosion of light flooded through the Mall. Alphonse screamed, shielding his eyes, the dark shapes of the Mallbeasts visible even through closed lids—

At the center of the light stood a roughly human shape. A man dressed in white deck shoes, crisp white sun pants, a short-sleeved shirt—matching, of course. He sported a gloriously golden tan, short sun-bleached hair, and the chest and shoulders of a lifeguard.

The thing that had been Thaddeus Dark hissed: "Nommo! Your kind have no business here! You dare violate the truce?" Other beasts hissed behind him, a venomous, swelling wave of sound.

The newcomer looked at them almost sleepily. "Chill out, dudes and dudettes. These folks are righteous. Truth is, they rescued two of yours, and what you're doin' is like *way* bogus."

Thaddeus Dark hissed. "Something is wrong here. You have no Sight into this level, unless a conduit . . ." The creature scanned the room. To Alphonse, it seemed that he grew larger as he did. His body swelled with rage. "Coral! Traitorous *dweeb*! You have betrayed the Mall!"

Beat. Nothing. Then Coral stepped out of the shadow. She couldn't face him; she talked to the floor. "Like, Tod is dead, man, except not really, he's in that yucky undead place, and it's all your fault—"

The run-on sentence was about to run further, but Thaddeus raised his hand. His teeth gleamed through a ruin of rotting lips. "I will see you dead. I will hang your skin on my wall, and your soul will writhe in torment for a thousand years." His voice rose to a thundering crescendo, then he stopped, suddenly thoughtful. "That's just a rough. I'll get back to you."

Coral balled her hands into little fists and balanced them saucily on her hips. "Thaddeus?" she said.

"What?"

"Bite my shorts."

The light subsided, and Alphonse could move again.

Nommo beckoned to them. "This way to safety."

The Adventurers shucked off their shock and gathered their gear, backing away from the hissing mob of Mallbeasts. Among Twan's group there was frantic whispered discussion—Appelion was doing all the talking, and he was grinning—then they were following, too.

Again and again the beasts tried to advance. Casual sweeps of Nommo's arm raised waves of light to drive them back.

Their rescuer backed toward a wall, which opened behind him. "This way," he said—without speaking. Alphonse heard it as a whisper in his ear, rather than an external voice.

No one questioned the command. They crowded into the room, and the door sealed shut. The floor began to lift beneath them.

Alphonse was scared. Something in the Mall was more powerful than anything he had ever faced. Only the direct intervention of— what? a God?—had saved them this time.

Next time, they had better the hell be ready.

Chapter Twelve

A Marriage Made in Hell

The cargo elevator doors slid shut.

There was a long, hushed pause, quiet breathing, no talking. Each of the hundreds of Mallbeasts listened or watched anxiously for some sign of approval, dismissal, or reproach. Doris Whitman's husky voice growled over hidden speakers: "All right, people—that's a wrap!"

Three hundred miscellaneous ghouls and were-creatures cheered. Thaddeus Harmony, sometime Chief of Operations of Dream Park, temporary leader of the Mallbeasts, exhaled a long sigh of relief.

Beside him, a slender Mallbeast smiled. Flabby thin lips pulled up in grotesque mirth, exposing yellowed fangs. It slapped him on the back, jovially. Harmony's was a large back, a reminder of his short, intense career in pro football.

"Not bad," the smaller creature said. "Ever wonder if you've missed your true calling?"

"Excuse me while I wring out my shorts. I'm not sure I can do this again."

The were-thing peeled off half a latex mask. Beneath it were radio-controlled air bladders. When triggered in sequence, they inflated and changed hue to nightmarish effect. Harmony knew that the face beneath the remaining makeup was very dark, very pretty, very feminine. It belonged to Millicent Summers, one of Dream Park's top financial-management officers.

Millicent said, "It's a little late to back out now."

"I know, I know," Harmony grumbled as he peeled makeup off. He winced as a bit of stickum caught on a real wart. He popped out a rather canine dental appliance. Most of the prosthetics were designed as three or four interlocking pieces for easy application and removal.

The crowd had thinned out. Dream Park employees who had opted to be Mallbeasts were drifting back to their amusements. On Mall level, there were plentiful amusements to be found.

Three of the restaurants were open for business. Games were available, video, holo, senso, and others. Music rang through the halls. Sensors built into the Virtual scanners kept track of the Gamers. If any of them approached this level, all employees would be altered. Meals, games, or naps would end, and the Mallbeasts would live again.

Millicent was right behind Harmony as he reached the commuter elevator.

"How's Alex?" he asked as the door shushed closed behind them.

"Not good. He's taking Sharon's death pretty hard."

"Getting pretty close, were they?" Harmony looked at Millicent more closely. Her makeup transformed her into a thing of nightmare, broken facial bones fused beneath puffy swollen skin. He dipped his fingers into a running sore and sniffed the glaze that rubbed away. "Smells like cold cream. Ah, my undead Nubian queen . . ."

She didn't smile, and couldn't meet his eyes.

He stopped chuckling. "Did it hurt? Alex and Sharon?"

She peeled away another section of mask. Only the forehead piece remained now. "Alex and I were always a . . . convenience for each other. We were both too busy with our careers. It was nice to have somebody nearby to take the edge off. We never considered it a romance."

"Oh," he said in the same tone another man might have said *Bullshit*. "And?"

"Well, Alex was in deeper than he thought. He's wrung out about it."

The doors opened, and they were in Gaming Central.

A ten-meter skeletal holo of the entire complex rotated majestically in the air. Within it, a glowing green matchbox-sized freight elevator ferried miniature Gamers toward the roof.

Tony McWhirter was at work coordinating the two primary labor pools: the Lopezes, who handled the electronics, and the Whitmans, who handled the Non-Player Characters. For the Gamers, it was a marriage made in hell.

Harmony liked Tony well enough, but would never completely trust him.

McWhirter looked up suddenly, grinning. "Mr. Harmony! I didn't know you had thespic ambitions."

"Yes, well, Millie convinced me that I was the right physical type, and I had to admit it sounded like fun. Who hasn't wanted to play Mister Big? Everything all right here?"

"Some interesting glitches, but we're holding on. And I don't suppose they'll reach Mall level again for twenty-four hours at least. Probably more. Got to sleep sometime. Hi, Millicent."

Harmony asked, "Aren't sleep breaks built into the Game?"

"Not this one. You take it when and where you can—but teams that try to get ahead by skipping sleep lose their creative edge. No way to make it through the whole Game in less than forty-eight hours. They had better sleep sometime, that's all I can say." Tony pivoted to face Harmony. "What can I do for you?"

"Looking for Alex. Is he on the roof?"

"No. He was supposed to be." Tony scowled. "Lucky I had a guy big enough. Harry Lessenger, he already looks like a surfer, but I have to keep feeding him lines." He whistled a short, high note, and barked, "Roof, roof."

The holo image cut to the top level. Revelers were partying throughout a primitive village mockup, making up rain dances, trying to climb the little glassy-smooth pyramid, sunbathing, and in general having a wonderful time. They were in a holding pattern: the five-minute warning buzzer had sounded, and they were ready for the ten-second trill that would put them completely in character, ready for the appearance of the Gamers.

"Sharon's death just flatlined him," Tony said.

"Easy to understand. So where is he?"

"At DP, I'd guess. He won't talk to *me*."

Harmony's big, round face drooped. "Well . . . hell. I guess we'll go and check in on him there."

Tony watched them leave. When they were out of sight, he used a monitor to follow them into an elevator and down.

Then he caused a tiny window to appear on another monitor

screen. Wearing a bland, not-quite-bored look, he watched statistics stream by.

The Army team had slipped from third to last place.

Now they knew it in Vegas: California Voodoo wasn't being played in Dream Park. Army's odds were falling. The Army had played dozens of successful games in Gaming A, but had a mediocre record elsewhere.

The Universities of California ran just behind the Troglodykes right now. Best odds. But Vegas didn't know what was coming next.

Whistling to himself, Tony manipulated his bank account, placed a quiet little bet against Tammi and Twan, routed through carefully constructed cutouts. With the right system in place, bets could be placed and collected without revealing his identity, without any direct contact at all. What he was doing was illegal, and unethical, and probably endangered his immortal soul. Therein lay the interest.

There were several kinds of bets he could place. How long would the Game last? Who would win? What would the point spread be? There were ways for an ingenious lad to make money, and all without hurting anyone. *Right, Albert?*

It was a thrill to watch the odds changing in Vegas or Atlantic City. Intoxicating to feel the constant ebb and flow of the numbers as a high roller dropped a really big bet, changing the odds. The bookies made their own adjustments. A bookie never lost big, never won big. The house always took a steady, even percentage, three to six percent or so. Suckers played the other suckers, unless one sucker was really a house in disguise.

Tony McWhirter felt like playing house.

According to Alex Griffin's secretary, he wasn't in his office and hadn't been in his apartment. He was still right there at MIMIC, in the personal quarters of the late Sharon Crayne.

Millicent pursed her lips. "Figures."

Harmony spoke briefly to the elevator. It programmed itself and headed off toward Sharon's apartment.

"You know . . ." Millicent was staring straight ahead. He'd seen her do that in confined spaces. "I've wondered if I broke something when I left Security."

"How so?"

"We were a team, sort of. Me and Alex and Marty Bobbick.

When Alex came down from Tacoma he slipped right into harness, but we were there to help. Always."

The box sighed to a halt, and the door slid open.

The hallway was empty and sepulchrally silent. When they reached Sharon's door, they were almost reluctant to open it. The diagonal red slash of a Security sticker read *Entrance denied*.

"And?"

"And I left. And right after, we found out Marty was rotten." She shivered. "And Alex hasn't been the same. It's not easy for him to let anyone in. Or even close. When he finally tries to open up with Sharon, *this*." She looked down again. "He and I were safe together, you know. We both knew it was going nowhere." Her brown eyes were very deep—and numbed. With pity? Pain? "Safe."

Harmony thumbed the door, and the Security sticker faded.

There was dim light in the hallway, with brighter light farther on. He heard a faint scrabbling sound, the kind of sound a crab might make scuttling across rocks.

Harmony stepped in, following the light, and found Alex near the kitchen. He was seated on a plastic chair, sorting a pile of paper and plastic. There was another pile, of discards, to his left.

He looked as if he hadn't slept in a day and a half.

"Hello, Alex," Harmony said quietly.

Alex nodded to them. Millicent hung back. Something in Alex's eyes had shifted unpleasantly.

Then their eyes met, and he was friendly old Alex again, smiling crookedly. "I'm just . . . cross-referencing."

"I see," Harmony said. "And you've been here all night?"

"Here, or on the horn to Tacoma, or on the computers."

"What are you looking for, Alex?" Harmony hitched his pants and squatted next to his friend.

"I—I've only got a couple of ways to look at this," Alex said mechanically. "First, her death was an accident. She went to meet a lover, and she slipped. Or else it wasn't so innocent." He blinked. "A: She was murdered by someone with no interest in Cowles Industries. B: She met with someone antagonistic to Cowles, but died accidentally. C: She was murdered by an enemy of the company.

"If she was compromised, I have to see how someone could get his hooks in her. I'm building backwards. I want to know if there was anything that she wanted . . ."

That you couldn't give her, Millicent said silently.

Millicent groped behind herself and found a box to sit on, and

Harmony a chair. They pulled up close to Alex in the synthetic dusk. Millicent stopped wanting to turn on the ceiling lights. Somehow, it seemed important to leave things just the way they were.

"This is the way I reasoned," Alex said dully. "Assume the worst. Assume that she got involved in something illegal. She met someone to exchange something. It had nothing to do with sex."

Why, Alex? Is it easier to think she was a traitor to Cowles Inc. than to your bed?

"The assumption I made," Alex said, "is that the timing of her arrival was important. She needed to be close to MIMIC, and—to me." He winced, blinking again.

"Why you, Alex?"

"She needed information."

Harmony scratched his head. "But all she had to do was wait a month or so, and she would have been second-in-command of MIMIC. And there would be more valuable information and material there."

Alex nodded. "She needed it faster. Why? She knew the security system better than I did. She knew more about the tenants who will move in. There's something here now that won't be here later, or someone needs something fast."

"She would have had access to accounting operations," Millicent said reluctantly. "Also engineering designs, confidential correspondence with participating corporations—not to mention Gaming Central."

"But the time pressure? I keep thinking about the California Voodoo Game."

Harmony's eyes were distant. "Yeah. Maybe she placed some bets. She knew secrets; she could watch the Game Masters. Maybe she was meeting a bookie, or someone to place a bet for her . . . nah. She could have done that over the phone."

"But it's an angle," Alex agreed. "If she had a partner, and she exchanged something physical, like a key or a bubble chip, then a face-to-face meeting might be valuable." He sighed. "There are just too many possibilities."

Millicent paused and then offered her contribution almost shyly. "Listen, Alex. I can go through payroll, find her bank codes. I could find out whether large payments were going in and out of her accounts. Might indicate gambling, blackmail, that sort of thing."

Harmony sat, silent, until he realized that both of them were waiting for him to speak. "As Head of Operations, I have a lot of indirect power. I just don't know where to push. What do you want?"

"Let's see if we can expand her dossier, Thaddeus. And then I want Norman Vail to go over it. I want to know if Sharon would have been vulnerable to blackmail, bribery, coercion of any kind. I want to know what her flaw was. After that mess with Marty, I ran a high-level check on *everyone* with access to critical data."

"Everyone at Dream Park," Millicent corrected gently. "Sharon was with Cowles Inc."

Harmony stood. "I'll get on it, Alex." Alex didn't look up. Harmony waited an embarrassed moment, then left the room.

Millicent remained behind. Alex sat staring at the objects in his hand. He seemed like a husk. All of his physical and mental potential was there, and deep within his private recesses the engines were roaring. But they weren't hooked up to anything. Without the engagement of gears he was like a glass shell over a furnace. If she touched the shell, it would be warm. Lukewarm. But there was a fire within that couldn't burn to the surface.

She laid a hand on his neck. His skin was cool.

He turned his head and looked up at her. His green eyes seemed almost black. "Could I have been so wrong?" It was a plea. He needed sleep, but was far too wound up now. She wished she could take his hand, lead him to bed . . .

But she couldn't. To see this Alex, this face he had never shown her, let her know that things could never be the same between them.

How had Sharon slipped past Alex's defenses as she, Millicent, never had? She could read his face: Alex was afraid it hadn't been his choice at all. That he had been snared as neatly as one of Harmony's marlins.

So for that moment of terrible vulnerability, she held his head, and he leaned it against her. Alex shook himself like a tired old horse and said, "I've got some things I need to finish here, okay?"

Almost as an afterthought, he added, "Would you help Vail? There might be things that a—a woman would spot that a man . . . you know," he said miserably.

She nodded. "Sure, Alex. I know." Without another word she left him there. She wished there was more to say, but there just wasn't. Somehow, she wasn't disappointed; rather, she was astounded that he had let her say or do even the small amount she had.

Her last sight of him was a silhouette: a lonely man sitting in darkness, sifting through handfuls of paper and plastic. Rereading this letter, reexamining that holocube, trying them this way and that and the other. Trying with diligent desperation to make sense of the jigsaw puzzle that was Sharon Crayne.

Chapter Thirteen

Mami Wata

"In my dreams mermaids often appear who want to drag me into the water . . . I am afraid . . ."

—Gert Chesi, *Voodoo*, 1979

Thursday, July 21, 2059—12:10 P.M.

Acacia was jammed into the back of the drum-shaped elevator. At one side the Nommo stood gigantic, glowing, and alone. The Gamers about him shied from touching a probable god; else there might have been room to wiggle. As it was, Acacia had barely room to breathe.

Thank goodness six of us got killed off, she thought.

Coral, the Nommo, and two rows of Gamers stood between Acacia and Nigel Bishop. She kept a nervous eye on him. Her heartbeat accelerated every time she looked at him, and she was no longer sure exactly why.

"Reveal passage," S. J. Waters said dramatically.

Nigel and Acacia both echoed: "All Scouts cooperate," and in the crowded confines of the elevator, the Scouts reached out and joined hands. The elevator car turned to glass.

They were rising along the wall of a structure with the volume of a dozen Astrodomes, a hundred World Trade Centers, enough to swallow all the whales in the ocean. Hallways and ramps stretched off in all directions, marking off spaces that were larger than most buildings.

The elevator floor lurched under her feet. Acacia braced a hand against the wall, a flash of acro-claustrophobia driving all other thoughts from her mind. MIMIC juddered violently, then faded into solid wall as the Scouts lost concentration.

"What the hell was *that*?" SJ muttered. "Thaddeus Dark?"

The shuddering faded out.

"Maybe just an old building," Acacia said, irritated by the tension in her voice. She had to get a grip. The Game was just *starting*, dammit, and they already had her rattled. Her initial adrenaline burn was wearing off, leaving behind a gritty residue of fatigue. Her second wind hadn't cut in yet.

The Scouts linked hands again. MIMIC returned, huge and frightening. How were they supposed to find anything in a building this size? The Scouts. They had to protect the Scouts, at all costs.

The coolly glowing ceiling swept down to give them a moment of darkness. Now the floors whipped by just a little too fast for them to *see* anything. Here was a tropical garden, here was the graveyard again; here a vast indoor pool, its silver surface roiled by . . . gone.

MIMIC had a shimmy to it. The car must be vibrating—and then it lurched again. Gamers screamed as it tilted to a side, and they crashed into one another, sliding into the wall in a scramble of limbs and swords and staffs. The Scouts must have been maintaining their link, because MIMIC still surrounded their tiny transparent bubble; but the vast transparent cityscape was tilted and trembling. An ear-ripping, whining, metal-against-metal vibration made the car dance, as if the tilted car were grinding against the shaft walls. The floor dropped six inches, and Acacia was the first to scream as she *thumped* back down.

Genuine fear lived in that elevator now; even Bishop searched the walls, seeking a way out.

Al the Barb was pasty-faced. "I'm dyin', " he gasped.

"Be polite," Tammi said. "Wait for me to kill you properly."

"Eat my—" The last word was lost in a scream, as the elevator clanged, dropped, and changed its tilt. The wall was solid again. Acacia was on the floor again. Arms reached past her nose as the Scouts doggedly attempted to regain their *Reveal* spell.

"This damned thing is coming apart!" Bishop muttered.

Acacia took emotional refuge in analysis. Al the Barb seemed mighty twitchy, but if memory served her right, his manic edge was as much shuck as his cowboy routine. She couldn't count on him to fold under pressure. Nor did she want him to, until they had a clearer idea of what they were up against.

Mouser, the little Thief who followed the Troglodykes around like a St. Bernard puppy, was grinning like a kid on a roller coaster, completely nerveless. Furthermore, despite his frailty, she knew that he could go for seventy-two hours without sleep, when there was a Game to be played.

The *Reveal* spell was flickering. MIMIC showed like hologram stills.

MIMIC's levels sank below them, giving hints of the building's complexity. Acacia was too busy keeping her stomach under control to do any mapping. She took what mental snapshots she could, storing away flashes of external detail, knowing that "Aces" Wilde would remember far better. Given the correct spells, "Aces" would reel back what she had seen as if it had been recorded.

Mouser was not likely to forget that she had killed him during Crystal Maze. Was there a way to manipulate that? Not yet . . .

Despite the chaos, Appelion had seen something. He was bursting with it. She'd seen Twan elbow him in the short ribs, warning him not to blurt secrets in the crowded elevator. What had he seen; what had Acacia missed?

The car slammed to a halt as if it had rammed a roof. The door slid up, grinding and protesting, on blue sky and a tilted horizon.

"Out! Get out!" Clavell yelled unnecessarily. They damn near trampled each other scrambling to safety, the elevator groaning behind them.

Mary-em was the last out. As her feet left the elevator floor, there came terrible sounds: shriek of old metal struts and braces giving up their rusty ghosts, cannon sounds of stressed cables snapping under immense tension. The car dropped from sight.

For a moment the silence was such that Mary-em crawled to the doorway to look. Then all hell broke loose in the elevator shaft.

The Gamers rolled away from the sounds, shaking their heads. Coral croaked, "I think I swallowed my gum."

Acacia heard laughter and water splashing behind her, and she turned.

A dozen giggling women stood hip-deep and flirted with a knot of men ashore. Music blared from hidden speakers: loud, heartthrob precise, but peppered with static. Off to the east were orchards of miniature orange trees, and fields of corn and wheat, and a pyramid—a featureless pyramid eight to ten meters tall, looking right at home in its cultivated fields, as if the whole set had wandered in from Mayan times.

They were on a roof, but a roof so huge that the edges formed a horizon. To the west the edge of the roof seemed to have crumbled, and the lagoon gushed over it.

A rooftop lagoon? Losing liquid at that rate? MIMIC had been built in an age when any form of power was subject to attack by various nut groups. Where had Meacham got his power?

Not hydroelectric, not in a desert. Not solar or wind; both were too weak. A nuclear plant? The Sierra Club would have freaked . . .

One of the revelers jogged toward them. A gaudy sarong flapped around his legs; a loop of seashells bounced around his neck. Otherwise he looked like a Westwood Beach surfer: white-blond shaggy hair and beard, wide bronze sunglasses, a muscular bare torso. His miniature nose was peeling from sunburn.

"Nommo!" The surfer stopped, stared, then dropped hastily to his knees. "You bring—strangers here. And this Mayombrera? Why?" He was angry, frightened, and fascinated.

"She brings you allies, Bobo," the Nommo said. "They may be the ones we need."

The man scratched carefully in his blond Jesus beard. He was still kneeling. "You're saying we can trust the Mayombreros?"

Their rescuer clucked in disgust. "Bobo, sometimes I think your mind is a few beads shy of a necklace. *Of course we can't.* But *Coral's* heart is pure. Trust the Gidget, not her people."

The Nommo moved another step closer to the waterfall. The sky above them was very blue. A hot, dry wind blew from the east.

Alphonse was the first one to speak up. "They call you Nommo. Are you a god?"

The Nommo laughed warmly. "No. We Nommo never claimed to be gods. The name is generic, by the way. My own name is Wannis."

"Can we trust you?"

Wannis grinned. "Believe only what you see," he said. His entire body began to shimmer, and Acacia suddenly realized that he had stepped back *onto* the water, hovering there rather disconcertingly. Beyond him was the edge of the roof, and the foaming waterfall.

His outline grew plastic. For an instant there was another shape, and then he had become six glowing feet of sleek muscular fins and tail.

That other shape . . . had she really seen . . . something like a catfish and something like a flatfish, ugly as sin. Then a dolphin leapt into the air, arced back down, and skipped across the water like a skimmed stone. It tail-danced at the crumbled edge of the roof, balancing at the edge of the roaring water. Wannis spoke, his voice rising into a buzzing Disney squeak. "Then again—believe only half of what you see!"

Then it was over the edge, and gone.

Acacia noticed that, once again, they were surrounded.

At least these were more recognizable as voodoun. They wore peasant garb—simple cloth with red and silver frills; jewelry of many shapes and sizes, made of gold and silver and polished shells. They'd come noisily; she'd heard it herself and ignored it. But why hadn't her Scouts . . .

Where was Corrinda?

She must have slipped away while Wannis was putting on his show. Off to investigate . . . what?

A huge, imposing brown-skinned woman with African features parted the crowd. When she walked, it was like a battleship cresting the waves. Bobo scampered hastily out of the way, *then* got to his feet. She didn't notice.

"And so," the enormous woman said. Her eyes sparkled in a nest of deep wrinkles. "The Mami Wata are friendly to you."

"Mami Wata?" Acacia asked.

"There are many, many names for the same creatures, the same gods. They are also called mermaids—and Nommo." She laughed. The sound was broad and warm and genuine. "Whatever you call them, today we celebrate their blessings. Come with me! You are our friends now."

Acacia wanted to let her guard down. She needed to! But magic walked here that wouldn't even register on a deep scan. She had to be careful beyond any ordinary sense of the word.

"I am Mamissa Kokoe," the big woman roared, "and I am what you would call the Fetish Priestess."

Some of the Adventurers introduced themselves. Coral hung back. Mamissa came to her, squatted, and brought her dark, flat face closer for an inspection. "You are not an outsider. Who are you, child?"

Coral seemed to draw into herself. "My name is Coral," she said in a strangled, little-girl voice. "They saved my life. They tried to save Tod, but he was like chipped beef, man."

Mamissa put her palms on her enormous knees and looked at the girl more closely, like a grown woman examining a doll. "Well. You come from the lower levels, don't you?"

Coral nodded nervously.

"And you helped these people, and you have no tribe now?"

Coral nodded again.

"I see. Well. These are hard times for you. If these newcomers had any power of their own . . ."

Mamissa and her followers led them across the rooftop. It was scattered with huts and small ponds and what seemed to be hundreds of acres of crops.

"What is this place?" Mary-em asked.

"This is our home. Some call it MIMIC. Some call it New Africa."

"The people down on the lower levels didn't seem to be very African," Mouser said. "If you pardon me for noticing."

Mamissa's massive frame shook with elemental laughter. It blended with the wind that rustled the leaves of sugar cane and whistled through stands of cornstalks and banana trees.

"Africa is in the heart, not the skin, little boy. The tribes of Africa are black, and white, and yellow." Acacia heard the words echoed in her earpieces and switched her belt pod to *Record*. These were notes from the Game Masters. You never knew what might be useful.

"Before the great disasters struck the world, the old gods warned the faithful, told us to come here. Taught us prayers to make the crops grow," said Mamissa Kokoe.

Nigel Bishop had shouldered in closer. "But there seem to be many . . . ways to worship," he said.

"As there have always been."

They had emerged from the fields and were now walking through a network of huts. Potbellied half-naked children ran barefoot through the streets. All of them were nut-brown, by birth or exposure to desert sun. They seemed healthy and happy.

"Are you completely self-sufficient here?"

"No." For an instant the smile wandered. "We need things from the lower levels. Most of us on the upper levels worship the gentler gods—we have even given up animal sacrifice."

"Sacrifice?"

Twan's ears had perked up at the word. They were surrounded by children now, coming out of the houses and the huts, curious as children always are.

Acacia found herself scratching a cornrowed head. Trevor Stone was sitting on his heels, whispering to a handful of the children, showing them something hand-sized that glittered. Many were coffee-skinned Hispanics, and they ran alongside the Adventurers laughing and smiling, rows of improbably white teeth gleaming, hands outstretched, touching strangeness.

"Pigs. Barnyard fowl. These are often sacrificed, and we have done away with some of it."

"Why?" Twan persisted.

"Greenpeace," Mamissa said soberly. "Save the chickens, man."

The ash-blond jogger—Bobo?—sprinted forward to block their path. "Mamissa," he said, "we cannot allow these strangers to witness our ceremonies!"

"Oh, hush your mouth. The Mami Wata have personally interceded. It would be rude to turn them away."

"You go too far!" Bobo called after them.

Mamissa paid no attention to him, and they continued on.

"You refuse to sacrifice to the gods, and now you allow strangers. You will bring grief on us all!"

So sacrificing to the gods was valuable, but they hadn't been doing their share of it? Acacia made a mental note, resolving to pay extra special attention. In all times and places, one must learn the religious laws.

Huts were clustered like coconuts just this side of a lagoon . . . wait. From this angle, the lagoon seemed an ocean. It stretched as far as the eye could see.

Acacia strode up to keep abreast of Mamissa; for all of her girth, the woman moved like a race walker. "What exactly *is* this ceremony?"

The village seemed to be gathering. The sun was high and sparkled on the waves rolling in toward the beach.

"The Mami Wata ceremony is a tribute to the water folk," Mamissa said. "If you would soothe your dreams, if you would know the future, if you would commune with the water spirits, you must participate." She turned and looked among the Adventurers. "What woman among you would join in the Mami Wata ceremony?"

Acacia weighed options for a moment and then stepped forward. "I will," she said.

"Waters," Poule snapped, and S. J. Waters stepped forward.

Mamissa shook her head. "No. Women only."

SJ shrugged at Evil Poule. Poule said, "Yeah. I thought your name might be lucky."

A high, moaning sound went up from the village, followed by a joyful keening. Perhaps fifty women rushed out of the huts. They were all races and colors—and all half-naked.

Acacia watched Alphonse's eyes bug out. *Here comes the main event,* she thought. She had been expecting this.

With studied casualness she stripped down to her panties. Every movement was a calculated tease. The Army men had effectively turned to stone. Al the B, paranoid as always, tried to keep his eyes moving, and failed. The Fool-Killer could have had him for free.

Gloriously long-limbed and bare-chested, Acacia turned and glared at the men. Their eyes bugged like gigged frogs. "Well, what are you staring at, you knuckle-dragging mouth breathers?"

Adam's apples bobbed. Nervous perspiration glazed wrinkled brows. *God,* she thought. *I love being a mammal.*

The Mouser managed a weak reply. "Uh . . . she said we can't join in . . ."

Mamissa laughed heartily. "True, but if you would watch, or help, shed your clothing. Otherwise, stand back! And allow the Faithful to worship."

"I remember!" Al the B said suddenly. Slowly at first, then with a growing frenzy, Alphonse started to peel.

Other men were following suit. One could tell from their expressions—puzzled frowns or secretive grins—whether they'd read the material on the Mami Wata rites or were just following Al's lead.

Only two people actively complained. One was Major Terry Clavell. "I'm not doing this," he said stubbornly. "I just won't watch the ceremony, that's all."

General Poule dropped his pants on his backpack, then his shirt, without taking his eyes off the native women gathering at the shore. He said, "Then *I'd* better watch. I might see something we need to know."

The other was a wrinkled, sun-dried nut of a woman, Mary-Martha Corbett. "There's enough sufferin' in the world," she muttered, "without askin' perfectly nice folks in China and England to watch my peekaboos on wide screen." Uncharitably, perhaps, no one argued with her.

Top Nun hadn't complained, but wasn't disrobing, either.

"Oh, come on," Mouser said. "Give it a try."

"You don't know my husband," she said wistfully. "Would he be angry? Hoo-ha!"

Poule said, "Dammit, Waters, they're all staring at my belly."

"It isn't soft, it's just big, right? General, why don't you ask Bobo to punch it?"

"Because he looks bloody strong."

★ ★ ★

Far below their feet, Doris Whitman requested a stat run from Tony McWhirter. Tony ran through the complete list of twenty-four survivors and evaluated them for magic and resistance to spells. He came up with three names, all males.

Doris ran a quick randomizer series to select a victim. She patched through to the individual lines, punched his code, and began to speak.

For an instant, Alphonse thought that he was going crazy. "Hello," a rather sexy voice whispered breathily in his ear. "The gods, here. You have been chosen for a demonstration of our power. You will do exactly what we tell you to do, when we tell you to do it, or you will take twelve hit points of damage right now. If you understand, please nod your head."

Alphonse nodded enthusiastically.

"Good lad. This is what we want you to do . . ."

Nonworshipers had been pushed to the rear of the crowd, with nothing to see but the backs of heads.

Participants were all lined up at the water's edge now. The entire three-quarters-naked lot of them were swaying and chanting to music that seemed to surround them, to flow from everywhere, from nowhere, and filled them completely.

The water roiled at the shoreline. Near-naked Adventurers separated themselves from their clothed companions and joined the legion of screaming, leaping, wailing women on the beach.

The waves seemed almost alive. They beckoned.

Back near the huts, Major Terry Clavell gave a harsh, flat bark of laughter. "Seems to me that this is going to give The Girls an unfair advantage," he said unpleasantly.

"Philips crossed us. She tried to show how good she was," S. J. Waters said matter-of-factly. "Her timing was lousy."

"Waters," the major said curtly, "we've discussed all this before. I'm not interested in it now. Whatever fucking mermaid nonsense this is, I don't care. Someone has to remain ready for combat at all times. However . . ."

Mamissa looked over the clothed Adventurers and motioned several of them forward. She shook her rattle at them, and they began to glow. "Aiiie!" she chanted, dancing about them. "The Mayombreros have infected you. I can lift the spell, but it will be expensive."

The major sighed with resignation. "What will you take in exchange?"

"From you? Perhaps a cookpot. A piece of fine jewelry . . ." She looked at the ring on his finger and then at the watch on his wrist. "This will do very well."

The major grinned craftily. "I don't think so. You take my watch, muck up my time sense with a spell."

"We are your friends."

"That's what the last guys said. Listen. I'll give you money—"

And in the depths of Gaming Central, Elmo smiled. "I think you can forget Alphonse, dear. The good major just volunteered." His finger crept near the microphone. His wife restrained him.

"Not quite yet. We have to give him a chance."

S. J. Waters leaned over. "Major, this might not be the best idea, sir."

"This is another trap, dammit! It's some sort of associative magic." Clavell dug into his pack and brought out a handful of pretty golden squares: diffraction-grating jewelry that glimmered in the sunlight like a handful of rainbows. He held them out to Mamissa. "Look," he said earnestly. "Beautiful, aren't they? Much more valuable to my people—"

Her eyes flamed.

Elmo grinned. "Now?"

Doris nodded sweetly. "Yes, dear. You can possess him."

Elmo switched on the microphone. "Attention, Major—"

The major's eyes widened. He scratched at his ear.

Mamissa spat at the major's feet and moved on to Prez, exchanging a pinch of dust from a purse at her waist for a golden Zulu armband.

Elmo said, "Clavell, you have just made a *major* error. Unfortunately, it is not one which you can remedy. In five minutes, during the middle of the Mami Wata ceremony, you are going to become possessed. At my command you will seize a weapon, anything handy, and begin killing the other Gamers. If you kill three before they kill you, you will emerge from the possession unharmed. You are not to discriminate between members of your own team and members of other teams. The person nearest you. If we judge that you are bypassing your own teammates, we will diminish your hit points and kill you out of the Game. Nod if you understand."

The major gulped and nodded.

"Very good."

A ghostly shadow peeled away from Alphonse as the Mami Wata priestess dusted him.

"You may relax," the voice whispered in his ear. *"The gods have changed their minds."*

The priestess had taken his boulder opal belt buckle! But he was glad he hadn't haggled. Only a fool would enter a Game without trade goods; he had more. He'd get Saray's gift back at the end of the Game.

There were other things to concern himself about—or, perhaps, rejoice in. The gods were about to put some kitticombotty on the good major's ass.

Chapter Fourteen

Nine-Tenths of the Law

"Now the crowd is seized by the call of the mermaid . . . will all survive, or will the mermaid keep one woman for herself?"
—Gert Chesi, *Voodoo*, 1979

The women stood at the edge of the marshy water, weaving back and forth, moaning softly. Acacia, naked to the waist, wove with the best of them. She had been given a headdress like the one crowning Mamissa Kokoe, with a fish tail protruding from the back.

She had no particular aversion to nudity: she was not a prude, nor was she an exhibitionist, at least where bare-breasted exhibitions were concerned. She was much more likely to get into the spirit of the thing if she stopped thinking of herself as an anthropologist on acid, and just stepped into the heart of the Game.

The music vibrated in her bones. The marsh tossed and foamed itself into waves and tide pools. Easy to forget that this was merely a free-form rooftop swimming pool. To Panthesilea, the Warrior-woman within her, it seemed the doorway into an ocean as deep and unknowable as the night.

The women around her moaned and swooned as the waves whipped into a frenzy. The sky rippled with dark, fire-fringed clouds. As they coiled, pulses of thunder shuddered through the air.

She sneaked a look back at the others. The men were gathered at the edge of the water in a great semicircle. It was kind of nice to have them completely left out of things, for a change.

Then—the waters parted, waves rearing up like glass walls. She was looking right down into the center of the lake bed.

All of the women began to scream hysterically, Acacia's shriek the loudest of all. A voice in her ear said, "You have been possessed. Please walk forward . . ."

In Gaming Central, El coaxed a young woman through a complex pantomime. She wore a body stocking laced with sensors that registered every shift in position. All reference data was fed by it into the main banks. There it was overlaid with the Virtual effects that changed her from a young woman into . . . something very different.

In front of her was a hologram of Acacia Garcia. Next to El was another young woman, this one coached by Doris. "Come on, put your hips into it. Possessed, not repressed. That's better . . ."

The actors played off the holograms, and the Gamers in turn responded, in a feedback loop that was one vital aspect of the DreamTime phenomenon, a blend of technologies that made total emotional immersion not only possible, but damn near unavoidable . . .

Acacia walked slowly forward. To her left, Tammi stepped gingerly into the lake bed, but Twan hung back, watching the proceedings suspiciously. One nervous thumb rubbed the hilt of her sword.

Acacia took another step.

The waves rippled, shifting almost shyly. Now, for just an instant, she could see a greenish-blue feminine form, legs fused into a broad, fleshy, muscular tail. It was only just beyond her reach now. If Acacia looked around, she felt uneasy: the walls of churning water stood far above her head, held back by magic alone.

The mermaid beckoned, its fingers waving her forward—

And the waves collapsed upon her.

Captain Cipher, half-naked and shrunken into himself, saw Acacia vanish into the waves. A moment later Tammi was gone, and then the other women.

Those ashore waved their hands and shouted deliriously. Several fainted.

Trevor Stone waded forward, waist deep in the waves. "Prez!" he screamed."Quick. I think the menfolk are set up for a rescue."

"Right! Ah—there's her hand!" It projected up from the waves, and waved forlornly. Captain Cipher called, "Mouser! Rope!" and the Thief obeyed instantly. They tied a lifeline together. Cipher anchored it to Prez Coolidge and edged down toward the water.

The first to die was Appelion, Troglodyke Warrior.

He didn't even see the major come up behind him, swinging his sword. His head was cloven from his shoulders in an instant. There were screams, and the others fell back.

"Keep him away from the beach!" Alphonse called out. Instantly, the Adventurers formed a protective barrier between the major and the entranced women.

"Crom!" Mary-em yelled. She popped a button on her telescoping staff, and it expanded to ready position. "He's possessed!"

Half of their best Magic Users were in the water. Black Elk tried anyway. A stream of sparks erupted from his fingertips, but Clavell didn't even blink. His sword glowed with power.

"Demon's work!" Black Elk shouted, scuttling back.

"Top Nun, can you help—" Mouser started the request, but didn't have time to finish. Clavell swung at them viciously, and the little Thief scrambled for his life.

Clavell shifted his grip on the sword and began to stalk. He looked red-eyed and hungry.

Women screamed in the surf.

"We don't have time for this," Trevor Stone yelled. "We've got to save the girls!"

Two Warriors approached Clavell, one sword, one pike. He growled at them and batted their weapons aside.

Ozzie the Pike lunged, tried to get in with a disarming cut. The major blocked low, blocked high, came in for a slash that was berserk-mean.

Ozzie went down in a welter of blood.

Two Warriors tried to get in disarms, and retreated with wounds at chest and thigh.

Alphonse Nakagawa screamed, "You can't capture him! Where's an archer? Mouser, get up here!"

Acacia turned and saw Prez, his dark cheeks bulging as he waded through the "water" to her side. She stretched out her wrist to him, and he caught it.

A voice in her ear said, "You may return to the surface. You are unharmed."

As she began to back up, she felt something pressed into her fingers. When she came sputtering to the surface, she saw the object in her hand: a wood-framed mirror four inches across. When she looked into it, she saw only her own face.

She waved her hand, made a *Reveal magic* spell. The image in the mirror shimmered, wavered, and there was another face there. The face of Coral's dead brother Tod. He waved.

She grinned. *This* was going to be valuable.

She waded up out of the lake and draped her arms around the shoulders of her teammates. Captain Cipher almost swooned.

"Thanks, guys, I—" She narrowed her eyes. "What's going on over there?"

"Major's gone nuts," Prez said.

Cipher seemed to wake up; he lost his sloppy grin. "Ridden by the Loa. He's killed two—Appelion and a Tex-Mits pikeman."

"Shit," Acacia hissed. "Somebody better take him fast."

That's just about it, Tony McWhirter thought. The major was too good for anyone else to take a chance. Mouser would fill him with arrowheads. Shame to lose a team captain, a Loremaster, this early in the game. Then again, couldn't happen to a nicer guy, and the lesson was a valuable one. Tony settled down in expectation of an excellent death scene.

Nigel Bishop strode forward, half-naked, and stood before the major.

"What's this, now?" Tony wondered. "Wants to show off? Get the kill himself?"

Bishop unbuckled sword and scabbard and laid them on the ground. He held up his empty hands, palms forward.

The control room was abuzz.

"Try to parley with a *possessed man*?" Tony was incredulous. "He must be psycho."

El moaned. "Are we going to lose two Loremasters at once?"

"That's the biz. Maybe he knows what he's doing." Tony's fingers danced as he performed a complete scan of Bishop's powers and abilities. Any magic held back? What could his strategy be? Bishop hadn't prepped or engaged any spells in the last few seconds.

About them was the clash of waves, and silence. Hundreds of native throats were quiet and closed.

The major faced Nigel Bishop, and though his face was mad and his slack lips dripped saliva, a slow smile spread inside him. Bishop thought he could persuade a man who was *possessed*? Well. He *had* been away too long.

On the other hand—did Bishop have enough Charisma points . . .

"Charisma?" Clavell whispered.

"Come, let us reason together." Bishop took a step forward. One more step would place him in sword range.

Tony McWhirter's voice came back over Clavell's earphones. "Negative. Insufficient Charisma points. Insufficient Magic points. Execute him now, or we will remove you from the Game."

The major's interior smile broadened.

Bishop took another step forward, and the major swung the sword at neck level.

And Bishop wasn't there. With an eye-baffling blur of movement, Bishop went under the swing. Missing an expected target, the major overcommitted. Bishop was in close, close enough to crowd the major's sword arm. Clavell couldn't reverse the swing without stepping back.

He did, and almost tripped: Bishop had slid his foot behind the major's ankle. The major stumbled back and hopped over the foot at the same time, fighting for his balance.

Where in the hell was—

Bishop had his sword hand. Powerful fingers gripped, bit in, and twisted hard. Bishop spun clockwise like a top, and the major felt his wrist, arm, and shoulder lock up and hyperextend. His balance was destroyed. Bishop dropped to one knee, still holding the wrist. The major flew over his shoulder. Clavell released the sword so that he could break his fall. Regardless, it was a bone-jarring thump, and he lay there, hissing breath, trying to focus his eyes. Before he could move, Bishop was on him again, twisting the captured arm into some kind of weird hold so that the major couldn't move at all.

Pandemonium erupted on the third floor.

"Goddamn it!" El shouted. "What the hell does he think he's doing? He's ruining everything!"

Doris looked a little pale. "Isn't that a rule infraction?"

Tony was livid, but controlled himself. "In Extreme Environment competitions, Gamers can engage each other in physical confrontation, by mutual agreement—I think. If the major lodges a complaint, Bishop would be in trouble, but Clavell would look like a lawyer. He won't bitch."

Doris had only a moment to spare. She was still guiding a pair of mermaids through their paces.

On the far side of the room, the Lopezes were making magic, creating water, the horizon, the sound, and the external effects, all of the "Cecil B. DeMille stuff." They were still completely engrossed. Player interactions were temporarily beneath their notice.

So it was Tony's call. He sat back, brooding. Damned Bishop had to show off. Risked his character, risked censure if the major complained. And what would happen? Nothing. Just another legend. Nigel Bishop, bare-handed, disarmed a former national saber champion gone berserk.

It was impossible not to admire the bastard. He was so confident, so utterly sure of himself. Intimidating as hell.

No wonder Acacia was laying him.

Clavell surged futilely against the pinning arm. A trace of self-control remained: he screamed incoherently, where a man not ridden by a Loa might have sworn like a soldier.

"We will save you," Bishop said, face calm, even though the effort must have been extreme.

Foam dribbled from the corners of Clavell's eyes, and his eyes were mad. "*Must—kill—you—*"

"Hurry!" Nigel screamed. Top Nun hurried to him, then Captain Cipher, and Twan. More women emerged from the lake, dripping, holding mirrors. They threw on clothes and gathered around.

"Healing spells. Dispel demon!"

They raised their hands, and arcs of flame played over the two men who strained on the ground, locked together in frozen violence.

Tony bit his fingers. They'd had it all worked out. The major was going to be killed out of the Game. He would return as a zombie, later. Now, thanks to Bishop, the lesson that should have been learned—respect local customs!—might be obscured.

The Magic Users arced their crackling bolts over the two struggling Gamers.

Tony didn't notice Richard Lopez coming up behind him.

"Let it go, Tony," Lopez said. "These things happen sometimes. You laid—*we* laid an excellent trap. Possession is only nine-tenths of the law. Why Bishop wormed through this loophole we don't know. But see them . . ."

Members of five different competing teams directed healing energies at the major. For that moment, there was no competition, and that in itself was phenomenal.

"It was spontaneous, it was spectacular. Let them have their moment of glory. And kill them later!"

Tony grinned back. "Aye-aye, sir." He leaned over to the microphone. "Now hear this. El. Get me a demon rising from Clavell's prostrate form."

El snapped his fingers, and a mime jumped to the ground, immediately mimicking the major's uncomfortable position. He began to stretch . . .

The major's body, glowed. Gradually, as if his soul were tearing loose from the flesh, a glowing shape pulled free. Its face was a silently screaming demon's . . . and then some terrible force had distorted it beyond recognition. Three meters it stretched . . . five . . . ten. It loosed its hold on the major just short of being ripped apart. It was a ribbon in the wind, rising, fading, gone.

Mamissa Kokoe pushed through the crowd. She examined Bishop, then Major Clavell.

"You have survived what no one has ever survived," she said solemnly. "The demon came upon you because you refused my protection. Your friends are powerful, but all power has limits. Beware."

Clavell glared at Nigel, hatred and admiration mingled in his eyes. The humiliation! he thought, and in the next moment:

That scene is going to be a classic! And at current royalty rates, by the time it makes the networks, I'll earn about ten thousand bucks for that one little dump on the head . . .

So he gave the moment a dramatic climax. He rose shakily to his feet, wobbled once or twice, and then held out his hand to Nigel Bishop.

"Friend," he said, smiling.

"Comrade," Nigel Bishop said, and they embraced.

And the major was thinking, *When you least expect it, asshole, expect it.*

Chapter Fifteen

Palo Mayombe

Thursday, July 21, 2059—1:17 P.M.

The mirror fragment in Acacia's hand shimmered. In one moment, it reflected the people around her, the sky, the mountains, the surrounding terrain. In the next, Coral's late brother, Tod, gave her a thumbs-up in the glass.

Twenty-two surviving Gamers were seated in a circle. Crystal Cofax, Tammi Romati, "Aces" Wilde—all of the women who had entered the water clutched their mementos and gazed into them.

Acacia's Thief, Corrinda, was back. If anyone had noticed her absence, it didn't show.

The Mamissa spoke. "You came here," she said, "to save us. You have been accepted by the Mami Wata. Your own warriors are strong enough to overcome the dark Loa, your magic powerful enough to overcome demons.

"You have each gained great honor in your fight with the undead, your rescue of Coral, and in risking your lives to save the major—" She paused and added significantly, "Especially since it would have been so easy to just let him die."

She began to dance. The natives ringing the inner circle swayed with her in rhythmic familiarity, as if hearing a story told many times before.

"Nothing. Pyramid's featureless," Corrinda whispered to Acacia. "A surface like glazed pottery. Eighteen, maybe twenty feet tall. No openings, no markings. Crops grow right up to the base, like the natives never notice it. I dug some around the base and found nothing but more pyramid."

"Long ago," Mamissa Kokoe said, "the gods, the Nommo, came to us. They brought creatures of earth and air and water, magical beings which did our bidding. The Nommo taught us the mystical ways. Bad men took the magic, and twisted it. The Nommo taught us no more, but remained our friends.

"Thousands of years passed. The gods and demons brought by the Nommo spread across the earth and sea. And we knew how to call upon them, and the magic in ourselves, and the magic in the earth.

"But knowledge can be used for evil as well as good. Man's love affair with violence and power is an ancient story. The Nommo knew that Man was set on destroying himself with war.

"They warned their followers, and we built this structure, this 'arcology,' New Africa. And the Nommo came here to teach us. When civilization fell, some of them remained here with us, determined to help.

"We allowed into New Africa all of those who knew the old magic. Some made promises that they would not keep.

"The Nommo asked us to avoid animal sacrifice. We agreed. But there were others in New Africa who would not stop the killing, and would not confine it to animals."

"Bobo called her a Mayombrera," Bishop said softly.

"Yes, she is of Palo Mayombe, black magic from the Congo. They worship bloody gods, made stronger and more terrible by the sacrifice not of animals, but of human adults, and even innocent children.

"They grew strong in secrecy. One day, when they felt that they had grown strong enough, they attacked us. It was slaughter. There was no force in New Africa strong enough to stop them, for they gained new, terrible power from the atomic machine in New Africa's basement. Only the Nommo could even slow their advance. They made a barrier between the Mayombreros and us. That line is all that has preserved us until now.

"But the Mayombreros grow stronger daily. We cannot hold out forever. When they find a way to destroy the Nommo, we will all perish."

Twan leaned forward. "Is there anything we can do?"

"Yes. In this building are objects of power. Find them, and you will be able to call powerful allies. Gods. Use these gods, or allow them to use you. Your magic, already formidable, will become fearsome. You will be able to confront even the Mayombreros."

Trevor Stone said, "And then what?"

Nigel Bishop spoke as if his subordinate hadn't. "This power source—if it were shut down, it would destroy the Mayombreros?"

"No, but it would weaken them."

"How dependent on that power are you?"

"We have our own sources—but thousands in New Africa might die without it."

Acacia leaned over to him. "That means an Engineer or maybe a Magic User could shut down the reactor."

"Why can't we just wreck it?" Corrinda Harding asked.

Bishop looked at her with disgust. "Don't you remember the briefing on the train? We'll need to turn it back on."

Alphonse thought for a moment, then said, "This building is too huge. We need help. Guides?"

"Those with mirrors will not need guides—the mirrors will talk in your dreams. But I will send Bobo, and Coral."

The blond bodybuilder was jolted. "Mamissa Kokoe! Is this only to be rid of me?"

She shrugged, and quakes ran across her body. "You may return a hero, or die a hero. I've never doubted your courage or your sincerity, Bobo. But what can a man like you do here? Wait for the Mayombreros to come to us?"

Alphonse pondered. Crystal had gotten a mirror, and Acacia, and Tammi. That meant that Clavell and Bishop would decide between Coral and Bobo. Fair enough. Which would be worth more, a native of the attic or of the basement? Or trade a guide for a mirror? Such talismans were links to the gods, often enough, and sometimes had information human guides lacked . . .

There was a moment in which everyone was weighing the odds and considering their options. Then they began to stand. First one, and then another and another, until all twenty-two Adventurers were on their feet.

Al the Barbarian was first to speak. "We hear you, Mamissa. You say it's gotta be done, that's good enough for me and the girls I go with. We'll shut down that reactor and recover those talismans—or like to die trying. Who's with me?"

The rooftop rocked with cheers, and as someone else had said under somewhat different circumstances, the Game was afoot.

★ ★ ★

"They're leaving the roof. They never even noticed the fish," Tony said.

Doris Whitman looked up. "They'll be back. There are talismans in the pool."

"Mmm."

"Goddamn touchy artist. *I* noticed the fish, okay? The fish is wonderful."

Tony smiled. *Nothing worse than a novice Game Master,* he thought, and said, "That'll have to do."

Chapter Sixteen

Long Odds

Tony McWhirter was becoming very twitchy.

With five top Game Masters to run it, Tony hadn't expected California Voodoo to give him this much trouble! But with five teams to keep track of, and glitches in the machinery, and prima donnas screwing up the story lines, Tony wasn't getting time to take a full breath.

The enclaves were clumping up a little. UC and Apple were descending via stairs, sending scouts for a quick look at each floor. Texas Instruments–Mitsubishi and Army, with more than their share of mountain climbers, were exploring the modular wall. General Dynamics was descending much faster, which meant they might miss something, unless Bishop had special knowledge—as was his wont.

Army and Tex-Mits had done badly in the trading on the roof. They had two mirrors and no guide. Gen-Dyn had Coral. She looked fetching in short shorts, a neon-blue daypack, and a raggedly chopped off T-shirt reading "Shop Till You Drop." Bobo, assigned to UC and Apple, did without the shirt. The guides shared a brainless look that fitted their roles nicely. Their information had great gaps in it and was not trustworthy.

Tony hadn't planned those alliances and hadn't welcomed them, but they'd make the Gamers easier to keep track of. He needed that, with all the distractions, failing equipment, missing NPCs . . . and a distracted, manic Alex Griffin.

Tony hadn't felt pressure like this since the South Seas Treasure Game eight years earlier, when he had been trying to slay monsters and steal corporate secrets at the same time. They just weren't giving him room to maneuver!

Through computer cutouts Tony had carefully invested five thousand dollars—with another ten sequestered—in various main and side bets, spreading the bets out around the country so that no one would ever be able to trace them back to him. Nobody who wasn't better at this than Tony, anyway. On one of four screens he watched numbers flow.

His nerves were screaming at him. It had been a crazy, self-destructive impulse, carefully worked out in anal-retentive detail over the last few weeks. He was betting his job, his reputation, his friendships, against a trivial profit. He'd lose it all if he was caught. He could even lose the bets. He had special knowledge, sure, but the odds . . . well, they weren't fitting the expected patterns.

Hey, now . . . was *that* what had been pecking at his composure? The numbers?

Most of the bets went down as he would have expected. Half-smart Vegas money, people betting as if this were just another sport. Idiots who assumed that if the sponsoring companies were high on the stock exchange, their teams were shoo-ins. People betting on past performance of a corporate banner before knowing the composition of the team. People betting for favorite Loremasters . . . and that was smarter money.

But . . . oh, take the odds against Army. They'd peaked at 7:45 A.M. Thursday the twenty-first, just about the time that everyone discovered that the game wasn't to be played within the Park.

Now, one could figure Army's chances in several ways.

They'd started in third place because they knew Gaming Dome A better than anyone. That advantage had evaporated . . . but the Army ran war games, too, in deserts and mountains, through ghost towns ruined by the old Quake.

But a gambler might also know—he could ask any soldier—that war games involve tens of thousands of warriors and a bare few wizards and Loremasters (called "strategists" and "generals"). Real Games are *personal*.

Then again, the oldest players, like Trevor Stone of Gen-Dyn, now became *really* valuable. They'd done this, too: they'd Gamed in desert terrain, and up mountains and down river rapids, before

Dream Park's domes had gone up in spring of 2040. Army didn't have anyone like him.

So figuring the odds was like herding rattlesnakes, and the pattern that emerged was bound to be chaotic. The odds against Army dropped, then bottomed out as more players took a better bet, then wobbled . . . but look at that bottom curve. It was as flat as west Kansas. When the odds hit that point, somebody had been waiting.

Something, some lost datum, had been gnawing at him, and this was it: roughly six hundred thousand carefully coordinated dollars skewing his numbers.

Timing. It was the timing that was unbelievable. So smooth had it been that the odds, which had dropped to 22–3, rose to only 14–3 before the last of the big money was recorded. If Army won, somebody was going to make a killing.

Now who could have done such a thing?

Nigel Bishop's unforgettable grandstand play. He had simultaneously saved and humiliated Army's Loremaster. Tony had been sure Bishop had done it for the cameras, a stunt for the fans and a record for the history books, but hey . . .

Money made a more satisfying motive. You could count it. You'd know when you won. Six hundred thousand dollars at, say, 20–3 odds . . .

Even if Bishop was fronting for someone, his cut could hardly be less than a million dollars. If Army won. But could he do it? Throw the Game to Army? Even if one of the other players—

Say Acacia Garcia—

Was aiding him?

Tony took the numbers off his number-four screen, to be replaced by a less damning view of the basement power plant. Nothing was happening there. No team would get that far for at least twenty-four hours.

El and Doris were working miracles, stage left. The Lopezes seemed to be loafing, talking to each other with one eye for the screens. Like Tony. But Tony's mind was seething.

If Bishop hoped to pull something like this off, wouldn't he need somebody on the inside?

Tony leaned forward in his chair and conjured up a file on Bishop.

The Art of Gaming, of course. Bishop's magnum opus, the piece of strategic writing that had secured his place in Gaming history. Tony hadn't read it in years, but a quotation flickered vaguely to mind. He summoned up the book and did a global search for the word *spy*.

Here:

> When gathering intelligence, know that reliable intelligence is the single most important factor in your success. Therefore, do not forget that there are factors which go beyond the stated rules of the game. You are engaged in a war, and those of you who remember this most clearly, without sentiment or fear, are the ones who will succeed.
>
> There are disaffected members in any Gaming organization. Get to know them, and their vulnerability. You can appeal to vanity, or greed, or a sense of adventure. And you can get them to give information that you would otherwise have had to sell lives to obtain.
>
> Treat them well, and never forget them, these spies . . .

Bishop's highest priority in Gaming was gathering intelligence. And because Bishop had been in retirement when he had written *The Art of Gaming*, he had been extraordinarily candid.

A spy.

Goldfish nibbled at Tony's adrenal glands. Minutes ago he'd been worried about a few thousand dollars' worth of bets. Now . . . Had Bishop corrupted Acacia? Screwing her was one thing. Tony would merely have flayed him alive for that. But forcing her to *throw a Game* was unspeakable.

For that matter, weren't they looking for a motive for Sharon Crayne's death?

Sharon had been scanning and possibly recording some of the building specs. That would certainly be a lovely piece of intelligence data for a Loremaster. And if she had sold it to Bishop, and the sale had gone wrong somehow . . .

Naaah. Why would a relatively innocent misadventure blossom into murder? On the other hand, with between one and four million dollars at stake . . . People had died for a whole lot less.

Tony gritted his teeth. He'd have to see if he could track that money.

It was, all in all, the thinnest string of supposition he had ever considered seriously. It would never hang together. And a poor, distracted Game Master just didn't have time to deal with it! Gamers were moving into MIMIC's bowels in little paranoid clumps. They'd want his attention . . . heh . . . they'd be trying desperately to evade his attention starting real soon now.

Then again . . . a mystery, a veritable mystery, and a shot at Sharon Crayne's killer? That could jog Alex Griffin out of his black mood. Griffin fancied himself a man of thought—but Tony knew him to be happiest in action. Get him to believe he was *doing* something.

After all, it had been a long time since the Griffin had stalked a Game.

Chapter Seventeen

Burning Love

"Chango is the god of fire, thunder and lightning. He . . . is used in Santería to overcome enemies, as well as for works of passion and desire."

—Migene González-Wippler, *Santería,* 1987

Thursday, July 21, 2059—2:50 P.M.

Al the Barbarian never got dizzy. It said so right in his character notes. This was of little comfort to Al Nakagawa's stomach, which wanted nothing more than to squeeze itself dry and empty, curl up quietly, and die.

He and S. J. Waters lay at the outer lip of a modular apartment on the seventeenth floor. It was an abandoned shambles, its dock open to the elements; and its intended mate, a portable office quarters, was a cracked half-eggshell dangling far down the side of New Africa. At a whisper of "Reveal treasure," the eggshell glowed green. There was something in there worth having.

Al slid away from the edge and rolled onto his back. "First talisman," he said drearily. "She's there, all right."

The wind whistled in from the California-Nevada border, hot and dry and hollow. The steel and concrete box creaked slowly back and forth. Two hundred feet below was the desert floor.

"Phew." The cables ran up to the modular wall track. It looked like some force had ripped the box free of the apartment and sent it tumbling down. Or a cargo copter had attempted to link it up, decades before, and the job had never been completed.

Modular apartments were the twenty-first century's answer to an increasingly mobile society. The living and office quarters of a house or apartment could be detached and shipped to the other side of the country within forty-eight hours, allowing employees to bounce from one job assignment to the next without leaving home.

But he'd never seen a modular wall as high as this one. It seemed to him now that the whole concept was idiotic.

Crystal's mane of unkempt red hair flagged around her shoulders as she coaxed secrets from the circuit box. It was plain metal and glass, disguised as a lamp by the edge of the open wall. The rolling sheet of weatherproofing protecting the apartment had long since worn away, and the box was uncomfortably close to the edge.

Crystal traced a line with her finger: Al wished that he could see what she saw, but that was one of her abilities. All Gaming categories overlapped, a little. Crystal's Engineering abilities gave her a little facility with mechanical things—less than a Thief, usually, but SJ had taken his crack and failed.

Major Clavell hovered over her, worried. "What have you got?"

"Problems," she said. "This diagram is complex. I'm not entirely sure . . ."

Al watched the major. He had suggested a truce, adding his Warriors to Al's team. Jockeying and trading had erupted the minute their conference with Mamissa Kokoe ended.

A truce between Clavell and Alphonse was a natural: Clavell needed Al's women. At the current attrition rate, Al would need the extra sword arms, but he didn't look forward to a power struggle.

Al the Barbarian touched Crystal's shoulder, and suddenly he could see the diagram. His heart fell: the glittering maze of circuitry was interrupted in a dozen places. A *real* Engineer would have seen a perfect model.

While the major conferred with Poule, Al bent to whisper in Crystal's ear.

"I notice the major is hovering. Problems?"

Crystal shook her head. "No! Man's made some useful suggestions. He's no dummy."

"Nervous?"

"Me or him?"

"Either."

"Both."

Al was nervous, too—nervous to have Army at his back—but Army teams tended to play straight, and he knew of no instance in which they had broken truce or sabotaged allies. That they left for

Congress, maybe. With Bishop and Acacia and, for God's sake, the Troglodykes out there, the Army was a welcome ally.

New Africa was vast, and he was glad to have three Scouts. The Tex-Mits/Army grouping had crept down the halls, following arcane clues visible only to the Scouts' eyes, or Crystal's mirror.

At the end of a dark corridor on the twelfth level, SJ found a locked door that glowed orange to his *Reveal location* spell.

He picked the lock under Clavell's approving eye. Al let Clavell enter the apartment first, hoping that the major would get first crack at a Beastie, and maybe a chance to reclaim a little lost honor. The scuffle with Bishop had been enough to bruise anyone's ego.

But there was nothing alive in the apartment. Crystal's spell of *Revelation* gave them the control panel, and when they looked out over the open lip . . .

Crystal passed her hand over the mirror, and the image of Coral's brother Tod appeared. "Hey," he said. "It's dull being dead. Thanks for calling."

Crystal held the mirror out over the edge. "What can you tell us about this?"

"Oh," the mirror said, "like I heard that we used to *live* in these dangling little boxes, but that was like back in the ice age or something. Then during some little cat fight between my people and the roof yokels, some of the boxes got ripped away. Long way to fall— like people pizza time."

"Is there anything valuable in it?"

"Not that I know. But who tells me anything? I'm just a mirror."

SJ inserted a probe into the panel, and it sparked gently.

"All right, let's give it a try." Crystal punched a button, and the ancient machinery began to creak. Cable rolled smoking through the winch, and the dangling box was reeled back up toward its berth.

Mary-em slapped Crystal's broad back in congratulation, and General Poule puffed up to make a short speech—

Twenty feet below them, the room stopped. A little glowing rectangle on the control panel blinked: NEED ACCESS CODE.

"Oh, crap," Clavell said disgustedly. "We need an Engineer to break the code."

"Only Peggy the Hook had enough experience," Al grunted. "Last time I saw Peggy, her face was being chewed off."

"Just great. Can you do it, SJ? You're a Thief—"

"Half-Thief. If a half-Engineer can't do it, neither can half a Thief. This happened because of a magical war. If anything's lurking about, trying to break that code without a scan would be suicide."

Al sighed. "I've got a notion. We can signal one of the other teams, and borrow an Engineer."

For a moment Clavell was preoccupied, then he shook himself out of it. "Hell with that."

He shucked off his pack, spun and unzipped it, and dug inside. "SJ," he snapped. "Let Al have your Spider."

Alphonse winced. "You're kidding, of course."

"Ah." The major stopped digging. He brought out a hand grip device that looked very like a dead spider: six stubby curved arms connected to a flat handle. On the underside of the handle was a Teflon gear device. It was a standard rappelling implement, adjustable to cables from $1/32$ inch to 3 inches, standard equipment for a Hazardous Environment Game.

Clavell grinned maliciously up at Alphonse. "You speak Spider, don't you? All we have to do is slide down twenty-odd feet of line and go in through the roof."

Alphonse's head hurt. "Now wait just a redheaded minute." Reality came popping back into his mind, tearing apart the carefully constructed illusions. In that very crystalline instant he remembered that he was Alphonse Nakagawa, acrophobic systems analyst for Texas Instruments. *That* Al had once offended his Sunday-school teacher by implying that it was hell, and not heaven, where people were forced to cling precariously to clouds.

Clavell's eyes sparkled with mischief. "We all knew that this adventure was risky . . ."

Translation: *This is a master's level Game. We've all signed personal liability waivers.*

"The easy thing to do would be trade with another team. Who? Bishop? Hasn't he got enough of an edge already? If we can handle this ourselves, we can even the score."

SJ was holding his rappelling apparatus out to Alphonse, an enormous grin on his freckled face.

Clavell's logic was compelling. Bishop, Panthesilea, and the Troglodykes were certainly ahead on points. If they could really pull this off . . . Al said, "Mary-em? You're our mountain climber. Can this be done?"

She looked down at the capsule swaying twenty feet beneath them. The floor, the dock's underlip, extended three feet farther than the ceiling. The cable winches ran at each upper corner, and the center of the roof. With a winch operating properly, the capsule should have been drawn up and into its place comfortably.

"I'll give it a shot, boss man," she said. The tiny woman doffed her rucksack. She tightened her sword belt and took the Spider from SJ. "Let's see this thing. Wrist thongs?"

"Or belt attachment."

"I prefer wrist."

"Go for it." SJ squatted down next to her and helped her stretch out her shoulders. He wrapped her wrist thongs snugly into place. "How've you been?" he whispered happily.

The little woman with the nut-brown skin grinned up at him. "Just fine, youngster. Haven't seen you since South Seas Treasure." She tested the connections on her wrists. "Hell of a Game." Her eyes twinkled with the memory.

"Hell of a Game."

The major was ready. "Fair's fair, Alphonse? One from each team."

Al's curiosity was piqued. "Why did you suggest it like that? You and SJ could have done this."

"Cooperation," Clavell grinned. "I figure that teamwork will accomplish more than backstabbing."

"And when it comes down to the wire?"

"Let's play it straight," Clavell said, wrapping his wrist thongs into place. "And let the gods sort it out."

Alphonse froze for a moment. Was Clavell saying "Let the Best Man Win"? Could he really be that much of a straight arrow?

Clavell bowed to Mary-em. "Ladies first?"

"Age before beauty? Blow balrogs, sonny."

Mary-em climbed up on SJ's shoulders and found the lower rung of the service ladder that took her up to a corner cable. She grinned down at him. "Got it."

The first thing that Mary-em thought as she clamped her Spider around the cable was, *Going down is easy. Coming back up will be a bitch-kitty.*

She twisted and locked the Spider's handle, ensuring that its Teflon and plastic gears were fully engaged. She slid it back and forth smoothly a few times, satisfied with its action. She rolled her shoulders, anticipating the strain when her weight hit her wrists. She breathed deeply, exhaled, and stepped off.

It was a long way down to a desert floor dotted with brownish green shrubs and cactus. The wind plucked at her hair. Peripherally, she watched the modular apartment's empty shell recede as she slid away.

She'd learned that the challenge in a Game was to keep the adrenaline level high. If her grip on unreality started to wane, she would tell herself over and over how real it was, to deliberately get her juices flowing.

But now, swinging two hundred feet above the desert floor, she needed just the opposite. She needed calm, and so she whispered to herself, "Aren't the illusions nice today? How do they do that? Look at the desert floor down there. Wayyyy down there. Nope, just another wonderful illusion from the mischievous boys and girls at Dream Park . . ."

Mary-em kept the Spider's braking action at about seventy-five percent, and the device vibrated just enough to make her nervous as it ate friction.

She was dangling in space now, halfway between the apartment and the modular box. She risked a look back up and saw her friends' faces disappear as she slid down out of sight.

Her toes touched the top of the apartment, and she felt it sway, then settle back down. She anchored a lifeline to the cable—no need to take unnecessary risks, now, was there?

Major Clavell landed a moment later, on the opposite cable. Their combined weight rocked the box enough to give her the willies, but they steadied themselves, brought the flash of panic under control, and saluted each other like cavaliers.

The desert floor swung dizzyingly, back and forth and back and forth . . .

And gradually came to a halt.

Clavell was vibrating with pleasure, really enjoying himself for the first time in the Game. "Let's get down to cases, shall we?"

The man was crazed. She liked it. "Why not?"

Both of them had safety lines attached by this time, cords that occasionally snapped taut as one or the other of them lurched or lost footing.

"This is the life, eh, Mary?"

"One teensy mistake and that'll be past tense."

There was a trapdoor in the capsule's roof. Clavell carried twenty pounds of tools on his belt. Mary-em wasn't complaining. The man had unexpected class.

The lock in the trapdoor was an antique, a circular design taking a special key. Mary-Em had never seen its like, but Clavell must have recognized it. He had it open in about thirty seconds. He wedged open the trapdoor and slipped inside, kicking a light fixture out of his way.

Lightly, as if afraid of jarring the room from its cable track, he jumped down. The major landed on the balls of his feet, instantly alert.

Mary-em followed a moment later. She dangled from one burly arm in almost simian fashion, sniffing for danger. "Oook oook," she chuckled, then dropped down as lightly as Clavell.

The transportation sections of modular apartments were generally office space and bedroom. This bedroom was walled in shatterproof Plexiglas, and the view out over the desert floor was spectacular.

She sighed. "My enclave could never afford such wealth," she said.

"If we can just solve this puzzle, wealth will come to both our peoples."

Good man.

"You take the office. I'll take the bedroom."

"Check and double-check," Clavell said.

Tony McWhirter bunched his shoulders, dreading the sound as the feet came tromping up behind him.

"Hello, Mr. Meyers," he said politely. He turned and held out his hand. Meyers ignored it. He was furious.

Mitsuko Lopez glanced around, lost interest. Richard and the Whitmans didn't bother. *They're no busier than I am. I'm low man on the totem pole; I'm the worst choice for playing dominance games with the IFGS.*

Ordinarily calm, the little man was swollen purple around the neck, and red in the face. He looked like a were-frog caught in midtransformation. "Just what the blazes do you think you're doing?"

"Ah . . . coordinating a Game?"

"Those two could have died sliding down that cable, don't you realize that?" He didn't say "I *knew* that we shouldn't have let someone like you run this Game." Perhaps he wasn't even thinking it. But he'd not been happy when he'd read the fifth Game Master's dossier.

Tony worked to keep the irritation from his voice. "I'm sorry you feel that way, but it was an internal decision."

Meyers sniffed. "If a player dies during a Game, it could cause a blot on the record of the IFGS—"

"With all respect, sir, if those two players had slipped, it would have made a blot elsewhere, as well. The risk was theirs. This is a Nekro-Max Extreme Environment Game, and everyone involved knows it. Waivers have been signed all around. If anyone, or anyone's heirs, so much as whisper the word 'lawsuit,' their firstborns grow tails."

"Are you trying to be funny?"

"No. Yes. Look—there's no need for conflict here." Tony McWhirter steepled his fingers. He'd finally realized *why* it was his turn in the barrel. "We both want to show Gaming in the best possible light. The audience likes the excitement, sir."

Arlan Meyers tried to calm himself. "The IFGS is a family organization, McWhirter. If parents see people plummeting from the sides of buildings—"

"Then the ratings will go up. Stop thinking of this as a chess match, and start calling it what it is: a sporting event. The risk-benefit ratio is—"

Meyers had heard enough. "We are going to revoke our sanction, Mr. McWhirter."

Tony examined him shrewdly, like a lepidopterist examining a new and rather ugly species of moth. "Um-hmm. And if nobody dies, will you give it right back, like you did for Ancient Enemy last year?"

Meyers flinched. Expressionless now, he squared his shoulders and said, "Good day." And stalked off.

Tony's whistle of relief was echoed all over the control room. The whistle wasn't enough. His whole body tingled with suppressed tension.

Then Doris was behind him, her strong fingers kneading his shoulders. "He's an idiot," she whispered. There was a sudden starburst on Tony's holo field, and a cartoon caricature of Arlan Meyers appeared. The field expanded, and Meyers was staked out before a firing squad. A further expansion, and a row of Richard and Chi-Chi Lopezes were pointing rifles.

Nice to know that he had the gods on his side. Better make sure the lawyers were there, too.

And if the IFGS revoked Dream Park's sanction . . . yeah. They'd claim that Meyers had acted from prejudices against one of the Game Masters: against the jailbird, Tony McWhirter. The Lopezes never missed a trick.

Back to work. Where had the wandering Adventurers gotten to now?

Mary-em had searched the cubicle of bedroom. From time to time she or Clavell would call out, "Find anything?" and receive a negative response.

She had torn back the bed sheets, emptied the closet, taken apart everything that she could find—and nothing.

At an almost subliminal level, a soft musical refrain had begun, a chanting sound that whispered in her ears:

Chango mani cote Chango mani cote olle—

She tapped at the earpiece of her Virtual set. Was this . . . Then she was on instant alert.

A rooster, red-combed and white-feathered, crawled out from under the bed and pecked its way across the floor, ignoring her.

. . . masa Chango mani cote olle masa Chango ara bari . . .

A closet door flung itself open, and above the hypnotic chant, she clearly heard *"baaaa . . ."* and a longhorn sheep wandered out, grazing at the rug. It sauntered across the room and into the hall.

The chant was loud now, drowning out thought.

. . . manicote ada manicote aran bansoni Chango mani cote Chango mani cote elle masa Chango arambsoni Chango Ara Baricote . . .

The air swam hazily in front of her. Where was Clavell? Didn't he hear the music? Hadn't he seen the animals? Where—

Then a voice behind her said softly, "I have what you seek."

Mary-em turned and faced the window.

A man stood there, a man who burned. He was African, fantastically muscled, utterly naked, and his skin crawled with fire. Mary-em was stunned. His body was perfect, his dimensions formidable in every respect.

"Who are you?" Her voice shook. At first she wasn't sure why, and then she knew.

Crom, but he was a fine-looking man.

It felt like her shorts were percolating, and Mary-em fought for control. She was a loner by nature, and even if men had come flocking after her, she would have been difficult to approach. But her age and diminutive size, not to mention her extremes of preferred activity, made her all but celibate.

It had been five years since her last lover.

A voice whispered in her ear: "You are bewitched. Let yourself go."

She relaxed, letting herself slip into the syrupy warmth of the illusion. No need to be so defensive—who the hell turns down a god? And as gods go, Chango was primo.

Woof.

How far did Dream Park expect her to go? For that matter, how far did she *want*—

"I am . . . Chango," he said, and smiled hugely.

And came closer.

He had to be a Virtual projection. With one shaking hand, she flipped her Virtual shield up.

He was still there. Hologram, then, with a Virtual overlay. That explained his graphic arousal. She was almost ashamed of herself for lowering the Virtual shield again. She hoped to God he was computer-animated. Could she maybe *meet* this guy, later?

"Come to me . . ." he whispered. His voice was intoxicatingly warm and exciting. "Take the gift . . ."

His hand opened, palm outstretched, and resting in it was a bloodred gemstone. A ruby.

Mary-em's head swirled. She heard herself say "yes" with a stranger's voice—

And took the step forward.

Her hand reached out, and the gem dissolved as she touched it. Her world exploded into flame. The chanting in her ears drowned out thought, clouded sensation as his downturned face came to hers.

There was no physical contact, nothing but the sudden heartbeat throb of the electric mesh in her costume. The air became a kaleidoscope of colors, raging, pulsing—

Major Clavell screamed, "Hold! Demon!"

The perfect face flickered away from hers. Fire jetted from his eyes, hammering Clavell squarely in the chest.

Clavell smashed back into the wall, jarring the entire capsule.

Dazed, Clavell raised his sword and chanted, "By the powers entrusted in me—"

Chango, still enfolding Mary-em in an embrace of cold fire, turned to look at him. "You? You think that you can best me? I will destroy you, mortal!"

Clavell was panicked. War games weren't like this; weren't this personal. This thing had seduced the indestructible Mary-em, and her body, convulsing rhythmically, was—

He had to snap his mind out of that track. The visual was designed to throw him off base.

Now. "Fire, god, lust. Which god?" He'd spent enough time preparing: the meager information sheets that they had been given, and the volumes the Army research team had found. "Chango, of course." *And can he be destroyed?*

Idiot. He's a god!

Bargained with? Frightened away? Ah!

Major Clavell pulled himself off the wall and spread his arms again, chanting.

The skin on Clavell's own head began to singe and peel away. Flesh rolled down in droplets, burning and spattering on the floor beneath him.

Incandescent in the narrow hallway, Clavell's head had become a naked, blazing skull.

Chango screamed, a high-pitched sound that shook the entire dangling apartment. He turned to run. In three steps he had dwindled to a point.

It was in the notes, Clavell crowed. *Chango fears skulls!*

Mary-em lay on the floor, apparently unconscious.

He rushed to her and did a quick scan. Magically speaking, she was alive and healthy, but . . .

"Oh, shit," he said.

The cable had started to creak. The modular room was being hauled back up. The gods had decided to be merciful, he guessed.

Mary-em raised herself to a sitting position. "What happened?"

"I've got good news and bad news," Clavell said.

"All right, give me the good news?"

"We defeated Chango. And we don't have to climb back up that damned line—which is especially good news for you."

"Why?" Her eyes crinkled at the edges. "Coming down was fun."

"Sure was. But now you're pregnant."

Chapter Eighteen

Puppy Chow

"Oggun is the god of war and metals. He favors black dogs as his food . . ."

—Migene Gonzáles-Wipple, *Santería*, 1987

Thursday, July 21, 2059—3:40 P.M.

Alex Griffin stared numbly as Tony McWhirter's image blossomed on the wall before him. "What is it?" He felt his lips moving, but it sounded as if he were speaking in someone else's voice.

"Some stuff just came in through personnel, Griff. I broke the seal on Sharon's files, and I've done some poking around. She might have been supplying someone with Game specs—that might mean betting. There's big money at stake, and that's the oldest motivation in the world. Second oldest, maybe."

Griffin's eyes were as cold as rifle barrels. "Can the humor. I'm coming down to Central. I want complete dossiers on everyone in that Game."

"It doesn't *have* to be someone in the Game, Alex. It *could* be an outside gambler who wants an inside edge."

"But it isn't, is it?"

Tony hesitated, then said, "No, Alex. It's not."

Alex Griffin was down in the office in ninety-two seconds. The personnel files were already flowing in the air in front of McWhirter.

Alex studied them, and Tony waited for his reaction as Acacia Garcia's file floated up. Alex's hands white-knuckled on the chair back.

"You didn't know she was in California Voodoo?" Tony asked.

"I guess I managed not to notice. Panthesilea . . ."

Acacia had been with Tony eight years before, until South Seas Treasure. Then Tony went to prison and Acacia went to Griffin.

She liked dangerous, manipulative Games. And maybe dangerous, manipulative men. Maybe she just traded up.

"Alex?" Tony said quietly. "Acacia has been linked romantically with Nigel Bishop."

"*The* Nigel Bishop? Who came out of retirement for this Game? *That* I heard about." Alex's green eyes narrowed as his brain went into overdrive. "I want into that Game. Now."

"Wait a minute—"

"For *what*? We're losing time, dammit."

"Give me fifteen minutes," Tony said. His fingers tapped independently. "I've got even less time than you do, but you especially have *got* to see this."

Replay: the Mami Wata ceremony, a view across the rooftop pond toward men who waited to rescue drowning women. Tony McWhirter's voice told Major Clavell that he had been possessed. When the voice said, "Now!" Clavell struck like a rattlesnake.

"The Army's Loremaster," Tony said. "Guess what it would do to Army's odds to lose the major?"

Clavell killed a second man. The Bishop stepped forward, dropped his weapons—

Tony's fingers tapped. Alex barely noticed when a second window popped up next to the first. Green threads wove through the air: the Las Vegas betting graphs.

Alex was busy watching Bishop as he trounced Clavell. "Very nice. Excellent, in fact. Aikido, maybe." Alex's tone implied grudging admiration. "Why would Bishop save Army's ass, Tony? He's Gen-Dyn's Loremaster."

"Weird, yes? Bad enough if Bishop bet on himself, but that isn't what we're looking at. Six million dollars got itself bet on *Army*."

Army's odds traced a jagged icicle: steeply down and steeply up as Army's Loremaster was doomed, then saved. A shallow stalactite on Gen-Dyn's line marked the moment when Bishop stepped forward with empty hands. *Vegas* had known the risks. And Tony was still talking. "I followed twenty trails so far, tracking the money. I got lost a few times, but the rest all went through Ecuador."

"Ecuador? Why Ecuador?"

"I haven't the remotest. You'd think he'd scatter his footprints more."

Alex mulled it. "Tony, could Bishop force a win for Army?"

"Alex, I . . . no. Yes. Hell, *I* don't think so, but I want to ask the

Lopezes what they think. A better question might be: Is Bishop egotistical enough to believe he can do it?"

"Okay. Call costuming for me, I'm on my way." The Griffin stormed out of Gaming Central.

For ten seconds Tony didn't move or make a sound, then he exhaled in a long, noisy sigh. He leaned back and stretched his fingers.

Why *not* Ecuador?

At least the Griffin hadn't asked him why he was studying gambling curves. But maybe he hadn't *needed* to ask . . .

Thursday, July 21, 2059—5:00 P.M.

Creeping on all fours, Acacia Garcia peeked around the corner of the hallway. The other Adventurers were behind her, eyes on her upraised hand—mostly. Several eyes were watching her delightful gluteal muscles as they clenched and released rhythmically.

She held up a palm, fingers outstretched, and then made a fist. *Get ready.*

The palm opened. *No immediate danger.*

The room was dark and quiet, an alcove off a main hallway on the fifteenth floor. The hallway was bordered by a chain-and-pipe railing, which lipped a sunken dining area complete with tables and chairs. Here, long ago, malted milks and slushed ice drinks had been consumed by doomed, famished teenagers. A sobering thought.

Metal boxes within the room flickered with light, occasionally sparking or smoking. Some of the boxes were as tall as Thaddeus Dark, and some of them were emblazoned with readable emblems.

XAXXON, one said. Another said MARIO BROTHERS CONQUER THE UNIVERSE. And another: WAR OF THE POD DEMONS.

A video arcade.

There had been earthquake damage. Two of the walls had a wavy look. Most of the third wall had collapsed, shattering several games and opening a way into an adjacent jewelry store. From beneath the rubble came a fitful flickering.

Acacia called Cipher to the front. There didn't seem to be any direct threat here . . . "What do you think?"

"Don't know," Cipher said. "Mamissa said something about demons that feed on power. Here's electrical power. I'd be careful if I were you."

"Talk to Tammi," she said. The Troglodykes had taken the roof-top surfer as their guide. "Where's, uh, Bobo?"

She cast around for him. "Bobo?"

Top Nun said, "He was here just a minute ago. Stepped over against the wall. Oh, here he . . . is?"

And Bobo stepped back out of the shadows. For a moment Acacia's mind didn't work fast enough. Bobo had changed size. He'd gained two inches (he stooped to hide it) and some breadth across the shoulders, and lost some belly—

And the face: bronze shades, peeling pink nose, short white-blond beard and—

Holy shit.

She fought to keep her composure. "Bobo," she said to Alex Griffin.

He looked at her without betraying anything, with that neutral NPC attitude. "Yes, ma'am," he said.

She scanned him. Definitely Bobo: she got the same clear iden-tification code. This wasn't a trick, it was a simple substitution, fully allowed by IFGS rules.

Even as they spoke, computers would be editing earlier Game records, implanting Alex Griffin's image over the old Bobo. There was nothing to do but accept the change.

"Does the electricity always work in here?"

"As far as I know."

"All right, then." Memory tickled at her. Every game she could recognize was a combat game, a war game of some kind. A clue? Electricity? Or maybe metal?

She drew her sword and moved into the video parlor.

First she poked her sword's tip, then her head, through the truck-sized hole into the jewelry store. Here were elegant dust-colored chairs, and glass-and-wood jewelry cases, all broken, all empty. Rubble was strewn across a case and two chairs; one chair bore broken human bone.

And that was all. Acacia judged it safe and turned back to the video arcade. Dust lay thick on the floor and revealed no recent footprints.

Acacia hissed for Captain Cipher to come to her. "What do you make of this?"

Tammi and Twan circled around to the other side, careful and alert.

Captain Cipher's answer was a rapid mumble and a waving of

hands: *Reveal magic.* One of the machines lit with a pale green glow. "Bingo, milady."

Tammi and Twan continued their prowl, seeking other dangers. Captain Cipher examined the machine. "Fairly advanced," he said finally, "given it's an antique. Circa 1995 video arcade game with full Virtual-reality helmet. Took dollar bills. Visual and auditory, of course, and pressure feedback for the hands, but no taste or smell. Anybody got a dollar bill?"

Nobody answered. "Shame. All the voodoo gods were greedy. Okay . . ." Cipher sat down in a pneumatic seat made of black metal and plastic.

It wrapped around his body and cinched him in until his face went red. Only his arms were free. He gulped. "Hope this was a good idea."

"Shall we get you out?"

"Wait one on that, milady." He was swathed in a black cocoon, facing the screen.

As his hands touched the fingerboard, the holostage flickered to life. Air churned into black liquid and fluxed into an inhuman, metallic face that was all planes and angles. It examined Cipher like a serpent contemplating a robin's egg.

"I am . . . *Oggun,*" it said. The voice was totally synthesized and bore no trace of human origins.

"God of war," Cipher said without hesitation. "God of metal."

"Do you dare to challenge me?"

Cipher smiled sickly. "I come not to challenge—"

Tammi had described a cautious spiral, zeroing in close enough to touch the floating head before it turned to face her.

"You," Oggun said. "You are a Warrior. Is this one of yours?"

"Cipher is under my protection."

"You will stand by it?"

Instant of hesitation. "Yes, I will."

"Good. Good. Then, let the Game begin."

Acacia heard a low pulse tone in her ear. The "activate visor" tone. She made sure her Virtual equipment was in place, and backed up until her hips and shoulders were against a wall.

Oggun's head was twisting, pulling, ripping itself free from the video game.

Living tendrils of light boiled out of the game's shell. Blinding, sterilizing light. It tugged and stretched and twisted, bulging out, dark lines and colors threading through the brightness, an entire world of two-dimensional computer graphics now expanding and rotating out into three dimensions.

Bobo was close behind Acacia. She burned to talk to him. *That security woman died, and now Alex Griffin is here. Why? If he wanted Nigel, he'd just pull Nigel out of the Game, wouldn't he? Does he want me? To watch me? To talk?*

Split attention would get her killed. *Concentrate!*

Light diminished in the video junkyard until she could barely see. If claustrophobia had been one of her problems, she would have been near panic.

Tammi and Twan were handling it better than she was. As if directed by a single mind, they had formed a back-to-back defensive posture and were waiting calmly.

"I am Oggun," a voice behind her said. She twisted her head in time to see the screen of an ancient video game extrude a giant yellow happy-face. Its teeth were shark-sized, and it made constant, famished gobbling motions.

"And I eat flesh."

Here it comes . . .

The happy-face Oggun laughed. "Not your flesh. I prefer other meat, and it pleases me to be witnessed."

Under the shattered wall, the sparking of a not-quite-dead machine cast a moving shadow. A miserable black mongrel dog crawled out. It might have been a mix of collie and spaniel, head too large and body a little too small. It limped toward them, whining, shuffling.

And then a second happy-face, this one with red lipstick and improbably long eyelashes, tore free from a game opposite. In a single smooth motion it scooped the mutt up in its teeth and bore it, howling and screaming, to the opposite wall. The two happy-faces kissed obscenely, passing the pup from one to another. There was a hideous chewing sound.

"Observe," Twan said steadily. "Our collective life energy just dropped."

General principle, Acacia said to herself. *Protect the living from the unliving.*

"All right," Tammi yelled. "Let's rock!"

Another black dog wriggled from a jagged inch-wide crack along a wall. A third video machine popped open, disgorging four masked, green, slightly anthropomorphic turtles. They brandished assorted martial-arts hardware. Acacia steeled herself for action.

Behind her, lights flashed and power bolts flew as Twan plied her trade against an endlessly multiplying centipede. For Acacia, steel would have to suffice.

Her blade glowed, and the dog scampered behind her, whining. A turtle approached, samurai sword leveled. It champed grinning teeth at her, canted its head sideways, and spoke. "Puppy pizza time. Back off, beautiful."

Acacia screamed and swung her sword, aiming at the junction of shoulder and neck. Her aim was true. As the turtle's head flew from its shoulders, it screamed, "Radical!" It bounced once. Its beak opened and closed, and opened and hissed, "Pizzaaaaa . . ." and it died. And . . .

"Cowabunga!" a second reptile screamed, leaping at her, slashing with a pair of sai. On the defensive again, Acacia fought furiously, the mongrel dog shadowing her the entire time, whining, its tail tucked between its legs.

Acacia was tiring. She managed to deflect a sai and lifted her leg high, smashing her heel into the turtle's breastbone. Well, her heel didn't actually make contact with anything, but the creature sailed backward and crashed into a pinball machine with a satisfying thump. Sparks erupted, and steam, as the evil reptile was electrocuted. The air reeked with the stench of scorched turtle flesh.

The battle was going poorly. All about them, the video machines were disgorging Tie-fighters, mercenary soldiers, and professional wrestlers. A Michael Jackson clone moonwalked off a screen, pirouetted, and rolled his snap-brim hat into his hand. He threw the fedora like a Frisbee. It skimmed through the air and struck Aces Wilde in the side of the neck. She crashed to the ground, dead.

Dogs were dying, borne screaming to the wall by Larry, Moe, and Curly. Their sinister *nyuck nyuck nyuck*s reverberated endlessly, drowning out the yips of canine terror.

"Cipher!" Acacia screamed. "Where the hell are you?"

The fabled Troglodykes were doing better than any of the others. Shattered, smoldering centipede segments lay heaped about their feet. Six dogs had formed a pack behind them, cowering but alive.

A statuesque brunette Amazon in red-white-and-blue spangled tights threw a golden lariat at Twan. The Troglodyke glowed, caught the noose, and spun, sending her attacker hurtling through the air. The Amazon landed in the lap of a grotesquely deformed sailor, his tattooed forearms swollen to the size of beer kegs. His eyes bugged, and he said, "Arf arf arf! Blow me down, little lady!"

Suddenly, Cipher croaked his reply. "I can hear you, but I can't see you . . ."

Twan knew that it was time to take a chance. To flip from this level of reality meant to blind herself to the very real danger of the video demons, but she had a hunch, and she'd play it.

"Tammi! Cover me. I'm going blind for a few seconds."

Tammi's breath was coming in shallow, controlled hisses. "All right, hon. Make it fast."

Twan switched off her Virtual field.

She could see no dogs, no miniature starships firing photon torpedoes. She was in the unchanged arcade. A pinball machine had collapsed. Captain Cipher was at the video game, playing desperately, enmeshed in his own Virtual world. The cocoon about his chest and shoulders heaved like a devouring mouth. His bound hands struggled with finger toggles, fighting miniature video images. The images came faster and faster, giving him no time for rest. No time for thought.

A video game, she thought. *That's exactly what this is.*

In certain video games, it is impossible to win. All you can do is survive as long as you can, piling up points, until you are eventually dragged down and killed.

Much like life itself?

She hit the floor in a flickering shoulder roll and came up next to Cipher's machine.

Twan conjured with her hands, chanting spells. The air crackled and leapt with blue and green power bolts, darkened with mystic smoke. Her feet slid around the lower edge of the video game.

She locked both hands around her sword, while her left leg edged around for the power cord. Carefully, she wrapped it around her foot—

Instinct made her flip her Virtual visor into place. Tammi was busy, trying to swat a tiny black, bat-winged helicopter from the air. Twan started to flip it back up, when a leering moose appeared next to her. It giggled like an imbecile and said, "Watch me pull a rabbit out of my hat."

What he pulled out of a black top hat was an abomination, some unnatural meld of lion, gorilla, and maybe squirrel. It snarled and leapt—

Her foot twisted in the power cord, and she *yanked*—

The mutant screamed, and froze, and spun backward into the hat.

The moose disappeared. Turtles, centipedes, Michael Jackson, all vanished.

"Iiii ammmm Ogguuunnn," Cipher's video machine groaned. The cord lashed and writhed across the floor like a wounded snake, searching for the outlet. Twan watched in horrified fascination.

Cipher, gasping, ripped himself out of the cocoon, scrambling out so fast that he fell to the floor, breaking his fall with his hands. There was genuine fear in his face. "Screw *you!*" he yelled. His aura flared, bolts of power arcing out and playing over the machine. It smoked and burned, plastic and metal melting, tiny video images in the flames screaming and writhing until there was nothing left but slag.

Acacia examined the ruin, and then Cipher. He was flushed, sweaty, heaving for breath.

Acrid smoke filled the air. The other Adventurers were silent. "Ah . . . Cipher," she said as gently as she could. "If it isn't completely dead, would you maybe like to torture it for a while?"

He considered for a moment. "Naw," he said finally. "That would be cruel." He dusted himself off and went to inspect the damage.

Acacia stared after, trying to figure out which was worse: the fact that he might be serious, or the fact that she couldn't be sure he wasn't.

Chapter Nineteen

Ile Ife

"And when Ile Ife, the place of creation, was complete and ready for life, the Great God sent his messenger, the Chameleon, to inspect it and be sure it was good . . ."
  —"California Voodoo," notes given to Loremasters by the IFGS

Tammi and Twan shot their fists into the air and gave a mighty cheer of "Ahroooo!" The human sound blended with one that was pure canine.

Alex realized that the dogs had vanished. Only one animal remained—a smallish black Labrador. It crept up to Twan and tried to lick her hand. It couldn't touch her, but she patted its discorporate head and spoke to it.

It arfed, turned, and burrowed under the shattered wall. It was into the broken jewelry case next door. In a moment it was out, dragging . . . a necklace. The necklace was made of metal beads: seven brown beads alternating with three black beads.

Twan hefted it. "Talisman." She handed the beads to Tammi. "God of war. Your turf."

"Bobo—what do you think?"

Alex Griffin, aka Bobo, tried to remember what he had been told. "Oggun challenged you. You won. He has acknowledged victory—your power will increase."

That sounded pretty good. Moreover, the voice of the Game Masters was silent.

His eyes met Acacia's squarely. Her lips moved silently. *Alex.*

Tammi made a T formation with her hands, and said, "Fifteen minutes, potty break. I saw a crescent moon back a door or two."

★ ★ ★

Acacia Garcia slipped away from her compatriots and found a quiet corner. She drew her belt knife and twisted off its handle. Within the five-inch hilt was two inches of hollow. She shook out a tiny cube with a standard tripronged electrical plug attached. She spoke into the cube rapidly, concisely, spitting consonants, then plugged it into the nearest electrical socket.

It was 5:30 P.M.

There were apartments on the eighteenth and seventeenth floors. Nigel set his team sampling them at random. Trevor Stone, Bishop's Sorcerer and second-in-command, found two sets of ancient scuba gear in a closet. Bishop flickered a smile at him, the equivalent of a pat on the head, and left him to carry them. Stone dithered, then handed one set off to Holly Frost; but he couldn't make himself get rid of both. The stuff was heavy, too.

There was no salt anywhere, not in any kitchen or dining or breakfast room, until Tomasan found lemon pepper in a fifty-years-abandoned spice rack. Not many Gamers would have had the wit to read the list of ingredients: the first named was salt.

Bishop decided to skirt the fifteenth floor's arcade, although his guide, the irrepressible Coral, had recommended it strongly. "Let Da Gurls do da work," he had said with a flat, hard smile. "Then, if they came up with anything worth having, we'll hijack them."

"Grody," she grumbled, "to the max." Stone had nothing to say . . . or maybe he lacked the breath. Nigel was leading them a stiff pace. The younger General Dynamics Adventurers were keeping up, but Stone was pushing his envelope.

By 5:50 P.M. they were combing an abandoned office suite on the fourteenth floor, finding nothing but cartons of paper cups and ancient computer disks. *Reveal information* spells reaped nothing but columns of accounting data. Disgusted, Bishop called a break.

He watched his team scatter to perform their various ablutions. There was a brief, mutinous glare from Trevor Stone as he dropped his pack and wobbled off.

Nigel wandered off by himself and leaned back against a wall, sliding down to a squatting position. He drew his belt knife and unscrewed its handle. He shook out his own tiny cube, and plugged it into the electrical outlet at his heel.

The tiny transceiver sent out a coded pulse along the copper wiring that webbed densely through the building. In a tenth of a second it had located and communicated with its mate, the device Acacia had plugged in at the video arcade. Acacia's transceiver uploaded its data in a supercompressed, encrypted format. ScanNet failed to differentiate this from ordinary static, although it did register the disturbance.

Bishop waited a few seconds and then plucked the transceiver from the wall, plugging it into his Virtual display equipment.

He listened to Acacia's voice: clipped, concise, urgent. It was time to make a move, but what?

He brightened.

It was time to let Trevor Stone's pent-up frustrations out to play.

For an hour the General Dynamics team had crept down empty hallways and narrow, unlit stairwells, ready for anything. There were no more apartments; no other Adventurers crossed their path; nothing attacked them.

The stairwell opened up into a grove of banana trees lit by rows of artificial lights. Their fronds rustled in a synthetic wind. Bishop moved out, testing the ground as he went, suspicious as hell. He spied other vegetation growing alongside the banana. Bamboo, and maybe coconut?

Bishop spared a glance for their guide, but Coral was hanging back, silent.

There was no natural order to the trees. Bishop suddenly realized that some of them—no, *all* were planted in rectangular wooden pots.

The ceiling crawled with clouds—distorted shapes, as with an old-fashioned planetarium ceiling. A distant crackle of thunder rumbled through the floors, but it felt more like Sensurround than reality.

Tamasan reached into the dust and retrieved a faded clapboard, like something from an old movie set. Silently he held it up. It read: *Scene 34, Ile Ife.*

The village itself was made up of storefronts and flats, imitation native huts built over fiberglass frames, and wooden shacks with three walls.

Holly Frost looked at it uncomprehendingly for a minute and then nudged Bishop. "Be damned. It's the set of *King Solomon's Mines.*"

Trevor said, "Hollywood refugees. Trying to get into the spirit."

"So where are they?" asked Holly.

It wasn't completely empty. There were dozens of statues or partial statues of human beings. Bronze busts of men and women and children were apparently half-buried in the earth. Their expressions were of exaggerated pain and terror, extras emoting for the camera.

"Touch *nothing* until our Cleric has scanned," Bishop said testily.

Trevor glared at him. "Aye-aye, sir."

Tamasan began an elaborate Shinto ritual, taking his time.

The set's most prominent feature was a gigantic cylindrical shaft, which jutted from the ground at an eighty-degree angle and pierced the ceiling twenty feet above them. The shaft was of pitted, weathered stone. About its base were the remains of dozens of baskets of fruit, long withered. The last one might have been placed there a year before, and only stones at the bottoms of the rotted baskets kept the wind—

Wind?

Holly touched Bishop's sleeve, and he peered through the artificial grove. Just barely, they could make out the shapes of giant wind fans, eight-foot monsters humming and pulsing with electricity, whipping air across the set.

She came close to the shaft, but didn't touch. "Wonder if this whole thing is a matte painting," she muttered.

The surface was studded with iron nails in patterns of wave and curlicue, driven to various depths.

Bishop came up behind her. "Language of some kind. Can't scan it."

"What about this?"

There was a stone tablet set in the ground in front of the shaft. Commentary in several different scripts was carved into it, including one in English: *The Staff of Oranyan.* And a smaller, older sign under it: *Wet Paint.*

"Scan," he said softly, and it began to glow.

He couldn't keep his eyes off those statues. Or busts. Or petrified people? If they had once been people, they were now buried to thigh or chest or chin.

The slate showed no residue of magic, nothing dangerous.

He scanned the statues next. Nothing. "Not transformed human beings," he said to Holly. "Statues. Just statues."

"Check out the set?"

Tamasan, a brown swirl of monk's robes, was scuttling about

checking buildings. Bishop remained in the center of the town. Thinking.

Looked like they had broken for lunch. Just about ready to film a scene? Did he have to guess hard to figure out which one?

Bishop raised his hand and whistled. Coral and his three remaining team members flocked to him. He squatted on the ground to talk. "Booty?"

Holly Frost's dark brown face was streaked with dust and sweat. "We haven't found a talisman, if that's what you mean. There's some costume jewelry, some plastic pottery. It's a movie set, all right. I suspect similarity magic. I'm not sure I want to see the special effect."

"Tamasan? Danger?"

"Nothing, Bishop-san."

"Ile Ife," Bishop began stentorianly, "was the mythical birthplace of the Ibo people. They were protected by a mighty god—" His voice was sonorous and dramatic, and he was starting to work himself into a roll.

"Excuse me," Trevor interrupted. "I believe that it is part of the Yoruba legends. Not the Ibo."

"No, I'm sure—" Bishop paused. "Are you certain?"

Trevor hid his smirk. "It wasn't in the notes. I can finish the briefing, if you'd like."

Bishop allowed a trace of unease into his voice. "Ah—yes. Why don't you do that—I'll be gone for maybe twenty minutes. I'm sure I don't have to remind you not to touch anything, Trevor."

Trevor's eyes were hooded.

"Right, then," Bishop said, and rose to his feet. "I want to do a little spying on Da Gurls. Coral, come with me."

Alex squatted with his back to one of the battered video machines, arms draped over his bent knees.

Acacia sat next to him. She smelled a little sweat-sour, and her hair was a ruin, but in a remote way he had to admit that she was, physically at least, as attractive as ever.

He knew that guilt wasn't acid: it might eat at the heart, but it didn't necessarily etch the human face. He searched for its signs, anyway. Where might it show? Around the eyes? Were those wrinkle lines a little deeper, more pronounced? Or was she just tired?

Tired . . .

Suddenly, and with a little shock, he realized that he hadn't slept the night before. When the adrenaline burned itself out he was going to crash, and crash hard.

Acacia offered him half of a tropical chocolate bar. "It's good to have a guide," she said, studiously avoiding direct eye contact. He nodded without comment. "It's good to have . . . someone that I can trust. Can I trust you?"

"Assuredly, miz. I'm here to help. For the good of all, and the survival of New Africa, and because the Mamissa doesn't trust my temper."

She nodded. "I've seen you before . . ." She wavered, and then lowered her voice to a whisper. "Hi, Alex. I can't play games with you, can I?"

"Games are all we've ever played, Acacia. Why change the pattern?"

Their eyes met sideways. For a moment they kept their expressions solemn, then she began to shake with silent ironic laughter.

"So. Here we are again. Just couldn't miss another chance to fight zombies?"

He made an expansive hand gesture that might have meant almost anything. "Hundreds of us are in it, Cas. Hell has let out for lunch; everybody's going wild."

What are you thinking, Acacia? There are so many possibilities. If you aren't dirty, you could be wondering if I'm here to bitch up your game. Could wonder if I'm trying to patch things up with you. Whether that will cause problems with Bishop.

If Bishop is rotten, and you are helping him . . .

Or if you're involved in Sharon's death, God help you. Don't bother trying to kill me out, Cas. I can take more hit points than Godzilla.

"So you'll be with us from here on?" she asked.

"All the way."

There was a sudden commotion at the front of the arcade. "Intruders approaching!" Mouser yelled.

"We seek parley!" That was Bishop's voice above the hubbub. Acacia cringed.

The line parted for Bishop and Coral.

He swaggered up to them. "Well," he said, examining Tammi's necklace. In his vision, it would glow like an aurora. "Looks like you've been busy."

"Should have been here," Tammi said.

"Would have. Too busy getting ahead of you."

"Get anything interesting?"

"That would be telling."

"So what do you want, Bishop?"

"Peace in our time? Surcease of sorrow?" He wandered farther back into the arcade and stood over Acacia. "Panthesilea." He bowed deeply. "So nice to see that you've survived."

Griffin got to his feet. He and Bishop studied each other for a second before the Loremaster turned back to Acacia.

"Coral suggested this place, but it looked more your speed. Congratulations."

"Cut the crap, Bishop. What do you want?"

"I was wondering whether any of your people would care to switch teams now, while they still have the chance."

Twan made a "hurry up" motion with her hand.

"I wanted to look over the damage," he said with deceptive casualness. "Make a body count. We've come a long way."

He examined the smelted video game. It was a barely recognizable heap of glass and plastic and scorched metal.

"My goodness. You had a time here, didn't you? And lost a Scout. Get anything beside the necklace?"

"That's for us to know—"

"Yes, yes. Let's not be tiresome."

He took Acacia's hands and squeezed, eyes twinkling. "Well. It seems you've fallen in with the right group, dear. And who is this? Your guide?"

For the first time he examined Alex carefully. Measuring. Categorizing. "My memory must be failing me. I could swear Bobo's changed since the Mami Wata ceremony."

"Changed?" Acacia asked. "How?"

"Why, he looks so much larger and more competent now. Intelligent, even." He enjoyed another moment's muse and then stalked back toward the front of the arcade. "Well," he said. "I can see that everything is in line here. I've learned everything that I want to know."

"Like what?" Twan asked.

"Ah, my little Asian jungle bunny, that is for me to know, and for you to never, ever find out." He smiled expansively. "I'll see you again, and sooner than you think!"

Still under the sign of truce, Bishop and Coral backed away.

Twan watched him go, chewing her lip. There was a game going on here, right under her eyes, and she didn't like it. And she didn't like the switch that Dream Park had made with Bobo, although it wasn't the first time something like it had happened. A guide got sick, or twisted an ankle, or screwed up a scenario, and an alternate stepped in. Still . . . she didn't have to like it.

"All right," she called out. "We move out in five minutes."

Trevor had propped his pack against a papier-mâché stone fountain, using it for a cushion. He said, "Anything?"

"Nothing, Trevor-san. No icons or talismans. No magic, not even in the signs and sigils. Even so, the place must be important. Work was done here."

"Might I ask, would you call me Mr. Stone, or Stone-san, or—"

"Stone-san, of course. Forgive me."

"Is Tamasan your first name or—"

"My nickname. It more or less means 'Mr. Ball.' My shape, you know, from Beverly Hills High School."

Holly Frost had climbed a potted tree. She slid down and came back to the fountain. "Zip."

"If there's nothing here, then something must be made to come here," Trevor said. "Some magical ritual associated with the Ile Ife legend, if we knew enough. Or . . . perhaps one of these trees is needed somewhere else in the building."

"Ugh." Holly flopped down against her pack. Stone had looked worn out when Bishop left. Now he had his energy back, she judged; in fact he was becoming twitchy. She said, "So we wait. Tell a story, Trevor."

"My turn? It'll be lovely not to be interrupted. All right, this was a long time ago, and the Gaming area was just a patch of high desert near Denver. No special effects really . . ." Trevor settled more comfortably against his pack. "Three groups of players had gone through ahead of us. Their corpses were scattered everywhere. This one chap was standing upright, not moving. 'Hi, I'm dead,' he said.

"He'd been killed in an patch of cactus, you see. Needles everywhere. He may have been dead, but damned if he was going to lie down."

Holly laughed. Was this really the only way to keep him from going off half-cocked? Bishop seemed to think so—though he kept interrupting the damn stories . . .

★ ★ ★

Bishop and Coral were halfway down the stairs when Bishop held out a restraining hand.

"Like, what's the prob?"

"I need to think," he said. "Let's wait a minute."

"Your dime, dude."

Bishop sat down and put on a thoughtful expression. But most of what he was thinking was, *Trevor Stone. You're boiling by now. Impatient as hell, and you want to show me up. How much longer before you make your move?*

Stone said, "Your turn, Tamasan."

"Hai," the monk replied. "I played in Japan once," he said. "It was all very formal, the ranks established very clearly. We were supposed to know the legend, I think, but I didn't. I fought when we were attacked. There was never any doubt about who was the enemy. Very different from Dream Park."

"You missed the mental challenge?"

"Yes." Tamasan stood up abruptly. "I wonder if there's anything about the fountain itself?"

There was nothing to do at the moment. The inactivity was wearing at all of them, especially Trevor Stone. Holly Frost, Warrior and Thief extraordinaire, hated playing baby-sitter. Such passive work really wasn't in her nature. She would much rather have been stealing something or killing someone.

Still, it had to be done. "My turn? Something I overheard from an old Game Master. 'The Orb of Eternity' was a twenty-four-pound bowling ball. Some teams carried it the whole eight miles before they realized it wasn't what they wanted, and it sucked the power out of magic spells . . ."

It wasn't exotic enough; she had lost him. "This whole level is an H. Rider Haggard movie," he said. "I think you were right, Holly. It was some kind of ritual. The fans are still running. Movie cameras still set up. So where are the actors?"

Holly watched him carefully. "Go on."

"We are the actors. It's been set up. The whole village is a ritual waiting to happen."

"This is voodoo?"

"Similarity magic. Reenactment of ancient events, Hollywood-style."

"So?"

"So let's put on a show."

Holly didn't much like the sinking sensation in her gut. Stone was dying to do something, anything. And Bishop had to know it. Why had he left like that? Something was wrong here, and Holly Frost was stranded in the middle of it.

"I think," she said finally, "that we had better wait for Bishop. Finish what you were telling us. You were halfway up a mountain? Before Bishop—"

"Yes. Fifty years ago, near as dammit. I wasn't a player, I was an Implementer, one of the chaps who makes the Game happen. I could watch the Gamers going up another peak a mile away, and I had a walkie-talkie to guide the NPCs who were going to fight them. I could also see a kind of black whirlwind, a real one, mind you, coming toward them. They couldn't see it, and I'm a Brit, you know, we don't get tornados, but I couldn't believe it was any kind of special effect . . ." Trevor stood up abruptly. "You wait if you want to. I'm going to start a ceremony. There are personal points to be won here. I was performing sorcery before he could *spell* it."

Trevor drew a circle in the ground with a sprinkle of powders, chanting softly as he did. The circle glowed and hummed. Lightning flashed overhead, filling the air with a sharp, stinging metallic scent.

"I call to the gods of this land. The Drama Cosmic unfolds! Your cast awaits! Ready when you are, CB."

"Trevor, Jesus—"

He turned on her, furious. "Go and hide if you want, Miss Frost. This is *Gaming.*"

Too late anyway. Out of the darkened sky an oblong shape formed and dropped toward them, a shape with stumpy legs and a thrashing black tail. It landed in the common with a thump. They couldn't quite make it out, despite the overhead lighting. It unfolded itself, a two-meter length of pinkish tongue whipping out and back repeatedly.

"What in the hell?"

It was ten meters of rather loony chameleon, multicolored, changing shades to match every object it passed in a steadily shifting, fractured rainbow. Big, but hard to see. It plodded toward them, enormous pop-eyes rolling. Its entire body flickered. Unmistakably, it was a stop-motion monster, a refugee from a Gumby film festival.

Tamasan was running toward them. He stopped suddenly and set his staff against the ground. "I'm scanning—"

"Yes," Trevor said sarcastically. "Scan it. Haven't you ever seen a Ray Harryhausen movie? Kill the damned thing!" He spoke a spell in some unknown language and hurled his sword. The sword burst into brilliant flame as it spun toward the thing's head.

The results were disproportionate. Flame singed the lizard from tail to tip. Its distended eyes bulged, and its entire claymation body rippled with agony.

Frost and Tamasan never had the chance to add their own power. The chameleon fluttered, glowed, seemed to electrify, and was transformed into a jet of lightning, crackling and arcing in the shape of a lizard.

Then, with a howl, it burst apart. Beneath its skin was a clock-work maze of metal gears and plastic knobs. It steamed and shuddered, and then was motionless.

"There's for you!" Trevor cheered it.

Holly eyed her teammates nervously. "Trevor . . ."

Trevor relaxed suddenly. "I know. Too easy. We've been had. *I've* been had, but I still don't understand—" He stopped, giving up, as the earth beneath them began to tremble.

The sound was as rhythmic as a slow drumbeat. Footsteps. Then a violent crackling, the sound of trees and shrubs torn up by the roots.

They could see nothing, but they heard a voice that crackled like thunder, coming from everywhere. "Haven't . . . you read . . . the script?" it asked.

Stone's voice was thin and cracking. "We are the defenders—"

"*Who* are you?" The voice was closer. Terribly close, and now they could see an immense shape forming in the sky. Staggeringly huge. Wearing a black beret and Brobdingnagian sunglasses; carrying a riding crop. A gigantic potbelly bulged from beneath a sun-bleached safari shirt. Bermuda shorts exposed knees as white as fish bellies, quaking with rage.

"Ohmigod," Holly moaned. "The director."

The Adventurers fanned out in the semblance of a defensive posture.

"Foolhardy . . . miserable . . . pitiful . . . *actors!*"

Trevor screamed at the others. "We can negotiate with this guy!"

Holly barked derisively. "I've gotta meet your agent!"

But by then the shadow of the director lay upon them, as dark as night.

The creature leaned down, its grin filled with gleaming, capped teeth a cubic foot in size.

And it hissed, "Strike the set."

Chapter Twenty

Oranyan's Staff

"An African tribe named the Dogon . . . were in possession of information . . . that the actual orbital period (of Sirius B) is fifty years."
—Robert K. G. Temple, *The Sirius Mystery*, 1976

"There are legends that other, specialized knowledge spread out from Africa. There are strange repetitions of the number fifty in the mythology of pre-dynastic Egypt. For instance, the Argo, the boat of Isis and Osiris, has fifty Argonauts . . ."
—"California Voodoo," GM's notes

Thursday, July 21, 2059—6:55 P.M.

Cautiously, Bishop and Coral entered the deserted village of Ile Ife.

It was exactly—*exactly*—as it had been when they first entered. The Panaflex camera sat deserted. Behind a stand of banana trees, the wind machines howled and churned the air. The General Dynamics team might never have existed at all.

Bishop made a megaphone of his hands and shouted, "Hello!"

His answers were echoes buffeted on the artificial wind. Then nothing. The planetarium sky/ceiling above them shifted. Tarnished statues and bronze busts, human figures caught in midscream, moved not, spoke not. Wept not.

Bishop scanned the set for living things, carefully suppressing his grim satisfaction at the negative reading.

"Like, ohmigawd," Coral said. "Where *is* everybody?"

"Time to find out." Bishop scratched a circle in the dirt with his sword, muttering a guttural mouthful of arcane words.

The wind died. The soil began to ripple and shift. Dust fell from the air, like dry tears shed by invisible eyes. In the dirt the falling many-colored dust began to shape a crude, impressionistic sand painting.

It became less abstract, became an accurate rendering of Ile Ife, with three human stick figures caught frozen in attitudes of horror. More sand fell . . . the painting took on detail: Trevor Stone and his teammates stood frozen in time. Bishop muttered again, folding his fingers together in a mystic glyph, and the drawing began to move.

Once again, Trevor hurled his grenade at the chameleon. The director descended upon them, enraged. And then—

"Shit."

Bishop scuffed the earth with his toe, obliterating the painting. He was drawn to the rows of statues scattered about the set. They *weren't* exactly the same. Three new statues were partially buried in the earth. Two men. One woman. Mouths gaped open in primal scream, as if voicing final pleas for mercy before consignment to the pits of hell.

Bishop held his breath, tensing his muscles to create a convincing imitation of rage. "The fool. That raving imbecile Stone. How could he *do* this to me?"

He tilted his face up to the ceiling, squeezing his eyes shut as if calculating odds and possibilities. Coral stood in silent confusion, not daring to speak. Finally Bishop's lips curled in a thin, vicious smile. "On the other hand," he said, "one might take the optimistic view: we have just separated the wheat from the chaff."

"Mr. Bishop, you don't have a *team!*"

Coral had slipped out of character there. Bishop patted her head. "So I don't. I shall adopt one. Come."

Bobo the guide stalked MIMIC's silent halls in a state of total concentration. He sought to pierce the veil of shadows, listened for signs of menace beneath and beyond the fading echoes of the Gamers' own footsteps. Every footfall offered new risk, every dust-sealed doorway concealed new danger.

It was a schizophrenic world Alex Griffin walked. His ache for Sharon and his need to perform his sworn duties were at war with the DreamTime illusions. If he submitted, he was betraying his heart, and his trust. And if he resisted, he could be killed out of the Game.

So he scanned for demons, or goblins, or zombies—and kept one unwavering fragment of his attention for Acacia.

She remained as skittishly alert as an antelope, avoiding his gaze, but always an arm's distance away.

Griffin whispered a quiet command. Information scrolled across the left lens of his mirrored sunglasses. He split-focused his attention, searching the halls for danger while he combed through data:

Acacia Garcia, 34, MA in Business Administration, had been top-seeded into the game. There had been little doubt that she would be one of the five leaders.

On the other hand . . .

Nigel Bishop, 36, with a master's in Psychology and a doctorate in Communication Arts from Columbia University, had stepped back into the IFGS after seven years of retirement. Had bribery or blackmail helped him win his slot? Unlikely—but he might have used his reputation, the *myth* of Nigel Bishop, for intimidation.

Tammi's eyes shifted left to right and back again, watching for clues or threats. She was point person as their column swept through an abandoned corridor. It was lined with abandoned shops: barber, beauty, comic books, massage, and something called a 7-Eleven store. A sign in its window promised a Big Gulp for eighty-nine cents.

Seven-Eleven? Big Gulp? That last had an unwholesome sound, but even in '95, even in California, surely eighty-nine cents wouldn't buy—

Sound ahead. Her staff snapped to the ready, but it was just Nigel Bishop again, with Coral tagging behind.

Ambush? Where was the rest of his team?

"Parley," he said.

"What do you want, Bishop?"

"A situation has arisen—"

Tammi aimed her staff at his throat. "A *situation*, eh?"

"Please." Nigel was using his very best let-us-reason-together voice. "While I last spoke with you, my second-in-command disobeyed my direct orders."

Tammi didn't relax, but the corners of her mouth twitched up. "Seeing as how you've distanced yourself from their actions, may I assume that they fucked up?"

"Big time. Only my guide and I are left. I have information and booty to offer, in exchange for joining your caravan."

"Standard deal, aside from that?"

"Standard."

Tammi shook out her mane of blond hair and seemed to be considering the offer. "Hold on."

Acacia and Twan huddled with Tammi, speaking in a hush, only occasionally peeking up at Bishop. Tammi sauntered back to Bishop, putting no more sashay in her walk than the average Barbary Coast fancy girl.

"You're on, big boy."

The caravan regrouped, ten players and two guides proceeding together through the darkness.

Griffin dropped back next to Bishop and took the opportunity to study the man carefully.

He was two inches shorter than Griffin, and weighed perhaps a hundred and eight-five exceptionally muscular pounds. His stride reminded Griffin of a two-legged lynx. Effortless grace, the lazy promise of blinding speed and crushing power. All his life, Griffin had earned physical skills through sweat and bruised flesh, and had the working jock's quiet loathing for, and admiration of, those who possessed such skills naturally.

He remembered the elegance of Bishop's victory over Clavell. What art might have spawned such a devastating move? It was similar to Griffin's home art of jujitsu, but there was a theatrical flourish, a fluidity, which he couldn't quite identify.

Bishop was whistling something between his teeth. "There's No Business Like Show Business," maybe. It was just low enough to be indistinct.

Still whistling, Bishop turned and examined Griffin from shoes to hair, wearing a mild, faintly ironic expression the entire time. Bishop's tune changed, and now he was rendering "Send In the Clowns."

And rendering it beautifully, dammit.

Acacia glanced back at them, uneasily, as if wondering when they would spring at each other's throats.

"Hold up!" Bishop called suddenly, and pointed out a doorway camouflaged as a wall panel. "This is the one." He peeled back a layer of plastic and scanned inside. "Nope, no beasties. Ladies first?"

"I think not," Acacia said icily, and curtsied. "After you, sirrah."

The Adventurers split into a fan formation for a careful search of Ile Ife. Bishop hung back, catching Acacia's arm.

"So, dear heart. Have you and Bobo been having a fascinating conversation? Catching up on old times?"

She twisted her arm, but couldn't pull it away. "We're in the middle of a Game, you idiot. This isn't any time for jealousy."

"Jealousy? Darling, your warm and supple body is the promise of heaven, but I prefer more mundane rewards."

"I made a deal," she whispered. "I'll keep it. I told you he was here, didn't I?"

His fingers slackened a bit. "Just remember whose team you're on," he said, and his fingers tightened again, with brief, shocking strength. Then he released her.

Acacia felt as if a motorcycle had run over her arm. She rubbed at it, trying to get the blood flowing again.

Her vision clouded, and she blinked hard to clear it.

You bought this horse, you crazy bitch. And you better be able to ride it home.

"What happened here?" Tammi asked Bishop. The stone column still jutted toward the ersatz sky. Bronzed actors still blindly clawed their way from the ground.

"Stone attacked a messenger of the gods. Bad move."

"So what's our move?"

"Begin a Summoning. When a chameleon appears, give gifts. That'll put you in square with the gods."

Bishop lingered back as the Adventurers gathered to begin the ceremony. Almost accidentally, he wound up next to Griffin again.

Strangely, Bishop seemed smaller than before. Was he slumping a little? A little tired and maybe worried? Suddenly Griffin saw Bishop as a Gamer—King of the Gamers, perhaps. Capable of projecting enormous self-assurance, but under pressure, that veneer could crack. Had it?

The sky rumbled, and the chameleon appeared. The Adventurers backed away to give it room to land.

Bishop straightened up, jaunty and invincible as ever. "What are you looking at, Bobo? Hadn't you better help your masters?"

Griffin tensed with anger, and then relaxed. Suddenly Bishop seemed entirely human-sized. A nervous Gamer, losing his Game in front of ten million viewers. The mingled sensations of relief and contempt washed over him—

And then receded.

For just an instant, half a heartbeat, Bishop had been watching him, appraisingly. Wondering which mask Griffin would accept?

One by one, gifts were placed on the bulbous tip of the chameleon's sticky tongue.

"They're doing fine by themselves," Griffin said. The hairs at the back of his neck crawled with alarm. What was he sensing? A shell of bravado, around a shell of insecurity, around—what?

I should yank your ass out of this Game, Griffin swore silently. *But I don't have justification. Maybe I just don't like you. God knows if I yanked you, you could claim I did it out of sexual jealousy, and cause a stink.*

So I'll watch. And wait.

The remaining Trogs crouched in a thicket of potted banana trees. Tammi and Mouser crowded close, blocking the view of any observer. "Bishop's off talking to Bobo the Second," Tammi said.

Twan nodded. She produced a palm-sized mirror. She made a mystic gesture.

Appelion lay in a double-shelled resurrection coffin. Tendrils of superchilled nitrogen fog writhed around him. His eyes were closed. His face was pale, the cheeks pink with rouge and dusted in frost.

"Ah, he looks so natural," said Mouser.

Twan said, "To wake the dead requires great power."

With eyes still closed, Appelion said, in a wintry, whispering voice like the wind from a great, dark cave, "Greater power yet, to put the dead to sleep. Be sure of your power."

"Wake, Appelion."

The eyes opened. "Even the patience of the dead has limits."

"It's been an active Game."

"I have seen."

"Have the Masters of the Great Game aught to tell us?"

"Seek the waters above and below."

"We thank—"

"That's from them. This is from me, so listen up." He still lay dead, his lips barely moving beneath his bushy black beard. "There's a book, *The Sirius Mystery,* by . . . somebody Church. No, Temple, dammit. Robert Temple. The basic idea is *Chariots of the Gods* with better logic and better evidence. Have you time to hear?"

"We'll *make* time."

"There's a tribe in Mali, the Dogon, who know far too much about Sirius. They know it's a double star. They know Sirius B is tiny and very dense—"

"*What?*"

"They put Sirius B, the white dwarf, in a fifty-year elliptical orbit with Sirius A at one focus. How does an African tribe come to know about a completely invisible white dwarf star? And Kepler orbits?"

"Is this for real?"

"Temple believed so, and did his research well. He tracked these legends back to ancient Egypt, and Sumer, and all over the Mediterranean basin. Does any of this sound familiar?"

Mouser and Tammi looked blank. Twan said, " 'California Voodoo,' the notes. They mentioned a recurrence of the number fifty in Egyptian legends."

"Egyptians?" Mouser was puzzled. "What does that have to do with voodoo?"

"Remember to be literal. Voodoo is fragments of African religion, filtered through other beliefs. Fragments, dammit. What was the reality? If a people without a written language played 'Telephone' with a bizarre occurrence ten thousand years old, and the result was the hundred different threads of voodoo, santería, Palo Mayombe, whatever, *what was* the original event?"

Twan nodded, one jerk of her head. "Go on, Brother."

The dead man said, "According to Dogon legends, knowledge was given to men by aliens from outer space. The Dogon called them *Nommo*. The knowledge givers apparently never claimed to be gods. They're given as benevolent and butt-ugly. And *aquatic*. They *sound* alien, don't they?"

"Nommo," Twan murmured.

"Did you notice the headdresses in the Mami Wata ceremony, just before Clavell chopped me open? Ridiculous little fish tails sticking out the back. The Nommo have dominion over water and the ocean, like Poseidon, like the Sumerian god called *Wannis*, spelled *O-A-double-N-E-S*. That fifty-year orbit wound up in a lot of legends, not just the Dogon calendar. Fifty Argonauts, fifty dragon's teeth—and fifty of Mamissa Kokoe's natives involved in the Mami Wata ceremony on the roof. I counted."

Tammi glowed. "Damned good, Appelion. Cipher couldn't have topped that. What does it do for us?"

"I'm not sure . . . The involvement with Egypt is very old. Remember the pyramid on the roof?"

"Yeah." Mouser had caught Twan's excitement, was vibrating like a little top. "I thought it was part of the air-conditioning system or something. I want a look."

"Corrinda disappeared during Mami Wata. You know, Thief, bad knee, with Panthesilea? Maybe *she* got a closer look. Watch her. Watch for pyramids and pyramid power. Watch for the number fifty. Temple published a Dogon sketch of a spacecraft with a rotating rim, 'wheel within a wheel,' but it looked to me like some savage tried to draw a helicopter. There was a lander, maybe: cross-sections of needle-nosed spacecraft with interior detail, but they're obelisk-shaped, so look for obelisks, too."

Twan said, "That's a lot."

"Yeah, and no guarantees. But it's the only place I've ever seen a word like 'Nommo'—and I'm out of ideas," Appelion said.

"Then go to your well-earned rest, Warrior."

The chameleon's mouth opened, and its tongue flashed out. Stuck to its tip was a staff, a miniature of the nail-studded column in the town square. He presented it to Acacia.

Captain Cipher inspected it without touching it. "This must be the Staff of Oranyan. This," he said, voice filled with awe, "this is *serious* power."

Twan was watching. Behind her impassive expression, she was exploding with excitement. *You're wrong, Cipher,* she thought. *The Staff of Oranyan is just another bauble. Knowledge is power.*

Chapter Twenty-one

Family Ties

Dr. Norman Vail was a man of singular talent and many responsibilities. Other employees sometimes found him intimidating, but no one had seriously suggested that he be replaced in his psychiatric capacity.

The bottom line was that Vail could get things done.

He was wondering why Thaddeus Harmony had ordered him to drop his other projects, to sift through the life of Sharon Crayne, the late love interest of his friend, Alex Griffin. He believed Harmony intended no more than a placebo effort for Alex's benefit.

It was always interesting to have unlimited access to another human being's secret workings. Because by violating the inner sanctum of Sharon Crayne, Harmony was of course giving Vail permission to take Alex Griffin apart.

Alex Griffin: born September 17, 2021, to Elliot and Darsha Griffin. Which made him . . . forty-three years old. Alex! We're older than we look! Father dead. Mother's whereabouts . . . unknown. Nothing dramatic here, Alex, just a career woman with ever-decreasing time for a young and demanding male-child. A child shunted into boarding schools? One who distinguished himself in military service . . . goodness, look at these classified files. Vail wondered if Tony McWhirter could do something about those . . .

"Cat's in the cradle," Vail hummed. Mummy made halfhearted efforts to reconcile with grown-up Alex, who would have none of it. Gradually they lost touch.

Alex Griffin, a man who had talents beyond the typical cop mentality. Perhaps with the right nurturing . . . of course, was it nature or nurture? The eternal argument. Even studies of identical twins begged the question: prenatal nutritional environment was essential for proper brain development, and twins shared that down to the last amino acid. Light and sound that reached the womb affected the brain of an unborn child.

Vail had once proposed an experiment that would resolve the question once and for all. Stimulate five thousand fertilized ova to produce quadruplets. Double-blind implant the little angels in mothers chosen at random from the Embryadopt lists—all income levels, all education and intelligence levels, all races.

Wait twenty years . . .

Vail sighed. He *supposed* he could understand why his colleagues were appalled by the notion. Such squeamishness often obstructed progress.

At any rate, Alex Griffin was what he was, and wasn't terribly likely to change.

On to Sharon Crayne. Thirty-two. Unmarried. Master's degree in psychology, University of Washington. Two years with the Washington State Police, recruited to Cowles Industries after a stint at a private security agency. No record of any problems at all. Six years there.

Vail sighed and leaned back in his chair, watching the numbers and patterns flash past. What was he looking for? A motive to betray Dream Park and/or Cowles Industries?

In Vail's opinion, motives nearly always broke down into three basic categories:

1) Relief from something
2) Revenge for something
3) Desire for something

Vail only knew Sharon socially, as a face at Alex's shoulder. He knew that she had climbed the ranks in Cowles Industries rather swiftly. She would have little to resent in that matter. Revenge was not a plausible motive.

Relief, then. From blackmail? A threat? Certainly possible. He would have to cull the data for a sign, for evidence. For . . . anything.

Desire? Ever since college, Crayne had chosen challenge over pure money-making opportunity. Her new position with the Barsoom project would entail nearly a thirty percent wage increase, and she wasn't spending the money she made now. Not desire for money, then.

Vail found his resentment slipping away. Here was a puzzle, the unravelings of this dead woman's sorry life. And somewhere in the maze lay the answer.

On level seventeen, S. J. Waters brushed a thin hand across his dripping brow. It was hot here.

The iron box in front of him had twice resisted their efforts to open it. Magic had failed: bolts from Major Clavell's magic wand had glanced off its surface, sparking uselessly. Brute strength had failed: none of the Warriors had a power rating high enough to rip the top off. A direct assault with a crowbar hadn't even scratched it.

But there was something in the box, and they needed it. It was now up to their Thief to try to pick the lock.

SJ muttered a prayer to Baal, god of thieves, and his Virtual vision exploded. He could see into the lock, peer into its most intimate workings, but that wouldn't necessarily be enough. There was no way to avoid a little genuine dexterity on this one.

The interior of the lock looked like a box filled with little gears. He extruded his lockpick and inserted it.

"Ah—people," he said after a moment. "This thing has a booby trap in it."

Lawrence Black Elk waved a handful of feathers over SJ. "We can heal you," he said positively. "Fear not, little one."

SJ glared at him. "Oh, thank you, great mage!" He didn't look at Mary-em, but he could feel her grinning.

He could see the probe as it snaked its way through the twists and turns. He paused. There was a throbbing red obstruction, and he snaked back a little. It was like picking a lock whose tumblers kept moving. In fact, it seemed as if the "tumblers" were actually searching for the probe—

He yelped as an electric shock jolted through his fingers.

A dark border outlined his hand. It was creeping up his wrist.

He continued to work the probe. Presently the box sprang open. SJ backed away from it. A black aura pulsated to a funereal rhythm around his arm and shoulder, spreading down his torso—

Black Elk screamed, "By the gods of sun and sky—bring the death into me, that I might conquer it!"

The black border flowed like ectoplasmic tar, down SJ's arm and into Black Elk. Black Elk danced; he shimmied; he threw powders into the air and twirled beneath them; and the black border settled into his body even closer.

His life energy flowed out through his fingertips, through his eyes, through his mouth and nose.

Then the aurora was solid black. He crumpled to the ground, dead.

Clavell scanned him. There wasn't a spark of life left in him.

SJ was stunned. "What in the hell was *that*?"

Clavell had to force himself to speak. "We can't challenge the magic here—it's just too powerful." He knelt by Black Elk and brushed two fingertips over the staring eyes. "He was a good soldier."

Mary-em straightened up. "Shall I?"

"Please. Waters, what did we get?"

SJ poked around in the box with the tip of his knife. His peripheral vision caught the motion of Mary-em's mighty swing; he cringed despite himself, and turned as Black Elk's head bounced toward him.

"In the box, Waters."

"Looks to me like we've got a map," he said. He turned it this way and that. "It says something about the land of the Nommo."

The major took the map and overlaid it on the general map that Loremasters had been given by Mamissa.

"Look," he said. "It shows a path. Hidden door here . . . stairway . . . what do you think?"

Crystal knelt and traced a finger along the twisting route. "I think that we have to go," she said.

"And there's another passage here," SJ said, his voice a reverent hush. "One which we can hardly afford to overlook."

The major examined the spot in question and agreed soberly. "Lead the way," he said.

The halls were deadly quiet here, long abandoned. Cobwebs spanned the walkways, and the shop windows were broken and dusty. But SJ followed the map, and followed the trail that blazed in the air in front of him, a trail that no other could see.

He held up his hand. "It's here," he said.

"Are you sure?" Mary-em tightened her grip on her weapon, real tension in her face for the first time that day. She felt the burn of a rarely encountered emotion digging at her, demanding.

SJ looked at the spot where the trail terminated. "I can't open this," he said. "It's going to need magic."

Major Clavell stretched out his arms and began to chant.

Almost too slowly, the hall began to rock. The winds increased in power, swirling about them like a miniature tornado. Lights danced from the ends of his fingers. Thunder crashed and shuddered, and the hall seemed to warp out of phase—

Then the wall peeled back, and there were two large metal boxes stacked one atop another there in the wall.

Al the Barbarian licked his lips. "Do you think . . ."

"If it isn't," Poule said, "we're in bad trouble."

SJ poked it open with the tip of his stick. They breathed a sigh of relief.

Nestled within a womb of foil were sandwiches, apples, and thermoses of coffee and soup. In the other container were pods of juice and soft drinks.

Dinner!

SJ and Mary-em sat together, tucked back in a corner of the hallway. General Poule took the forward watch to ensure their privacy.

"Been a long time," Waters said happily.

Down the hall there were rooms marked off-limits with hourglass radiation symbols—a guarantee of lethal roentgens for the first person foolish enough to pass the portal. Other doors were a part of the game: they might hide booty or information. For now the most important were the doors with a half-moon stenciled upon them.

It felt strange to let the adrenaline burn out, wear down, and to evaluate the fatigue behind them. SJ felt that, but it was balanced with a spring-steel sensation as well: he had trained hard for this, and was looking forward to whatever the day might bring.

Mary-em said, "Scout/Thief?"

"Code-name Aquarius, but nobody ever uses it."

"Used to be Engineer."

The wrinkled little woman seemed even harder and more deeply creased than when he had last seen her—what, five years before? Her hip was stiff when she walked, and he was concerned. But her eyes were as bright as ever. It was difficult to waste too much sympathy on her. Chances were that she would run him into the ground.

She'd left him time to answer, and he hadn't. "Been traveling," she said, and rolled onto her back. "Still a lot of mountains that I haven't tried. K-4 in Tibet."

"Everest?"

"Naw. Been done too much. You know exactly what you're up against. I prefer a different kind of challenge. K-4 without oxygen is perfect. After Patrick died—"

"Sorry to hear—"

She waved his sympathy away. "What can I say? We both knew that it was coming, but that doesn't make things a whole lot easier. I stayed away from Gaming for a while. Wanted to do something real."

"So the mountains?"

"So the mountains."

SJ drained his pod of soft drink and groped about in the metal locker, looking for another one. "My Engineer was killed out," he said finally. "I came back as a killer cyborg—"

"The Cyberyakuza Game."

"Who's telling this? They put me back in the game as a cyborg. Kill Gamers. But I ran across a metaprogramming disk that could have left me running the whole city like it was part of my body!"

"Hospitals?"

"That, too. I could have regrown my body. I violated my programming. Ran for the nearest phone booth. It was smashed flat. Walked toward the Control Center. Cyborgs cut me off. I was so tired, I crawled into a booth that was blinking error messages because I just couldn't go any farther. And it erased my program."

Mary-em said nothing.

"I'd have made it if I wasn't such a *potato*. Six years building him, and *bang*, dead-dead, no more Engineer. I'd been spending my life in front of a terminal. So I joined the Army. And they half killed me, but I'd *win* this time. And now they've got me Gaming again. And what brought you back, Mary-em?"

"This Game," she said. "You can laugh, but . . . I had a feeling about California Voodoo. That it might be special. Then I found out you'd be here, and Acacia, and I've played with Tammi and Twan . . ." She sighed contentedly. "It feels like family," she said.

SJ considered making a mocking comment, but saw how very

serious she was, and thought again. Instead, he raised his second pod and said, "*Salud*, then. To family. I'm glad you came." He had said it just to say something, but as soon as the words left his lips, SJ realized he had spoken the truth.

Chapter Twenty-two

The Obelisk

On the twelfth floor, stalks of corn and sheaves of wheat grew from hydroponic tanks, beneath a network of track-mounted lights. Goats and chickens roamed placidly between the rows of tanks, occasionally chased from the checkered tiles back to a grazing pen by healthy-looking barefoot children.

The air was scented with the mouth-watering aroma of Mexican food. Spanish guitar and castanets and the almost-inaudible heartbeat rhythm of drums pattered from a loudspeaker.

Everything was very clean. The hydroponic tanks were capped with glass, and pale green lights flared irregularly in the rows, perhaps sterilizing or driving away insects.

As the Adventurers approached, muscular young men appeared, blocking their path. They wore lab smocks and carried clipboards. Pens were tucked behind their ears, and their breast pockets were jammed with pencils. They also carried twenty-four-inch black batons.

Tammi raised her hand. "We come in peace."

A young, pale woman in a lab smock pushed through the guards and answered her coolly. "Greetings. We are a simple farming people, señorita." She was plain and fair-skinned, her hair pulled back severely in twin braids.

"I see. And can you perhaps spare us a little food?"

"Oh, no, señorita. We are obliged to our neighbors down the way. We give them chickens, goats, and grain, and they refrain from eating our children." She seemed to consider a new thought. "But if you could help us with them, then it is possible that we would then have food to give you."

"This augurs not well," Prez whispered.

Corrinda agreed. "If we have to fight, why not here and now?"

Acacia watched Corrinda's face. It was, increasingly, a mask of strain. *Damn it. That knee must be killing her.*

"No way," Bishop said. "Major faux pas. Even the gods can only fight defensively. Clear cue for our own behavior. We march."

Tammi and Twan nodded agreement.

"Tell us of your enemy," Nigel said. "Describe them."

"Oh, señor, they are very fierce, and they eat people." She shuddered as if it were just too terrible to relate.

Nigel waited, but she said no more. "Very well. Can you draw us a map?"

"Yes. Juan!"

A tall, broadly built young man stepped forward and conversed with the girl in rapid-fire Spanish. He pulled a piece of paper from his pocket and scratched a series of lines on it, involving a big square with a piece missing from one corner.

Lab Smock translated his explanations and then said; "Juan says that the path is dangerous, but that if you are brave and strong, you may succeed. May Orisha-Oko go with you."

"Prez" Coolidge, Zulu Warrior, led the way. The remaining Adventurers stretched out in a line behind him. The village bordered on an air well. The railing was rectangular; a blank wall bit a piece out of one corner. Looking over the railing, Mouser could see the neon glitter of the Mall several floors below, and the well dropping a couple of stories farther than that.

Graffiti and pictoglyphs marred the walls, many of them representing sun and crops and meat animals, speaking to simple peasant concerns.

But as they traveled around the Mall's edge the Latin flavor changed, becoming something else, something older and more sinister.

A forty-five-degree turn took them past an unmarred stretch of blank wall. Mouser trailed and, unobserved, reached out to brush his hand along the surface. It was ceramic, but not brick: smooth and hard, perhaps too hard to take frescoes, and easy to clean of paint or charcoal dubbings. Not quite vertical, it leaned back at five degrees or so.

The path turned again, and there were more graffiti carved painfully into soft stone. The symbols looked older than contemporary Mexican—Mayan, perhaps. Angular, jutting faces and spear-carrying warriors in frieze. But the wall behind them, Mouser saw, was as smooth as glass and tilted at five degrees from vertical.

Virtual imaging—his Thief's power—showed him a small round door thirty yards down; but Bishop was leading them in the opposite direction.

Mouser brushed Tammi's elbow. He whistled a single, very low note and then pointed by shifting his eyes. Her gaze followed his and registered comprehension.

Her nod was barely perceptible, just a hairline tilt of her jaw. But it told him everything that he needed to know.

The floor beneath their feet throbbed with an odd, distant beat. Irregular and yet organically steady. Perhaps a stuttering piece of machinery. Perhaps something else.

They descended into night. What little illumination there was struck busts and statues lining the corridor and cast a tangled, prickly forest of shadows.

"I've seen this one before," Bishop mused. The thing was five feet high, and balanced on a diamond-shaped brass stand. It was a warrior's mask, with a broad, curved axeblade ornament projecting from the helmet. The face was strong and severe.

"Where?" Prez asked. "No, wait. My . . . citadel had a collection of art from the old world." He squeezed his eyes shut, then looked again.

"From Gabon," he said. "A people called the Bakota."

There was another a little farther on. This was a complete figure, squatting with its hands in a prayerlike position. Prez had no comment.

Bishop ran a hundred images past closed lids. "Bayaka people. Zaire."

Prez nodded approval. "You know the motherland, my brother."

Bishop's smile glittered, and it was too dark to see how devoid of warmth or humor his eyes truly were. "Like coming home, isn't it?" He clapped Prez on the back, thinking, *Jigaboo*.

★ ★ ★

Prez held up a hand. "We've got something up here—"

And there was a scream behind them.

They turned in time to see Mouser lifted off his feet, carried up and toward the ceiling by fanged shadows.

Instantly, Corrinda snatched her bow and notched an arrow. She aimed carefully and fired it into the shadow figures flitting around Mouser. It struck one, to no effect.

"Quick!" she yelled, and handed a fistful of arrows to Top Nun.

The little cleric screamed, "You should pardon, God—no time for the whole *shmeer*. Bless these arrows!" and handed them back. Corrinda took aim and fired one after another.

The wounded shadows fluttered like crippled bats; they lowered the screaming Mouser back to the deck. He was covered with wounds, great claw marks that wept blood.

Top Nun immediately hunched over the wounded Thief and began to glow. Tammi asked, "Healing?"

"I should be playing dominoes, maybe? Excuse me for asking, but is all this trouble worth it for a little nosh? Could we maybe find a nice deli?"

Prez examined another frieze and crooked his finger at Tammi. "I *don't* like this."

"What have we got?"

It was a collage of metal and plastic, an impressionistic rendering of a head with two faces, a braided topknot of hair linking the foreheads. Eyes were inset hollows; teeth splayed out from angrily parted lips.

"This looks like a burial symbol," Prez said uncomfortably. "Someplace in Nigeria, I think. I think we've stumbled into another cemetery. But every one of these statues and images seems to be from a different culture, as if . . . as if . . ."

Coral began to back up. "*Oh,* grody."

"What is it?"

"Look. This is like McCannibals, you know?"

"She's right," Bishop said. "They raid the other villages. But in Africa, the dead are never really dead. Their souls can haunt. So they bury the bones here and steal idols from their victims, sealing each soul in with its own familiar god. Don't know what kind of spells they use to hold it together, but *Watchit!*"

It was too late. Coral shrieked as the frieze groaned and shivered. Dust and bits of plaster flaked from a thick, stubby arm as it grabbed her. "Eeeooowww!" she screamed, flailing with her hands to no effect. It tightened its grasp, and there was a terrible crunching sound. It threw Coral's limp body aside like a Barbie doll, blinked thick, crusty eyelids, and groaned again, wrenching itself from the wall.

It was an immense, ragtag spectacle of flattened tin cans and human femurs and ribs, brass and copper tubes and wiring, with squat stubby arms and legs.

It climbed down out of the wall, shook itself like a wet dog, and lumbered after them, teeth dripping dust. It groaned in a voice like splintering bones.

Ponderous it may have been, but with Corrinda's damaged knee and Mouser's injuries, it wasn't much slower than they were. Without hesitation, Twan and Tammi went to either side of Mouser. Shoulders set in his armpits, they heaved him up and carried him at a scamper.

Their allies were paces ahead of them. Bishop screamed, "Get it moving!" back over his shoulder, just before he rounded a corner.

Behind them they heard that ghastly cacophony, the splintering bone sound. The monster was at least twenty seconds back. The rest of their allies were out of sight. In gasps, Mouser began to whisper secrets.

"The stairway is blocked," Acacia said. "Bobo, what the hell *is* that creature?"

There had been something in the briefing, but it had gone clean out of Alex Griffin's mind. He would have been lost without the notes scrolling across his bronze shades. He read, "We entered the burial ground of the Ikoi tribe without performing proper ritual—"

Now he remembered: it was scripted as a battle, with no tricky little puzzles except that winning would give them access to a small round door. "We run, or we fight. There is no other option."

Distantly, but growing closer, they heard *crunch rriiip crrrunch* . . .

The knot of Adventurers stood with swords and staffs and magical implements at the ready, everyone snarling defiance and trying to get behind someone else.

"I think we can fight that thing," Tammi said. "We've got the Staff of Oranyan and"—another glance at Twan—"Oggun's Necklace. Let's go for it."

Acacia shook her head. "Not now. Not here. Let's find out more about combining the magic. We've lost too many people."

Bishop leaned out over the balcony, dreamily peering down into the next level. Mist roiled below, and, beneath it, cackling human throats.

"Listen to me," he said, spinning around. "We're *supposed* to fight that thing, but we're not *required* to."

Tammi frowned. "What are you babbling about?"

Crrrunch.

He tapped the door behind them, a sealed stairwell emblazoned with a radiation sign.

Tammi grimaced. "Nigel—are you blind? That's a Nekro seal. Instant death for the person who opens it." She lowered her voice. "We're not supposed to go through that door. You know that. This is an encounter. We fight!"

"Think about it," Bishop said urgently. "If we have this encounter, we'll lose maybe two people, maybe half of our healing points. My way we lose one person, sure. But *only* one person. You have to think flexibly."

Tammi paled. "That isn't done. You never throw away a member of your team."

"I'm not throwing him away. I'm *investing* him."

Alex couldn't believe his ears. Or his eyes: his bronze mirror shades were innocent of any hints from the GMs. "Ah—" Remain in character. "This symbol is *death*, Kahuna."

Rrrippp. Cruuuuunch.

"Yes, Bobo, we know. And so is that creature." Bishop took a quick scan of the Gamers. Corrinda was sitting against a wall with her leg straight out. The Mouser was getting up. Red still glowed in patches on his torso and right arm.

Bishop pulled them aside. "Listen. So far this Game has made hash of your abilities, Mouser. You're holding your team back. Corrinda, your knee is getting pretty bad; you know you'll have to drop out by tomorrow. Why not be sensible? Take this way out—I can offer you the chance to be voted 'Best Player' and win the Game Masters' discretionary award. What do you say?"

Mouser bared his sharp little teeth. "You say that to me again, you're gonna fall downstairs for a *month*."

"Another time. Corrinda?"

She narrowed her eyes. "Is this within the rules?"

"Nobody's ever tried it. *Next* time it'll be illegal. This time, it's a free ride."

Where does that stairway go? Alex thought. *Into the residential quarters?*

Jesus. And then out through a false wall into the next Gaming level. He couldn't think of an excuse to stop them. As long as they didn't vandalize . . .

Corrinda was weighing her options. "Let me get this straight. I sacrifice myself for the good of my team, and I'm a guaranteed hero."

"And you go down in the record books. This hasn't ever been done before. It will probably result in the 'Harding Principle.' "

She grinned evilly. "I like it."

Where was McWhirter? Dammit, Elmo thought, they were in the middle of the Game, and here came another problem. McWhirter deserved his breaks, yes, but Elmo had never seen so much rule-bending in all of his life.

McWhirter seemed to be preoccupied elsewhere, with some problem that had to do with the Security man now playing Bobo. The DreamTime routines were working automatically, but . . .

Elmo was getting the fits about this. Bishop had found one lulu of a loophole, and now that he had it, it would fit his profile to use it up. The only option was to change the rules concerning the Nekro seal, next time. This time it was too late.

Elmo wanted to do this one personally. "Doris, I'm going in," he said. He switched off his throat mike and stepped up onto the Virtual stage. Doris stepped back and watched: Elmo wasn't a masterful mime, but he was great fun to watch.

He adjusted his goggles. A Virtual Corrinda knelt in front of the door, actually picking the lock. Not a simple task, either—the locks were both mechanically and electronically sealed. Game locks could be just as difficult to crack as real ones; many Thieves developed actual criminal skills.

Corrinda used a combination of fiber-optic probe and computer tap. She anchored herself into the data line, opened it up, and used a processor in her belt pod to determine its protocol.

Twenty seconds later, the door clicked open.

Elmo spread his arms . . .

There was a thing in the doorway, a creature made of dust and cobwebs, something so old that it had fallen almost completely apart, holding itself together only by the application of dark magicks, arts beyond the ken of man.

Corrinda's triumphant expression gave way to terror.

She tried to scream, but it was cut short by the touch of a spectral hand. She and the creature both fell to dust.

Corrinda's ears buzzed. The buzz became Elmo's voice, a voice as warm and welcoming as a blizzard. "Kindly roll to the side. Your character is irrevocably dead. Not just for this Game. Corrinda Scout/Thief has been registered as dead in the IFGS computers."

Her Virtual world went gray. In dull confusion, she watched her companions travel on in the land of the living without her.

The door shut behind them.

As soon as it did, a black-suited stage troll popped out of a hidden door and hoisted her to her feet.

"That," he said, "was the stupidest stunt I've ever seen."

"I—I reinjured my knee. It was locking up again, *click* every time I move. I would have let my team down."

"You should have," the troll said disgustedly. "You're not just out of the Game. Your *character's* dead."

He led her through a side maze of passages, leading her ultimately to Security, and Gaming Central.

She was fascinated by the room, by the huge arc of ceiling and the background sounds of computers and human activity.

Richard Lopez examined her curiously. "Congratulations," he said. "You have just made history."

She managed a smile.

"Bishop played you very well."

Her smile faltered. "What do you mean?"

"He got you kicked out of the Game. People have made it through with injuries before. Worse, you are dead-dead, lady. Corrinda the Thief is gone. Forever. You spent eight years building her up into a Thirteenth Level Thief? Gone. Start over from scratch, if you can." His dark face was even darker with rage. "I talk to my friends, and I know everyone." His tone was deadly quiet.

"But Bishop suggested it!"

"And you can be sure he knew the consequences. To you. If you were the Bishop, you might get away with it. You're not. There is only one Bishop."

He paused. Temporarily, his anger had been leavened by pity. "And that may be one too many. *Well.* You might as well break into civvies. Settle back, take care of that knee, and watch the

Game." He motioned with his head to the troll: the audience was over.

Corrinda was escorted out. She felt confused, uncertain, and more than a little scared.

Lopez returned to his palette. Everything was working smoothly right now. All of the routines were running, and he was just beginning to feel fatigue. How long had he been on duty? Twelve hours? That was fine. Gamers should start breaking down for early dinner soon. With the Game divided into two main groups, that was manageable.

He scanned the room. Everything was going well, but—

Where was McWhirter?

Tony McWhirter was exhausted. It had been a long, tiring day so far, and it wasn't over yet. Game Masters were allotted breaks during the eight to sixteen hours of daily up-time. In California Voodoo there would be more free-floating optional breaks than usual, because the Gamers had been given no solid down-times. Even so, he felt guilty being away from the desk.

But he had to see Millicent.

He used a holo wall in one of the empty offices outside the Game regions. Dream Park was closed down, but many of the executive offices were still open.

She answered after three beeps, just a still photo of her face and a voice saying, "Yes?"

"Don't worry about your makeup. It's just Tony McWhirter."

The air rippled, and the real Millicent appeared in front of him, still wearing elements of her Mallsters makeup. Despite his fatigue, Tony giggled.

"You've found yourself. How did it go?"

Her smile was marginal. "Fine. I liked it a lot better than I like this." She tapped a stack of paper on her desk.

"What have you got?"

She had two computer screens on simultaneously. "I've been tracing back her financial records, including a few things that I really shouldn't have been looking into. Thanks for the passkey program, Tony. I'm now a partner in crime."

"I've wanted to corrupt you for—well, months. What did you get?"

"I did a search for unusual deposits or withdrawals in the past six months, anything to indicate sudden pressure. Nothing. I did come up with a smallish check to a private detective agency, anno-tated 'services rendered,' but that was over a year ago, and there was no repeat. No idea what that might have been."

"Can we get Vail on this line?"

Millicent typed in Vail's number and got a busy signal, followed by an encode that he would be off in a minute. "What did you get, Tony?" she asked.

"Odd pattern of betting on California Voodoo. Somebody with insider knowledge has been betting on Army to win. Big money. I've told Alex, and now he's in as a rooftop guide."

The air fizzed again. Norman Vail wasn't in his office at Dream Park. He was at CMC. His home office there was roomier than the one allotted him at the Park. "Good evening, Tony. Millicent."

Tony inclined his head in acknowledgment. "I've found some-thing of interest. Maybe. I think."

"Yes?" Vail said noncommittally. His perfect, even teeth glis-tened, as if he brushed them with glycerine.

"I was looking, ah, looking into the gambling patterns for California Voodoo."

Vail's lips twitched. He'd caught the hesitation. Tony plunged on. "I came across some weird shifting in the odds."

Vail listened as Tony explained. "Yes. I see what you mean. Mil-licent? Anything so far?"

"No extraordinary expenditures, no unusual patterns of absence for Ms. Crayne."

"Hmmm." Vail sat back in his chair, rubbing his fingers along the bridge of his nose. "I am attempting to fill in the blanks on the unfortunate young lady. Harmony arranged for her confidential medical and psychological records to be relayed from Tacoma. At this point I have a complete autopsy. Millicent, I assume we can have financial and telephone records eventually?"

"We already have all transactions or calls made from Cowles terminals. I'm hunting down the rest."

"Fine." Vail folded his hands. "We are looking for an influence which might have caused an employee of Cowles Industries to betray a trust. To violate security in a very specific manner. McWhirter?"

"If my guess means anything, she pulled a copy of the interior security map of MIMIC out of the file and copied it." Tony paused. "How long did Alex know her?"

"Just eight weeks, as far as I can tell. She was hired in Tacoma after he left. She came down here to pave the way for the eventual opening of MIMIC to the Barsoom Project, and to establish liaisons with Alex Griffin."

"She certainly managed *that*," Millicent muttered. "Would she have taken over Security?"

"No. She would have assisted the eventual chief."

Tony said, "She could have resented that—"

"Suspicion of sexism or some such?" Vail's lips pursed. "Not a rational position—there were a half-dozen people with greater seniority. I'd like to examine your data, if you don't mind."

Millicent and Tony nodded. Millicent immediately began to feed the material over to Vail.

Tony doodled up a window and watched the numbers flow through the scenery, Millicent's office, and Vail's rec room. He hoped that Norman Vail could do something. The man was ruthless, and absolutely committed to Dream Park.

"That's it," Millicent said. "Anything else, Doctor?" When Vail shook his head, she popped out. Tony was about to do the same—

"McWhirter, would you pause for a moment, please?"

Tony paused. Vail templed his fingers and smiled pleasantly. "Tony," he said, "I think that we have much in common."

Tony didn't see it that way. He said nothing.

"Neither of us cares for the niceties of social restriction. Both of us believe in getting the job done. I was wondering if I could count on your . . . unusual skills, if need be."

Computer skills, of course. "If it will get the job done."

"They may be the only thing which can."

Tony nodded uneasily and winked out.

Norman Vail watched information flow through the air before him. A printer in his desk was spewing out sheets of paper, fanfolding into a neat stack. He sighed, pulled an oversized pipe out of his desk drawer and stuffed it with contraband tobacco, lit it, and took a drag.

With McWhirter in the fold, he could count on an endless supply of information. McWhirter wouldn't ask too many questions. One merely pointed such a person in the proper direction and gave him an excuse to do what he wanted to do in the first place.

Vail closed his eyes, and unbidden, his mind formed thin blue lines against perfect black.

Some were vertical, bisected a moment later by a series of horizontals. Along the horizontal axis he wrote *Crayne*. Along the vertical, *Griffin*. As an afterthought, he expanded the imaginary construct into three dimensions and on the third axis wrote *Bishop*.

What could Bishop have offered Sharon? Not money—that had been established. She earned more than she spent, and had no regular savings program.

Sex? Bishop had retired to Toronto. He had only been in the United States three times in the last two years—and Sharon Crayne hadn't been in Canada at all. Hardly a torrid romance.

What did Sharon Crayne want?

What had attracted her to security work? Or better yet, driven her from police work?

Ah. It was there in her personnel record. She had been injured in the line of duty. Clean wound, beam weapon, but it had damaged her uterus. She would never bear children.

Vail examined that. Sharon Crayne had come from a family of four children. She was the second child. Happy childhood in a conservative Catholic family. How would she feel about childlessness?

Not a serious problem. Healthy ovaries; hire a bearer mother . . . hmm?

There were other avenues to explore, but for some reason, that one stuck in Vail's mind. He wondered why. There was something of interest there, he was certain.

Norman Vail trusted his hunches.

Chapter Twenty-three

Mouser

"Riddle me this," Captain Cipher said, merrily scouring the pantry. "How should one react to rumors of an imminent zombie attack?"

Twan stopped searching, eyes narrowed, then widening. "Alimentary, my dear Cipher," she said. "I would take that notion with a grain of salt."

"Yesss!" and they both broke up chortling. The apartment larder was well stocked, containing every seasoning imaginable. More to the point, its inhabitants showed their contempt for their blood pressure—they had samples of every sodium product imaginable: salt, celery salt, onion salt, garlic salt, lemon salt, and rock salt. Lopez's zombies were in for a rough, if flavorful, time.

Food was the next priority. Refrigerators and pantries were raided as Gamers stocked up on their supplies. When the backpacks were filled, the nine surviving members of the UC/Apple/Gen-Dyn caravan split off to bedroom or bathroom or dining room as preference dictated.

There was no vandalism, and very little gratuitous mess. After all, the owners of these apartments were probably watching and might well request a private conference with any vandals.

Coral's mirrored brother assured the Adventurers that there were comestibles on the twelfth level. Griffin watched Twan wrestle with that one: her partner, Tammi, was hot for the challenge. Their teammates were exhausted.

"And what kind of danger do you see?" Twan asked.

Tod's image did its best to keep them on track. "Nothing too gnarly, dudes."

Tammi made an anxious-puppy sound to Twan. Twan shook her head regretfully.

"Oh, all right," the warrior Trog sighed, giving in. "No more challenges today."

"Praise the Lord," Top Nun said, and pulled on an apron. She began to rummage through the kitchen.

Bishop sprang the lock on a closet door and grinned in satisfaction at three sets of diving equipment inside. "We're in luck," he said. "My partners were carrying the scubas when they—" Forefinger across throat.

Prez frowned. "You found diving equipment in the Gaming areas?"

"Yes. It follows that we are to do some diving, yes? There was probably treasure in the lake, topside. There is talk of 'flooded levels' at the tenth and eleventh. Anybody noticed that we're starting to run into technology? Better be ready, eh?"

He prowled through the suites. Everyone was slowing down. Eyelids drooped with fatigue. The aroma of cooking food filled the suites. If he dropped a little of his own control, Bishop could feel his own fatigue. But there was still so much to do . . .

So he dove into the cooking with great good humor, whipping up a batch of dinner omelets that had Mati and Prez cooing in admiration. Cooking was, after all, just another skill, another way to display excellence.

And excellence is my business, Bishop hummed to himself. *My only business.*

Alex sat against the wall with his knees drawn up to his chest. He had done his own cooking for so long that the prospect of sampling someone else's—especially Bishop's—actually made him nervous.

The apartment was one of a double suite. It was the most that he could do to keep them confined to this area. "Bobo" had relayed a stern warning: "The gods do not take mischief lightly. Take what you need, but leave offerings, and leave things exactly as you found them."

Weary nods all around.

There was a joint recreation room between the two suites. Twan and Tammi set their sleeping bags near a central fireplace there.

Prez took the first watch, to be relieved in two hours by Tammi. Official down-time was declared.

Tony McWhirter got back to Gaming Central, somewhat surprised by the general air of bemusement. "*Qué pasa*, Sis?" he asked one of his assistants.

"Welll . . ." "Sis" was a lantern-jawed, rawboned Oklahoman. With another thirty pounds he could probably place third in a Conan the Barbarian look-alike contest. "Looks like Bishop just found another way to break the rules."

Tony rolled his eyes. "What is it this time?"

Sis explained. Tony's first impulse was disbelief; his second, admiration. "Never thought I'd see kamikaze Gamers. We'd better find out who those rooms belong to. Offer compensation out of the discretionary fund. Full reimbursement for any foodstuffs—hell, and housekeeping for a month. Aarrrgh!"

Sis was startled. "Tony?"

"Bishop's found scuba. They won't have to go back to the roof. Dammit! They'll miss the fish. All that frigging work and they're going to miss the fish." He saw Sis staring and said, "Never mind. Anything else?" An isolated dot in an external hallway caught his attention; he pointed. "That?"

"That's Tammi Romati's kid, Mouser," Sis said. "Wanna play-back?" Sis made magic; the scene wound back at terrific speed. "This is just before they broke into the apartment."

Mouser, carried between Twan and Tammi, lost his patchy red glow: healing spells had taken effect.

Tammi watched for the monster, while Mouser shared secrets with Twan. "Appelion said to look for an obelisk, right? This one would have to be about the size of the Washington Monument. And the door's on this level! If—"

Twan laid her finger across Mouser's lips, her eyes sparkling. She slipped Oggun's Necklace over his head. "You're the only one who can do it. I believe in you, Mouser."

The boy glowed with pride.

The allies trooped through the forbidden door. The Troglodykes lagged, with Tammi and Twan carrying the Mouser's weight. As they passed through, Mouser dropped back . . . and ran like a Thief, back the way they had come . . .

Tony said, "Solved it, did he? Bright kid. I wonder if Bishop knows? Those ladies hold everyone's attention. You hardly notice any of the other Trogs."

"They've been whittled down to four. Bishop'll know the kid's gone. Believe it."

"Maybe. Thanks, Sis." Tony swung his chair around and watched the Gamers as they prowled through the suites in present time. Prez had barricaded the door. Food was warming on the stove. Showers were running.

These folks were down for the night.

A parallel display detailed the actions of the seven survivors of the Tex-Mits and Army teams. They were skulking toward the fourteenth level, with nothing between them and their dinner cache. It would take them an hour to eat. Dinner was heavy on the protein, designed to make them feel logy, to encourage sleep.

A third display showed the Mouser moving toward a circular door. It was set flush to that tilted wall; nobody but a Thief would have seen it. The Mouser was injured, with lowered hit points, but he was wearing the necklace and carrying one of the magic mirrors—enough magic to light a city. The door was close, but a towering monster made of trash was closer yet. Would the Thief's power protect him?

Tony's body cried for sleep, but this was what he lived for. He watched.

With myriad creaks and groans, the trash monster had shoehorned itself into the wall again. Only its flattened-tin eyes still shifted, comically huge. They were looking right at the Mouser.

The Mouser was a statue, perhaps of a Viking, a small warrior propped on his spear. His nose twitched, itching to sneeze. He kept the air moving in and out, without turbulence. He was the image of Wisdom, or maybe of Calm, a statue whose pedestal resembled the enameled white brick of a washer-dryer.

The monster's eyes swiveled away, glacially slow.

The Mouser dropped softly to the concrete and moved away like a snake. There was no cover here—nothing to protect him but his Thief's talent as augmented by Twan's spell. In moments he was beneath the faintly glowing circle on the tilted wall.

Virtual imagery revealed a tiny hole, a niche big enough to admit, say, a forefinger. It was maybe six feet above the floor.

Mouser pulled a set of probes from his pouch. He selected one, then stretched his arms straight up and began to work on the lock.

He clicked about in the hole, but he couldn't *see* what he was doing, and couldn't really *feel* what he was doing, with his arms straight up like that. He felt silly. This wasn't working . . .

The trash monster *skreek*ed like an automobile being crushed. It began to pull itself out of the frieze.

Mouser's head whipped frantically around. He needed a new idea, and fast. In a shadowed corner there lay a fallen statue, a copper bust of some queen of the dead. He scampered over to the head and pushed it back under the circular door. It felt like papier-mâché, much lighter than he had expected, but it supported his weight.

Now he could see into the lock while he probed.

The trash monster strode toward him.

Craaack. Rrrrip crrrunch . . .

He had no time. And then, when it was almost too late, he remembered something: the Necklace of Oggun. This was a physical talisman, a warrior's talisman. Maybe he was thinking too damned much like a Thief?

He twisted his thin lips into his best approximation of a fighting snarl and smashed his fist into the door.

And through the surface.

God *damn*.

He swung the other fist, and that penetrated, too. Emboldened by success, he ripped the door from its hinges and sent it rolling at the oncoming terror. It struck the monster's thick stubby knees; the trash monster went down in a shapeless heap. Mouser giggled and clapped his hands with glee.

He could hardly wait for puberty. Strength was *great*.

He stepped inside.

He was nose to nose with a blank flat surface, without even a sign of a lock to be picked.

The trash monster was getting up.

Mouser looked up and realized that he was at the bottom of about forty feet of near-vertical shaft. A set of knobs could serve as a ladder, badly, he decided. But the trash monster was about to reach through the shredded doorway. Mouser's thews swelled, anticipating the challenge—

Then a Thief's good common sense reasserted itself. He shifted his bow into a more comfortable position across his back and scampered up the shaft like a little monkey.

The knobs were finished to provide good traction, better for climbing than he had feared. Better still, ten feet up they became indented rungs, even more secure. He was panting a little by the time he reached the top and found himself facing another circular doorway and three glowing buttons. With his free hand he fished out a small, ornate mirror.

"Appelion? Wakey wakey."

A swirl of smoke, then a small silent flash of lightning. Appelion's frozen face reappeared, eyelashes dappled with frost. "The dead sleep soundly, Mouser. What have you done *this* time?"

"Listen: there was an airlock in the base of the obelisk at the sixth level. I climbed up the shaft, and I'm hanging at the top now." He looked down over his shoulder. It was a *long* way to the bottom. "I should be about to enter the tip, which should be the control cabin. The tip of an obelisk is a pyramid, and there was a pyramid on the roof."

"Ni-ice!"

"Yeah. Anything you'd like to warn me about before I open that door?"

"You're ahead of me, actually. Pyramids have deadfalls, right? Watch out for security. And if you didn't close the outer door, the inner door of an airlock shouldn't open."

"Aargh. Okay, stand by." Mouser tucked the mirror in a vest pocket. "Can you hear me?"

"Yeah." Muffled.

Mouser looked down at the bottom of the shaft, to the ruined doorway. Crap. No way to seal that *now*. "I'm going to use brute force."

"*You?*"

"Twan gave me the necklace from the jewelry store." Mouser set himself, then slammed the heel of his hand at the thick circle of door. The door ripped free and fell inward with an almighty clatter.

A slanting beam of sunlight lit his way as he moved inside.

The interior was a maze of stairs and platforms at different levels. A grillwork elevator shaft ran up the wall, and Mouser cautiously stepped onto the platform. There were two glyphs on the elevator's wall, one reminiscent of sky, the other of earth. Cautiously, he brought his palm near the "sky" symbol. The symbol glowed orange, and the elevator began to rise.

He rose past storage tanks, and weird computeresque constructs of ceramic glass, and what might have been huge engines. When he reached the top, the platform sighed to a halt. Mouser disembarked and found himself in the main cabin.

It was more than just a control center—it was living quarters, as well. On the platforms—he counted nine—were banks of equipment in a horseshoe array, primitive hardware compared to what one might find in a Gaming Central; and flat couches.

One of the couches had an occupant. It was held in place by a score of flexible white straps: a web of seat belts. It might as well have been mummy wrappings; the occupant wasn't going any- where. It was a skeleton. A flatfish skeleton, it looked like, though with an uncharacteristically large skull and a wide hollow spine, and odd pocks along the bones of the jaw.

The pilot had worn a crown of sorts: an ellipse of gold studded with gems half-covered its long, capacious skull.

Sunlight poured through a slit of a window, high up. Mouser climbed to that level and looked out. Then he pulled out the mirror and faced it through the window.

"Appelion?"

"Excellent, kid. You're on the roof!"

"But of course. The tip of an obelisk is a pyramid, *I* always say."

"Everybody loves a smart aleck, *I* always say. What's next?"

"There's a crown. It's sitting on the skeleton of a Nommo, maybe the pilot or captain. Maybe it runs the ship, direct nerve induction or like that, but it *looks* just like every crown you've ever seen. I'm going to take it."

"Careful, kid," the dead man cautioned. "This has all been too easy, so far."

"Watch this, Unc."

Mouser doffed his cloak and spread it on the elevator platform; he was going to need some cushioning for the next stunt.

Then he tiptoed back to the crown. Deep breath . . . shield his hand with his soft cap . . .

In a single smooth motion, he snatched the crown, flicked it into the elevator, and dove after it.

Something slapped his heels.

He rolled into the platform before he looked behind him.

The captain's bones were wearing translucent flesh. Hot damn, a Nommo zombie! Ectoplasmic tendrils writhed around the mouth. The thing's tail swiped futilely at where Mouser had been; and then it flopped off the couch and humped toward him.

Mouser pushed the lower button. He set the crown on his head, then reached for his bow. Try *everything*.

The elevator began to descend.

He heard a babbling; his vision was obscured by green line-sketches and pink hieroglyphics. The crown must be trying to talk to him. He snatched it off; he couldn't handle distractions now.

The dead Nommo flopped through the doorway and braced itself in the shaft with its tendrils, crawling after him. He held his breath. It was going to be a close race . . .

He nocked an arrow and aimed, prepared to sell his life dearly. The mass of a zombie flatfish dropped toward him, sank as if through water—and light bathed his feet.

The falling elevator had given him the top twenty inches of lower doorway. He rolled through it, landed on hands and feet, and kept rolling.

Ghost-tendrils groped out through the widening opening. Mouser could see the Nommo trying to slide under the door. In a moment it would be through. Mouser ran to the ladder, whooping.

Chapter Twenty-four

A Lie

A fire roared in the rec room's artificial fireplace, throwing vaguely human shadows onto the walls. Griffin sat with his back to a bookcase, finishing an omelet. He hated to admit it, but Bishop was a hell of a cook.

A soft voice above him asked, "Mind if I sit down, Bobo?"

Before he could answer, Acacia sat down next to him, balancing a plate of food on her knees.

"So," Alex said. "Your name is Panthesilea?"

"Yes. I come from the domed cities, an enclave far to the east. We came in peace." Her brown eyes were soft. "*I* come in peace, Bobo."

She chewed thoroughly, giving it her full attention. "I was wondering . . . if there is more than one reason for your presence."

Alex's tongue teased a scrap of bacon from between his teeth. He should have felt numb at Acacia's proximity, but instead the sensation was closer to dry heat.

"Duty," he said, vaguely disassociated. "I am here for duty."

"And not adventure? Or love?"

In the recreation room behind them, Top Nun had found a guitar and was beginning to strum. He hadn't noticed when it started, but his ears perked up when she said, "I've got one for you, Cipher. Listen to this—"

Letitia has a large one, and so has cousin Luce.
Eliza has a small one, though large enough for use.

Beneath a soft and glossy curl, each Lass has one in front.
To find it in an animal you at the tail must hunt . . .

Acacia grinned. "Mati's riddling Captain Cipher again. It won't do her any good."

"He's good?"

"He's a freak. He's got no practical skills at all, but throw him into a trivia game, or funny math, and there's no one better." She caught herself. "And he is a mighty Wizard."

"The world needs more magic," Alex said, a little surprised at himself.

Hermaphrodites have none; Mermaids are minus, too.
Nell Gwynn possessed a double share if books we read are true.
It's used by all in Nuptial Bliss, in Carnal Pleasures found.
Destroy it, Life becomes extinct, the world is but a sound . . .

Acacia had finished her food, and she daubed at her mouth with the corner of a napkin. She stood and extended her hand to Alex. "Walk with me?"

"Wait one," he said, and whispered, "Tony?"

A cricket-voice in his ear said, "Here."

"Watch Bishop."

"Absolutely."

"And get an inventory on these apartments."

"Got it. Out."

"Ready," he told her.

Lasciviousness here has its sources, Harlots its use apply.
Without it Lust has never been, and even Love would die.
Now tell me what this wonder is, but pause before you guess it.
If you are mother, maid, or man, I swear you don't possess it."

Cipher lazily said, "The letter *L*." And Top Nun groaned.

Acacia laughed and led Alex out.

She collected her bedroll in both arms and threw her head back, hipshot, in an attitude of naked challenge.

Alex followed her out into the hallway and down past the other bedroom, into a modular living room.

The modular capsule hadn't been fitted in. Acacia punched up the safety code, and the weather wall rolled up, exposing blue-black desert sky and night-gray mountains.

Stars clustered beneath and above them in uncountable thousands, like handfuls of diamond dust floating on a warm pool of oil.

Acacia busied herself in creating a nest, pulling together cushions, a mattress, pillows, and her bedroll. Finally she sat down, drawing him to sit next to her.

"Hello, stranger," she said, suddenly shy. She seemed a little smaller, more vulnerable.

"Am I talking to Acacia or Panthesilea?"

"Acacia. You're not here to play, Alex. What is this?"

Alex sighed. Relief was surely not the proper emotion, but it was as if the burden of maintaining an impossible deceit had lifted from him. He stretched; his shoulders relaxed; his spine seemed to expand upward. Acacia watched in astonishment.

"I need to know, and I need to know now," he said bluntly. "Was Bishop with you Tuesday night?"

"Part of the time." She kept her voice even. "I came in late. Then he went out, and came back in. There were a lot of parties going, Alex."

He watched her eyes closely. "One of our security personnel died Tuesday night. There could be a connection to this Game. Can you account for your whereabouts?"

She shook her head slowly, for the first time feeling her disquiet blossom into fear. "I was in my room, alone."

Alex cursed to himself. Acacia was as much of a suspect as Bishop. And with thousands of Gamers in the hotels, and hundreds of parties, how hard would it be for Bishop to establish an alibi? Or a dozen alibis?

"I'll only ask this once," he said. "Are you fixing this Game?"

Acacia's stomach sank. It had all come down to this. Bishop was a Thief, a liar, a manipulator. But he wasn't a killer. She was certain of that, as certain as a woman could be of a man she . . . cared for. She could never have opened her heart like that, never have responded like that . . .

Then, why were you afraid? You have no proof, she told herself. *And if you say anything, and Nigel is innocent, then millions will be lost, to no avail. And even if he—*

If he did it . . .

There would be time later for prosecution. Buy time to think.

She knew damn well she had hurt no one, but she might still be implicated. She would need that money for her defense. As Nigel would need it for his. *And after all, he's innocent until proven guilty.*

Mother of Mercy, Nigel just couldn't . . .

It isn't difficult to fool a lie detector, or a superb inquisitor. One technique involves deliberately misunderstanding the question. The question Alex had asked was, "Are you fixing this Game?"—a question she had anticipated.

The question she *answered* was, "Does Gaming bore you?"

"Jesus, no," she said fervently. "Alex, I love competing, more than anything in the world. Don't you know me better than to ask that?"

Alex searched the beautiful face he knew so well. Something flickered there, some unease . . .

But he couldn't call her reply a lie, and his gut instinct told him that she was no murderer. Whatever she was concealing, it was not that.

He wanted to believe her . . .

And he wanted to believe her a liar. It would have made everything so damned simple. Case solved. Sleep well, Sharon. You made a mistake—and paid for it. But I brought the bastard down.

Now, he felt lost. Where to start? Unless there was physical proof, or a solid motive, or a link between victim and prospective perpetrator . . .

He had zip.

He felt tired, and old, and beaten.

A dot of light flashed across the horizon—the real horizon, wasn't it? Could there be a hologram going? It would have to be *huge*, and to what end? So that was a flying car zipping just above the horizon, heading over to Yucca Valley.

There was a glow over the hills to the north. Was that the new spaceport? And what would be coming in there? There was a very distant hum, perhaps the sound of a helicopter. They were building things out there, things that would have some meaning in the new world that was coming.

And he, Alex Griffin, wouldn't be a part of it. Sharon would have been. But Sharon was dead now, had been cold for sixty hours.

Clutching at straws, Alex bore back down: he and Acacia had met during the South Seas Treasure Game. There, Tony McWhirter had used her to get in and commit industrial espionage. Tony truly believed she had been duped. Could it be happening again? Or could she be partially guilty, and afraid to talk?

"So now you're with Nigel Bishop?" he asked casually.

She smiled. There was only moonlight and starlight and the distant glow around them. Alex rolled over and looked up at the luminous height of MIMIC, allowing himself to feel awe.

"As much as anyone could be."

"Where is he now?" He watched her starlit face flicker with uncertainty. And then he was sure. *She doesn't know what he's done. She has no idea.*

"I'm cold," Acacia said, her voice a child's. She had snuggled up closer to him. Her body smoldered, like a coal wrapped in cotton. She draped the sleeping bag over them both, concentrating enough heat to bake potatoes.

Someone had found a music system, and from one of MIMIC's other alcoves drifted a soft, seductive rhythm. It seemed to wrap around them, separating Alex from the pain and the suspicions. He gazed out over the desert. It seemed so open, so direct and unsullied. It reminded him of another Alex Griffin, a younger Alex Griffin. The night's chill enveloped him.

Acacia sensed his withdrawal. Her head lowered, until she was staring down the blanket, at the floor.

The moonlight silvered her hair, her eyes, the long elegant line of her throat. He remembered the times of holding, and striving together. Remembered when they had tried to love each other.

They had failed. Failed each other, and themselves. And what, if anything, did he owe this magnificent creature now? The benefit of the doubt?

"Are you ever sorry we didn't work out, Alex?"

"I was. I'm not."

She chewed on that for almost a minute. Then: "Do you—have someone?"

"No," he said quietly. "No one."

Alex felt that chill penetrate into his bones, transforming him, as if with some subtle Dream Park magic, into a man of ice.

"I'm sorry about us, Alex." She laid her head on his shoulder with surprising tenderness. "I'm just your garden-variety man-eating adrenaline junkie." She choked back a small, sad laughing sound. "That's not what you need."

He smiled bleakly. "And what *do* I need?"

"If you knew what you needed, you'd find it. And hold it."

If you knew . . .

If truth had been spoken in the past hour, it was contained in those three words. *If you knew.* And in the paralyzing light of that truth, all thoughts of lies died quiet deaths. And Alex Griffin, flensed of lies and thoughts of lies, gazed unblinkingly into his own heart.

They stayed that way for a time, and then she pulled her face away and looked up at him, their lips an inch apart. She kissed him, not passionately, but with her lips parted slightly. Her eyes shone.

We're both in a box, Alex, they said. *We both hide in a world of dreams. We can tell lies about that, but we know the truth. And always have. But couldn't we tell just one more lie, just to each other, just for tonight?*

He shook his head silently.

"I'm through with lies," Alex said, so softly that the words were lost in the breeze howling in from the east.

So they sat there, sharing the moonlight. Acacia turned her head away from him. Alex thought he heard, or saw, or felt her crying.

But he couldn't be sure. It might, after all, have been the wind.

A few words to "Brother" Prez, and Nigel Bishop was out the door. *A little reconnaissance, if you please.*

Nigel Bishop moved through shadows. Considering all that had happened, he was at peace. Sharon Crayne's death had been tucked down somewhere inside him. He would deal with it later. Later . . .

(But from time to time came an image, a stray memory. Just the sight of Sharon Crayne, submerged in water, a thread of blood drifting, curling up from her nostril, dispersing in the warm, oily water . . .)

Later, dammit!

He forced that phantasm from his mind. He triggered his Virtual apparatus, its slimline visor and auditory channels. Sharon's map floated, superimposed upon reality.

MIMIC's security system was not yet completely in place. There were still pockets where the various line-of-sight, auditory, and infrared devices failed to overlap properly, giving an incomplete image or, better still, no image at all. Given further adjustments and modifications, all of those gaps would be filled in.

But for now . . .

Bishop floated through the hallway, remaining in shadow, picking locks to move through fire doors after disabling their alarm systems.

He knew which doors, which hallways, and which passages to challenge. Always. He was never deep-scanned. A few cameras or sensors picked up his ghost, but then there were Gamers in the building anyway, weren't there?

It wasn't strictly *illegal* for him to be out and about, was it?

The computer pod on his belt sensed the scans, targeted them, and recorded their points of origin. He slipped here and there and there, and as he went, he busied himself with the real function of his trip, the true intent, unguessed by all.

Although Sharon, in her final moments, had had a glimmer of a clue.

Sharon, her dead eyes staring at him, that thread of crimson drifting from her left nostril. It had been so bright. Terribly bright.

Bishop ground his knuckles against his temples, swallowed hard. *Bitch. You twisting, faithless bitch. It was* your *fault, damn you to hell. It was—*

Leave me alone!

Careful. He had almost screamed it aloud, that time. Almost. Close, close, tippy-toe.

Horrified, he heard his thoughts devolve to a giggle.

He had to be calm. He had to finish what he had begun. He should be safe: there was no evidence. Acacia and Griffin would be making the naked pretzel by now, and that suited him fine. Griffin would doubtless try to pump her for information. And that slut couldn't keep her legs together with a C-clamp.

Griffin.

Bishop pulled out of the way as a roving spy eye glided along a track in the upper corner. He steadied himself. It would be a bizarre coincidence if he fell afoul of a Gaming trap just now, wouldn't it? And he wouldn't be surprised if the Game Masters were figuring out how to bend the odds to get to him. They must be foaming at the mouth by now.

Griffin.

He was annoyed with his mind. It didn't want to obey him. Why the interest in Dream Park's rent-a-cop? True, Griffin had a certain style. A spark of challenge.

Not intellectual challenge, of course. Griffin was no match there. But the man had a certain brute physical cunning, combined with enough desperately cultivated coordination that he was probably competent in combative movement. Bishop thought little of physical combat, although he was, of course, a master of its intricacies. Alex Griffin's head might be a trophy worth having . . .

Damn it! There was no time to think of things like that. It was insanity. There was only the job. And if the Game had become unexpectedly lethal, that was just more spice, wasn't it?

Wasn't it?

Alex Griffin.

There was unfinished business there, something for the two of them to say to each other when all of this was through. Bishop wiped his hand across the back of his neck, and it came away cold and clammy.

Bishop heard that giggle percolating again. He was beginning to *like* the sound.

And that scared him most of all.

Chapter Twenty-five

Autopsy

Power had always fascinated Dr. Norman Vail. It delighted him to see what power could accomplish in the right hands. His hands.

In less than twelve hours, the money and leverage of Cowles Industries had opened Sharon Crayne's life like a filing cabinet, inundating him with a mountain of information.

Vail had pored over it for three hours before Millicent, Harmony, and Tony McWhirter joined him.

All were exhausted but driven by an almost morbid curiosity. What might the psychologist have to say that was so damned important, this late at night?

Vail's skin had a translucent quality, as if fatigue and strain had aged him in a manner that mere time could not.

He waved them toward his desk. "Come in, please. Come in."

They seated themselves, dragging. Harmony looked askance at folders heaped on Vail's desk. Sharon Crayne had been a human being. How could anyone's life survive such scrutiny?

A citizen's only hope for privacy was the sheer volume of information. Gathering data was easy and cheap. Sorting and culling it was a multibillion-dollar industry, resulting in AI systems like ScanNet.

"There are patterns here," Vail said. "Lots of them. It would be difficult to explain the exact path of my reasoning, but I may have found some loose threads. With these in hand, we can begin the unraveling process.

"The question is: Was Sharon Crayne bent? The probable answer: Not in the sense of selling us out for money. She worked too hard, for too long, and her basic reward seemed to be the work itself. Her personal liaisons were usually brief, intense relationships connected with work, perhaps reinforcing her conception of Job as Family."

"What about her real family?" Millicent asked.

"This is where the pieces began to come together. But remember, please: this is a fabric of supposition."

"Understood," Harmony said. "Please proceed."

"All right. Sharon Crayne, twenty-six years old. Never married. Little contact with her family, especially her father. There is strong evidence of guilt or shame in connection with her relationship with her mother. Strained. Competitive 'outsider' would probably best describe her relationship with her two sisters and brother. Second of four children. Eldest daughter. Evidence that she assumed many maternal roles around the house when her mother, an architect, buried herself in her projects. During the latter years of her family's stable period, her father was unemployed."

Vail paused, focusing upon his guests as if just discovering their presence in the room. "Does any of this strike a pattern?"

An unpleasant notion surfaced in Millicent's mind and then submerged again, like some particularly large and ugly serpent.

"All right, then." Vail tapped a button on his desk, and a color image of Sharon Crayne's naked body appeared behind his back. Harmony was aghast. Vail barely seemed to notice that it was there. "Full autopsy of Sharon Crayne noted a fully healed, professionally rendered surgical scar, approximately ten centimeters long, in the abdominal cavity. The scar would have been made when Sharon was approximately fourteen years old. According to a medical interview at the time, she claimed it was an appendectomy scar."

"Ah . . . is that unreasonable?" Harmony choked.

"Dr. Eva Reeves, the pathologist, noted that the scar is atypical in size, shape, and location for appendectomy—although the appendix went, too."

Tony McWhirter wrenched his gaze away from the levitated dead woman. He looked pale. "I don't get it."

"I believe I'm prepared to offer an opinion."

Harmony felt embarrassed and nauseated. Sharon's body rotated in front of them like a Thanksgiving turkey.

"Dr. Vail," Tony asked, voice strained. "Would you please provide some shielding for that hologram?"

Vail looked back over his shoulder. "Is there something—oh. I see." He tapped a few buttons, whispered a few words, and Sharon's body became an anatomy text, a technical drawing—just as explicit, but quite impersonal.

And that might have been even worse.

"Now—this was the clue. Dr. Reeves performed a standard tissue-typing for the transplant banks. Since Sharon had been dead for hours before discovery, it was unlikely that much could be recovered. The body changes rapidly at room temperature."

McWhirter looked a little green.

"But when Dr. Reeves typed the placenta, here—" The illustration expanded. "She found that Sharon's DNA fingerprints didn't match."

Harmony leaned forward, and Millicent shook her head. "Oh, shit," she whispered.

McWhirter asked, "Mill? *What?*"

"Placental transplant?"

Vail looked at her the way a teacher might beam at a promising student. "And how far can you take that?"

She paused, thinking.

"Here's a hint: in her fourteenth year, her mother and father were separated."

"Fourteen. *Twelve years since then.*" Millicent said, and her face went into her hands.

For almost a minute there was no sound in the room. Then Millicent looked up. "Ugly," she said.

"Yes?" Vail said encouragingly.

"Catholic family. Sharon adopting the maternal role. Her parents, Catholic parents, divorcing at the same time that Sharon got that scar. The placental transplant."

McWhirter was almost livid. "For God's sake, will you stop talking in code?"

"Fetal transplantation," Vail said, and for once his voice was gentle. "Very much an accepted alternative to abortion—an expensive one, though."

Harmony was fascinated but still confused. "How exactly did you come to this conclusion?"

"When Dr. Reeves got odd results for the DNA scan, she went looking for clues—and found them. A surgical scar, on the uterus near the cervix. You see, abortion is easy; the techniques are thousands of years old. The process of reducing the risk for the mother was gradual but sure—but the possibility of keeping the fetus itself alive existed by the end of the last century.

"One answer was to transplant the fetus's entire support mechanism, placenta and all. Rather than remove the baby from the uterus, the entire uterus is transplanted. An extracorporeal oxygenation device is needed, but that's just engineering. A new uterus is sewn in and attached to the fallopian tubes."

"Where was the operation performed?"

"Here's the clue: Nowhere."

"I don't understand."

"Sharon and her family lived in Utah. The operation was illegal there. Chances are that she went out of state and had it performed by the Embryadopt foundation. Sealed files."

Millicent seemed to have gotten herself together. "Another clue that Embryadopt was involved is the cost. Of removal, of the new uterus. They must have pre-sold the embryo. Healthy white fetuses are at a premium."

"Their security is complete," Vail said. "We can't get to their files, and no private agency can."

Harmony thought, *Tony.*

"No," Vail said, as if reading his mind. "McWhirter can't get at them. The files are *physically isolated.* No direct phone or computer lines into the banks."

Millicent began talking, almost to herself. "A Catholic family with a successful mother and an unemployed father."

"A father who probably stayed around the house a lot," Vail suggested.

"Sharon became pregnant, and gave her baby away. Something happened during the same period of time that was so traumatic that the . . . mother?"

Vail nodded.

"—sued for divorce."

"Sharon was raped by her father," Vail said quietly. "Probably repeatedly, over a period of years. When she became pregnant she gave the baby away."

Millicent continued in a pained voice. "So when Sharon Crayne was fourteen years old, she underwent a live fetal removal?"

"She fits many of the classic patterns. It would explain a lot. Her psychological tests from as far back as college imply a cyclical depression centering around March. Her parents were separated in April of '47. I'd bet that the surgical procedure was performed sometime in March of Sharon Crayne's fourteenth year. Her family was destroyed by the incident. Typical of incest victims, Sharon may well have blamed herself."

"And this might give a blackmailer material?" Harmony asked. "That she was an incest victim?"

For the first time Vail looked annoyed. "I would have thought bribery, not blackmail. If no legitimate private-party query can break through Embryadopt's legal shield, and even computer theft would fail, someone who *could* deliver such data would have an irresistible lure. Sharon lost a family over this trauma, and has never been able to sustain another relationship. Every year, on the anniversary of the operation, she plunged into depression, regretting her past and yearning to see that child. Someone with the right connections, and no scruples at all, might just be able to find that child of incest and rage. And offer Sharon Crayne her salvation."

Dr. Vail studied his fingernails for a moment before continuing. "Sharon Crayne stole something from Dream Park's files? Something of great value?"

"Great, but limited," McWhirter said. "A partial map of MIMIC's defense system. It will be obsolete in a month."

"And this rapid obsolescence implies it was needed in connection with California Voodoo?"

Harmony was aghast. "Cold-blooded murder over a game!"

Vail smiled coldly. "How much money is at stake, Thaddeus?"

McWhirter said, "Six hundred thousand gets someone four million dollars."

"Which team?"

"Army."

"That makes sense . . . perhaps." Vail closed his eyes. "Let me think. Sharon was prepared to exchange her stolen data for . . . something. My first guess would be information that the child was all right. But that just isn't enough. She could probably have gotten that through Embryadopt."

"Millicent and I have looked at her finances," Harmony said cautiously. "Sharon Crayne owned a house in Salt Lake which she rented out most of the time. She had nearly half a million in equity in that house. Another eighty thousand in the bank, a hundred and fifty thousand in various investments. At first we just thought this interesting, and considered it more evidence of her invulnerability to bribery."

"You see something else?"

Millicent said, "She didn't *use* the house. She's got *one* fur coat and a four-year-old Chrysler. She's got stocks, but she didn't play with them."

"She's not spending it," Vail said. "So let's stop looking at the house as a house, and look at it as a savings account. In that case she has a total of three-quarters of a million dollars in savings, and an emotional hunger to be reunited with the child she gave up. If money wouldn't get it for her directly, but she met someone who could give her information she needed, then that money could be used to, say, purchase a new life with her child."

"And a good life, too," Millicent mused. "But she would have to destroy the child's current family in order to do it."

Harmony seemed shocked. "Could she *do* something like that?"

"I have an idea," Millicent said quietly. "Instead of 'the child,' why don't we substitute 'the girl,' and see what happens."

McWhirter looked stricken. "Ah."

"Very good," Vail said. "A girl, who Sharon feared might be subjected to the same sexual degradation. Who is presently almost twelve years old. Perhaps the age the abuse began? Now then, I ask you: if three-quarters of a million dollars couldn't find the girl for Sharon, what might?"

"Nonmonetary pressure. Political favors maybe. Someone with military connections? Government connections . . ."

"Army. And who is the head of their team?" Vail pulled Clavell's file up and began to scan it with interest.

"You know," Tony said carefully. "One really strange thing has happened. Nigel Bishop placed himself in danger to prevent Clavell from being killed out."

"Nigel Bishop." Vail tapped out the name on his desktop console, and a slew of information began to rise. "Half the planet thinks he's unbeatable. Tony? Is he?"

"Bishop just lost his entire team."

Harmony looked shocked. "What? Wasn't Bishop supposed to have the biggest balls in Gaming?"

"Yes, but it was his second-in-command's fault. Disobeyed Bishop's direct orders. Bishop might have anticipated it would happen, but that's truly bizarre. But Bishop *likes* truly bizarre."

Vail said, "All right. We'll look at Army. We'll look at this Nigel Bishop. We'll find out whether Sharon could have met Nigel Bishop—or some Army strategist, for that matter. Then we go the other way, try to find someone with a connection to Embryadopt. Anything else?"

Nothing.

Tony McWhirter walked Millicent and Harmony to the elevator. All three were tired, but Tony pulled Millicent aside for a moment. She came without question, saying good-night to Harmony.

"Yes, Tony?" She looked at him, feeling mixed emotions. Tony was a victim, too, in a very special way that even he didn't understand.

"It's not Army. I've got tape—Clavell moaning when he first saw MIMIC. Christ, *he* didn't have any damned map."

"Could that have been for the cameras?"

"It's Bishop. I've got a bad feeling we'll never be able to prove a damned thing. He's got his tracks covered nine ways to hell, but *I* know. Trust me, I'm a Game Master." He stopped and frowned. "There's another problem—it's got to be Bishop, but I can't believe he placed that six-hundred-thousand-dollar bet."

"What do you mean?"

"You've got five teams in there. Bishop can't ride shotgun over Army the whole time, even if he wanted to. Be too suspicious, and besides, he's not even *trying* to control Army."

"Not trying?"

"He's nowhere near tracking the Army team. He's led two of the teams out of the Gaming area. Made us look like fools, of course. Also saved them a deal of trouble. You know, I can't even see his ego letting him throw a Game."

Millicent was leaning back against the wall, thoughtful. "Maybe he wouldn't be losing the Game. Maybe he'd be winning a bigger Game. It's all a matter of perspective."

"Yeah. I can see him thinking like that. *Never let the enemy know what your true intentions are* . . . But I can't see him believing he could pull it off."

Acacia, he thought suddenly. "He's got help. Acacia Garcia is in the Game with him. I mean, they're sleeping together, but Loremasters for opposing teams."

"So if she was in on it?"

Christ. There'd have to be a lot of money in it—and there was, damn it. "They'd have to kill out the Troglodykes and Tex-Mits, throw the Game, and leave everything to Army. Any idea how delicate and dangerous a backstabbing like that would be? One misstep, and complete scandal. IFGS invalidates the Game. Vegas doesn't pay off. Civil suits. Bishop loses six hundred gees. Nobody ever plays with Acacia again. Millie, Gaming is her life!"

"Everybody grows up, Tony. People have bet a lot more for a lot less."

"Maybe. She likes danger. Excitement. Maybe. *I* don't believe Bishop could pull it off, but maybe *he* believes he can. He's egotistical enough. And I hate to say it, but he might have Acacia hypnotized enough to believe he can do it."

"You just don't buy it."

Tony rubbed his eyes. "Everything I know says he can't pull it off. I'll ask the Lopezes, too, but . . . he can't. Influence the odds, yes. He could have another player paid off. He might be in the computers. But Millie, the safer it is, the more complex it is. The more complex it is, the more dangerous it is." He rubbed his temples. "Ouch."

"I'm trying to think like Alex here," Millicent said slowly. "Couple of different choices, assuming you're right about his aims—that he's involved in the gambling, that he involved another Loremaster in his plans. One, he's better than you think he is, Tony. He *can* pull it off. Two, he's overrated himself, and he *can't* pull it off."

Tony rubbed his eye and yawned. "My brain feels like scrambled eggs. When I close my eyes I see sheep screaming and running in circles. Call me if you get anything, would you?"

"Sure." And then she thought to herself, *You're jealous of Bishop, Tony. He's sleeping with the woman you loved. You'd hate Griffin for having done the same thing, but you owe him too much. Transference.*

But does that make Bishop more or less of a suspect? Was Tony trying to frame him, or to convince them that Bishop wasn't clever enough to be guilty, or *what?*

At that instant, she knew that despite massive medical evidence to the contrary, headaches were communicable.

Get some sleep.

Chapter Twenty-six

The Indirect Route

"The greatest difficulty in winning a war is forcing an indirect opponent into direct action, or an aggressive, straightforward adversary into excessive subtlety. The key is to take the indirect routes. Lure opponents to the attack with hints and clues and shows of possible weakness. One must be able to leave the starting blocks after an opponent, and arrive at the finish line before him."

—Nigel Bishop, *The Art of Gaming*, 2052

Friday, July 22, 2059—5:55 A.M.

Dawn had come to the Mojave. It painted the eastern mountains a burnt orange, with the promise of greater, warmer light and life behind it. Slowly, long before the temperature of the air began to rise, the light silvered. The radiance spread up behind the mountains, the shadows began rolling back, and back, and daylight marched toward MIMIC.

Alphonse was awake and packed, ready to move.

Three of his compatriots had formed a seated triangle: S. J. Waters, Crystal Cofax, and Major Terry Clavell.

SJ was Scout and Thief. Clavell was Magic User and Warrior. Crystal was a Scout. All had special sight, special powers of discernment. For some fifteen minutes they had been locked in magical ceremony.

In the center of the triangle, uncomfortable and a bit squat, sat the pregnant Mary-em.

"This is ridiculous," she said.

"Shut up," Crystal replied politely.

SJ cocked his head sideways. "Did you know that you glow when you're pregnant?"

"SJ," Mary-em said calmly, "I did a paper on exotic torture methods once. Care to contribute to its sequel?"

"Is that any way for a mommy to talk?"

The three joined hands around the edge of the triangle, and chanted. Somewhere in the universe, the powers that be evaluated their ceremony and intent and decided that they had enough of whatever such gods decided it took for them to achieve their intended goal.

Mary-em's tummy began to glow. The embryo within glowed more brightly: Chango's unborn boy-child. He had developed with preternatural rapidity. His eyes were open, his face aware and alert, if annoyed.

"Why do you awaken me?" he whispered. "I have need for sleep."

Alphonse said, "We need to know our next destination."

"Seek the water people," the embryo said. The vast brown eyes were heavy-lidded, threatening to flutter closed. "And let me rest."

"We are afraid. Afraid of ambush, by others of our kind. We need to know where they are."

A light pulsed out from inside Mary-em, turning her entire body transparent. Organs and bone structure were available for perusal. A translucent ghost of MIMIC formed around them, floor to ceiling, as if Mary-em were embedded in Jell-O.

"Here. They are here, on the twelfth floor," the fetus said dreamily. A patch of the floor blinked. "The Nommo are a level beneath them."

"The water people?"

"Yes. Seek them, and you will learn what you must. I . . . hope that you . . . swim well."

And then the light faded away.

Mary-em's heavy mouth creased with amusement. "Well. My son, the godling."

The general asked, "What do we do? How many of us swim?" Hands went up.

"Fuck that," Clavell said. "We're not there yet. How many of us can fight? As far as we know, Bishop and Da Gurls have all banded together, and they're going to wipe us out, first chance they get."

"Which will be in about half an hour if we go down there," said Poule.

Clavell said, "We're not defenseless either. We have a talisman that probably can't be beat. And we can be sneaky."

"Listen up," Alphonse offered. "We consider ourselves one team till the end of the Game. No backstabbing, no bullshit. Help each other earn points, watch each other's backs. This time out, there's enough goodies for everybody—if y'all don't get greedy."

"But how do we get past Apple?" Crystal asked.

"Good question," he admitted. "Twan's read a book—she can track us. Even if we sneak around t'other side of the building."

"Now look." Clavell drew a simple map on a sheet of paper. "There's something else that we can do . . ."

Trevor Stone refused to speak to a Game Master.

Tamasan hadn't seen anything that led up to the disaster. The Cleric had come running when Trevor and Holly were suddenly surrounded by showy magical effects . . .

Holly Frost had slept badly, and not in the Gen-Dyn quarters. She'd refused to be near "that maniac" Stone. She slumped in a web chair and studied Tony through pink, bleary eyes. "I know you. You're the asshole almost ruined the South Seas Treasure Game."

"Years ago. Holly, I'm a reformed soul. Now I *save* Games."

"Like you saved this one, *Game Master*?" She couldn't wait for an answer; she bounded to her feet and screamed, "Can you *believe* that maniac? All we had to do was sit tight and wait for Bishop. Stone just didn't know how to handle it. Like this was a fat-ripper special instead of the goddamn Olympics of Gaming! He killed us *all*. Can you believe this shit?" Her whole body shook with rage.

"I want you to think back over California Voodoo. Could Bishop have set you up?"

She froze; she stared; she shied back and into herself, as if suddenly remembering that Tony had done more than ruin a Game. "You *have* gone nuts."

"Okay."

"Wait."

She sat down. When Tony poured a paper cup of coffee, she took it without comment. She sipped, and thought, and said, "I've never heard of anything that insane."

Tony nodded. He felt embarrassed.

"Bishop never does what anyone expects," she said.

"Right."

"You think he manipulated his way back into the Game? He wouldn't need to. Hell, I jumped at the chance to play on the Bishop's team. But did he set us up. McWhirter, *why*?"

"I—I could be way off here—"

"Game Masters don't leave a running Game for no reason! What do you know, McWhirter?"

"Not enough. Not enough to start a rumor or risk a slander suit, Holly. What do *you* know?"

"*We* didn't make any mistakes." Her dark pretty face was composed: Holly had gotten a grip on herself. "I tried to keep Stone calm by getting him to tell Gaming stories. It worked for a while, but then he just *had* to show Bishop up. Those two got along like balrogs and paladins.

"I warned Bishop not to call him Trevor. He's not a Californian, he's a Brit. Calling him by his first name is an imposition. It's like scraping a nerve every time."

"What did Bishop say?"

"He thanked me politely and said he'd try to stop. He hadn't realized. Goddamn you, McWhirter."

"Being sarcastic?"

"Not so I could see. I wondered."

"What can you tell us about working with Bishop?"

She nodded to herself. She said, "Gen-dyn *forced* Stone on Bishop. Second-in-command. Sooner or later Stone had to take the com, and it happened at Ile Ife. If Bishop—if he suckered us, there's no way to blame him.

"He's confident. Unbelievably so. But he's usually dead-on about anything to do with Gaming. One hell of a sexy man." She grinned at him, a shark's grin. "If I'd had an opportunity, I was going to make a play."

"What was he like to work with?"

Holly rolled one long, shapely thigh over the other and stared up at the ceiling. "Intense. Perfectionist. When the name 'California Voodoo' came down, Bishop set into research like a crazy man. Ancient African myths, Haiti, New Orleans, 'The Last Days of the Late Great State of California.' And yet . . ."

She seemed to be deciding whether or not to continue. Tony remained silent.

"Just a feeling in the back of my head, like a—a taste? There was a lot of movement, but it never felt directed, focused. It was all logical. It all made sense. But this is *the Bishop*, right? The Bishop does crazy things. The unexpected. The intuitive leap. The deceptive gambit. And he didn't really come up with any of that. It made me wonder. Either he had lost it—"

"Did you believe that?"

Holly smiled and shook her dark, pretty face. "The man was on fire. He is so smart it's scary. Hell of a sexy man. No, I thought he must be planning something crazy, something unexpected, something that it would take a genius to guess. But killing off his whole team? Why?" Her brow furrowed. "Does he think he can win single-handed?"

"Could he think that?"

She laughed at herself. "Even Nigel Bishop isn't that crazy."

"What if he's changed the definitions?"

"Of what?"

"Of winning. Like, oh, suppose he bet on another team, for instance?"

"What, on Acacia? That's who he's with now." Her face twisted in what might have been grief. "Damn you, McWhirter."

Tony only nodded.

"He's risking a perfect reputation if he throws this Game. It's tarnished no matter what happens now. He lost his team!"

"You're looking at this the wrong way. In the context of the Game, winning is important. Bishop quit because winning was too easy. No challenge."

"What would be more important?"

"Money?"

She shook her head. "Power. For Bishop it's power."

To Tony that was a new thought. He suggested, "Enough money is power . . ."

Holly was thinking, her eyes closed. "If Bishop is cheating. If you are seeing him outside the Game, gone rogue, then don't stop at the first easy answer. Bad mistake. He'll leave a false trail. He'll give you an answer you'll buy, and then hit you with something subtler, and bigger." Again, that predator's smirk. "Much bigger."

Chapter Twenty-seven

Alarums and Excursions

"Knowledge of the Gaming territory is of paramount importance. If the Game is to be played in Dome A or B at Dream Park, you have some idea of the Game Master's limitations and advantages to the Game Master. If it is to be held in another location, failure to acquire proper intelligence is an invitation to disaster."

—Nigel Bishop, *The Art of Gaming*, 2057

Friday, July 22, 2059

Promptly at 6:00 A.M., the combined party of General Dynamics, Apple, and the Universities of California moved out of their comfortable quarters on the thirteenth level and began their descent.

At Griffin/Bobo's insistence, all utensils were cleaned, all beds made, and everything that was possible to place back in its correct position was so replaced.

They had, however, taken every grain of salt in the cupboards. There wasn't a tin of canned meat, a bag of hard candy, or a jar of pudding left behind. Griffin decided that there was no practical way to prevent such petty pilferage.

Once again, Acacia Garcia had slipped completely into Panthesilea mode, a dark and dangerous place, one that fascinated him in spite of his headache and fatigue.

Alex wasn't sure he had gotten any sleep the previous night. He may have slipped off now and then for a few moments, but the least sound, the hint of an approaching footstep, snapped him awake.

It made for a dreadful evening. He pulled himself out of Acacia's bag in the morning feeling as animate as a Yule log.

But the nine Adventurers in the caravan were moving along now, cautiously but steadily. The rate of attrition had been staggering. Doubtless there was worse to come.

Alex kept a sliver of attention reserved for Bishop. The man seemed completely involved in his Game. Absorbed, even—but there was something else, wasn't there? Some dark inner light, the relaxed smugness of the gambler who has rigged the table . . .

Alex's earpiece buzzed. He cupped it to isolate himself from outside conversation. "We've got two choices," Tony McWhirter said. "Army, or Bishop."

Alex whispered his reply, the throat mike filtering and amplifying. "Any link to Sharon?"

"Just that map. Most logical choice for cheater is Army, but they've always been straight arrows. I don't buy it. Sentimental choice for cheater is good old Bishop."

Griffin thought about that. "I don't completely trust Acacia. I think she's in trouble."

"Alex . . ."

"No, I don't think she knows anything about murder. I just have a bad feeling about the whole thing. Don't worry, I watched out for her last night."

"Right."

Griffin knew that wounded tone and the confusion of emotions that hid behind it. "Tony—when this is over, you and I are going to have a long talk."

The chill was still there. "Any time." Then the line went dead.

Griffin caught up with Tammi: tall, blonde, physically superb, and in the lead as usual. The halls were deserted, but there were sounds just up ahead.

Just beyond the next corner, electric candles flickered in a storefront window. Above the niche was a sign which said, in extremely neat script: *Botánica.*

The Adventurers gathered around. After a swift huddle, Tammi, Acacia, and Bishop entered the store. After a moment's hesitation, Griffin and Coral entered, as well.

The room smelled like incense and peppermint. The walls were papered with glowing black-light posters in psychedelic array. From speakers in every corner of the room, heavily synthesized electric guitars bleated arrhythmically.

"What the hell is this?" Acacia asked.

Tammi examined a necklace of human teeth. "Looks like a cross between a santería minimart and a head shop."

A very dark, slender woman with flowing dreadlocks, a flowered robe, and love beads glided from behind the counter. "Peace to you, brothers and sisters."

A thousand-odd geegaws crowded the room, everything from statues of saints to hash pipes.

There were Baggies of "smoking mixtures," various legal blends which, when set afire, smelled remarkably like illegal substances.

There were incense, and glass tubes, and voodoo dolls; there were cigarette papers in a hundred different flavors and configurations, eye-boggling posters in Day-Glo orange and violet, and jars of owl's claw. There were pamphlets on the cultivation of psychedelic mushroom, books on the Orishas, dog-eared volumes on flotation tanks, charts of energy meridian flow, and books on African mythology. There were tomes by Timothy Leary and Joseph Campbell, tiny gold-plated coke spoons, crystals, pyramid-power manuals, silver-plated razor blades, stash jewelry, one-hit minibongs, and other accoutrements.

"Last chance, heading down, mon," the dreadlocked clerk said dreamily.

"What do you mean, 'last chance'?"

"Well, the Nommo like for the people around them to keep a clean head. And lower than that . . ." She clucked. "Gets deadly, mon. Like we do some trading."

She winked an eye, reached down under the counter, and brought up a pipe, made out of a humerus bone. "Now this pipe, she be special."

Bishop waved his hand over it, and it glowed. He turned back to Acacia. "We've got to have it, Panthesilea."

"How much?" she asked.

"Oh, no, she has no price." The storekeeper stuffed it with some herbal mixture and lit, puffing away peacefully. "She sure is fine."

"All right . . . you won't take money. What will you take?"

"Riddle me," the woman said, her voice singsong. "Riddle me for your life, mon, and the pipe, she might be yours."

"Riddle you . . ." Bishop smiled at the shopkeeper. "Does it have to be me?"

"You be afraid?"

"We have a better riddler."

"You be afraid."

Bishop wagged his head regretfully, controlling his irritation. "There is one far better suited than I. Captain Cipher?"

Cipher strutted forward. The dreadlocked shopkeeper examined him with interest.

"Ah, so you riddle with me?"

"Madam, I will."

The shopkeeper reached out a finger and drew a rectangle in the air. Thin, flaming red lines formed as she made even vertical and horizontal strokes. Four rows, four columns. She then brushed the top two boxes: they blazed red. The bottom two rows she similarly tinted green.

She gave them a toothy smile. Then she very carefully printed the following words so that each letter fell into one of the squares:

R A T E
Y O U R
M I N D
P A L

Cipher watched her carefully. "All right, now what?"

The shopkeeper licked the tip of her finger, reached out, and began to scramble up the letters. Her fingers moved faster and faster, sliding one square at a time. There was no sleight of hand, but her speed at the end was inhuman.

When she was finished, the squares read:

R A I U
M E L
T R P Y
A O D N

And the colors, of course, were thoroughly confused.

The shopkeeper grinned wickedly at him. "Three minutes to solve it, no less and no more—

"If failure is yours, then damnation's in store."

Captain Cipher reached out and nudged the Y experimentally. When it responded, he began to move other pieces, faster and faster, building on the R in the top box, trying combinations on combinations.

Griffin watched the Adventurers who had crowded into the doorway. Quietly intent, they studied a master craftsman at work.

At thirty seconds, the box seemed no closer to being solved. At forty-five Cipher had RATE in the top box, and then . . . scramble scramble . . .

A minute and fifty seconds, and the puzzle looked nearly solved. It now read:

R A T E
Y O U R
M I N D
P L A

Cipher froze. His hands hovered motionless. A sheen of perspiration had appeared on his brow. Griffin's heart went out to him. Here, in front of all of his friends and the cameras . . .

Suddenly Cipher's eyes spread wide apart, and his fingers blurred. What in the hell? He was taking all of his carefully structured work apart. Griffin couldn't be sure, but it looked an awful lot as if he was running the previous moves backward, as though he had photographed the entire thing and had the moves stored away in his mind.

Why would he be doing that?

Then when Cipher had the letters in the *RAIU MEL TRPY AODN* configuration, with thirty seconds left, he went back to work, moved the *R* in the third line into position in the top left-hand square, and then zipped the other letters around and around the grid.

With five seconds left on the clock, the puzzle once again read:

R A T E
Y O U R
M I N D
P A L

And Cipher grinned. "You shifted the first and second *R*'s," he panted. "Trick . . . kee! Milady, I nearly missed it. Change any two blocks, you change parity. With the second *R* in the top left square, it's hopeless, but your mind still wants to leave well enough alone, work around it. Gotcha."

The shopkeeper's smile was dazzling. "Very good, mon. The pipe, she is yours."

She handed Cipher the bone.

"Now," she said. "As long as you are here, would you care for any of my other items?"

There was a moment's pause, as if they couldn't believe their luck, then the Adventurers descended like locusts.

★ ★ ★

Bishop, Tammi, and Prez formed a protective shell about Cipher as he packed the pipe with herbs, then puffed it into life.

The smoke whirlpooled in front of them. Colors began to form . . .

Within black, oily-looking water, sleek and powerful fish shapes slid sensuously. There were human beings at the water's edge. They were looking at part of an indoor swimming pool, with diving boards and a tiled edge. The Adventurers could hear the beat, but not the melody, of half-familiar music.

"Our next stop," Twan said.

Tammi had a thought. "Wait. Try to find out where the other teams are."

Cipher puffed and puffed.

The image was faint at first, then swelled and became stronger.

Clavell and Poule might have been human spiders, trailing ropes down MIMIC's external wall. They jumped carefully, pushing out hard and then sliding down, legs braced and bent to absorb the shock.

Cipher choked on his smoke. "What in the hell are they—"

Bishop recovered first. "They're going straight down to the flooded levels. Don't you get it? They're going to get there first, and ambush us. We've got to move!"

The major and "Evil" Poule went down first, tightly, professionally, as if they had practiced the maneuver a thousand times.

In Poule's case, that might have been true. He may have grown a little soft in the intervening years, but there was clearly one hell of a man under those extra twenty pounds. He used a more traditional carabiner, hooked to the side of his belt. He wasn't able to use a classic rappelling position. Instead, in each hand he held a miniature Spider. The line was far too thin to control with his fingers. It would have cut his hands and thighs badly.

Clavell kicked out from the wall and bounced as he dropped about five yards. He swung back in, braked with his calves, and bounced out again.

Twenty feet to his left, just the other side of the crease, General Poule was similarly engaged—and having the time of his life.

Clavell paused, looking down at the desert floor below him. Its patches of brown and tan and dull green spun lazily as he pivoted on the line. He sighed. Life was rarely so placid for him, even though he was a peacetime warrior. He longed for the simplicity of action. Long ago, Clavell had accepted the fact that peacetime was a time of boredom. If he did his job well, boredom was all he was going to get.

So peacetime it would be, because Clavell was, above all, a man who appreciated competence.

He would not, therefore, have appreciated the actions of the stock clerk at the Mountain High sporting goods store in Denver where he had purchased Falling Angels monofilament climbing cable.

The Army team was composed of military personnel, but was not directly sponsored by the government. Only in that way could Clavell claim any winnings as his own personal income, to split it with his team instead of with his ubiquitous Uncle Sugar.

The downside was that the Army wouldn't supply him with military equipment. Good civilian substitutes were generally available . . . but his request for 500 feet of climbing cable had reached Mountain High at a time when their stock was low. They didn't have four 500-foot lengths. What they had was three 500-foot lengths, and two 250-footers.

An enterprising clerk took it upon himself to epoxy together two 250s and repackage them.

And this was, although innocent, a major blunder. Falling Angels monofilament was made from single-crystal iron fibers bonded into an epoxy matrix, creating a thread of fantastic strength. The adhesive chosen by the clerk, while ordinarily enormously strong, simply reacted badly with the matrix, creating a weaker bond than that guaranteed by Altex Chemicals. Altex had given very specific instructions, albeit in small print, not to use this particular cement on the variety of epoxy used to coat single-crystal cables.

When Clavell's Spider—and weight—hit the bond, the cable snapped.

He twisted in midair, wrenching his back as he flailed blindly for support. His left side slammed into a balcony railing, and the air *woof*ed out of him. Pain exploded in his ribs as he rebounded, and he tumbled out toward the edge.

A frantically outflung hand found window-gutter: barely an inch and a half of shallow trench. Skin ripped on his fingers; his thumb felt broken; his lips and teeth and nose and toes banged against thick glass.

Hanging by his fingertips, face pressed to the glass, he blinked. The glass was slick and cold with spray from the waterfall. A capricious wind blinded him with freezing water. He blinked it away, unable to spare a hand to wipe with. He clung there, shoulder flaming, sight blurred, trying to remember the appropriate prayer.

He shivered, heart thundering in his chest.

Oh God, oh God would just have to do.

Alarm klaxons split the air. Wonderful. Dream Park to the rescue. With cameras. Decorated war-game hero makes idiot of self and team. Tape at eleven. For about one second he considered the advantages of simply letting go.

A hovercar hummed down from the roof, carrying a three-man emergency rescue team. Clavell, clinging to the gutter, watched its reflection in the glass and tried not to whimper. Desperately, he surveyed his options.

Below him were the immense raised stone letters that spelled out MIMIC. Much farther down, and to his right, cars from their maglev train lay like something assembled from an erector set, then destroyed in a fit of pique.

He gazed longingly at the hovercar. It represented safety, and life—and the end of Army's chance in the California Voodoo Game.

All he had to do was nod, and they would take him in. They hovered there, faces masked with concern.

By God, he was going to finish this Game. He was going to win.

From the far side of the crease, Poule yelled; "Major! Are you all right?"

"Fine," Clavell lied blatantly. He panted, trying to catch his breath. What to do?

He tested the window. It was secure: no hope of getting in through there. He could just barely see Poule. The general had reached his target: an open bay for a missing modular capsule. The weather shield was down, but that wouldn't stop them.

He shifted his weight, trying to distribute the strain and keep his sore muscles from seizing up on him.

Nothing was broken. The right shoulder throbbed, but what the hell: one of the positive things about stark terror is its tendency to make almost any pain a minor annoyance. Come morning, the hounds of hell would romp in his joints, but tomorrow was another day.

He peered up along MIMIC's face. High above him were the concerned faces of his teammates. He wished he could wave at them. For that matter, he wished he could trade places with them.

A second aircar—Cowles Security this time—joined the first.

They floated just far enough away to be out of camera view. It was still his show.

Thirty feet down and ten feet to his right was Poule, and the open bay.

Clavell began to inch toward his right along the gutter. There was a narrow, decorative ledge between the windows. It was just wide enough to rest his right toes upon, taking some of the weight off his fingers. He sobbed for breath, steadied himself, lifted his left foot. He pulled his belt knife with his left hand, reached down, and gingerly cut the laces. He slipped the shoe off and watched as it fell to the desert sand 130 long, long feet below.

The right foot required considerable contortions, but he finally managed to shed the second shoe. Toes sufficed to remove socks.

And then he was ready.

His every movement was coldly deliberate. There was no room for another error.

He wiggled his toes. They felt strong. Limber. It had been years since he had last free-climbed, but since boyhood, mountaineering had been a favorite hobby. He remembered years in Yellowstone National Park, climbing barefoot, his toes hardened through grueling summers under the tutelage of a favorite uncle.

Now his uncle was with him again.

"Terry, you've got the easy part. Goin' down's a cinch, long as you've got light. Here's what you do. Wall's your friend. Press into it, like a lizard. Every inch of yourself you get against it, that's another inch you don't have to hold up.

"Reach out. Make sure you've got a good grip. Both hands, see . . ."

He had a good grip. The rain gutters and the weather etching on MIMIC's surface meant that there were a fair number of grips for hands and feet—or, more accurately, fingers and toes.

All right. He reached out and down with his right foot, feeling along the wall for a grip. One thing about man-made buildings: they tended to be too regular, with too few handholds, but those holds were reliable. The letters were raised almost eighteen inches away from the building wall, enough room for a decent grip. His toes found the groove of the *M* and braced themselves. All right. The diagonal line slid slowly to the right, and he eased himself into it, as carefully as he had ever done anything in his life. He braced a knee to either side of it and slid as if it were a fireman's pole glued to the side of a cliff. He gasped as he touched the bottom of the notch, and braced himself there for a moment.

His knees hugged stone outcropping, his thighs already burning. All right. All right.

Slowly he released his death grip. Hugging the wall, he leaned carefully over to the opposite stroke. The last, vertical stroke had a little horizontal foot. His toes clawed for purchase on the cold stone, and he pushed himself across.

There was a two-foot gap between the *M* and the *I* stroke. Clavell braced himself between the letters, muscles cracking with the effort, sweat streaming down his face. Then he was wedged between the letters, heart hammering in his chest. He risked a glance at the desert floor beneath him.

And looked right back up. He felt dizzy and weak. He had to focus. All right. He stretched out with his right hand until he was braced between the bottom of the *M* and the *I*. Then he gingerly shifted himself across. Easy. Forget about the fall. There was plenty of room, right? He reached up and around, gripping the *I*. It was weathered, lots of gripping points for toes and fingers, and the gap between *I* and the next *M* was no farther. His wonderful Falling Angels gloves were designed to grip cable. They were absolutely nonslip, and they gave him a grip on the weathered stone that an octopus would envy. He loved those gloves. He planned to marry or, at the very least, have carnal knowledge of them as soon as his toes touched Mother Earth again.

The little crossbar on the bottom of the *I* gave him a chance to rest. He heaved for breath, feeling pitifully grateful.

He shimmied around the *I* and over to the second *M*.

Now came the tricky part.

General Poule was peering up at him but wasn't making a sound.

"Anchor yourself, General," Clavell called. "I think I can make it down from here, but I might need some help."

The general disappeared for a moment, and then was back.

"Lashed myself to a crossbeam. Come on down, Major."

Clavell gulped air and began to descend.

His toes searched for purchase. His gloved fingers clung to cracks that should have sliced them to ribbons.

Then his toes were hanging over space, over the upper lip of the yawning modular cavern.

And there were no more grips. He stretched his toes out, and General Poule still couldn't reach them safely.

Shit.

He began to swing, metronoming from side to side. There was

a little slant to the wall here. Just enough to create a little friction. It would slow his descent, and he could get another handhold . . .

He threw himself sideways, belly and arms flat against the wall, sliding, fingers gripping to find the rain gutter above the modular opening. His fingers were numb and torn, but they still found a grip. His shoulder screamed. But he came to a stop.

Pain shot through his body, and he saw red, as if the strain had burst a capillary in his eye. Pain exploded in his shoulder. His fingers slipped, and panic overwhelmed him, control shattered as he realized he was *falling*—

But then "Evil" Poule's strong hands were on his legs, arms around his waist, under his arms, scooping him up and in to safety. "I think," Clavell gasped, "that I need to rest—"

Then the shock and fear and fatigue hit him all in a rush. The blood drained from his face, and Major Clavell fainted.

Chapter Twenty-eight

"Do We See This?" (part II)

Friday, July 22, 2059—7:30 A.M.

Crystal and SJ hovered about, caring for Mary-em and encouraging her. "Got to be careful," Crystal said soberly. "After all, you're climbing for two."

"Hee hee," Mary-em growled, fingering her belt knife. *The very worst part,* a traitorous voice whispered in the back of her mind, *is that you love it.*

SJ soberly triple-checked both lines, Poule's and Clavell's. He studied the faulty epoxy weld while cursing most inventively. Just for safety, he disassembled and reassembled the Spiders, checking every component three times.

Mary-em sat back, doing her best to project a maternal glow. Not a difficult task—her tummy was, after all, emitting a soft and lovely radiance that intermittently took the shape of a humanoid infant.

"Hell of a woman," SJ said soberly, patting her shoulder. "Glad to have a breeder in the tribe. Now. We've got a sling rigged for you, and it should be fairly comfortable. What does it take to miscarry a godling? Don't know, don't want to find out. You're our walking talisman. Just hope you're up on your Lamaze."

While Mary-em's reply did indeed have something to do with motherhood, it could hardly have been considered complimentary to SJ.

They had rigged her a sort of basket, anchoring down one of the Spiders to act as a stable braking platform. Mary-em sat in the makeshift seat. At a signal from Poule and Clavell, they began to lower her out of the lip of the modular apartment.

This was humiliating. She had watched Clavell's free climb, and knew it would make him famous. Mary-em's descent would be laughed at—unless she played it for all it was worth. She composed herself with an aplomb worthy of a queen. The pulleys creaked, and she began her descent down the weathered face of MIMIC.

Clavell reeled Mary-em in with a coat hanger rigged to the end of a mop handle. Poule had already lifted the weather shield, and as soon as she unhooked herself from the sling she wandered back into the apartment and checked the refrigerator. Empty.

The basket went back up, and Crystal got into it, and the procedure was repeated . . .

Alphonse Nakagawa was the second-to-last Gamer to take the ride down; SJ worked the brake mechanism.

SJ had no one to work the brake, and that was just fine by him. He rode down on the Spider, whooping all the way, the morning desert spinning below him. It was glorious. Best of all, for the very first time, they were ahead of Bishop and Da Gurls.

Alphonse and the major braced themselves beside the front door, opened it gingerly, and peered out.

They were greeted by a strong marine smell. Faint echoes: sounds of laughter and water play. Clavell, his wrenched shoulder wrapped now, raised an eyebrow at Alphonse. "Well, Civilian, what do you think?"

"Nommo."

Clavell called Mary-em up to the front, and they formed another circle around her.

Alphonse knelt by her side. "Hail," he said. "Holy infant, holy mother." The shape of the infant reappeared.

"I'm going to be sick," Mary-em said.

The baby covered its little eyes. "I'm sleeping," it said petulantly.

"We need your help."

"I want a song. If you want my help, you be nice to me," it insisted.

Alphonse pursed his lips. "Does anyone know a lullaby?"

SJ cleared his throat and sang:

Mary had a little lamb,
Her father shot it dead.
Now Mary takes the lamb to school
Between two hunks of bread.

The infant looked at SJ with disgust. "Is that any kind of poem to tell a small, vulnerable child?"

"Mary-em. What are your views on abortion?"

She narrowed her eyes and placed her hands over her tummy. The flesh flowed around black finger bones. "Not another word, twerp."

Crystal smiled, came forward, and knelt by Mary-em, putting both hands on her stomach. And she sang, in a surprisingly clear and sweet contralto.

Oh, the queen is giving a ball today
and the talking flowers are there!
We'll play croquet with guinea pigs
and all the cards will stare.
A bird will be my mallet, and I will win the game!
But the queen will have my head, just the same . . .

After she finished, the infant rolled over and looked at her with its star-child eyes. "Insane but nice. Now. Here's what you do . . ."

Up in the control chamber, Doris Whitman had curled into a fetal position. Remarkably agile and limber for a woman her age, her alignment and action of limbs precisely duplicated an unborn infant's.

The DreamTime Virtual system translated every motion, every flicker of a finger, with a time lag of less than three thousandths of a second. Doris was the unborn godling, the spawn of Mary-em's loins, and her performance was flawless.

She spoke as she rolled. The DreamTime system altered her voice, raising it in register and pitch until it became a sleepy, childlike whisper.

For a moment the entire control room stopped, leaving all programs on automatic loop routines.

Doris was something very special. Her entire body arched, muscle control so complete that she could imitate weightlessness. Heavy as she was, it seemed absurd that she should move so effortlessly.

And when she finally stopped, allowing her body to rest once again, the entire control room exploded into applause.

Tony McWhirter was heavily in conference with Mitsuko Lopez, studying one of the skeletal diagrams of MIMIC.

"All right," he said. "They're all playing California Voodoo outside the boundaries. *Everybody*. Weird."

She laid a comforting hand on his shoulder. "But still playing a damn good Game," she said. "So. We have to help them get back onto the track. Start with Army/Tex-Mits."

Tony pointed, his forearm sinking into the model. "They're here on the tenth level. They've gotten around all of the traps we laid for them, but they also can't get to the Nommo. For obvious reasons, we sealed the doors and shored up the walls *here* and *here*. What do we do, and how do we keep them on camera?"

Mitsuko thought for three seconds, then pivoted and punched out a code on the main board. "Mitch Hasegawa, please report to Security."

Tony cocked his head. "I know Mitch," he said. "He's a nice guy, but don't we need someone a little higher?"

"Sometimes rank isn't as important as communication," Mitsuko said.

"You know Mitch?"

She twinkled. "He's my little brother."

Mitsuko and Mitsuo "Mitch" Hasegawa hugged briefly, then he sat down to consider their problem.

"I can do it," he said, "but I'll have to activate some of ScanNet's maintenance relays on the tenth."

"Aren't they already on?"

"Naw. The way the system is now, it would overload. They're on manual. In fact, most monitors on the tenth have been turned over to the DreamTime system."

"So where's the security?"

"Well, we've got the entire exterior sealed, of course. We know the instant anyone moves into one of those peripheral units, let alone the wall. And then we have spot checks throughout the inner building. As soon as the whole thing is activated, we'll be able to scan you right down to the blood cells, big sister. Forget metal detectors—we'll know whether you had secret sauce on your cheeseburger."

Tony scooted forward. "Now listen to me. I need to get our Army group from here—" He indicated a sector in the tenth level that was coded blue. "—over a restraining wall and back into the Gaming area. To do that, I want to take them through a service tunnel. Here. I can guide them into it, but I don't have cameras to follow them inside. Whatever shall I do?"

Mitch tapped out commands on the main console and then grinned. "All right. We have maintenance 'bots in there. They've got cameras, of course, and some other senses, too. We'll let the 'bots follow your Gamers around. You'll have to give them one of those 'you can't see this' orders."

Tony laughed. "It's been a long time since we've had to use one of those. Can I see this maintenance unit?"

Tap tap. It looked like a crab on roller skates. It was intended to motor along a tunnel two feet in diameter, cleaning, inspecting, providing routine maintenance.

Mitsuko raised one lazy eyebrow. "How strong are those arms?"

"Exert about fifty pounds of pressure."

"How precisely controllable?"

"Very. Good for close work."

"And how resistant to damage?"

"Well . . ." Mitch's eyes narrowed at her. "Chi-Chi, what are you—"

"Just answer the question, little brother."

"Well, anything really valuable is inside the central casing. Pretty well shielded. The external arms are all replaceable. Maybe a thousand bucks, tops."

"And can you get a second one into the area?"

"To watch the first, right?"

She smiled expansively.

Tony was slow, but caught on. "Ah, Chi-Chi—Mitsuko, he's right . . ."

Her smile had broadened further. "Players aren't the only ones who can improvise."

Fast as a snake she twisted, calling, "Owen! We need some Virtual imagery here!"

In Mary-em's womb, the godling rolled back over toward them, its eyes as vast as a moonless sky. "Is there one among you who is a pathfinder? One who seeks?"

SJ came forward.

"Touch my mother's stomach."

Mary-em growled, said growl disturbing the beatific expression she had cultivated so carefully. "Watch yer hands, buster."

"Sorry. Heh heh."

"Now," the child said. *"Reveal!"*

A map of the entire tenth level rolled out before them like the ghost of a carpet. Their route through it was plainly mapped. A line of green dashes pointed SJ's path, and he stood—saying, "No offense, Yer Godliness"—and followed the dashes to a wall grille set too high for him to reach on tiptoe.

The major threw him a chair.

SJ tested the screws at the sides of the grille. They were fairly standard, but probably hadn't been worked since the original replacement two years earlier. SJ dug into his backpack and found a multihead screwdriver.

He hummed happily when he'd finally levered the grille free. He snapped an electric lamp headband above his visor and said, "Boost me up!" Clavell and Poule boosted him, and he eeled into the duct.

He wiggled in, elbows and knees braced against cold metal. He adjusted his Virtual visor. The green dashes bobbed in the air before him.

After a half hour, SJ's back was sore and his knees and elbows were a little skinned up. He was grateful that the duct was clean. He didn't relish the notion of getting an infected cut.

Newer ducts would have rounded corners. These antique ducts were square. Steel sheeting, and maybe rivets, under new insulation. How *did* they clean these ducts? Did they get midgets to crawl around in here with wet rags, or what? Had the squatters managed with dirty ducts?

The other six Adventurers of the Tex–Mits/Army combine inched along behind him. SJ found himself slipping into fantasy.

Corporal Waters, at great risk to life and limb, leads the way for the major and the general, crawling across no-man's-land, under barbed wire, and through a minefield under heavy machine-gun fire, to retrieve a live grenade . . .

A humming sound up ahead had grown steadily louder, finally crossing the threshold of his attention. Belatedly, he wondered what it was.

He was suddenly uncomfortably aware of the cramped, night-dark space. He widened his flashing beam.

Nothing. From a distance throbbed the soft, regular, hushed pulse of the air-conditioning. Somehow that was a reassurance, akin to the comforting rhythm of a mother's heartbeat. The building was alive. It breathed.

He called, "Hold it!" The column behind him stopped.

Scratch scratch.

There it was again, damn it. Closer now.

He turned onto his side and held the flashlamp out ahead of him, eeling forward until he came to a branching pathway. From here he could see up, down, right, left . . .

Left. The sound came from there. And now it was closer.

There was no way to get everyone all the way back down the vent before whatever the hell it was made its grisly entrance. The only real option was to keep going, and hope . . .

Then he remembered Mary-em, the soft underbelly of their column. If he kept going straight, whatever was down there might very well intersect their line right in the middle, with lethal results to Junior.

SJ made his choice—and turned toward the sound.

His Virtual goggles pumped a vaguely greenish light into his eyes. Irritated, he flipped them up. The scratching sound grew louder. Something emerged from the left side passage.

The low-pitched "engage Virtual shield" buzzer sounded in his ears, but SJ only stared.

It was a maintenance 'bot. He had seen them often enough, a six-legged steel and plastic critter that roamed tunnels and halls, repairing, cleaning, inspecting.

He was confused. This wasn't part of the Game . . .

He turned to stared back at his compatriots. "Do we see this?"

Alphonse said, "The buzzer, you dipshit. Flip your visor down."

SJ did that, and sighed in admiration.

It was half metallic, half fleshly tentacles. Whatever it was, this wasn't the product of an ancient African imagination. This was from a world of aquatic intelligence: a cyborg octopus.

It extruded a tentacle toward him.

He couldn't get to his bow. The passage was too narrow, and nocking an arrow would have been a topological riddle to boggle Captain Cipher.

Then the thing had wrapped its arms around him. Maybe they *felt* slender and mostly metallic, but they *looked* green and reptilian.

A head evolved out of the churning mass, and it hissed—

"Duck!" Alphonse yelled behind him. SJ turned his head to the side just fast enough to avoid a stream of hissing green venom.

(Funny. It smelled like ammoniated glass cleaner . . .)

When it struck the side of the tunnel, the metal there smoked and glowed.

"Crom!" he screamed, and grabbed the acid spout before it could eject again.

No matter how he braced himself, he could only get clumsy, partial leverage. No matter what he did, the damned thing always had another arm to attack with.

His breathing sobbed raggedly, echoing in the enclosed space. Behind him, his teammates watched helplessly. How to beat this thing? He thought of the knife in his belt. He didn't dare release either of its arms. It was all he could do to keep this damned thing off balance.

Balance. Yes. SJ fought his way to his knees, then bent his arms, getting all of the leverage that he could, wedging himself solidly in the duct—

And hoisted.

He tilted the creature sideways, so that it was on edge in the cramped space. His back was sore, and the muscles in his arms ached. The friggin' machine must have weighed fifty pounds, and without proper leverage it was a bitch to lift and control. It screamed and scrabbled like a beetle flipped on its back, and he watched as its claws attacked his hands, tearing flesh away. Blood spurted.

But S. J. Waters, mighty Scout, would not be denied. He managed to brace his elbow against the machine, wedging it into the wall. With his right hand he finally got to his belt knife.

The thing's underbelly was softer than its back. He wedged his knife into a crack, shrieking with concentration, loud enough to drown out the sounds made by the beast itself. He waggled the blade back and forth—

Green foam bubbled out of its innards, and suddenly that ammonia smell was everywhere. Acid blood spurted, miraculously spraying him with only a few mild droplets.

"Back! Back!" he yelled, and his comrades retreated as far as they could.

The creature was both smoking and screaming now, and then—

Its carapace burst open. Its metal legs trembled, shook, groped out one final time . . .

And were still. The acid blood streamed away in rivulets, leaving a harmless residue.

SJ examined his wrists and arms. Where the claws had gripped were tiny red welts (which looked *much* worse in DreamTime), and his eyes stung from the ammonia—but he was alive.

"All right . . ." He nudged the beast with the tip of his knife and began to push it along in front of him. When they reached a cross-path in the tunnels he pushed it to the side.

Much softer, but still ahead of him, he heard another clicking sound. He could just make out the image of a second beast, its pseudopods pulsing with rage. Had he slain its mate?

The beast retreated, wanting no part of the mighty Scout.

"Come back, you coward!" he screamed.

It stopped, and one of its pseudopods formed into a hand. Four of the fingers bent down, leaving a single digit standing straight up, in a universal symbol of disapproval.

And then it was gone.

Chapter Twenty-nine

The Larger Game

"The strategic arts are: first, measurements; second, estimates; third, analysis; fourth, balancing; fifth, triumph.

"The situation gives rise to measurements, measurements give rise to estimates, analysis gives rise to balancing, balancing gives rise to triumph."

—Nigel Bishop, *The Art of Gaming*, 2052

Friday, July 22, 2059—10:30 A.M.

Tony was in the break room with Lopez, surrounded by screens, sipping very good, very strong coffee from a vending machine. A nap would have helped more, he thought sluggishly; but not yet. That black magic coffee would have to do. Tex-Mits and Army were about to reenter the Gaming area—and *nobody* was about to get any rest.

"They've nearly reached the Nommo, and they've got their diving gear," Tony said. "They're never going back to the roof. So they'll miss the fish. So I've extended the Nommo's speech, but I haven't—"

"Let me see."

Tony brought it onscreen. "Haven't inserted it in the script yet."

Richard Lopez skimmed it, then began to chop. Tony flinched, but he watched. Richard had cut the speech to half before he could blink.

"There. That will tell them much of what they *need* to know. Smile."

Tony spoke through a wide rigid grin. "They'll miss the island. All that frigging work and they're going to miss the island fish."

"Nothing is lost, Tony."

"Twenty million viewers aren't going to know how clever I am, Richard. It was so wonderful! The floating island is an adult Nommo. That's why they can't go home, they get too big—"

"The Gamers always miss half of what we put in. They can't

take *every* path, Tony. The home viewers will get it when they buy the cassette."

Richard Lopez must have been exhausted, but his eyes and his smile were very bright. Tony asked. "What keeps you going?"

"You are playing your own Game," Richard Lopez said.

Say what? "Sure. Everybody plays—"

The little man's eyes glowed. "It involves Nigel Bishop, and the Army team. It involves gambling. It involves Alex Griffin, who entered one of my Games once before, and is a remarkable man."

He knows. "Yeah," Tony said dryly. "I think that I can remember that Game."

"You need my help."

"Richard," Tony said, "we've got a Game running here. You've got to focus your attention there, or the whole thing will come apart."

"Come, now," Lopez chided. "Something has occurred which might damage California Voodoo's integrity. I should be involved."

Tony sipped more coffee. His thoughts crawled in slow circles. What should he do? Get in touch with Griffin? Harmony? Vail? Summers? The little man was hovering, awaiting an answer.

"I will tell you a secret," Richard Lopez said. "This is my last Game."

"*What?*"

Lopez's smile was small, sad, wearily regretful. "The doctors did not want me out of my bed. They have held me together as long as they can. I'm afraid I am out of time."

Tony fumbled for words, and didn't find them before Lopez held up a hand. "It is all right. The pain is manageable, and my mind is clear."

"That makes one of us." There was no way he could deny Richard Lopez his request. His last request? "There's a dead woman. Alex was in love with her, but there's more to it . . ." Haltingly, Tony began to lay it out. Lopez leaned back, closing his eyes.

"I wondered why the betting money all went through Ecuador, but maybe there was more I didn't see. But I can't find it, and six hundred thousand is about what you'd expect Bishop to scrape up, and the tilt in the Vegas odds is about right. But . . . he'd have to be crazy. Stark crazy, and that would explain his killing Crayne too. If he did. Richard, *can he do it?*"

"Not Army," Richard said, with his eyes still closed. "Only Clavell or Poule can control that team. Neither are gamblers. I cannot imagine either routing six hundred thousand dollars through Ecuador, stealing maps, killing a Dream Park security woman—and then playing this Game as they have. There is no compulsiveness—" He stopped, considering. "Except for Clavell's accident on the modular walk. He risked his life to finish the Game. Yes. That makes it possible."

"And Bishop?"

"Psychologically capable. But capable and culpable are two different things. I agree that he can't force a win for Army. But if he cooperates with Army, and has Acacia Garcia . . ."

He shook his head again. "Absurd! Acacia and Bishop and the Army all in conspiracy? Too complex—and the winnings split too many ways. A team of two, perhaps. Bishop and Acacia? But Army alone?"

His eyes opened. "There is something wrong here," he said quietly.

"What you got?"

"This feels too much like a logic puzzle. *'If A and B cooperate, then C and D can't win. But if D gives A a bribe . . .'* That sort of thing. It . . . is superfluously complex. Deliberately complex." He grinned. "A trap for excessively clever minds, I shall look elsewhere."

They both glanced at the screens first; but Tex-Mits/Army were still crawling through pipes, wiggling legs filmed by an insectile cleaning robot. Now Lopez took control of a small break-room monitor console. His fingers blurred as he accessed the IFGS library, Master's level.

"In the library are computerized versions of every book germane to Gaming. We know about Bishop's *The Art of Gaming*. What you may not realize is that since 1960, over a dozen different game versions of the source material, *The Art of War*, have been created. The entire book has been rendered into a series of If-Then propositions."

"Meaning?"

"*The Art of War* was uniquely suited to a man like Bishop, who sees the entire world as a zero-sum game, and more importantly, as a black or white proposition—that is, he divides all actions into those things which are good for Nigel Bishop, and those things that are not. I propose to you that we run those routines, especially the best AI version, which is called, I believe, 'Sun Tsu.' It was designed to give opinions of gaming strategies—chess, go, role playing. You submit the Gaming scenario, and it offers an opinion. I suggest that we enter a synopsis of 'California Voodoo,' available in my own file—"

Tap tap tappity.

"And the moves made thus far—"

He went into fast-playback mode, following Bishop around MIMIC.

"And see what happens."

Tony licked his lips. "Ah—Richard. It may be more than that. You have to expand it outside the realm of the Game."

"To include the gambling, yes." At first enthusiastic, Lopez had bogged down. He was staring at the screen. "There are too many variables now," he said. "Too many to feed them into the computer. Yes. Too complex for the machine. We must trust our own minds, yes?"

Richard Lopez sipped his coffee, thinking, and then, very lazily, asked, "The money was routed through Ecuador?"

"Yes."

"Why Ecuador? Drug money?"

"Fifty years ago, maybe. Now it's old money, and there are service corporations running parts of the government."

A long pause. "Is Ecuador part of the Barsoom Project?"

"Heard a joke about that." Tony leaned back. "The Barsoom Project is much like the European Space Agency, circa 1990 or so. That is, countries put in *x* amount of dollars, and they get back a guaranteed *x* dollars in the shape of contracts."

"Sounds fair."

"But it doesn't really work out. Some countries simply don't have sufficient industrial base to produce the goods. Ecuador is one of them. I heard someone say that Ecuador had put in like three hundred million dollars—and that Barsoom was gonna end up with enough Ecuadorian toilet paper to gift-wrap Phobos. They want a launching base for the Phoenix F. Being near the equator, it might actually save a little fuel, but Ecuador simply can't cut the mustard—not in the next forty, fifty years. Then it might be a different story."

"I've been in the hospital," Richard said in nonapology. "What—"

"I only meant—they're on the equator, Richard. That's why it's Ecuador, and that's why they might be king of the walk when the Barsoom Project is ready to start testing skyhook devices on Mars. I know of at least six ways of getting to orbit without rockets. Mostly they involve tether technology, none of them can be built yet, and they all *have* to be on the equator to work. But of course there are other countries . . ."

Lopez's brow wrinkled. "Corporations. How many of the countries and companies involved in the Barsoom Project have moved in at this time?"

"Practically none, although some of the spaces have been tailored for their use."

"But Ecuador would be in a better position twenty years from now if they had better technology now. Could they *buy* what they need?"

"A lot of it is proprietary. They'd have to steal it."

"Just thinking aloud. Listen: I will confer with Mitsuko. If she gives permission, I would like to see more information pertaining to this situation. Perhaps . . ."

He closed his eyes again. "Just perhaps. Security is an interesting Game," he said approvingly. "A larger Game. I think I begin to like Alex Griffin. Very much."

Chapter Thirty

Ambush

Friday, July 22, 2059—11:10 A.M.

S. J. Waters kicked the ventilator grille free of its housing, and it clattered to the ground.

He scooted around in the vent until he could just poke his nose out. He sniffed, and smelled water. An enormous bank of fluorescent tubes overhead cast hard shadows.

SJ pushed himself out and landed on the balls of his feet. The hallway seemed empty. "All clear," he whispered.

His head jerked, and he notched an arrow to his bow, pointing it down the corridor at the unexpected splashy-giggly sounds.

Seemed harmless. Merry. Still, his nerves burned.

Alphonse Nakagawa emerged just after him, followed by Major Clavell, and then General Poule.

They formed a protective pocket around Mary-em, who crawled out just before Crystal.

"What do you think?" Poule asked when the last of their party had emerged.

"We think that you had better remain very still," Tammi said, stepping out of a door to their left. In a flash, they were surrounded and outnumbered.

Poule was deadly quiet. "An ambush?"

"Call it a hijack," Bishop said lazily. "We want your icons. All of them."

Alphonse glanced at Mary-em; but no, he'd keep that secret for now. He said, "You can't just kill us, you know."

"And why not?"

"We were told very specifically: the gods don't take murder lightly. On the other hand . . ."

Prez the Zulu had fixed his attention on Alphonse just one instant too long: Poule leapt into action.

His sword was out in a flash, and he had slashed Prez's right arm. Prez deftly tossed his assegai into his left hand and lunged at Poule. Clavell blindsided him, and the fight was on.

The hall was too narrow for effective maneuvering, and Alphonse knew their cause was lost. Regardless, Poule and Clavell teamed brilliantly. They had Prez Coolidge, an accomplished Warrior, down and dead in a moment. Then they broke through the opposing line, using a confused Twan as a shield. They pivoted to another twin-prong attack, and then another . . .

Still, it was hopeless. Al's heart went out to S. J. Waters, who quickly found himself surrounded.

SJ was no great fighter. He simply didn't have the reflexes for it, but he had played enough Games that his Shield and Recovery ratings could see him through. Twice Tammi struck him, and twice the computer disallowed or healed her touches. Then Acacia was beside her, and SJ was doomed. He died before loosing a single arrow.

Crystal Cofax hadn't room to swing her staff. She sobbed in frustration as she tried to get a clean shot in on Bishop. Finally she screamed, charged through the line, and ran down the corridor toward the sounds of laughter and music—

And skidded to a halt, her eyes wide. She balanced at the edge of a vast swimming pool ringed with diving boards and lounge chairs. The boards vibrated as bronzed beach boys bounced off, sailed high, and somersaulted in midair, plunging into the water. On every chair reclined a golden girl, oiled and sun-haired and masked in bronzed plastic, perfect breasts and hips swathed in wisps of bikini gauze.

They saw her at the same moment she saw them. For a moment the tableau was frozen, and then—

Led by Bishop, the battle spilled out of the hall, and the sun-bathers—

Yawned, and returned to their tans.

Crystal feinted a figure-eight pattern. Bishop faded back, deflecting the tips skillfully, never committing himself. Crystal lunged—

Bishop slid his blade down the staff and grazed her fingers. They glowed red and black, and might as well have been twitching in the dirt, for all the good they'd do her now.

Panting, Crystal dropped the staff. Bishop saluted—and ran her through.

He turned to Griffin. "Watch out, Bobo!"

General Poule, enraged by the ambush, even more incensed by the hopelessness of his situation, had attacked the only unarmed member of the enemy party: their guide.

Griffin backpedaled. What were the rules about this? Weren't guides off limits? Wasn't he protected by the gods or something?

There was no more time to think.

Poule lunged with his sword, and Griffin snatched up a beach chair to deflect the blade. Twice more Poule attempted to breach his defense, and each time Griffin frustrated him neatly.

"I can't get used to this fighting with furniture," Poule said nastily. "Where did you learn it?"

"Macy's School of Self-Defense."

Poule tried a low-line attack, aiming at Griffin's left foot. Slamming the chair down, the security chief disarmed him.

And now everyone was watching. Poule was enraged. Exhausted emotionally by the long crawl and the fight, the general was determined to take someone with him to hell.

Poule leapt forward, drawing a foot-long dagger from his belt, holding it underhand. His weight was balanced as neatly as a prizefighter's. Once again, Alex ran the Voodoo Game's specs through his mind: this was a Level Ten Hazardous Environment event. Physical challenges between players were acceptable. But between players and NPCs?

Griffin backed up until he was against the wall.

"Got no guts?" Poule taunted.

Griffin was facing a professional military man with a twelve-inch fighting knife in his hand. If he wasn't careful, his guts were going to be very much in evidence.

Bishop threw Griffin a knife, and Alex snatched it out of the air. "Here you are, Bobo," Bishop said cheerfully. "Go to town."

Griffin balanced the "blade" carefully. It was twelve inches of plastic dowel, set within a holographic image of gleaming, curving steel.

Poule had every reason to go for the kill. His team had been neutralized, but a good personal combat would fatten up his Wessler-Grahams; and his enemies would lose a Guide.

He slid in, blade held underhand in the right, left hand forward and flat as a spade.

At all costs, Griffin had to stay in the Game. He stood, lowering his hand. "I am no Warrior. I cannot fight this man."

"Die, then!" Poule laughed, stabbing viciously for Griffin's arm. Griffin scrambled back. Despite the potbelly, Poule was lightning. Damn the man!

Contempt flashed in the general's eyes, and Griffin suddenly realized something:

Unlike Bishop, Poule didn't know who Griffin was. To Poule, Griffin was just another actor. He could feed that overconfidence, and maybe, just maybe . . .

Griffin flipped his knife around into classic "ice-pick" configuration. It was a mug's game, a John Wayne Indian position, a Hockey-Mask Killer position, completely wrong for any sophisticated knife fighting. It limited the arc of approach and confined the defender to stabbing only. Or so said conventional wisdom.

Griffin and Poule circled each other.

Alex's attention screwed down to a point so intense that the rest of the room ceased to exist, became a gray fog. And in the center of that fog . . . General Poule.

Confident. An ex-Beret, perhaps? Combat specialist? Griffin wanted this to be over fast, and his only hope was to keep Poule overconfident.

Poule tested Griffin's perimeter, slashing in with the blade, smiling grimly when Griffin merely jumped back again, almost stumbling, knife still held like an ice pick.

Then the general went for the kill.

The ice-pick knife position allows only for stabbing, but if one folds the knife back against the forearm, it becomes a tool capable of vicious slashing defenses. Because of the shortened reach, one must wait for one's opponent to approach. One must have great speed, very precise timing, and a keen eye for distance.

Alex Griffin had all three. Poule lunged in, his left hand high to deflect. Griffin sliced Poule's left wrist, and in a single fluid, swerving stroke brought the blade down and across the attacking arm.

Red and black light spilled from the wound. Poule groaned and dropped his knife.

Griffin grabbed Poule's right wrist with his left hand. He stepped in, driving an elbow to the jaw and a knee to the groin.

(The man played fair, and had great reflexes! Griffin thought.

Poule knew he was beaten, and responded to Griffin's mimed blows like a professional stuntman.)

With Poule doubled over in pain, Alex raised his knife high, ready to plunge into the nape of his unprotected neck—

But instead let Poule fall to the ground. "Bind this man's wounds," he said. "He is a brave enemy. I would not have him die."

He looked over at Bishop and saw his secretive, meaningless smile.

Griffin tore strips from his own shirt and began to bind Poule's wounds. Top Nun completed the binding and knelt beside the general, threw her hands into the air, and said, "Abracadabra. So I'm making a *broch* already. If you're not too busy, heal 'im up. We might need him. Maybe not now, maybe Tuesday, but why take chances?"

Griffin took stock of the survivors, and it didn't take long. That last ambush had been bloody. Only eleven players remained: Mouser, Mary-em, Al the Barbarian, Acacia, Top Nun, Twan, Tammi, Major Clavell, Captain Cipher, Bishop, and General Poule. The Game had become a slaughter.

Finally there was time to examine his surroundings.

It might have been the biggest indoor spa in the world. It had a makeshift look: no one had planned to put a pool here. But someone had diverted water flow into a vast sunken region of the tenth floor. The resulting pool dwarfed an Olympic standard. The inhabitants had carted in tanning machines, and sets of gleaming chrome weights, and steam cabinets. Stand-alone Jacuzzis bubbled along the rim of the pool like yeast clusters; rowing machines, stationary bicycles, and massage tables grew like weeds.

But along the ceiling, and all along the walls, tiny gleaming creatures scampered about. They seemed part machine and part animal and were busying themselves with repair and rebuilding. The entire level had an organic honeycomb look, crinkled and textured and pocketed. Shifting, multicolored waves of slow lightning crawled behind the walls, painting everything in the vast room in ethereal, electric hues of red and blue and yellow.

The air was as humid as a sauna, with wisps of steam curling from the water itself.

One of the muscular poolside loungers uncoiled himself lazily and sauntered over. He was well over six feet tall. On his face was written bland, unconcerned amusement.

"Name's Biff," he said. "Gettin' into serious hassles, dudes. Just hang loose, huh? Keep those bad vibes rolling in, the Nommo won't like it. Like, kick back, and we'll get some tasty waves up for you."

For once, Bishop seemed to be a little off balance. "Make a wave?"

"Totally tubular, dude."

Even as they watched, the pool's surface rippled, swelled, and reached up for the ceiling. It crested, boiling with froth.

One golden surfer had been balancing on his board in the middle of the pool, waiting patiently for a wave to happen by. As it expanded he rode the crest up and took the stance: right leg forward, left back and slightly bent, arms spread for balance. Fifteen feet of water ridge rolled him along a thousand feet of indoor lagoon, and then—

The wave turned itself inside out, flowed through itself, turned back, and headed the other way. The surfer pulled off a maneuver that Griffin was quite certain no other had ever managed. He leaned into the board like a skateboard artist doing a wheelie, his weight sinking back to the rear. The board stood up on end, pivoted, and he sailed back the way he'd come.

Griffin gathered his jaw back off the floor and followed their host to a cluster of chairs and tables. Biff snapped his finger, and a bevy of giggling, bikini-clad bunnies scampered forward to do his bidding. Twan, Tammi, and especially Acacia bristled at the performance.

The girls disappeared, then reappeared with platters of sushi and carrot juice.

Griffin tried the taste combination and decided he could gag it down. Something beneath the water glistened for a moment, but when he turned his head, it vanished.

Twan leaned toward Biff. "You're only two levels above the Mayombreros," she said pointedly. "How can you be so . . ."

"Laid back?" He laughed heartily. "This is Nommo country. Everybody's pretty mellow here."

Something that looked like a meter-tall mollusk cruised up to Alex, serving drinks from a nipple on its side. Griffin sampled it. Delicious and martinilike. Did it eat grain and sugar, ferment them in a second stomach, and then regurgitate alcohol?

Acacia tasted her California roll gingerly, then bit in. "We'd like to see the Nommo. Would you call them for us?"

"No can do," Biff answered regretfully. "The Nommo don't like coming out all that much. Maybe if you wait around for a day or two . . ."

"No can do."

"Well, then—I guess you better go in after them. I hope you can swim."

Twan punched Bishop's arm lightly. "You know, right about now I'm glad we brought you."

Seated, Bishop managed to bow gallantly.

Alphonse, still seething with anger, noted the booty bags that Bishop and others had brought to the tables. A gleaming regulator poked out of the top.

Scuba gear.

The first self-contained underwater breathing apparatuses had, of course, used compressed air. The development of cheap nuclear batteries had made those obsolete: a rebreather driven by a really powerful pump could last for twenty hours on a charge, far beyond the capacity of air bottles.

At first he wondered if these would be the classic, older devices, lost in MIMIC since 1995 . . .

Biff had the same question. He examined one of the rebreathers and raised an ironic eyebrow. "Not what I expected," he said. "I was going to tell you about some scuba gear guarded by a local fire demon."

"Not interested." Bishop grinned.

"Can't say I blame you."

Bishop checked over the apparatus. "We've got three sets of gear here."

Major Clavell, who had been miserable, took an interest again. "Does the word *anachronism* mean anything to you?"

Bishop beamed. "Not a thing. Working fine," he announced. "Who's coming?"

Twan inspected the gear, hesitantly at first, then with a growing excitement. "I want in," she said.

Bishop nodded. "And we need a guide. Coral having departed this vale of tears, I believe that Bobo is our only choice."

Griffin smiled coldly and began to strip.

The poolside surfers gathered around to watch them, with the sounds of old Beach Boys and a little Jan and Dean still playing over the loudspeakers.

They were down to underwear, with the exception of Twan, who had borrowed a swimsuit. Her body was petite but taut, a swimmer's body, in fact the body of a swimmer who might have done weights and running merely to keep in shape for more swimming.

The rebreather gear looked slightly oversized on her. Of course, on Mary-em it would have been absurd.

Alex slipped himself into harness, balanced the gear in place, and checked to make sure that everything was operating smoothly. Acacia handed him a hand lamp, and he splashed its yellow beam across to the far wall.

He noticed that Bishop was treating him with just a hair more respect. Was that the result of the little episode with General Poule? Or was it something else? He took this opportunity to examine Bishop more closely. In the swim trunks he was a very dark black man without an ounce of useless tissue on his body. Probably a high-metabolism type, seething with testosterone. Any level of exercise would make his body bulge with muscle. Perfect coordination. A precise mind driven by a monstrous ego. He probably weighed twenty pounds less than Griffin and was possibly as strong.

Griffin didn't like to think about that. As strong. Possibly faster. Probably smarter. But there had to be a flaw there. Griffin felt the stirrings of a sour cold knot of fear in his belly.

Bishop nodded to Griffin and slipped feetfirst into the water. Griffin went in a moment later, followed by Twan. The water closed about him in warm embrace.

It was fresh water, unchlorinated and murky. He couldn't see anything in it but submerged walkways and corridors. He shone his lamp around, and the beam stretched out like a yellow finger, briefly touching first a statue, then an ancient, rusted bank of computer terminals.

The water rolled. For a moment he thought, *Wave!* and readied himself for the turbulence to follow.

But it wasn't that. Something like a textured torpedo brushed past him. It was rough and slick at the same time.

Griffin kicked back and reached out for it, but it was gone. When he switched his light around, the murk had already concealed it. Gone.

He hovered there, sucking cold, flavorless air from his mouthpiece. What had it been?

Nommo.

He pushed a button on his wrist, and a line of green arrows projected in front of him, taking him down farther into the depths.

Bishop was a few feet off to his right, moving beautifully and having no trouble keeping up. The setting was so ethereal that for a few minutes Griffin was able to forget the mission, forget the job at hand, and just submerge himself in the underwater world.

Twan slid alongside him and extended an arm, pointing out a building that looked something like a cathedral dome.

Bishop stopped, floating, and made a very broad gesture. *Reveal magic.*

The dome glowed weakly at first, and then more strongly, until they were all but blinded.

Griffin shielded his face, the hiss of air muffling his hearing.

But when the light died down, they were surrounded by—

Dolphins. Alex tried to touch one of them. His hand slid along its body, and it darted away. There were six of them. With gentle nudges, they herded the three Adventurers down to the glowing dome.

Chapter Thirty-one

The Nommo

The dolphins seemed as friendly as Flipper. They coaxed the swimmers through the water with gentle bumps and nudges. Despite their incredible delicacy, one could *feel* the power of a dolphin moving past: a wall of muscle, capable of smashing bone with a flick of a tail.

Their inner sanctum was tropically warm, a lagoon within a lagoon. Wisps of steam rose from slow, swirling, oily whirlpools.

Imitation rock slabs rose from the surface of the water, forming broad rough steps. Lounging on the steps were—something was wrong with the light—a man and a woman? But their arms and legs were—well, flattened, a little like the flukes of a whale; and their faces were unforgettably ugly; and their skin was not white or brown or any human shade, but a dark blue reminiscent of the dolphins themselves. They whispered to each other in high-pitched, gobbling, squeaking sounds.

One of the dolphins arched backward out of the water and danced on its tail as it skipped across the surface. It balanced upright at the edge of the stone steps, shimmered, melted into an amorphous cloud of blue light, then became another of . . . those. The Nommo. Her face, like theirs, seemed immobile, the eyes lidless and staring, the mouth turned up in a rigid meaningless grin. Without a shred of self-consciousness, she lounged back on one of the steps and grinned at them, challenging.

She gave a dolphinlike burbling chuckle, and then addressed them in a very human voice. "Betcha like this tons better."

"May I?" Bishop indicated the steps out.

Twan said, "Go for it."

Bishop settled himself on the steps. Griffin continued treading water, working off restless energy. So did Twan, for whatever reasons.

"We are—from the outside," Bishop explained.

The blue woman found that funny. "Oh? Outside. And we are from *Queeepzz*—from outer space, from the worlds circling Sirius Little."

Back on the surface, eight remaining Adventurers were as relaxed as might be, considering the circumstances. There was little to do until the two Loremasters resurfaced. Only a nominal guard was placed on Alphonse Nakagawa, Clavell, and Poule. They were, after all, disarmed and helpless.

All this water: it seemed likely that they'd all be under it sooner or later. Al wasn't the only Gamer who had changed into his swimband. Slender and muscular, he looked almost as good as Bishop. He'd spent a few minutes making eye contact with Tammi and Acacia and Top Nun. The ladies weren't responding; they were ignoring him, in fact.

So no one seemed to be watching Alphonse as he stood watching the water, or knelt and stirred it with one hand, near the piles of discarded clothing and costumes.

Bishop had left all of his gear behind. Al the Barb's fingertips wandered through side pockets in the Loremaster's pack. A spare shoestring . . . a dirty sock . . . good. They went into his waistband. And what's this—a long-toothed comb? Humming a silent, joyous little song, Alphonse teased it out with two fingers, keeping his eyes carefully fixed on the water's surface.

Still nobody watching? He peered down. Caught in the black plastic tines were six black, curly hairs.

He plucked them out. For an instant he held them in his open palm in full view, not of any passerby, but of some omnicient deity, some hypothetical ceiling camera. The Game Masters could play it back if need be. Nakagawa's Law #4: *If the GM didn't see it, it didn't happen.*

Then he rubbed the hairs into a tiny ball the size of a pinhead and tucked the ball under his right thumbnail. His folded hand returned to Bishop's pack and emerged empty. A lost comb would be noticed.

According to voodoo lore, a single hair was enough for a charm.

Mess with me, Bishop? My daddy put a rattlesnake in a man's pocket once, then asked him for a match. And he's the family wimp.

Al the Barbarian edged back from the pool. Nobody watched him too closely, and why should they? He wasn't close to any weapons, or anything valuable at all.

"Sirius Little?" Bishop asked, momentarily confused.

"The Dogon," Twan said with deep satisfaction. "Appelion was right."

"Oh, yeah," the blue woman said. "We thought we'd zip on down here. Earth looked like a party planet. We'd catch some rays . . ."

The blue male behind her rose, stretching until joints popped. She slapped him smartly on the buns as he passed. He jumped up, flipped, and took a header into the water. In mid-arc he transformed into a dolphin. The dolphin nosed up against Bishop, who stroked it affectionately.

"Our folks—damn near ancestors, now." The Nommo woman grimaced. "Some of them have even *died*. Well, they were only supposed to stay for a few months, but they took a bad splash when we landed. Couldn't repair the lander."

"Why not?" Twan asked.

"Dig it. It's not like they were some high-dome expedition. They were a buncha kids, out for a good time. Weren't supposed to be here at all. There was a mother ship, stashed up in orbit. When the lander crashed, they must have gotten scared, zipped back to the motherland." She chuckled. "I'd like to hear the story they told the folks back home. Most of the tech they brought was biomech— you've seen some of that? And the Ethereals. You folks call 'em demons and angels and so on, but they're like roaches and rats where we came from. Useful, but they breed too damned fast. And we have some little tricks, mental matter-energy conversion stuff, too minor to do a really big repair, but your folk—your ancestors seemed to like 'em."

"I'll just bet they did," Bishop murmured.

"Now, the lander crashed in the Atlantic, off what you called the Ivory Coast. Good people. Like the food. We just played around with them, taught 'em a little stuff, and, well . . ."

The male's dolphin-head popped up. "Our ancestors thought your ancestors were being polite," he buzzed. "Excessively polite, but you know, local mores . . ."

"They worshiped us. This was a long time ago, back around what you call the Ice Age, and I guess we were kind of unusual. We didn't catch on fast enough."

"Our ancestors taught them our technology," the male explained, and spit a mouthful of water. "What you'd call magic. The mind tricks—sound and visualization and so on—what you'd call spells. Summoning the Ethereals, who were rutting out of control by then, but don't have much to do with humans unless someone calls 'em."

"Years passed," the female continued, "hundreds of years. Our folks couldn't go home even if they could get the ship repaired—"

"Why not?"

"Too big. Adults of our kind get as big as islands. As for us, we were having fun. Lots of sun, and water, and good company. Ever been treated like a god?"

"Not recently," Twan said.

"From time to time," Bishop admitted.

"Addictive, isn't it? We got lazy. Some of us—a *lot* of us—started making babies, going out further into the ocean where there was room for them, goin' native, I guess you'd say. They forgot even the simple magic, or didn't teach it to their kids. Not many of us even remember what we really are."

"How could that happen?" Griffin asked.

"Easier than you think. Hey—the ocean was warm, the fish were slow, and nothing had teeth big enough to bother us, not even us kids. Humans are fun to play with. We've had a great time teaching you tricks!"

She laughed warmly, then grew serious.

"Then something that we hadn't really expected happened. One of the big things about what you call magic is that it takes life force to create life force—I mean, it can be amplified or converted, but not actually created. Back home, they breed a sort of hive beastie. Lots of individual bodies, one big life-form. We could 'kill' pieces of it, but it was only like trimming toenails, you see? It died out quick here, and then we actually had to sacrifice animals, harvest their life force."

"Santería?" Twan asked.

"And the rest. All magic spread out from Africa. A lot of your magicians don't really remember anything; it's like cargo-cult magic and aeronautics. But we were the beginning. Through sacrifices and rituals—"

"Rituals?"

"Certainly," the were-dolphin said patiently. "Imagine, for example, a cube . . ." The water fluxed, and a glistening, rubbery cube of water popped up from the surface of the lagoon. It floated there, suspended apparently by the force of mind alone. "Now, divide it into octants . . ." Concentrating, the Nommo put on an amazing display, dividing the cube of water into ever more complex geometric shapes, while keeping it suspended above the surface. It finally evolved into a crystal castle, its component shapes rotating, dancing, and dividing all at the same time. Her blue-black face was screwed up in concentration.

Then with a tinkle the entire structure dissolved, the castle crashed back into the water, and the older male slapped his tail repeatedly on the water, applauding her performance. It sounded like a chorus of cherry bombs.

"What was *that*?" Bishop asked, for once impressed.

"An advanced exercise."

"Needs work," the male said lazily.

She stuck out her tongue at him. "Anyhow, it's one of the mental exercises that calls up the Ethereals, and some of the other powers."

"What about the sacrifice?"

"Our ancestors laid this big trip on you guys: it is like ultra cool to sacrifice animals with big brains. But we couldn't be everywhere at once, and some of you guys tumbled to the fact that the smarter the beastie, the more you can milk its pain."

Twan seemed to be studying the ground as she spoke. "And conscious animals, like human beings, would be the most powerful yet."

Bishop and Twan looked at each other simultaneously. "Excuse me," Bishop said. "But wouldn't the sacrifice of Nommo—of your own kind—be the most powerful of all?"

"Gag me with a jellyfish. That's like *disgusting*." She smiled upon them as if they were simpleminded children. Her expression reminded Griffin of one of his aunts. A woman who could look straight at the truth and not see it, blinded by the light of her own assurance that The World Doesn't Work That Way.

Bishop was thinking again. "If you kill the creature quickly you release all of the energy. How about slowly?"

The Nommo grimaced. "Uncool. I don't even want to talk about it."

Twan was aghast. "You're suggesting this is the real reason for torture?"

"Have you just *got* to hear this? All right, all right. You people look so funny, act so friendly, but you get hooked on that death-energy stuff so easy, it's scary. Do you realize that your planet's most popular religion uses an act of torture as its central symbol?

"We did what we could, you know. Kept you in small groups. Limited the techno stuff. Tried for centuries. Results, zip. We kept really nasty weapons from being developed in Africa, but the rest of the world just . . ." She trailed off.

Bishop's eyebrows flew up. "Prez would have loved this. Africa was conquered and colonized because you limited their technology?"

"*Mea culpa.* Like, 'oops, we're sorry.' We folded our tents and snuck away in the night."

"We didn't forget you," the male said. "We watched. And when you developed some heavyweight tech of your own, we figured, Hey! Maybe we can get home now. The children, anyway. We still had that crashed shuttle offshore from Cameroon.

"So we traded little teensy bits of magic and got our worshipers back. It was easy; our families had been in the god biz for generations, after all. We got our shuttle repaired enough to hover. Got this building partially constructed and then walled in the shuttle in the dead of night."

"What happened?"

"We were too late. That big collapse came, you know? We saved as many of our people as we could, but . . ." She shook her head. "We just don't have the technical skills here to finish the repair job."

"Why don't you control this entire building?" Griffin asked.

"The Mayombreros. Bad dudes, man. They know all the oogy sacrifice stuff. It's been all we could do to keep 'em at the bottom. They need the roof folks to grow fresh food, roof needs the basement for power—for a long time it worked out."

"You know," Twan said. "Our enclaves have powerful scientists, but we lack power. Perhaps together . . ."

★ ★ ★

Mgui-Smythe was nervous. He'd run stress-analysis programs under a wide variety of assumptions. His crew had shored up the walls and floors of MIMIC until they were twice as strong as the computers said they needed to be. Still, what they were about to do was way outside standard engineering texts.

On the plus side: if MIMIC stood up to this, the building would take anything the Barsoom Project might require of it.

Sections of both the ninth and tenth levels of MIMIC had been flooded. All furniture and statuary on the submerged floor of the tenth were constructed of light, breakaway material, weighted with sandbags. Even the IFGS had finally, reluctantly, given their approval.

The floors of the first ten levels were all retractable, intended to allow the construction of enormous machinery. Under the right circumstances, they could accommodate whole rocket engines and shuttle craft. They could also survive the calculated insanity of Dream Park.

The countdown began.

Bishop held quite still, just sensing, not reacting, as the walls began to rumble. Griffin thrashed about in the water. The water was carrying vibrations through his whole body, humming in his bones. "What in the hell—"

And then the very floor beneath them gave way, and they plunged screaming into darkness.

Chapter Thirty-two

Death from Below

Friday, July 22, 2059—2:12 P.M.

Al the Barbarian heard a sort of magnified gurgle. His nimble fingers froze, then tucked his nearly finished weapon into a plastic bag in his day pack. Al's guilty conscience would have flinched at *any* sound. Someone must have seen! He was doing black voodoo here.

He twisted the bag and sealed it, one-handed. The floor was singing against his bare feet. Other Gamers were listening for a gurgle that was becoming a roar—

The surface of the pool lurched down by six inches, as if the bottom had been ripped out.

The water foamed and churned hideously, and a gigantic whirlpool formed. Beach boys and bunnies thrashed toward the nearest ladders and were dragged down, drowning.

In Engineering, a team of experts led by Ashly Mgui-Smythe oversaw the massive water dump. Sluice vents fanned open at MIMIC's base. Thousands of gallons a second flooded out onto the desert floor.

When supports for the tenth level's sliding floor were withdrawn, the Gamers fell down into the ninth, also half-filled with water. Every object they could possibly bump into was either soft, slick, rounded, or all three. The net effect was like spinning down a three-story water slide.

Their howls of consternation rang through the speakers in Engineering, and the visual effect was horrendous. What remained of the floor looked as though it had been torn away by giant claws.

Mgui-Smythe popped a beer open and saluted, wishing them luck.

Griffin hit the water fast, but not hard, guided down safely by a chute of torn floor. He was planning the murder of Tony McWhirter. As a first step he righted himself, blew air to clean out his mouthpiece, and thrashed three hundred and sixty degrees in the water, searching for enemies.

Floating near him was a Nommo in its flat-catfish shape. The ugly creature seemed almost helplessly dazed, but not too badly injured.

Twan had regained her equilibrium fast and had screamed out a spell. A golden halo of protection surrounded her as she splashed to keep afloat.

Where was Bishop? *There*, floating on his side. Griffin swam over to him and helped him right himself. Water poured from Bishop's half-open mouth. His eyes rolled back, eyelashes fluttering weakly.

"Good going," Bishop whispered. "We'll make a Gamer of you yet." Shamming for the camera, dammit.

Splash!

Alex bobbed around in the water and saw the ripple, but nothing else. Something was in there with them.

Some of the Nommo had seen it, too. Those less dazed were changing from that flat-catfish shape into dolphin mode, from tool user to fighter.

The water exploded, and driving up from the depths came a creature of nightmare, twenty feet of pseudocrocodile, an abomination stitched together from human arms and legs, a patchwork monstrosity with great black liquid eyes and jagged mosaic teeth. A grinder, a destroyer, something that belonged in no world that knew the light of reason.

It had a Nommo in its mouth. Its mutant dolphin shape writhed and streamed blood and screamed in supersonic agony. The grotesque teeth clamped shut. The Nommo was sliced into two; its tail fell in a dreadful hail of viscera.

The surviving Nommo formed a barrier between the croc-thing and the human beings. They screamed, a high-pitched, keening noise, and the beast recoiled in seeming pain. The magic of the Nommo, even if merely defensive, was mighty.

But if the Mayombreros could create one such beast, why not . . .

Bishop had reached the same conclusion at the same moment. "Defend yourselves!" he screamed. Twan was momentarily frozen, watching the display.

A floor and a half above, their compatriots gaped down at them. And one, Tammi, screamed urgently to Twan, "Behind you!"

A zombie croc rose dripping from the water behind Twan. This one was an undead were-beast, closer to human size, but it looked as deadly as its giant cousin. It chomped at Twan's defensive shield and actually ripped a hole in it.

A dolphin-Nommo smacked into its flank, an animated torpedo, and flitted away before the monster's tail could snap around. In that instant of distraction Twan raised her hands defensively. Golden energy poured from her palms into the hole in her defenses.

"Salt!" Bishop screamed. "Dammit, get some salt down here!"

The water level on the ninth floor was dropping slowly but steadily. Partition fences and statuary began to rise like Lemuria from the deep. The walls of the lagoon were laced with ladders and catwalks, making it easy for their companions to descend.

As the water level dropped, it turned black and oily. The Nommo still held the gigantic creature at bay. Now Griffin could see their magical blockade more clearly: it resembled a curtain of glowing jellyfish, a living barrier to the horrid teeth and claws.

Bishop was unarmed but hardly defenseless: he screamed, "Gods! Give me fire!" and a man-crocodile was struck with a devastating wall of flame. It rolled back under the surface, smoke curling from its cracked and sizzling skin.

"Look out!" That was a woman's voice from above them. Tammi plunged into the water carrying a sword in either hand. "Here!" she yelled as soon as she had her balance, and tossed one to Griffin. He delighted himself by catching its hilt; he saluted her and plunged into the fray.

Tammi fought like a whirlwind, cleaving her way through an army of demon crocs to reach Twan's side. Griffin fought his way toward them.

Sudden turbulence behind him. He spun in time to see a black, scaly shape writhing through the water. Before it could strike, there was a thudding sound: one of the Nommo had attacked, butting with lethal force. Their magic might have been merely defensive, but their physical power was stunning. The undead man-croc burst asunder.

The Nommo danced up out of the water, trilling with glee.

Splash. General Poule was in the water, and then Clavell. Crocodile shapes were rising everywhere now, and—

Twan screamed shrilly and vanished underwater for an instant, then—

Bobbed to the surface again and struggled to reach Tammi. She screamed out something Griffin couldn't quite hear, another spell, but this time the golden glow of her barrier barely showed.

Griffin slashed at a croc. His sword passed through the beast without really damaging it. *Already dead,* he thought. It turned on him, gaping, and he flailed with his blade. *Holes don't hurt it. Cut parts off. Hack, don't thrust.* It surged over him like a mountain of spoiled meat, and he threw himself to the side as its jaws snapped at him—

Then it rolled over onto its back and was still.

Spitting water, he saw Top Nun, half a story above them and crouching on a landing. She was holding hands with Cipher, casting spells of protection around Acacia, who screamed, "Panthesilea is here!" flexed her knees, and dove glowing into the water.

Two crocs went after her, but their teeth couldn't reach her, their tails couldn't flail her—and she sang her Warrior song, sword flickering too rapidly for sight to follow.

Captain Cipher cast handfuls of white powder out from the heights.

Salt.

It was killing the zombie crocodiles. They were melting. They actually disintegrated, losing both human and amphibian characteristics in the same dreadful moments.

Twan gasped for breath, spitting water and losing her concentration for a moment.

A hulking, blackly malevolent shape rose behind her and dragged her down. She surfaced a few feet away, screaming, then went down and under again.

She was being dragged backward in the water faster than any of them could swim, and although they tried, the next time she went down . . .

She stayed down.

Mouser, high on a ladder above them, screamed, "Twan!" and splashed into the water after her. He didn't get five strokes before vanishing himself.

Tammi seemed frozen with indecision. Then she plunged into the murky water and swam to the spot where Mouser had disappeared. She came up, cast about, and dove down again. And stayed down.

The carcasses of the zombie crocs floated, partially eaten away by salt. In places the water had drained almost to the floor. Chairs, tables, and ancient lighting fixtures rose up like ghosts of the deep.

In the deeper water, the seven surviving Nommo swam back and forth, or crawled painfully onto furniture in their human form, shivering with exhaustion. They had lost much manna, and they knew it. The black-white woman who had lectured the Gamers seemed to be deep in shock.

Above them, at the eleventh floor, dozens of beach people stared down at them, faces paled with fear.

One of the Nommo danced upright and spoke to them. "The Mayombrero are more powerful than we dreamed," he said. "They have learned to feed the Ethereals power from the reactor. They have learned necromantic secrets beyond our knowledge. They will cut off our water, and we will die."

"No," Griffin said, surprised to hear his own voice. "We can get through them and shut down that reactor long enough to weaken their creatures. Would that give you the opportunity you need?"

Bishop's contempt was a pressure on Alex's skin. He said nothing—and Alex thought he had a point. *I'm an NPC, dammit. Let them play.*

Several of the Nommo consulted. Then they turned back. "That may be the only chance that we have. Otherwise they will destroy us, and after us, the upper levels . . ."

Into Alex's pointed silence, Bishop said, "They'd control the whole building. We can't allow that."

Tammi burst up from the slime, spewing water, sobbing with the effort to draw air into her lungs. Her bodybuilder muscles were slack, and glistened with muck. "They're dead," she said disbelievingly. "They're both gone." In her hand she held Mouser's pack. It was torn and bloodied, but she hugged it to her chest, eyes casting about uncertainly.

The Nommo nodded kindly. "Come," they said. "Show us the talismans you have earned so dearly."

Acacia beckoned to Cipher, who had carried her pack down from poolside. She sloshed back and presented the jagged club from Ile Ife, the Staff of Oranyan. Captain Cipher presented his chillum pipe. Mary-em simply waddled forward; her tummy glowed with the life within.

And finally, Tammi peeled open Mouser's bloodied pack as if ripping out an enemy's heart. She brought forth Oggun's Necklace, and . . .

The Nommo crown.

There was a moment's pause during which no one spoke, no one moved. *So*, said Bishop's silent lips. Acacia's eyes glittered greedily.

"The crown," the Nommo said reverently. "With it, you can all function as one family, one mind and heart. You cannot survive in contention. Do you understand?"

They nodded.

"Then this is what you must do . . ."

Chapter Thirty-three

ASA

Harmony and Millicent were back in full Mallster makeup, which lent a bizarre and almost surreal air to the conference.

"Do you really think you'll be on call again today?" Vail asked.

Harmony spread his fingers. "Depends on when they decide to break for dinner. The Gamers have been racing through that building about thirty percent faster than anyone anticipated. It pays to be ready." He placed his enormous hands flat on the table before him. The overhead light gleamed on long, ragged black fingernails. "Millicent. McWhirter. Dr. Vail . . . as Chief of Operations at Dream Park, I have allowed you unusually open access to information. Only the time factor involved made this palatable. I ask you again. What have we learned about Sharon Crayne, and Army, and Bishop?"

McWhirter cleared his throat. "Considerable. Also, we've got an additional ally, if we want him. Richard Lopez wants in."

Harmony squeezed his eyes shut. "Great. And why not a brass band while we're at it? Might as well call in the vidzines, too."

Tony shook his head. "With all respect, Mr. Harmony, Richard Lopez is the closest we can get to having a Bishop on our side. We may well need him before this is over."

Harmony ground his teeth, then nodded. "All right. Dr. Vail— you and Millicent have been working. What results?"

Vail tapped a short stack of printed plastic sheets. "We believe that Nigel Bishop pierced the security around Embryadopt and offered Crayne access to and/or custody of that child."

"How in the hell did you come to that conclusion?"

"Sharon's own words," Tony said. "We've got them on tape." He consulted handwritten notes. "While making her copy of MIMIC's security systems, she said, quote: 'I'm coming, sweetheart. Mommy's doing everything she can.' Unquote."

"You found that?" Harmony asked, impressed. "Good work, Tony."

McWhirter glowed.

Harmony grew thoughtful again. "I thought Embryadopt was completely secure."

"There's no such thing as absolute security," Tony said. "Sufficient bribery, or political clout, could manage it. Or maybe Bishop lied to her."

"Political?"

Tony said, "Millicent?"

It was disorienting hearing Millicent's cool voice emerging from that monstrous countenance. "Six hundred thousand dollars in gambling money was routed through Ecuador, whose economy is based more on agriculture and mineral resources than high-tech manufacturing. Suppose a money source in Ecuador was bankrolling Bishop?"

Tony chimed in. "Bankrolling or employing him. Remember— *Bishop can't make Army win.* But there were rumors in the Gaming community that he was involved in spy stuff during his retirement."

"All right. If it was someone in Ecuador—and financial clout buys political clout anywhere in the world—he has access to enough power to pierce any security shield, if you can find the right button to push."

Tony said, "Finding buttons is Bishop's peculiar talent."

Harmony drummed his fingers. "So the only question remaining is, How did he know Sharon Crayne's vulnerable spot? And what the hell does he want? Two questions."

"Acacia Garcia, too," Tony said. "He hunted her down. She was a way to learn about Griffin, or get to Griffin. Or . . . distract Griffin. And she likes dangerous men."

"Shit," Harmony said quietly. "But what about Ms. Crayne?"

"We came up with something interesting," Millicent said. She consulted her own sheaf of notes. "Six years ago, in March of '53, Sharon Crayne belonged to an organization called ASA. Tony and I got into some of Bishop's bank transactions. We didn't find any guilty associations, but did reveal a series of small deposits to the account of an organization called ASA, during the same time period."

"And what does ASA stand for?"

Vail chose his words carefully. "There once existed an Adult Survivors of Abuse. Primarily a support network for incest survivors. Disbanded now."

Harmony sat back in his chair. *"Bishop?"*

"Mmm."

"Dr. Vail, isn't that stretching coincidence a little?"

"Not particularly. Our Nigel Bishop sounds to me like a smiling sociopath. Incapable of forming any truly significant relationships, but brilliant. That kind of brilliance, omnicompetence perhaps, combined with perceiving the entire realm of human endeavor as a game, a win-lose proposition . . . implies an extremely stressful childhood. I picture a little boy who was never loved for who he was, only what he did."

"What he did . . ." McWhirter whispered.

"Yes," Vail said dryly. "And for whom. Without knowing more it would be difficult to say. But if he was an adult survivor of incest, I would guess that the incest was perpetrated upon him by an aunt, an elder sister, even his mother. That he did everything to please her, and she used the dual positions of authority figure and lover to manipulate him, forcing him to perform like a puppet. That the relationship was eventually discovered and ended, leaving him emotionally devastated, with a terrible ambivalence toward female sexuality. I'd think he's tried to control and subvert women ever since."

Harmony interrupted. "So Bishop is just trying to win the Game? For *that* he killed Sharon Crayne?"

Tony was shaking his head violently. Vail said, "According to McWhirter and Lopez, whose judgments we must rely upon in these matters, he *can't* win, and should have known it. He lost his own team—possibly by design. He has no talismans. He can't force Army to win. Whatever he wants, it's not in the Game."

"Then what is this all about?" Harmony looked ready to explode.

"This is where we ran down," Tony said. "What did he want that was outside the Gaming area? He broke every rule to get there. Maybe he's stealing something."

"It would have to be small," Harmony said. "Gamers don't carry much out of the Games, do they?"

Tony shook his head. "What's in MIMIC to steal?"

"Some of the spaces have been modified. Some computer systems are in, but there isn't much in them yet."

"He could put taps on them. *Now*, before ScanNet goes fully operational."

"All right, then," Vail said, getting into the game. "Industrial plans? Equipment? Sabotage?"

Millicent looked uneasy. "Sabotage? Where's the profit in that?"

Harmony cleared his throat. "You throw another country behind schedule. They can't make their deadline. Come next bidding time, you might look a whole lot better. In the long term, it could be Ecuador against Sri Lanka for the ground site of an orbital tether."

"All right," Vail said finally. "We'll have to get Griffin in on this. When is the next rest break?"

"I don't know, but soon," Harmony said. "They've got to be dead." He grinned wearily. "Which is appropriate. Their next stop is a graveyard."

Chapter Thirty-four

Baron Samedi

Friday, July 22, 2059—5:00 P.M.

Steam rose from the wet graves like a pall, and the nine remaining Gamers, and their one remaining guide, plodded through the muck with hands up to their noses. The entire fourth level reeked of corruption.

It had taken two hours for them to creep down from the ninth level. Through stairways and hallways, avoiding things that shambled in the distance or groaned in the depths, they followed a Virtual trail of green arrows. At the end of that trail they found the graveyard, where their adventure had begun a day and a half earlier.

Muck had seeped down from the ninth level. The floor was sopping and slippery. Partially decomposed, inhuman corpses had washed from the graves and lay moist and rotting in the park lanes. Eyeless sockets stared at them; tongueless mouths screamed in silence.

Acacia held her sword ever at the ready. Captain Cipher had much of their salt supply. He sprinkled bits of it, just a pinch, on each corpse that they passed. Where the salt fell, a puff of smoke rose, reeking of corruption.

A trill of laughter wafted from across the boneyard, a sound even more inhuman than the warped and withered objects around them.

"Oh . . . so clever you are," a voice called. The word "are" dissolved from vowel sound into insane laughter. "You have salt, and salt stops my people. So clever . . ."

"Twenty-toed Moses," Cipher said. "I wish they'd hurry up and attack. I don't know how much more of this—"

"Shhh."

Most of the fourth level had been a park of some kind, a place where people might have come on holiday, to celebrate, to picnic. Now it was a place of stinking death, of corpses that clawed their way back from perdition.

"What do you think?" Tammi inspected one of the skeletons. "It looks like it was changing into one of the crocodile things." Tammi wore the Nommo crown. The Warrior-woman had powerful magic now. With the crown and the Necklace of Oggun, she was the single most powerful Adventurer.

They had tried spells to waken Mary-em's godling child, but it never stirred. "He's just a baby," Mary-em said sheepishly. "Maybe he's just taking a nap."

The entire caravan of Adventurers was suffused with Top Nun's saffron, protective radiance; it illumined the landscape, as well. The blasted, ruined graveyard was so depressing, Acacia almost wished the light would go out.

Captain Cipher's tuneless voice rang out: *"Hi ho, hi ho, it's off to die we go—"*

"Is that your voice?" Al asked wearily, "or did you have beans for lunch?"

With a sudden rumble, a tombstone rose out of the muck. A man-sized ball of cobwebs bubbled out of the mud in front of it and then began to unfurl. Like a butterfly emerging from a cocoon, a human being stepped forth from the ball and smiled.

He had *been* a man. He was part skeleton, and through gaps in his body and tattered greatcoat they could see the tombstone behind him. He had been of African blood, but there remained precious little blood in him, or flesh for it to course through.

He bowed expansively. "Welcome to my domain," he said. "I am Baron Samedi."

"Lord of the dead," Acacia murmured.

He flexed stiltlike legs and bowed creakily. He held his hand out for hers. She held out her hand nervously, and the rotting thing touched its protruding teeth to her softness. There was just a hint of warm, sticky breath against her skin, and then he straightened.

She had regained her composure. "Did you send the crocodile things to attack the Nommo?"

"No," he said, smiling. "I watch. I enjoy the spectacle."

"Of what?"

"Of . . . life. All life ends here, in my domain. I enjoy watching the living ones try to forestall it for a few hours, or days, or years. It means nothing. All ends here, you know. I serve Babalu-Aye. He should have protected the dead from the Mayombreros, but they have greater power now. Much greater. My master has become their servant." His voice was a delighted whisper.

"Where is your master?" she asked.

"Bound. Perhaps no longer my master. We shall see."

Top Nun crept up and whispered in Acacia's ear, "Babalu-Aye. Protector of the sick."

"What do you think?"

"The Mayombreros are going for the whole *shmeer*. We know that the gods are really just energy fields, but this one was made to heal, and to protect the dead. A sort of embalming demon, maybe? 'Baron Samedi' must be a kind of golem subprogram. Something that *shmoozes* with both the living and the dead, for Babalu-Aye."

"But without any real loyalty."

"So how could it have loyalty? It's just a golem, a robot, a made thing. Any energy that sustains it—"

"Energy . . ."

Top Nun's brown eyes narrowed shrewdly. "The reactor?"

Baron Samedi stood aside, cackling, waving them on their way.

The graveyard steamed as the Adventurers entered it; mud sloshed around their ankles. The trees were as bare as wheat fields in winter, and canted sideways. A dim wind whistled through the naked branches.

A scream behind them. Panthesilea saw Top Nun, eyes rolled up in her head, ankle grabbed by something from under the muck.

Panthesilea was on her in a second, hacking and slashing at the loose soil. Top Nun screamed, *"Oy!"* and light exploded around them both, driving the attacker back into the ground. She staggered back, panting. The rest of the adventurers set themselves in circular array.

Here they came: crawling up from under the ground, up from the slime, creatures half human corpse and half crocodile, in states of hideous decomposition.

The Adventurers fought for their lives.

The creatures were no larger than men, but they writhed from the earth like maggots from meat, in apparently endless profusion.

But there was a new factor now: Acacia and the rest of her compatriots had survived the worst that the Mayombreros could throw at them, and their power had increased as a result.

That which does not kill you makes you stronger . . .

Captain Cipher still had salt. He flung it, chanting at the top of his voice. Where it touched the corpsodiles, their skin blistered and peeled back. A sword or staff stroke on a salt wound caused the unfortunate creature to die a second swift agonizing death.

Griffin, shoulder to shoulder with Bishop, watched the man go into high gear. His sword was a flicker of liquid light. Griffin swirled his own borrowed blade in narrow arcs, smashing the corpsodiles until there was a wall of bodies—

(There was no real resistance to the creatures. Almost as if they were phantoms . . .)

—and finally there was no more movement from the graves. No movement, but a low moaning sound that came from everywhere and originated nowhere, filling the room.

"Something's coming," Acacia whispered. "Oh, shit, I don't like this."

"Stay strong," Tammi said tersely.

At first there was nothing but empty graves and stacked zombie crocs, then two pony-sized black figures came bounding along the park path toward them. Dogs. Brutes. Two-hundred-pounders, pit bulls the size of mastiffs. They stopped, hovered out of range of the Adventurers' weapons.

A shape appeared at the top of the hill, dimly backlit by a dying street lamp. A one-legged man on crutches. Slowly, painfully, he made his way to them. Every step was an effort.

He was an old, old black man, and the dogs at his sides seemed more guardians than pets. They sniffed at Tammi, and at Mary-em. When they nuzzled her tummy, one of them sat on the ground and rolled over to expose its belly. She bent and scratched.

Real dog, by God.

"You have destroyed many of the undead," the old man said. "You are powerful. I think not powerful enough for what you try to do. But powerful."

Captain Cipher piped up. "Are you Babalu-Aye?"

"I have taken that guise, yes. You know the truth about us now. You saved, or fought to save, many dogs. I love dogs. They are my friends. And you have weakened the bonds that hold me. I offer to you—this."

He held out one of the battered wooden crutches to Top Nun. "It magnifies the power of healing. You will need this before your task is through."

Top Nun slipped the crutch under her arm. It was dark, stained, heavily knotted wood. Her protective glow amped up until it was almost uncomfortably bright. With a wave of her hand, she brought it down to a milder level. She turned back to Babalu-Aye—but he, and the dogs, had disappeared.

"Such a *mensch*," she whispered, and fingered the talisman softly.

A decision was made: with Top Nun's new protective power at their command, they would take a final break, preparing for their ultimate assault.

They found a gazebo, a rickety white framework in the middle of the desolation, and the Adventurers shucked their backpacks and sat heavily, as though the fatigue had flooded over them in sudden waves.

Griffin was watching carefully. Nigel Bishop seemed to have no desire to relate to Acacia, or to Griffin, either. Alex would have liked it better if one or the other of them had been killed out of the Game. He had to get out for a conference, and he needed an ally. There was only one choice.

He walked over to where Mary-em sat, unfolding her bedroll. She was gazing across the mud-flat graveyard, the scene of recent battle, one hand resting gently over the unborn child within her.

"May I sit?"

The little woman glanced at him slyly. "Absolutely."

"Better still. Can we go for a little walk?"

"Could be dangerous. Could be buggies about."

"We need privacy."

"I'm a mother now—" she started, then saw how serious he was. She hitched herself up, following him out of the gazebo. They found a bench a hundred feet away and sat.

Alex pressed his earpiece. "Message for Tony," he said clearly. "McWhirter. This is an emergency time-out, security matter. See we're not disturbed."

There was a pause. "McWhirter isn't here, chief," Mitch Hasagawa said, "but I'll pass the word along."

Mary-em was watching him shrewdly. "So. What is it *this* time?"

He laughed. "I keep messing up your Games, don't I?"

"Is that why you're here?"

"No, but you know that I'm the head of Security, and Acacia knows, and . . . Bishop knows."

"Uh-huh. Cut to the chase, Griffy."

He sighed. "Right. Bishop has conspired to fix this Game somehow. Acacia is in on it, or was. That's not all. Someone died."

Her eyes narrowed in unspoken question.

"A security officer for Cowles Industries. Bishop might have been involved. If Acacia can implicate him . . ."

Mary-em was thoughtful. "A Game like this wouldn't be a bad opportunity to take someone out."

"I want you to stay close to Acacia. Don't let her out of your sight. I know that Bishop wouldn't try anything with a witness."

She nodded, her nut-brown face crinkling. "You've got it."

Bishop watched as Griffin and Mary-em and Acacia did their little minuet. And laughed to himself. He excused himself from the group to do a little scouting. There was no reason not to, and Acacia's relief was a delight to see. He walked out into the graveyard, then disappeared into the shadows beyond.

Chapter Thirty-five

Conference

Griffin found one of the hidden wall panels and thumbprinted for entrance. It slid back, admitting him to a sealed corridor. A second door yielded to him, and he entered a deserted office. He flicked on one of the monitors and punched up Harmony's number.

Harmony appeared in the air in front of him, looking startled. "Man, you look like hell. When was the last time you slept?"

"I—got some sleep last night," Griffin said lamely. If he looked half as dead as he felt, they should have played him alongside Baron Samedi.

Millicent's image appeared, followed by Tony—and Richard Lopez. Griffin wasn't happy about that, but it took only a minute to understand the sense of it.

"Mr. Lopez," he said finally. "We assume you will hold the following discussion in strictest confidence?"

"Of course." Lopez's image flickered a bit, and Alex adjusted it.

"All right. Thaddeus, what have we got?"

Griffin fought to maintain concentration while Harmony brought him up to date. God. All he wanted to do was crawl under a bush somewhere and sleep. "So Bishop might have known Sharon. Big coincidence. And he *can't* con himself into believing he could pull off this Army thing? Because that was the obvious . . ."

Tony shook his head, an emphatic negative.

Richard Lopez spoke carefully. "Understand, Mr. Griffin, that much of Bishop's strategy originates in his reverence for Sun-tzu's

The Art of War. One reason that *The Art of War* is so easy to computer-model is that it suggests a very specific set of reactions to certain stimuli. For instance: 'If you outnumber the opponent by a factor of ten, surround them. When five times greater, attack them. When two times greater, scatter them. When fewer in number, avoid them,' and so on. The combination of reactions creates infinite tactical variety. The basic reactions are If-Then propositions. At the very core is the constant reminder to never do what the opponent expects."

"Reasonable enough."

"But do you really understand it? The American military officer who came closest to Sun-tzu was probably Douglas MacArthur. During his Philippine campaign in World War II, he committed to retaking Manila. 'I shall return,' and so forth. The Japanese had prepared a series of reinforced military obstacles on his way there—and he simply leapfrogged over them, never engaged at all. This strategy is typical of Sun-tzu. Bishop has had months to study your defenses, and is probably prepared to leapfrog them."

"How?"

Lopez shrugged. "It will probably be conceptual in nature. You are already swimming in supposition, which has clouded your perceptions."

Griffin sat back, thinking hard. *First, Bishop is just playing the Game, with Acacia as a lover. Then he's arranged to win, with Acacia throwing the Game. Then he's throwing the Game to Army, with Acacia's help. Then maybe he's not interested in the Game at all—but if not the Game . . .*

"We're wondering if he's after something in MIMIC, Alex," Harmony said.

"Then he's already got it."

"You *know* this, Alex?"

"Close . . . Bishop's turned flaky. He's just playing now. Whatever he wanted . . . Please stand by," Griffin said apologetically, and put Lopez and McWhirter on hold. Both of their images fizzled out.

He turned to Millicent, although he spoke for the computer. "I want a list of everything moved into MIMIC during the last eight months."

"On it, Alex." She performed magic, and a seemingly endless list began to scroll through the air before him.

"Shit. Sabotage?"

Millicent shrugged. "We wondered about that."

"Bugs. We'll have to sweep."

Harmony slapped his desk with his palm. "Dammit, why didn't we have ScanNet up by now?"

Griffin closed his eyes. "We got it in as fast as we could, Thaddeus."

"Yeah. So—somewhere in that mess of possibilities is what Bishop wants."

"Maybe. Probably information; it's so portable. How long has Bishop spent off the scanners?"

Harmony consulted some figures in front of him. "About three hours total."

Alex brought McWhirter back on line. "Tony. None of the scanners have been disabled, have they?"

"No. Working perfectly, or close enough. We've had microburst static in several sectors."

"Analyzed for patterns?"

Tony's voice was small. "No. Security was waiting for you, I think—"

"*Do* that, dammit! What sectors? Pipe it in!"

The familiar holographic model of MIMIC appeared on the desk before them. "So . . . ScanNet picked up microburst transmissions . . . when?"

"Often when Gamers were moving through the areas. Probably RF static from Gaming equipment. Not all of that stuff is properly shielded, Griff."

"Still, dammit—Tony, I trusted you. You know how important this is." Griffin's head was throbbing. "If you don't have enough sense to study those bursts—"

"I've b—"

Alex cut him off coldly. "Get on it, McWhirter, or suggest someone who can."

Tony stiffened. "I think that . . . if you feel like that, maybe Hasegawa should be doing this. He's already involved."

Alex massaged his right temple and felt the blood pulsing against his fingertips. "Yeah. You stick to the Game."

Tony nodded grimly. "I'll tell him." And he winked off.

No one spoke. Then Richard Lopez cleared his throat. "I think that I should return to my Game. Thank you. It has been . . . interesting."

Griffin nodded his head as the little man winked out.

"What now, Alex?" Harmony asked uneasily.

"I want MIMIC sealed. Most of the Gamers and NPCs are still there, waiting for the final scenes. Well—nobody leaves until the Game is over and I've had a chance to think about this. Do you understand me? Nobody."

Tony McWhirter was angry, and hurt, and, more than anything, scared. Scared for Alex. Scared for himself.

Scared for Acacia. He had to admit it. Griffin had been pushed too far. Had he slept at *all* in the past three days? He was riding on the rims, and that wasn't rare, but Tony had never before seen Alex take it out on an employee.

In the main control room he gathered his things and said good-bye to the Game Masters, and spent a few minutes watching Sis. No worries there: the Oklahoman was handling six things at once without any visible strain.

Maybe Tony McWhirter wasn't needed at all.

Nobody had told him to leave the building; Griffin hadn't even insinuated that Tony was no longer an employee. After everything had cooled down, there might even be an apology.

If there was an afterward.

Tony wanted to do something, anything, to keep images of Acacia out of his mind. He had to talk with her again. Somehow. And if he could be a hero, could rescue the fair lady from her own stupidity, he might be rewarded with a kiss . . .

Or something. Dammit.

Now he was out of the loop altogether, and that was perfect for Bishop. While Bishop couldn't have counted on it, he had to know that Griffin was overloaded enough to make mistakes.

Everybody else playing this Game was playing by the rules. Tony McWhirter had promised himself a long time ago that he would play by the damned rules. Now a man who understood those rules was beating the hell out of the best minds Dream Park could offer.

So Tony McWhirter would have to even the odds.

He went up to level fifteen, now deserted. Guards lurked in the building, and extra monitors had been quietly placed in position.

Tony found an unused console and used his security key to get in. It didn't take him long to access the recent conferences. He studied the security charts, noting the areas where microburst transmissions had been recorded.

All had been recorded while Gamers had been in, or minutes after they had been through, the area. Could Bishop have planted something to interfere with the Gaming computers? Making his own magic more effective, perhaps, overriding the on-boards . . .

Tony wanted to see one of those areas for himself.

On the thirteenth level, he found the Hollywood mock-up of Ile Ife. He grinned, remembering the chaos their stop-motion monster had caused. Tony kept to the shadows. The fields of reception weren't completely overlapped, he knew. There were places where a reasonably quiet person could move without being noticed by security apparatus. After all, ScanNet's chief problem was to determine what was and was not fit to be sent on to the next substation. They couldn't send everything. So with the system only forty percent operative . . .

Dream Park's blind spot is its Gamers, Tony thought grimly. *We're soft on them. It has to stop.*

Tony sidled up to one of the monitors. It was a substation computer, set up to coordinate information sent to it by other monitors on this level. And it had sensed inappropriate static?

Disruption? Information? If Bishop had wanted to do something inappropriate during the Game, might he have wanted to disable the main processors?

But they would have known if a station was outright disabled.

But what if the information was distorted a bit?

All right. Say Bishop is after a piece of information stored in one of the Barsoom Project areas. *Outside* the Gaming sections. He transmits it during a melee. The sensors are overloaded; no one will notice.

Transmits it where? He can't get it out of the building.

How about one of the modular apartments? He steals information, breaks into a modular apartment, lifts the weather shield, and tight-beams the data to a waiting receptor miles away. On line-of-sight he could use a laser without tripping an alarm . . . could he? Maybe not.

But he couldn't have *counted* on it when he was preparing for California Voodoo. Whatever Bishop had, *it was still in the building.*

Tony began to scan the monitor. Nothing obvious, dammit. How about the surrounding area? A disruptor device wouldn't need to have physical contact with the equipment . . .

He crawled along the floor, checking connections. It was dark here. He was grateful for a tiny night-light plugged into the wall, and flicked it with his finger before going on.

He looked at the monitor itself. It was much more than a mere visual camera, but there was a standard, easily recognizable multi-vision receptor in plain sight. Made the tenants comfortable.

Nothing looked amiss. In fact, the cord looked very new, the joints of the rotating scanner arm as shiny as the day it had been installed.

In fact . . .

Tony looked at the scanner joint and traced it back into the wall. At the wall everything looked kosher, but the more he looked at the scanner, the more it disturbed him.

There seemed to be an extra metal collar around the output cables. Tony flicked a penknife out of his pocket and pried at it gently. With a click, it fell away.

Jesus. It was a bug, no question about that—some kind of tapping device. Short-range transmitter. To what receiver?

It could be anywhere, dammit, and the intent . . . What was it waiting to see? The only thing going on now was California Voodoo. The bug must be in place for later use. The microburst transmissions: mere noise . . .

But they'd led Tony straight here!

So the bursts were system tests? They had to be tests. There simply wasn't anything worth scanning here. Just a bunch of Gamers, fighting monsters in Ile Ife . . .

Mmm? A rival Gaming company? Disney Japan? Could Dream Park secrets be revealed by—

But dammit, every feed going out to standard monitors showed everything there was to see! Unless the ScanNet cameras showed things about special-effects techniques that ordinary cameras wouldn't?

What if, Tony thought, the real purpose of the entire exercise was to use ScanNet to analyze DreamTime, Cowles Industries' patented holographic and Virtual technology?

He had to find an office, call someone. Mitch. This tap could record information, and then maybe relay it to a transmitter that could reach outside MIMIC's cocoon of protection. *At least I've got this!*

"Let me get this straight," Hasegawa said. "You think Nigel Bishop is tapping the security lines to get a better look at DreamTime technology?"

"Yes."

Mitch Hasegawa shook his holographic head. "I don't buy it. In order for that to really be profitable, he would have to have access to the main banks. He only had access to the substations. They gather information and pass it on, get it? They filter out, to keep the main banks from overload, but they don't interpret. And that's what he'd need."

Tony sighed.

"And anyway, why all of the rigmarole with the gambling, and the impossible bet?"

"It's a blind," Tony said. "He had to figure that somebody might see through part of his plan. This gives us a maze to chase through."

"But we won't chase through it forever."

"It keeps us busy for long enough. Till the Game's over."

"Makes sense." Mitch reached for his cutoff switch. "Gotta get back—you know, you're not really supposed to be working on this. Not anymore."

"That makes it easier, Mitch. No pressure."

Mitch winked out, leaving Tony with wheels still spinning madly in his head and a silent giggle bubbling in his throat. No pressure!

Sharon Crayne, who needed help finding the child she gave up.

Nigel Bishop, who needed information only an insider could give him.

Acacia Garcia, partnered with Bishop . . .

In an impossible venture?

As a blind, the "forced win" scenario was a good bet. Say Bishop could get five to one on Army. Bishop knew his own team was doomed: that's four to one. Any move Bishop made—nothing too overt, but no obvious opportunity ignored either—would help their chances. Three to one? A good bet, if you didn't bet your ass.

He couldn't make it a certainty, and he had to know it. *But Acacia didn't!* What if he had her so dazzled she believed that he could pull it off? He'd have a perfect accomplice, one who would bend the rules supposedly for money, while helping Bishop cover something bigger. Nastier.

Something involving the Barsoom Project and its billions of dollars. And some entity in Ecuador powerful enough to pierce Embryadopt's defenses through diplomatic channels.

Or something involving Gaming: say, DreamTime Virtual display techniques . . .

Both had something in common. Tony could *feel* it, could taste its shape. A territory of the mind, an area bounded by Ecuador, Sharon Crayne, Acacia, MIMIC, the Barsoom Project, the California Voodoo Game—and Nigel Bishop.

He could hear Richard Lopez saying, "It will be simple. Very simple. It will only appear to be complex."

He rubbed his temples. "Why can't I see it? Goddamn it, Richard! I'm a Game Master, too."

Chapter Thirty-six

The Barn Door

There were ten minutes left in the hour break when Alex Griffin returned. Mary-em was in animated conversation with Acacia when he came upon them. They exchanged a brief glance, and Mary-em wandered off to get some water.

Griffin pulled Acacia aside. His fingers were tight on her arm, his voice deadly urgent. "Bishop is up to something, Acacia, and you're in on it. If it's gambling, and that's all it is, I'm not interested. Keep your goddamned money. But I have to know. Now. This is your last chance. If you lie to me now, and I find out, with God as my witness I will nail you to the tree. Do you understand me? Last chance."

She opened her mouth, closed it again. Searched for lies, searched his taut, strained face for mercy, and found neither. Abruptly, all of the terror she had repressed came bubbling to the surface. She had trusted Nigel. Alex asked her to trust him. And he said that he didn't care about the gambling. That he was after something bigger.

She had to take the chance.

Acacia took his arm and led him away from the gazebo. They found a bench and sat. She began to whisper. "Right after the Game was announced," she said, "Nigel called me. We hadn't had an affair or anything, but I knew him, and I'd heard the stories." She stopped for a moment, as if lost in memories.

"Go on," he said flatly.

"We became lovers. I guess that's what you'd have to call it. I—don't know what he thought."

Alex had the urge to push her a little more, to coax her. He made himself wait, and finally that patience was rewarded.

"I guess I fell in love with him, with his way of being, of doing things, and of seeing the world. He convinced me that there were bigger games to play, and that together we could play them. I guess I fell for it."

"I can see where this is leading."

"I'm sure. He felt that if we could both get into a Game together, we could fix a superbowl, force a win for one of the other teams. He showed me how it could be done, theoretically . . ."

"How?"

"The first step is to consolidate three of the other teams into a caravan. Then, on some pretense, capture the team you want to force into the winning position. It gives you an excuse to protect them, see? Then create weaknesses in the other teams so that a vital skill, necessary for the winning of the Game, can only be found in the 'captive' team."

"Sounds simple."

"I hope you're being sarcastic."

"Ss—"

Her voice rose. "It's *unbelievably* complicated. You have to have a very precise understanding of the makeup of all of the other teams, and advance knowledge of the Game itself, particularly the end-game."

"How much inside data did Bishop have?"

"Hard to say what he knew and what he extrapolated. He might be the smartest man I've ever met."

He looked into her eyes, and there was a brief shrug, but no apology.

He tried another tactic. "You know that a security officer died. What you don't know is that a model of MIMIC's security setup might have been stolen. Did you see anything like that?"

She shook her head. "No. He has a lot of information. He's had it for months, on the Game, on the Gamers. The only thing I can say is that the night that the security woman died—"

Griffin grabbed her wrists. "I didn't say it was a woman."

Acacia talked very fast. Hysteria was creeping into her voice, and she couldn't meet his eyes. "I knew from one of your own security people—Hasegawa, I think—that something was wrong on

Wednesday, Alex. I used one of Nigel's programs to break into your communication lines. I listened. I'm so sorry, Alex." She was starting to cry.

"Jesus." He slackened his grip.

"She was important to you, wasn't she?"

Alex nodded.

Acacia said, "I'll tell you anything I can."

"How did you communicate? Did you have a dead-drop system, or what?"

"One of these," she said. She unscrewed the hilt of her belt knife and shook out one of the little three-pronged communicators. "It uses MIMIC's electrical circuitry."

"I'll be dipped in shit." He held it up to the light, marveling. Could McWhirter have been wrong? "Can Bishop really pull this off?"

"Why not?" Acacia said. "It's not even strictly illegal. Gaming isn't licensed by the state athletic commission. I might get blackballed from the IFGS, but this has been the biggest Game ever. Maybe it's time to go."

"And what about Sharon?"

"I don't know more than I've told you, Alex. Maybe he didn't— didn't. Maybe it's nothing."

"Has he tried to kill you?"

"How can I tell? *Everything's* trying to kill me. I'm a Gamer." But the question hadn't surprised her. "I don't think so, Alex. And if he wanted me dead, wouldn't he have drowned me? That was the easiest place."

Alex sat back. What to do? Unless and until he got more information, his hands were tied. Even if Bishop had fixed the Game somehow, there was no proven connection to Sharon Crayne, and there might never be.

Bishop moved carefully around the inner periphery of MIMIC's fourth level. He was in shadow now, invisible to the unaided human eye.

But that wasn't what he was up against. He heard the purr and looked up. A maintenance robot glided along the crease of ceiling and wall. Its camera eyes stalked him, watched him. It would make no mistakes.

And it would not be alone. So. The forces of Dream Park were alert, but it was too damned late.

He had to keep moving. Had to stay in motion. By now Griffin must know all that Acacia knew, but that wasn't enough.

He could hear his own breathing, hear his own heartbeat, but somehow the sound of his crepe soles against the floor, the loudest sound of all, eluded him. *I've made it. I've beaten them all.*

And still he was second-guessing himself, going over it again, every move at the motel, every countermove. He had compartmentalized all information so that even Sharon Crayne's reanimated corpse couldn't tell them everything they needed to know. He had taken safety precautions, the irony of which Alex Griffin would appreciate, if he was bright enough to appreciate irony.

Nigel Bishop crept through the halls, paying no obvious attention to the roving camera eyes. He checked doors, drew maps of the hallways, made secretive preparations with his equipment. He was back in control. He could feel it. He was safe. All he had to do was hold out another hour or two, play the fucking Game, and get out, get far away, get away from where the woman had lain, submerged in water, blood oozing from her left nostril, her terrible blue eyes staring at him, through him . . .

He stopped, shaking, and wiped his palm across his clammy forehead. He had nothing to worry about. And it was too late for Dream Park to start being clever.

There's a parable about horses and barn doors, he thought. *Griffin should learn it.*

Chapter Thirty-seven

The Final Assault

Captain Cipher had packed his chillum with herbs and settled back to puff. Around him, his companions were enjoying the last of their rude, makeshift dinners. It was still break time, but he wanted to experiment.

He puffed hard a few times and then exhaled. The smoke hovered in the air . . .

And turned slowly red. And then black. And then red.

And sank down into the ground at his feet.

And seeped back up again. Not just at his feet, but—

"On your guard!" he screamed. "The graveyard is smoking, the graveyard is smoking!"

Tammi threw her dinner place aside and had her staff in "guard" in the blink of an eye.

The Adventurers collected at the gazebo. Major Clavell peered out at the wisps of smoke rising from cracks in the mud. His fingers itched for a weapon. There was an extra sword in Tammi's bundle, and her eyes were elsewhere . . .

He stole it, hoisted it, feeling a terrible pleasure.

Top Nun bowed her head and pressed her palms together against the sides of Babalu-Aye's crutch. Golden light spilled from her fingertips, her eyes, her open mouth, and spread to surround them in a cocoon of protection.

Tammi kept her staff tucked under her right arm and clutched her magic necklace with her left. "Into place! Now!"

In the graveyard, smoky things appeared, wavered for a few instants, and then disappeared again. They leapfrogged from grave to ruptured grave. Will-o'-the-wisps? Vaguely human outlines quavered and became enormous, silently screaming mouths without lips or teeth or even faces to support them. They trembled to come closer and then backed away, like flames flickering in a breeze, or coyly flirtatious shadows. They circled the gazebo, locked in a ritualistic dance without music or rhythm.

Then one of the things broke free of the circle, attacking.

Tammi gripped the beads, and a bolt of light erupted from her chest, striking the creature a shattering blow. It shredded into fragments of black, leaving only an outline, which stood for a second and then collapsed.

"This is it!" Bishop said. Griffin swung his gaze to the man: he hadn't seen Bishop until that moment, wasn't sure exactly when he had reappeared.

In wedge formation, the Adventurers plowed toward a corner exit. The shadow things flitted in and out of existence, swooping on them, repulsed by the light.

"What have we got here?" Acacia panted.

"Don't know." Cipher said. "The Mayombreros have too many tricks right now."

They had almost reached the stairwell when the door burst open, and Thaddeus Dark stood before them.

He was massive, swollen, twisted with animalistic hungers, face distorted with rage and killing-fever. His fingers were crooked into beastlike talons. He shambled hunchbacked from the shadows with unmistakably lethal intent.

It would not do to laugh, Alex thought; and Thaddeus did look fearsome. Behind him came a flood of Mallbeasts.

They struck Top Nun's protective dome and rebounded. The shadow demons were utterly foiled, but the Mallbeasts raked with fang and claw, and some of them fought their way through.

There was a thunderous melee, a dizzying flux of swords and staffs and knives, fireballs, sizzling shafts of light, and the howls of the damned and dying.

Blood flowed freely, slicking the dirt and the cobblestone paths as they fought through the press, and Griffin found himself face to face with Thaddeus Dark.

A hideous growl—and then a swipe of claws. Alex slashed with his sword. Dark grabbed the blade, wrenched it—a voice in Griffin's ear said, "Let it go!"—and pulled it from his hands. Thaddeus Dark brought the sword down across his knee. It snapped like a twig; he lunged at Griffin; Alex stumbled back, tripping over the bleeding body of Major Terry Clavell.

Clavell bore four diagonal slashes across his chest, and they pulsed blood in cardiac rhythm.

"Here . . ." he said weakly. "Take mine." He handed his sword to Alex, then went limp.

Alex spun and found himself shoulder to shoulder with Acacia. She had a long, limber fighting style, graceful as a dancer. He felt more like a trained bear, but was actually almost as quick. Together they smashed and cut and hacked their way through the ranks.

A female Mallbeast came at Acacia, and Griffin vaguely recognized the huge dark eyes and dark skin beneath the ashy complexion. This creature had once, in another life, been his friend, Millicent Summers. Scoundrels!

Acacia slashed at the transformed Millicent, and Millicent hissed and slashed in return. They circled each other, searching for openings.

Alex didn't have a chance to watch. Thaddeus Dark had found him again. The man-beast was fast, and strong, and—

"One side, Guide!" Bishop said behind him. "I'll take care of this."

Alex gritted his teeth and stepped back.

Bishop went after Thaddeus Dark with power bolts lancing from his aura, lightning blasts that struck Dark's flesh and exposed bone. The scraps of flesh actually attempted to knit themselves together again, and then again, and Dark roared, losing even more of his human countenance, becoming totally bestial as his lifeblood pulsed from a dozen wounds, as smoke drooled from gaping saucer-shaped burn holes.

Finally, Dark slumped to the ground, dead.

All about them, the tide seemed to be turning. Top Nun shouted, "Hoo-hoo!" and then—

The door crashed open again, and their own dead shambled forth.

Here was SJ, his torn body reanimated, his head slumped onto his right shoulder. His eyes burned with terrible new awareness. He carried a club studded with nails and broken glass. And there was Holly Frost, body mashed by some unimaginable pressure, eyes bulging from her head, sword trembling in her dead hand. There were Crystal Cofax, Friar Duck, Tamasan, "Aces" Wilde . . .

Shambling, lurching toward their former friends, hell-bent for blood.

Griffin found himself beside Top Nun. She and the crutch were glowing fiercely, extending power to her allies. Again and again, wounds that should have been fatal healed on Acacia or Tammi, and once on Griffin.

Demons, Mallbeasts, and zombies batted and scratched hungrily at her shield, struggling to get in, trying to claw their way to the meat . . .

SJ lurched against Top Nun's barrier, snapping his teeth. "Brains," he mumbled, black fluid drooling from his mouth. "More brains. Fresh brains." And slapped against the barrier again. "Sweetbreads?"

Some zombies were specially marked, sporting Virtual symbols on arms or legs that only Adventurers could see. Griffin struck a glowing head, and it burst. Spiders and snake-things sprayed out in ghastly profusion, and the zombie fell to its knees, twitching.

Alex leapt in, striking at the glowing designated limbs (*just cut on the dotted line!*), getting a spectacular nauseating effect every time.

In the center of the fight, unable to contribute, were Mary-em, Alphonse, and Poule. Alphonse watched the action nervously—he had been disarmed, but it was getting too much. He pointed to Poule—Acacia had disarmed a Mallbeast, had a long and a short sword, and was wielding them like a Fury.

Poule came from behind and wrenched one of them from her hand. She gasped in surprise, seemed for a fraction of a second to consider fighting him for it, then came to her senses and turned back to the hungry dead.

"Cipher! Give Al his damned sword!" she screamed.

Cipher shucked it from his back without losing a word in his spell and tossed it to Al the B. Al snatched it, dropped it, almost lost his head picking it up, and then went on the attack.

And just in time. Top Nun had run out of juice. The golden shield failed, and she tumbled to her knees atop the crutch, exhausted. General Poule got an arm around her waist and carried her as if she were a child.

Alphonse was fighting like a fiend, but Alex saw him stop and adjust something at his belt. Griffin glimpsed a sandwich-sized Zip-loc bag, and something within. A doll?

Then they had fought their way to the door, and Tammi led the way down the stairs. The stairwell was narrow, lit from overhead by a row of little yellow bulbs. Shadows flowed from one landing to the next. They stopped to catch their breath, and Twan came lurching up the stairs.

She was still slicked with rancid water. Her mouth gaped. A chunk of meat was missing from her midsection, and viscera bulged within. Her almond eyes were alight with a terrible fire, and she was encrusted with filth. She was carrying two shields—two trash-can lids.

Her eyes found Tammi—

Tammi came at her, snarling, swinging her blade. One shield came up, then the other, in no obvious haste; but Twan had the sword trapped. Her foot came around—and found nothing. Tammi had leapt back, dropping the sword.

A moment later it was over. Tammi had remembered her other defenses. Flame burst from the Nommo crown and enveloped Twan. The undead woman slammed back into the wall. Her eyes bulged from their sockets, and exploded—

Alex was saved from looking at the rest of it. The lights had gone out.

"They killed the power," Acacia whispered.

"Enough already with the darkness. A little light, maybe?" Top Nun's force field came to life again. It might have been too weak to offer protection, but illumination it could provide.

They continued past Twan's smoking corpse and found their way down to the Mall level.

The ceiling was cracked, and great mossy sprays of graveyard dirt hung from the cracks, matted with mud. Water ran in sticky puddles on the ground and had ruined many of the shops. It dripped into the central well with a steady echoing sewer sound.

Tammi and Acacia were on the point now, Bishop taking up the rear.

Griffin's eyes were as open as he could get them. He was watching everything around him.

Then came drumbeats. Hot, rhythmic, jungle sounds, hypnotically alive and compelling. It seemed to Griffin that they came from every corner of the third level at the same time.

"What do you think of that?" he whispered.

"Catchy. Makes you want to dance," Alphonse said, but he stood in fighting stance and his eyes were wide.

Captain Cipher's arms shot into the air. Another dome of light covered them, and the music was muted.

This murky light—Griffin started to flip his Virtual shield up. "Keep shield in place," a voice whispered in his ear.

Then the Mayombreros came out of the murk. They charged from every angle; they were everywhere at once, slavering and hungry, a living carpet of enemies fighting and dying for their terrible cause.

The Adventurers fought as a unit now, and with the power of the talismans they were strong. They ripped a hole through the Mayombreros in a whirlwind of fire and steel. General Poule shook blood and sweat from his scalp, panting. "There!" he screamed, and pointed to an EXIT sign twenty feet away.

It was the last thing he said. In the next instant he was down, buried in a forest of fangs and ripping claws.

The rest reached the stairwell. Bishop slammed the door shut on a hairy arm. It dropped to the ground, writhing and trying to crawl to the attack. Cipher's magic burned it.

"Seal the door!" Bishop yelled. Magical bolts hit it from three directions, slagging it shut.

"That won't stop them," Acacia said, sagging against the wall.

"Yeah," Tammi said. "But it'll take them a minute. Maybe. And meanwhile . . ."

Alphonse was gasping. That had been close. Very close. Mayombrero talons had nearly clawed his belt loose.

And that wouldn't have worked at all. Not at all.

I've got something for you, Bishop. It's almost payday.

The base of the stairwell was abandoned. Tammi touched the closed door gingerly. As she did, they could hear the ringing of an alarm klaxon. Insistent. Frightening. "This is it," she whispered. "Everything depends on what happens next. Any last thoughts?"

There was an awful silence, in which only the klaxon spoke. Then Mary-em raised her hand.

Griffin stiffened. It would be good to hear the clarion call to battle, as spoken by this redoubtable Warrior-woman. What would she have to say? Words to stir the blood, no doubt. They all leaned close.

"Ah . . ." Mary-em said, mouth twisting into a rueful smile. "I think my water broke."

Chapter Thirty-eight

Endgame

Friday, July 22, 2059—8:23 P.M.

The upper door was being battered in, one shuddering crunch at a time. Cipher lit Oya's chillum pipe and puffed smoke to form a magical window. It showed them the Mallbeasts slamming their bodies mindlessly against the portal. Horribly, they seemed to ignore the fact that their own flesh was tearing, their own bones breaking with the effort.

But at the bottom of the stairs, a delicate miracle was taking place.

Tammi stood with her back to the Adventurers, scanning the landing above them. The Mayombreros would have to get through her first. Bishop and Acacia stood guard at the bottom. Top Nun focused all of her energies on the task of bringing Mary-em's child into the world.

"Push!" she coaxed. Mary-em gave a convincing imitation of a woman attempting to pass a watermelon. She bucked and writhed, she held her breath until she purpled, and she screamed and clawed the ground, gasping.

Then her abdomen glowed. Within that glow, curled sleepily, was the child of Chango, an ethereal infant who looked at them with huge star-child eyes and said, quite clearly, "I've changed my mind. I'm not coming out."

Mary-em blanked with shock. "What?"

"I'm perfectly comfortable right here, Mom."

She sputtered, searching for words that didn't come. "Well—what am I supposed to do?"

"Sit back," the babe suggested, "and watch the show."

Above them there was a rending shriek, the unmistakable cry of a door being wrenched from its hinges.

"Whatever you're gonna do, better make it fast!" Tammi yelled.

And something did happen. The light in Mary-em's stomach expanded, and expanded—became a seething cascade thrusting against the bottom door. Griffin watched disbelievingly as it bowed outward as if pushed by a giant's hand. Its hinges screeched, and it was ripped entirely away in a shower of plastic and metal, flying a dozen feet before clattering to the floor.

And then they were in the reactor room. The warning klaxon grew loud and insistent. *"Warning,"* a synthesized voice said coldly. *"The reactor has entered a terminal overload state. You have five minutes to initiate shutdown . . ."*

The light contracted again and formed into Chango junior. Tucked safely in Mommy's tummy, he sucked his thumb. "Did I do good, Mom?"

"Ah . . . what can I say?"

"By the way—I'm not fragile anymore. Neither are you."

Mary-em's nut-brown face creased in a smile. "You mean I can fight?"

"Does the term 'Mommy Tiger' mean anything to you?"

With a vast sigh of relief, Mary-em pulled her staff from her back, balanced it in her hand, and touched a hidden button. It expanded to a four-foot length.

"What'll I call you?" she asked.

"Junior will do. Kick butt, Mom."

She grinned a feral grin. "You gotta love 'im."

The reactor room was a living sea of swarming demonic forms, clotted like weeds in the Sargasso Sea. Only Junior's radiance kept them at bay.

A swarm of Mayombreros boiled down from the top of the stairs, howling. As Junior's light expanded and touched the other talismans, they burst into new light. The Staff of Oranyan talisman blazed at Acacia's neck. The Nommo crown, the Oggun Necklace, and the crutch of Babalu-Aye shone like captive stars. The Adventurers pushed their way into the control room through a raging, foaming swarm of demons.

Top Nun raised her voice. "That reactor has such a mad on. Gonna get a lot worse, real quick."

"Can you protect us?" Griffin asked.

"Maybe yes, maybe no."

"Dammit, try!"

"Warning. You now have four minutes to initiate shutdown . . ."

Completely covered by a series of interlocking shields, Griffin and the surviving Adventurers fought their way slowly across the room. It was paved and walled in white tile. Stinking water covered the floor in puddles and trickled down the walls into the electrical connections, which sizzled and popped and reeked of burnt insulation.

The Mayombreros had backed away from the energy barrier. Tammi could slash at them through it, but they couldn't reach her. They watched with hungry eyes as the party edged across the floor.

On the far side of the room, there was a panel almost entirely shrouded with the wispy demonic forms. They seemed to feed at it, to leech upon it. As the Adventurers watched, the shadows suckled, expanded, divided and grew teeth, flew at them and were beaten back by the shields.

But with every attack, the shields buckled just a little bit more before regaining strength.

"Can we get close to it?" Bishop held his sword in both hands, blade slanting at a seventy-degree angle.

"I'm not sure," Top Nun said. She gasped and stumbled before she caught herself. She was buckling with the effort.

The reactor's main panel pulsed and glowed, and the air around it shimmered with demons. One managed to squeeze its way through the shields and attach itself to Top Nun's chest. She turned gray and then white, the life-force leaving her in a visible current. Then Mary-em's hand touched her arm. Color flowed back into Top Nun's face, and the vampiric demon crumbled to dust, falling to the ground.

"Warning, you now have three minutes to initiate shutdown sequence . . ."

A few more steps, and they had made it to the main panel. Light streamed from the Nommo crown atop Tammi's head, and the Plexiglas shield over the controls slid to the side.

Captain Cipher examined the motherboard. He touched a dial here, a switch there—and the wall opened up.

Beyond it lay a steel-lined corridor. It hummed with energy. Water lay in puddles. At the hallway's end, lights glared bright enough to blind. Pulsing, deadly, irresistible. Hourglass Nekro symbols lined the walls.

"The motherboard has shorted!" Cipher said. "Damned Mayombreros have cut their own throats." The computer screen cleared, and a mathematical equation appeared, with a blinking cursor at its end. Cipher screamed. "I can't handle this now!"

"Isn't there an emergency cutoff or something?" Griffin yelled above the growing din.

"Down the corridor. Can't get to it—when everything shorted, the gamma shields went up. It's radioactive as hell. I've got to try to route around this blowout. Double-donged Demosthenes—the cube root of *what*?"

"Damn!" Panthesilea screamed. "The entire hall's another Nekro trap! Cipher, we've *got* to go through the motherboard!"

Their protective shields began to bend. The godling within Mary-em grew steadily paler. "Mother," it whispered. "I can't hold up much longer . . ."

"Cipher?" Mary-em said, alarmed. "Can you or can't you?"

Still examining the screen, Cipher shook his head. "This is straight math. I . . . I don't know."

"Warning, you now have two minutes to initiate emergency shutdown . . ."

Cipher looked up at the wall speaker. *"Will* you shut the fuck up?"

In Gaming Central, all Game Masters were off duty. Every Gaming routine was automatic now; all of their jobs were done, and they hovered around the main screen, watching avidly as time ran out.

Sis was suddenly jolted from his state of passive interest by an alert light.

"We've got a special request from Alphonse Nakagawa," Richard Lopez said.

"What the hell?"

"Alphonse Nakagawa. He . . . hmmm. I'll be damned. He seems to have constructed a voodoo doll."

"That's interesting."

"More than you know." Lopez conjured up a holo window. On it appeared a succession of freeze-frames: Nakagawa's hands holding a comb; holding half a dozen black hairs; holding a fist-sized doll of twisted cloth, crude but unmistakable. "He registered it with the computer about an hour ago, during their last break. It's Bishop."

★ ★ ★

Nigel Bishop scratched at his ear. *"Attention, Bishop,"* Richard Lopez said with unmistakable relish. "You have exhausted most of your protection points and are now vulnerable. You have been possessed. According to the dictates of your new master, you will now attack and kill Panthesilea."

Bishop's eyes widened. He spun around, scanning the group, and saw Alphonse—seated cross-legged, expressionless, staring at something in his fists.

But there was no time to waste—the penalty for resisting the will of the Dream Park Gods was fearsome. Bishop drew his sword and struck at Acacia.

Her response was almost instantaneous. She dodged, as if she had been expecting the blow—expecting sudden death from the Bishop. Fencing, blocking, she retreated in the only direction she could— into the radiation-flooded Nekro-blazoned corridor.

She tried to stop herself, and couldn't. "No, Nigel!" she screamed, once only. She took a lurching step and found herself in the middle of a lethal radiation field.

"Damn!" she screamed, real fear in her voice. "Damn, damn damn damn damn!"

Bishop stood frozen, unable to move or speak.

Panthesilea collapsed into herself in slow motion. Her body began to steam.

"You bastard!" Tammi said, wheeling on Alphonse.

"Stop!" He called, "I can pull this out. Cipher, you can't break it in time, can you?"

Captain Cipher, sweating, shook his head. "I don't know. I really don't."

"Warning—you now have one minute to initiate emergency shutdown . . ."

"My way, we win for sure."

Tammi and Mary-em looked at each other. What did they have to lose? Their shields were cracking.

"What do you have in mind?"

"Give Bishop the Oggun talisman," he said. "Enhanced physical strength. Stand still, Bishop!"

Bishop's eyes flamed hatred as the beads were slipped around his neck. "Now," Al the B said with naked malice. "Walk into the corridor, Bishop, and pull the fucking emergency switches."

If looks could cut, Al would have pulled First Soprano in the

Vienna Boys Choir. Bishop ground his teeth, almost vibrating with hatred.

"Now," Al said gently.

Then Bishop relaxed, a reluctant grin of admiration half-hidden as he turned. *Showtime!*

Bishop the Possessed lurched convincingly down the corridor, blistered by killing waves of radiation. On monitors the Adventurers watched his cheeks begin to bubble and run, the skin to blister and peel. He staggered, but the strength in the Oggun Necklace kept him erect.

In seconds he stood before the open shields, bathed in unholy light. He fell against the wall, hands with no flesh remaining digging into them, tearing away metal restraints, grasping for control rods, yanking—

And then he collapsed to the ground, disintegrating as they watched.

The shields slid shut. The control-panel lights dimmed. The lights in the room dimmed.

"Attention. Emergency shutdown has been activated. Have a nice day."

The demons circled them in a howling mass. They slowed, and faded, then vanished altogether.

The shrieking alarm siren slowed, and then lowered its pitch and died.

Griffin spared a brief, pitying glance at Acacia. A double black border surrounded her. She looked melted, but her skeletal shoulders heaved almost imperceptibly.

Mary-em, Top Nun, Tammi, Al Nakagawa, and Captain Cipher were all that remained of the party.

Their magical shields failed. The magic was worn out. What next? They had nothing, and—

A glowing form appeared in the air before them. It was the image of a Nommo, the majestically hideous flat-catfish form balanced on its tail.

"It is over," it said. "And you have won."

Chapter Thirty-nine
Wheelbarrows

Griffin reached Gaming Central in time to see the Game Masters packing and preparing to leave. "I heard," he said softly to Richard Lopez, "that this was your final Game."

"It is what the doctors tell me." The dark rings beneath his eyes lightened, as if his reply pleased him.

"He's cheated them before." Mitsuko held his arm tightly. In affection? Or to help him remain erect? Alex wasn't sure. All he could be sure of was that they wanted no pity. They were the best. They had presented their masterpiece to the world. If it was their final work, there were worse exit lines.

He squeezed Richard's hand warmly, and they left.

El and Doris had already dismissed most of their mimes and were busily gathering their props and character sheets.

Then Alex was alone with Vail, Thaddeus Harmony, Millicent Summers, and a handful of noisy workmen dismantling the Virtual theater platform.

Alex took a tiny metal collar out of a foil wrapper, gazed at it, and held it up to the light. "McWhirter found this?"

"Affirmative," Millicent said.

"Wish I could claim prescience, say I wanted to get him out of the control room and into the field, but the truth is that I'm so tired I can hardly think. I just blew my top."

She nodded without speaking.

On a viewscreen between them was a shot of a celebration party whipped up for the Gamers in one of MIMIC's apartment suites. All the Gamers were there, and only two or three seemed aware that they were detained against their will. Security had politely informed them that transportation would take a couple of hours, and requested the honor of their company at a special party.

You're not leaving MIMIC yet.

A little grumbling, a couple of protests. Al Nakagawa called his wife; Clavell and Poule had to alert their superiors and subordinates.

Then the party began.

Alex had yet to change out of his grubby costume as he scanned the information before him. Vail, quiet for once, watched him with professional curiosity. Millicent and Harmony, still in partial makeup, sat in uneasy silence. Millicent spoke first.

"What are we going to do, chief?"

"Use the hours that party buys us," he said. "Time to think."

"He was trying to force a win," Harmony said. "Or cheat."

Alex finished scanning Vail's report.

Harmony leaned forward. "Whatever it was, we stopped him. And ScanNet stopped him."

Griffin sat back in his chair.

ScanNet may have stopped him. He hadn't acted like it! But Bishop was all poker face—and if Dream Park didn't *know* he'd been stopped, they'd have to act as if he'd won.

He might have been after some piece of the Barsoom Project, hired by an Ecuador concern to get it. He might have a map of MIMIC's defenses. He'd tapped the security cameras. There was little in MIMIC for him to steal. ScanNet was only forty percent operable, but even so, it had probably stopped him.

Unless . . .

Alex Griffin's eyes flew wide open.

"Griff?" Harmony asked, alarmed. "What is it?"

A light dew of perspiration had appeared on his brow. "Oh my God. Wheelbarrows. It's been under our noses the entire time."

"Wheelbarrows?" Vail asked, genuinely confused. "What are you talking about?"

Alex stood up, shaking. "Get Tony McWhirter in here. He's earned it." His voice cracked, and he smashed his fist down on the control panel. The picture of the partying Gamers fizzled out. "Can't you see it? Bishop is stealing goddamned wheelbarrows!"

* * *

Mitch Hasegawa was very polite to the Gamers as he conveyed the news of another unfortunate delay.

"It's going to take a little more time. There are some things to work out."

Tammi and Twan, huddled by the artificial fireplace with Mouser, grinned up at him. "Just keep the champagne flowing, bud," Tammi said. "We can party all night!"

Twan corrected her: "And grape juice for the Sprout." Mouser glared.

All thirty Gamers were mingling with the NPCs from the previous day and a half.

Thaddeus Harmony kept popping in and out. He cheerfully admitted that they were being held at his orders; but somehow it wasn't easy to whine complaints at Thaddeus Dark.

Mary-em, Top Nun, and SJ sat together in a triangle, scarfing down canapes. "So . . ." SJ said, a huge grin splitting his freckled features. "How does it feel to be a permanent mommy?"

She patted her tummy. "M'power just went through the roof, sonnyboy. As far as I'm concerned, I won this Game. Know what this means? I've got more than enough points to go for Loremaster now! Got my eye on the Terminator Game coming up next year. Heh heh. Me and Junior are gonna kick robot butt!"

She was glowing. Texas Instruments–Mitsubishi had come in first, due to a last-minute maneuver by Al the Barbarian. The only Loremaster to emerge with a surviving team member—Mary-em— he had simultaneously saved the day and destroyed two opposing Loremasters. Mary-em's perpetual divine pregnancy hadn't hurt things at all.

In second place had been the Troglodykes. Then Acacia's UC team, then Army, and last, Bishop's General Dynamics team.

Who weren't talking to Nigel Bishop.

Bishop himself stood next to a video window currently displaying an alpine scene. He seemed lost in thought, for once without an epigram or a joke on his lips.

Occasionally someone would approach him and offer condolences. He accepted smoothly and made it clear, with subtle tones of reply and closed body language, that he wished to be left alone.

And so he was. He stood staring, as if trying to imagine himself flying down the slopes. From time to time he would check his watch, or take a sip of champagne.

The flow pattern was a curdle around Corrinda. She'd found a chair and she stayed in it. Friends brought her drinks and rice crackers. Her left leg was stiff and straight, swollen at the knee.

Acacia Garcia floated through the room like a wraith. When she smiled, the mirth went no further than her lips. Tammi watched for a while, and then rolled out from under the blanket and went to her.

"Listen, Acacia—sorry about Panthesilea," she said. "It'll take you a while to work back up to Loremaster again, but I wanted you to know—you're welcome on my team anytime."

Acacia tried to respond, but couldn't seem to get her face to cooperate. When she replied, it sounded as if she had a sore throat. "Maybe it was time she died," Acacia said. "She was starting to think she was immortal. Like she could get away with anything." The left corner of her mouth flickered up. "Guess she learned, huh?" There were tears very close to the surface now. Suddenly she surrendered to the grief, letting Tammi hug her hard.

"Dammit," Acacia said, fighting for control. "I hate that bitch, and I'm going to miss her so damned much. I'm just going to . . ." She couldn't speak any more, and just held on, and let the tears come.

Griffin met Tony McWhirter at the door and held out his hand. "I made a mistake," he said. "I've made a lot of them, lately. I hope to God I can correct them."

Tony shook the hand and took a seat, without saying a word.

Harmony seemed to stop breathing. "Now. He's here. Will you finally tell us what you meant about wheelbarrows?"

"It's an old story," Griffin said. "There was a man suspected of being a smuggler. The chief of police had his men watching at the borders for him.

"Well, the first day the man came by, pushing a wheelbarrow full of straw. And they said, 'Wait! Let's take a look.' And they looked through the straw, but it was just straw, so they had to let him go. And the next day he came with a wheelbarrow full of straw, and they searched it. And the day after that, and the day after that. Every day it was straw, and just straw.

"Years later, the police chief ran into the thief in another city. He said, 'Listen, we know that you were stealing something, but we can't figure out what it was, or where you were hiding it. You're safe now, come on. What was it? Gold, gems?'

"And the thief laughed, and said, 'Wheelbarrows.' "

There was a moment of silence, finally broken by Millicent's small voice. "I don't want to sound stupid, but—I still don't get it."

"Not yet? We thought Bishop was trying to beat ScanNet. Later he can get at whatever we use ScanNet to protect, right? The answer is yes and no. He's stealing ScanNet!"

Tony's eyes were still cautious. Griff must be running on fatigue poisons. "Why? How?"

"Let's—call them Ecuador. *Whoever's* behind this. Ecuador, maybe, or some industrial forces within Ecuador. They want proprietary technology, which will be coming in when the Barsoom Project starts in two months. To do that they have to beat ScanNet. Once the system is in place, they can't beat it, but maybe they can get someone into MIMIC before the system is entirely operational. That someone is Nigel Bishop."

"Shit." Tony slapped his palm against his forehead. "Of course. I've got it. I've got it. Here's what Bishop wants—he wants to measure the output from the ScanNet sensors and compare them with the input, what they're seeing. That's the standard Game tapes. That will tell him how ScanNet selects its data, what it sends on to the next substation."

"How does that help him?" Vail, for once, seemed baffled.

"The p—" Griffin began.

"If h—" Tony bit it back.

Griffin said, "The problem with an automated security system is teaching it what information is irrelevant. No processor could handle the insane amount of raw data that ScanNet can pick up. So every sensor is intelligent. It decides what to send on to the next station and what to ignore. And each successive station handles input from, say, a dozen sensors, and it sorts through *that* and sends on what *it* thinks is important. And so on through maybe a dozen generations of substations, until you get to the main processing unit. Development of the sensors was easy. Developing the intelligent software was a miracle."

"It took seven years," McWhirter said. "Over a million manhours. If you can tap the sensors and run some stimulus in front of them—"

"Say a special-effects extravaganza?"

"Perfect. Sound, visual, warm human bodies doing all manner of strange things. Sort through all of that. Find out what's being kept, what's being thrown away. What does the system pay attention to? What has it been told to ignore? You can reverse-engineer the software, find the conceptual holes in ScanNet, and beat the system."

There was silence around the table.

"Did he get it?" Harmony asked.

"This is where the real dilemma begins," Alex said. "Don't you see? We can't afford to assume that he *didn't* get it. But if he smuggles it out to his employers, we have to rewrite the entire software scheme—and we don't have time to do that. Or we could implement another, inferior system."

"Could he have already smuggled it out?"

Tony shook his head slowly. "Bishop has a reputation for being a loner. Trusting no one. He let Acacia into part of his plan, because he needed a spy, a distraction. I think—I *think* it's safe to assume she was his only confederate. If that's true, then I'd guess it went like this:

"First night, Bishop slips out and plants his taps. The next day his team, or someone else's team, fights monsters in front of ScanNet, and his taps pick up their information. Record it on any kind of storage medium."

"Could he broadcast it out of the building?" Millicent asked.

"MIMIC is shielded. If he was near an external window he might use a line-of-sight laser transmission or something, but he was never near one once the Game began the second day, and he didn't get back to the roof."

"You'd know, I guess. Tony, couldn't he have gone down the modular wall with Army and Tex-Mits?"

Tony barked laughter. "Al the Barb would have cut his line!"

"Oh. Right. Then . . . his recordings must still be somewhere in MIMIC. On him, or one of the other Gamers, or one of the extras—"

"NPCs."

"Or hidden in a tool, or a wad of chewing gum stuck to a wall . . . or spilled out with the water when Mgui-Smythe blew the tenth level."

Tony said, "Millie—"

"We'll check it, Alex."

"Jesus. Or *all* of the above! Why not make a zillion copies and hide them everywhere?" Alex lowered his head into his hands. "There's no way in hell we can scan this whole building for something that might be the size of a thumbnail. We're screwed."

Vail drummed his fingers. "Tony—could we conduct some kind of massive magnetic pulse through the entire building, wipe out every piece of storage in the whole thing? We don't have anything irreplaceable . . ."

Tony wagged his head. "We don't know he's using magnetic storage. Why would he? More than likely some kind of laser holographic storage system. EMP won't touch that."

"Shit."

Griffin was staring at the metal collar and finally said softly, "Damn, he's a tricky bastard. But there's a hole. There's something we're not considering."

"What's that?" Millicent asked.

"If we can't afford to have our system stolen, Bishop can't afford to fail. At least six hundred thousand dollars has been invested—and that was just the bait to bring in Acacia and cloud the issue. How much more to get the information for Sharon? And his equipment? Call it at least a million dollars. Remember—as far as Bishop's primaries are concerned, his mission fails if we even *discover* the information is stolen. If we can change the system, or switch the system, or prevent any high-security data from being stored at MIMIC, Ecuador's stolen goods become worthless. There has to be enormous pressure on him—he was willing . . ."

Griffin faltered for the first time, and he lowered his voice. "He *might* have killed Sharon to protect the secret. If he doesn't deliver the goods within a reasonable time, it could cost him his life."

For the first time, some of the tension left Harmony's face. "Bishop's as nervous as we are? Poor bastard."

"He's *got* to have a backup plan. More than one way to get the information out of the building." Alex called up the rotating model of MIMIC. "Picture information recorded on a disk as big as a quarter but thin as plastic wrap. Push it on a flat surface with your thumb, it sticks. Now picture a handful of quarters—"

Tony said, "Why not a hundred?"

"No. If we found *one*, we'd search. Find *two*, we might bite the bullet and change the whole system. He can't afford that. He wouldn't hide more than a dozen, maybe, and he's been careful where he put them."

"Well, that's not so bloody bad. What we need to do is eliminate most of his choices, then lead him to the one we want."

"Tony, we don't *have* one."

"I know, I know. Jesus, I'm tired. Well, we'll search. Meanwhile, try this . . ."

Smiling security personnel met the Gamers as they left MIMIC. El and Doris Whitman met them, congratulating each Gamer in turn.

"Your attention, please," El said.

They were half-looped from the free-flowing champagne, but ready to get back to the hotels, to husbands and wives and lovers and friends, to hot baths and real beds.

"You probably noticed that we were using some new technology during California Voodoo." Doris waited for the inevitable nods and murmurs of appreciation. "We were lucky enough to get permission from Cowles to use some of these techniques, on the condition that no raw recordings be made. Some of the illusion technology hasn't been patented yet. So as per section six subparagraph twelve of your contracts, we're exercising our options to confiscate all recording apparatus. They will be erased and returned to you."

"Sorry about this," El said, "but it's the only way we can protect ourselves. You will all receive free recordings of any Game perspective you choose, of course."

There were a few grumbles, and then Bishop shrugged. "What the hell," he said. "Only a Game, right?"

Everybody laughed. "Tell that to my hamstrings," Tammi said.

And some made speeches or threw tantrums, but every Gamer did hand over his equipment, and then passed through a doorway lined with scanning apparatus.

All weapons, costumes, and Gaming computers were thoroughly scanned. Nobody and nothing left MIMIC without going through the procedure.

The entire process took over an hour for the Gamers. In the black wee hours they boarded a ground shuttle and returned to their Dream Park hotels via the same track that had fired them into a talus slope a little more than forty hours earlier.

Alex caught six good hours of sleep in his own bed. It wasn't nearly enough . . . but he was almost smiling as he answered the doorbell.

Tony looked grouchy but clear-headed. "Come on in," Alex said.

Dawn light glared through the bay-window wall. Tony stood closer than Alex would have, looking down, sipping coffee.

"Tony, don't you have *any* acrophobia?"

"Not when I'm inside. I'm just picturing it the way it must have looked to Clavell when his rope broke." He turned back. "So we've locked Bishop out. Right?"

"He didn't leave MIMIC with anything," Alex said. "If he planted something on another Gamer, it didn't leave either. We can't seal MIMIC off forever, but a month will screw him just fine. What's next?"

"Acacia?"

"She should have let Bishop cut her in half. Panthesilea would have been killed out, not dead-dead!"

"She must have thought Bishop wanted to *kill* her." Tony rubbed his jaw. "How's she taking it?"

"Like a death in the family. Tony, *I'm* not going to hold her hand. Sharon—"

"She didn't know, Griff." Tony sat. He gulped coffee. "Where were we?"

"Say a dozen disks. Say we've blocked him from eleven. Where's the other? Why does he think he can get it?"

Tony nodded. "Play a game with me. What's outside of MIMIC that we think is inside?"

"We should be asking Captain Cipher!"

"Can't. Sewer system?"

"Ask Mgui-Smythe. It probably recycles."

"The water from the flooded levels—"

"That was a good thought," Griffin said. "He only had to drop one of the disks. How would he find it, though?"

"Chango only knows. We're guarding that patch of desert. Griff, he didn't go back to the roof, and he *could* have. There were talismans, one in the pool and one in the cornfields. It would have been legit."

"Yeah?"

"Yeah. Maybe he never had a transmitter at all. Just the bug and a dozen record disks, of which I would dearly love to find at least *one* as a sanity check."

"We'll search. We'll keep him out of MIMIC. I don't know what else to do except go toddling back to Dream Park like some cyborg turtle."

The coffee must be helping. Somewhere in Tony's muddled mind, two things connected. "Griff? There's something more we might try . . ."

Chapter Forty

The Snake Is Alive

Friday, July 22, 2059—11:27 P.M.

MIMIC was almost deserted. Voluntarily, all of the employees had accepted scans. Only security men and women moved in and out, and they subjected themselves to repeated inspections. A good pick-pocket can place something *on* a person as well as take it off. Even an innocent employee can be used as a mule.

The building was searched for hours, but without real hope: in MIMIC's vastness, an elephant could have evaded a search for days.

"We can't keep this up forever," Alex said to Mgui-Smythe. "Eventually, the work crews are going to have to come back."

"So what do you want me to do?" the little engineer said softly.

"The Snake is alive," Griffin said. "You just found unexpected earthquake damage. Nobody comes in the building until we have a full reappraisal."

Mgui-Smythe nodded. "Could take weeks."

"Six weeks," Alex said. "Give me six weeks. By that time, one way or the other, it will be over."

Acacia had stopped crying by the time the shuttle reached Dream Park. During the entire trip she had remained on her side of the car, not watching anyone, enmeshed in her own thoughts.

Bishop had kept to himself as well, but as they began to file out, he gathered up his gear and crossed to her.

"Well," he said quietly, fiercely. "You managed to screw yourself out of a million dollars. I hope it was worth it."

Then he turned and left the car.

She felt like a stranger. Security had kept her Virtual projection equipment, her pack, her weapons—most of her costume. It was as if she had left the corpse of Panthesilea to be buried at Dream Park. How appropriate.

Panthesilea, dead. Years of growing and fighting, gathering power and experience, all nothing. Dead. She would have to start all over again, from the bottom.

Oh, God. She didn't know if she could do that again.

"Excuse me," a voice in front of her said. "I was wondering if you need a lift."

Acacia looked up and for the first time in eight years faced Tony McWhirter. She saw his tentative smile slip and guessed how she must look.

"A lift," she said. "Yes. Definitely."

Griffin slept for twelve hours, then awakened to the buzz of the telephone. He awakened instantly, relieved to find himself in his modular apartment, returned to CMC once again.

Moshe Osterreich, chief of the Yucca Valley Sheriff's Department, was on the line. "Sorry, Griff. The hookers who saw the man enter the motel identified the car. It was stolen. No prints, no traces, no damage either. Owner never even knew it was gone. Ladies can say it was a tall, slender person, but no description beyond that. Not race or even sex. I'm sorry."

"So am I," Alex said, and punched off the line, and went back to sleep.

In parties throughout Dream Park's peripheral hotels, music, laughter, and debates raged far into the night. Bishop made a few low-key appearances, then slunk back to his room. No eyebrows rose, and few tongues wagged. With so few previous defeats on record, how could his present behavior be judged? Depression and embarrassment seemed as likely as tantrum or bemused resignation.

He packed his bags and checked out. He took the shuttle to Los Angeles, and there changed cars to the Denver line. Two more shifts took him to his condo in Montreal.

Once there, he carefully scanned his luggage and his personal clothing for bugs, and found nothing. Griffin was either as ineffectual as he seemed, or very good indeed—and so Bishop discarded luggage and clothing and bought all new.

He walked from the mall to a nearby office building. On the second floor was a lawyer named Trapman, who had accepted Bishop's cash retainer a month before. Trapman admitted Bishop to a soundproofed room with a com screen. Bishop spoke a telephone number that connected to a number in Ecuador via satellite.

"It was a good Game," he said when the line was eventually picked up. No face appeared on the screen. "Looking forward to playing again. Maybe next year."

Year meant *week*.

"Those of us who follow your exploits," a heavy voice said, "are disappointed that it will take so long. There is great interest, Mister Bishop, which every day grows greater."

"Next year," he said. He hung up.

He templed his hands together and clapped them over his mouth. The operation could wait another week, damn it. But that was his timetable, not theirs. For the sake of this very special operation, close to two million dollars of *their* money had been invested.

He had succeeded, but the information on ScanNet was not in hand. There were multiple copies of it. There was no way that Dream Park could find them all, or shield them all.

It was a waiting game.

Now, as at no time during California Voodoo, Bishop felt the cold tight feeling at the back of his neck, at the pit of his stomach.

He had to control himself. Control the vision, and the dreams that he knew would come. Now was not the time to crack. Not now, when he was so close to winning that he could *scream*.

It was the size of a quarter, made of stiff plastic, almost transparent. A hologram. Mgui-Smythe held it up in two fingertips. "You'll never guess where we found *this*."

Tony walked around the image. "Oh, Lord, I'm sane. It's not just mob paranoia," he said. "Where?"

Alex Griffin's spectral head popped up next to the engineer's. *"Ah. Very good, Mgui-Smythe."*

"Where?"

"We found it when we were taking the nuke plant apart. It was in the radioactive tunnel, near the far end."

"He planted one *then*?" Tony found that awesome. "He does have nerve. Griff, we want a number of people to look that over."

The engineer rang off. Tony stayed on.

"So it's all real," Alex said. "But we still don't have anything actionable. Legally."

"Legally. But give me that disk for a while. Trust me, I'm a Game Master."

Even Norman Vail hadn't suggested taking Bishop to court, and under the civilized veneer, Vail was the most vindictive bastard it had ever been Griffin's pleasure to meet.

Even this last, desperate gambit had been Vail's idea. It had taken every bit of convincing, and Tony McWhirter and the entire tech team at Cowles were working on it.

He hoped Vail was right. Alex Griffin was out of ideas.

Chapter Forty-one

A Visit

Monday, August 29, 2059

Alex Griffin usually left CMC at seven in the morning. It was as much of a pattern for him as anything in his life. CMC was an insular community, each of the units nestled into its spread of trees and shrubbery with minimal line-of-sight interference from the other units.

So no one saw the man who was a hundred yards away from Griffin's door that morning, a slender figure in green and brown camouflage cloth. When he shifted position, crawling against a patch of white rocks, the clothing changed color. He didn't approach the apartment, just watched it. He had scanned it, thoroughly, and didn't like what he saw.

The electronic burglarproofing was dazzling. Griffin seemed to be a gadget freak. It made sense for the head of Dream Park security to be a paranoid, but this was absurd. There was no way a fly could get past the cameras and microphones and sensors without triggering *something*.

He wondered if Griffin was frightened. He'd been living in his apartment even while it crawled home to CMC, and he hadn't left it since.

What the hell is wrong with you, Griffin?

Nigel was breathing too hard, although there had been no physical exertion. He took a minute to calm his breathing. This was a time to be calm. And precise. MIMIC was unapproachable, true. His principals were screaming at him. Probably looking for him. He would have to go to *them*, data in hand, or . . .

Once again, his breathing annoyed him. He was very proud that he didn't think about the dead woman anymore. Never thought about her eyes, or the single thread of bright red . . .

The slender man lay panting in the shadows, forcing his mind back on track. A frontal assault would surely fail. There was a surfeit of hardware. A trap could be brewing.

But perhaps the human factor could be engaged. Yes. It had worked before. A pity he'd lost Acacia.

Tuesday, August 30

Alex Griffin rarely left the grounds owned by Dream Park—too rarely, it sometimes seemed to his friends. It meant that his contacts were limited outside of Cowles and Gaming.

So when a stunning blond free-lance writer entered his office, it was something of an event.

She stopped at his secretary's desk, his secretary being an attractive black woman with infectious energy. The plate on her desk said *Millicent Summers*.

"Hello," the blonde said. "I'm Penny Addington. I have an appointment with Alex Griffin?"

She was in Alex's office for an hour, and the two of them left later for lunch, by now chatting like old friends. She touched Alex's arm proprietarily, and Millicent hated her. By walk and dress and tone of voice she broadcasted that she was a bundle of sexual tension held under inadequate restraint. A man looking into those sharp blue eyes must feel he was peeking into a blast furnace.

He would come back cheerful, relaxed. Millicent thought she was braced for that.

Alex returned to the office two hours later, whistling merrily. "How's my favorite temp secretary?"

Millicent glared. "You're late."

"Any sacrifice for Dream Park."

"I'll just bet."

"You wound me. I was all business. I was too stupid to take hints. And oh, Millie, was I glad to see her!" He smacked his palms together in delight. "Bishop doesn't have it! And time must be running out *fast*."

"Excuse me for asking, but—what if she's really a vidzine editor? What if she *likes* muscles without brains?"

"Then the two of you could barhop together. Hahaha . . . Seriously, you should have seen her. Her hints got broad enough to make me blush. We made a date eight nights from now. She wanted sooner."

"You animal."

"God—if I wasn't me, I'd wish I were. Give Tony her address. I want all her personal records razed."

Millicent stood and moved next to him. When she spoke, her voice held no trace of amusement. "Why don't you just disable a couple of the alarms, Alex. Wouldn't it be . . . safer?"

"He doesn't like safety, or he wouldn't have sent that woman to get at me. He thought he could take on all of Dream Park, and he just can't do that. I want a chance at him, Millicent. And I'm going to get it."

Millicent started to speak, but then swallowed the words. There was more to this than Alex could ever say directly.

There was Sharon Crayne.

When it came to that little piece of unfinished business, Dream Park, MIMIC, the Barsoom Project, and shadowy Ecuadorians mattered not a damn. In that realm, all that mattered was a final, terrible question which Alex Griffin needed to ask of a man named Nigel Bishop.

Wednesday, August 31

At three in the morning, Alex Griffin awoke from a sound sleep. A holographic window had opened in the air next to his bed. Even before his eye focused, he knew who it would be.

"Um-hmm." He rose, staring at his hands as he swung his feet to the floor.

He pulled on his underpants, and as an afterthought, a supporter with a plastic groin protector, as well. And a set of sweatpants, curling them up over the long, hard muscles of his thighs, to just under his flat, ridged belly.

He pulled a sweatshirt over his head and down his arms, and finally all the way down to his waist.

He gargled a mouthful of water, and spit it out.

Got to be presentable, he thought dourly.

His body creaked. He turned on lights and punched up the coffee maker. He disabled the alarms and opened the front door.

"Good morning," Nigel Bishop said flatly. "I thought that we should . . . talk."

"Talk?" Alex asked. "What do we have to talk about?"

Bishop walked through the open door, eyes moving constantly, evaluating without comment.

"Perhaps about Acacia. She's an interesting subject." He studied the furniture, the numbered prints, and finally an eighteenth-century ceramic statuette Griffin had acquired in Kyoto. It was a samurai, sword held in baseball-bat position, the kendo attitude known as *hasso*, or eighth phase.

"It's a forgery," Bishop said helpfully. "I hope you didn't pay much for it."

"I don't need an art appraiser. What do you want here?" Alex was fully awake now. There was a hot, tight feeling in the pit of his stomach. And an unholy satisfaction in having lured Bishop into his lair.

Bishop gave Alex a meaningless smile and continued to examine the apartment. "Isn't there something you'd like to say?" Bishop asked.

Waiting for me to make a move, Alex thought. *Doesn't want an assault charge. No breaking and entering. Smart.*

Alex poured himself a mug of coffee and went out onto the balcony. His unit was on a slope, and he gazed out over the rolling hills. It was a good life, all in all. He had done stupid things, risky things, and become many different men along the way. And all of those moments had brought him here, to this.

"Yes." Alex said. He nosed at the coffee, but didn't sample it. It was still much too hot to drink. "I'd like to say something. I can't prove it, but we both know you killed Sharon Crayne. I don't know whether I loved her or not. I don't know if it could have worked. But she was young, and lovely, and very alive, and now she's dead. And you killed her."

Bishop made no denial, offered no affirmation. He merely waited, silently.

There weren't going to be any verbal games, then.

His left leg felt a little looser than his right. *All right, then. Let's get it done.*

Alex threw the scalding coffee at Bishop's left eye, then whipped a low sweeping kick into his right knee as he dodged.

But Bishop was rolling, under the coffee and over the kick. The man was as agile as a monkey, a tight springy rubber ball that bounced once, feinted left, and with eye-baffling speed slipped behind him.

Bishop pounced on Alex's back, hissing like a cat. His thumbs and fingers dug for Alex's windpipe, his carotid artery, gripped and tore at the muscles themselves. Griffin fell backward, slammed to the ground, trying to smash the air from Bishop's lungs. Bishop squirmed from beneath him, and Alex lurched up, roaring.

Bishop had his arm in some kind of hold. Alex didn't have time to recognize it before Bishop spun and threw him. Alex felt as if his fingers, wrist, and elbows were all being torn apart. The pain made his whole body leap, and he spun through the air. He slapped the ground with his left arm, hard enough to make a bad breakfall against the carpet. Bishop was already jerking him up again, by the fingers this time. Alex's fingers were torqued into a *sankyo* wristlock, and in a moment, his head was going to be through the wall.

With a desperate surge of strength Alex went against the hold, wrenching his hand loose. He felt his index and second fingers *snap* under the unearthly torque.

Alex's mind went blank. He abandoned technique, smashing into Bishop shoulder-first, tackling him, carrying him back over the couch, sprawling on the floor with him, and crashing his elbow into Bishop's face: once, twice, thrice. Bishop's eyes were wide and wild, his face split, blood drooling in a mask from eyes to chin. He snapped forward and butted Alex in the mouth, mashing lips against teeth and driving his head back.

Bishop struck the exposed throat with the web between thumb and forefinger, and Alex retched. Bishop arched his back massively, heaving Alex up and into a table.

Bishop tried to regain control, to return to some kind of a balanced posture, but Alex drove back in with no concern for pain, or injury, or anything except the primal urge to finish what had begun.

They thundered against the wall, into the corner, upsetting another table. Bishop strove to get the distance to use his superior technique, to no avail. Griffin time and again took fearful abuse to ribs and face to hammer Bishop back. To hurt him, punish him, make him forget all of the carefully learned combat maneuvers and force him to react on the animal level. This wasn't a dojo ballet. This was two cats in a sack, and Griffin was beyond concern for life or limb or anything but smashing the man before him.

Alex's face was a mask of blood, but with head bowed he worked Bishop's body, left hooks and right elbows, grunting with the effort, broken fingers standing out at an angle, not thinking, not feeling, a perpetual-motion machine that went on and on and—

Bishop's nerve broke.

He screamed, forgetting his human skills, forgetting everything except the blind urge to get away from the maniacal *thing* that Alex Griffin had become.

Alex slammed a knee into Bishop's crotch, the hardest and most heartfelt blow of his life.

Bishop went limp, gagging. Alex stepped back with his left—

And his foot slipped on the coffee.

He fell, and Bishop twisted under him, sobbing with the effort, foot striking up and into Griffin's groin in a modified *tomoenage* stomach throw, arching up and back, throwing Griffin high—

Alex smashed through the patio glass, somersaulting out and over the balcony.

Bishop lurched to his feet, vomited, and almost choked on it. He managed to steady himself and focus his eyes.

He had only seconds, if that. He spun a chair into the center of the room and reached up to the ceiling next to the lighting fixture. There, hidden in a shadow, was a piece of white glue no bigger than a thumbnail. And upon it was a tiny beige plastic chip. His hand shook as he pried it loose.

With agony in every joint and muscle, blood oozing from his nose, Bishop managed to crawl over the balcony and drop to the ground five feet below.

Griffin lay at the bottom of the slope, his head twisted at an odd angle. Maybe the bastard's neck was broken. Bishop didn't have time to check. No time! He had to escape, to find a doctor, to get his precious data into the right hands before someone put a bullet in his brain.

Fingers clutching bruised ribs, Bishop limped into the shadows. Every step hurt. He made his way along a line of retreat secured far in advance. Within minutes he was in his car, had punched in an address and collapsed against the seat, tears of pain starting from his eyes. *I'm alive,* he thought. Alive and flying now, as the car began to rise. Flying away from Griffin, away from Dream Park. Away from the clamor of alarms and yapping dogs, the steady panicked cry of first two and then a dozen throats. As fast as the car could travel he flew, away from that one thing worse than an honorable defeat: a humiliating victory.

Epilogue: Part One

Tuesday, September 27, 2059

The house was a rambling, Spanish-style two-story dwelling with a red tile roof and enormous bay windows looking out over a cliff above the Malibu beach. It belonged to Millicent Summers, and although she had tried for years to get Alex Griffin out for a week, this was the first time he had accepted the invitation.

The sun was minutes above the horizon, swathed in orange clouds, so that Alex could look almost directly at it. Millicent and Tony seemed as torpid as he, lounging in wet swimsuits and dampening terrycloth robes, listening to the hard, steady roll of the waves below.

Alex felt exposed. There was a part of him that wanted to go back to Dream Park, to its safety and consistency. To be able to reach out and touch a button and change the image: now a beach; now a mountainscape; now the far side of the moon.

But you couldn't control the tides. You rode them, or avoided them, or they drowned you.

They were all pleasantly tired after a day of snorkling and swimming and roaming in the hills. Smelling real air, chasing real birds. Running on a real beach. Watching the sun set on a real horizon.

He felt so *small*.

"I don't know," Tony was saying. "I know what I want to do. I know what Cass wants. I just don't know if I can give her a chance."

"Then don't do it for her," Millicent said. "Do it for yourself.

You have a chance to see whether there was ever anything there. If it doesn't work, fine, but let it be real this time."

Do it for yourself, she thought. *And if you don't know who you are? Then you'd better the hell find out. There's always someone ready and willing to fill an empty cup.*

Alex donned a happy expression as Acacia Garcia came back from Millicent's house with a platter of margaritas. Alex tasted his, licked at the salt along the rim, and said, "Compliments to the mixologist."

Acacia dimpled. She was thinner, by maybe six pounds. She had lost some of the sass, and her cheekbones were a little too sharp. Her hair often looked a tad disarrayed, as if she had only fussed with it as an afterthought. Some of the carefully cultivated seduction ploys were still in evidence, but the frayed edges were showing. And often, she caught herself in mid-posture, mid–calculated sigh, mid–knowing wink—and stopped.

Shorn of her artifice, there was something wistful about Acacia. She was still an exquisitely lovely woman, but she seemed . . . frailer somehow. And loud noises or sudden shadows made her flinch.

Tony took his drink, and her hand. She sat next to him on the lounge chair. They didn't speak; they hadn't spoken much around Alex or Millicent, but they had taken long walks together, and after four days at the beach house, Tony had moved into her room.

He stood, still holding her hand, and motioned with his head toward a cut stone path winding down to the beach. She nodded, and they started toward it—and then she stopped. Acacia turned and faced Alex, as she often had over the last five days, and during the weeks since the end of California Voodoo. She looked as if she might be about to say something: "Thank you," perhaps, or "I've changed," or . . . maybe something else. Alex couldn't guess. Apparently Acacia couldn't, either; she just broke eye contact and led Tony to the stairs and down to the beach, where they would walk together, talking, until long after dark.

"What do you think?" Millicent asked finally.

"I think that they'll be together as long as Acacia is frightened."

"Of Bishop?"

He nodded.

"Should she be?"

"He's a pretty scary guy," he said, trying to be light about it. Despite the attempt, his mood darkened. He stretched his right hand out, examining the fingers. "I still have trouble typing. Swimming today, my ribs felt full of broken china."

"I'll bet you're glad you put breakaway glass on the patio." She grinned. She could see that he was still locked in that memory—not a pleasant place to be. "How long will it take to heal, Alex? Not your body. I mean inside. Where you feel beaten."

"Millicent, you know I threw that fight."

She sipped. "Uh-huh."

"I used Sun-tzu against him. 'It is inferior to destroy an army—it is better to capture it.' We'll end up with the entire Ecuador connection."

Millicent said nothing. He was annoyed with himself for rushing to fill the silence with more words.

"Mill, I *planned* it all. Between Vail and Lopez and Tony, we knew that he would have multiple copies. He went mountain climbing before the final assault. The bastard put one in my own apartment! By the time we found it, Tony and the tech boys had already cracked the cipher on the disk he left in the reactor. We put in our own version of the data. He had to come for it—MIMIC was all sewn up."

"And?" She was watching him. She was listening to his words but paying attention to his expression. His ears burned.

"Anyone who tries to use the ScanNet data gets mousetrapped. After that, nobody will trust Bishop. Even if he recovers a genuine copy of the data, who'd buy it? They've lost everything. With any luck, they'll kill him." The word "kill" was spoken too flatly, with too much control, and Millicent knew.

"It hurts you, doesn't it?"

"Millie, for Christ sakes . . ."

"Naaah." Her voice tautened. "Bishop scared you, Alex. He was too smart, too fast, too strong. You had your little schoolboy turn at him, and he drop-kicked you through a plate-glass window—"

"I wore a cup—"

"Shut up!" Her intensity was shocking. She had turned away from him. Alex reached out and turned her face. A tear had formed in her right eye, and she tried to blink it away. "You listen to me, Alex. It's time you learned what everybody else knows."

Alex felt a great void open within him, and he stood, face a mask. "I'm not sure I want to hear this."

Millicent locked glares with him, and before her sudden, unaccountable fierceness, he had no defense.

And he sat down.

"Bishop," Millicent said, "is the perfect loner. Trusts no one.

Uses everyone, and everything. Life is a game, and the only rule is to win. And there's some part of you that envies him that, that *total* freedom. What you've never considered is the cost."

"What cost?" he muttered.

"Love. Friends." She took his hand. "*Family.* Alex, you could have been Nigel Bishop. All you'd need is to live in constant fear. To see the whole world as a battleground. He beat you in the battles—and you beat him in the war—because you're stronger than he is."

He looked at her quizzically. "Stronger?"

"Why can't you see it? Don't you know how much courage it takes to care? To let other human beings in? Bishop is what he is because he has *no options.* You had me, and Tony, and Harmony, and even Vail, dammit. You had family. We care about each other. And together, we took him apart. Why do you think that you have to do it all yourself?"

"Because . . ." The next thought was stuck within him. Unspeakably anachronistic. And too damned real.

Millicent's eyes softened. "Because that's what a 'man' does?" He couldn't look at her. "Well, you're not a man. Look at me! You're not a unit—you're a human being. A 'man' is just part of what you are. Don't throw the rest away, like Bishop has, Alex. Don't throw the people who love you away. Let us in."

He still didn't, couldn't, face her. Alex felt as if that void within him had suddenly widened. As if he were tumbling now, uncontrolled and uncontrollable.

A cold breeze blew in from under the dying sun, and he began to shake. "I—need a blanket," he said lamely.

"Alex?" Her voice was low, almost a whisper. "I watched you hurt yourself with Sharon, and with Acacia, and I think sometimes that you only open yourself when you know it won't work."

The sun was lower now, and the orange of the clouds had deepened. More of them had clustered there, obscuring what little light remained in the day. "Seems like that," he said finally, almost to himself.

"Maybe I've done the same thing. And maybe that's why we've managed to avoid each other. I just wanted to say—it's over, Alex. I can't sit back and watch anymore. I can't be your friend anymore—"

"Oop. Hello? *Millie—*"

"Not if you don't trust me enough to know that we're family!

That if things don't work out between us we'll *still* be family. But if we never even try, it's a waste of your life, and mine, and I'm afraid that you'll go right out and find someone else to use you, Alex. Someone to make you close up even tighter." She rested her hand on his. "I won't hurt you, Alex," she said. "I'm your friend."

"Millicent—"

"I'm not finished," she said, but the anger and pain were gone. In its place was a mischievous grin, and eyes that sparkled with challenge. "I've thought about this for a long time. And what I've decided is that I love you, and I intend to seduce you. Tonight, in that four-poster bed upstairs. I'm going to lock the door, and stuff a washcloth in your mouth to muffle your cries for mercy. Do you understand me?"

"Why—"

"Am I saying this? Because if I wait for you to say it, we'll both be talking through liquid nitrogen!"

Alex's head spun. She looked so small and fierce and determined. And beautiful. And afraid of what he might say, or do, next.

Shit.

"So, mister . . . what do you say?"

Alex Griffin sat up and wrapped his big arms around his knees and buried his face there, peeping out between them at the sunset. The clouds had cleared, and the sun was almost down. It was only a partial disk now, but it shone as brightly as it could, even at the end of the day. It painted the sea in copper, and the beach in gold, and for a moment the air seemed not so frigid, the day not so near the night.

Alex stood up. He took her face between his hands and kissed her long enough and hard enough that when he pulled back they were both a little dizzy.

"Well, it's certainly worth a try."

"And if it doesn't work?"

He kissed her again, tasting salt and tequila. "We'll still be family."

The pink tip of her tongue darted out and wet the end of his nose. "Damned straight!" Millicent giggled and jumped off the couch. He grabbed for her. Shrieking, she eluded him and dashed barefoot across the grass to the house.

Alex watched that tired old sun disappear and downed the last of his drink in one swallow. *Fair's fair. Give her a head start,* he thought. The end of a day meant the beginning of a night.

He spun up off the couch and sprinted after her. And if Millicent hadn't stopped to shed her swimsuit, she might well have made it all the way to that four-poster before he caught her. Or she caught him.

Or . . .

Epilogue: Part Two

Quito, Ecuador

Saturday, October 8, 2059

Nigel Bishop sat in an oak-paneled waiting room, beneath a gigantic neomodernist rendition of a bullfighting scene. He hadn't studied it.

Beneath the broad double windows to his right, street musicians were playing, vying with the horns and motors of a Tuesday's evening traffic. He paid no attention.

For the first time in weeks, when he breathed or moved his face, he experienced no sharp stab of agony. He felt no gratitude.

What he felt, instead, was a niggling feeling of doubt. Somewhere, somehow, something was wrong. It wouldn't come into focus, but he was almost certain . . .

Bishop cursed softly. Why couldn't he see the flaw? His mind just wouldn't perform with its usual clarity and precision. When he closed his eyes he saw Alex Griffin.

He had to think . . .

A door opened, and a pretty, light-skinned, almost Asian Hispanic woman beckoned to him. "Señor Bishop? They are ready to speak with you."

Nigel stood and brushed invisible dust away from his coat. He gripped his suitcase with hands that were suddenly cold and wet.

There was something. He was certain of it, but—but it kept eluding him.

"Excuse me. Señor Bishop?"

"Yes. I'm ready." He breathed deeply, banishing his doubts.

Vague fears and uncertainties often accompanied major life events. Victory, he reminded himself, belonged to the bold.

And so thinking, Nigel Bishop strode across the threshold.

> There are Paths that should not be taken.
> There are Armies that should not be confronted.
> There are Fortresses that should not be attacked.
> There are Battles which should not be joined.
>
> —*The Art of Gaming*, Nigel Bishop
> (2052 translation of Sun-tzu's
> *The Art of War*)

Afterword

One of the challenges in writing *The California Voodoo Game* was the very nature of voodoo itself. There seems, on the surface, to be no single logical core from which to extrapolate. Books such as *Santería* (González-Wippler), *Rituals and Spells of Santería* (González-Wippler), *Voudoun Fire* (Denning and Phillips), *Secrets of Voodoo* (Rigaud), *Voodoo—Africa's Secret Power* (Chesi), and *The Serpent and the Rainbow* (Davis) paint pictures that are frustratingly incongruent. Shaping a Game from such stuff was like line-dancing with jellyfish.

To the rescue came *The Sirius Mystery* by Robert K. G. Temple. A well-researched tome that presents some fascinating possibilities of alien contact, and which has nothing at all to do with voodoo, Temple's work became the core for an entirely new way to look at voodoo, and is largely responsible for the shape and feel of the novel you have just read.

There are other minds at work here, and other contributions that should be mentioned.

In connection with Dream Park Corporation and Tower of Night, Incorporated: Sue Potter, Mark Matthew-Simmons, Eleanor Wood.

The members of the International Fantasy Gaming Society, whose stories helped to shape ours, and whose organization continues to promote the Dream. These terrific people can be reached at P.O. Box 3577, Boulder, Colorado 80307-3577.

In August of 1990, Steven Barnes had the opportunity to play in what many consider to be the ultimate Live-Action Role-Playing game, *Ancient Enemy*, produced by a group of talented folks who call themselves Emerald Isle. It was conducted along the Snake River in Colorado. *Ancient Enemy* was a combination of Gaming and white-water rafting, two solid days of chases, ambushes, midnight ceremonies, dreadful sacrifices, monster attacks, sword fights, magic duels, cliff-climbing, and hair-raising adventure. It was one of the most exhausting, invigorating, and entertaining experiences Steven has ever had.

It wouldn't be fair not to mention the people who made this experience possible: Game Master Mike McGee and scorekeeper Vicki Cade, transportation coordinator Melanie Pappas, production supervisor Kevin Taylor, and most certainly game designer Dirk Hovorka. Steven's stalwart teammates in this adventure were John Cade, Paul Hayes, Martha Lauer, Mike Kimble, Dave Holt, Larry Streepy, and Rick Shelton. Mention should also go to "Shaman" Fred Welch and "Man With No Bones" Cat Kaufman.

More research material and input was provided by Harley "Swift Deer" Reagan, Nigel Binns, Darnell Gadberry, the staff of the UCLA research library, the staff of Dolphins Plus in Florida, and others too numerous to mention.

In the time since *Dream Park* and its sequel, *The Barsoom Project*, were published, Virtual reality has become a buzzword. When we first envisioned Dream Park, the illusions were maintained with advanced hologram technology. Since that time, it has become glaringly obvious that some manner of Virtual technology will be up and running a lot faster.

One more thing: the 1985 quake that ruined California has been postponed to 1995.

Oh, well . . .

We'll leave the prophecies to Jeane Dixon and her ilk. Writing novels is a lot more fun.

—Larry Niven and Steven Barnes

ABOUT THE AUTHORS

Larry Niven was born in 1938 in Los Angeles, California. In 1956, he entered the California Institute of Technology, only to flunk out a year and a half later after discovering a bookstore jammed with used science-fiction magazines. He graduated with a B.A. in mathematics (minor in psychology) from Washburn University, Kansas, in 1962, and completed one year of graduate work before dropping out to write. His first published story, "The Coldest Place," appeared in the December 1964 issue of *Worlds of If*. He won the Hugo Award for Best Short Story in 1966 for "Neutron Star," and in 1974 for "The Hole Man." The 1975 Hugo Award for Best Novelette was given to "The Borderland of Sol." His novel *Ringworld* won the 1970 Hugo Award for Best Novel, the 1970 Nebula Award for Best Novel, and the 1972 Ditmar, an Australian award for Best International Science Fiction.

Steven Barnes attended Pepperdine University and now teaches writing at UCLA. He has written for film, television, stage, comics, and radio, and has collaborated with Larry Niven on two previous Dream Park books as well as other projects. This is his ninth novel. He lives in Canyon Country, California, with his wife and daughter.